FOREVER 51

Fiction
Skjolsvik,
P.

Editor Twyla Beth Lambert

Cover by Fresh Design

Print ISBN 978-1-945419-62-1

Ebook ISBN 978-1-945419-63-8

LCCN 2020940164

FOREVER 51

PAMELA SKJOLSVIK

FAWKES PRESS

For Erik

"Despite all my rage, I am still just a rat in a cage."
William Patrick Corgan

1

—————

At the counter of Tropi-Tan, Veronica eyed the polished, caramel skin of the young blonde as she rushed through the details of their transaction. The girl remained oblivious to her gaze, even as she placed cash and a "buy three get one free" redemption card into her hand. When their fingers touched, Veronica could feel herself slipping into self-will. It was never a good idea to try something new when she was hungry.

"Your hands are really cold. Are you sick?" asked the girl.

"Besides the fact that I will be wearing a bright yellow bridesmaid's dress tomorrow night, I'm fine." She tapped her fingers on the counter and forced a smile. "What can I say? Cold hands, warm heart."

The girl chuckled, exposing her freshly bleached teeth. "Is this your first time spray tanning?"

"Yes." Veronica's brows knitted. "Is that a problem?"

"Well, you don't look like you get out in the sun much, which I guess is a good thing, you know, with cancer and all that." The girl nervously flipped long strands of flat-ironed hair off her tanned shoulders, revealing her name tag—"Brittany," scrolled in thick Sharpie, with a heart dotting the I. "We close in thirty minutes, but I'm pretty sure you'll have time to dry. Anyway, um, here's a shower cap, nose plugs and some goggles. Did you by chance bring your swimsuit?"

"I don't swim," Veronica deadpanned.

"Um... I... it's not a problem." Brittany laid a pair of paper briefs on the counter. "Take your pick of any room and I'll be down in a minute."

"I imagine that you will." Veronica swept the items into her oversized purse and sauntered down the empty hallway, eyeing each identical room along the way. Halo-blue tanning beds. Weird black hoses hanging from the walls. Mirrors everywhere.

This was not what she signed up for.

"Which room has the machine? I don't see it." Irritation was building.

"It's out on repair."

"Oh." Veronica felt trapped and uncomfortable with the idea of a younger, more attractive woman witnessing her exposed, aged flesh in this last-ditch attempt at vanity. A hot flash rose inside her, beading her upper lip in sweat. She hadn't eaten in a week, which didn't bode well for anyone.

"Don't worry about it." Brittany called out from the front counter. "I've seen a ton of naked women and a lot of them were way bigger than you."

Veronica sucked her teeth, her thoughts careening between escape and homicide. But there was no turning around now. It would look stupid and prudish if she left after cash and paper panties had been exchanged. It didn't help that they were closing in thirty minutes and the wedding was tomorrow night. *Fuck it.*

She shuffled inside one of the tiny rooms at the end of the hall, closed the door and bolted the lock. The fluorescent bulb flickered its sick light, illuminating a compact compressor, a cedar bench, and a long thin mirror so patrons could observe their sticky, sunless metamorphosis.

Or not. Veronica yanked a long trail of paper towels from the roll by the sink and tucked it in at the top edge of the mirror. She shucked off her yoga ensemble, hiked up her two-ply big-girl panties, and tucked a prayer between the despondent folds of her cleavage. *God, grant me the serenity to accept the things I cannot change…*

"Ma'am? Are you ready in there?"

No. "Yes."

Brittany breezed into the room, flipped on the compressor and assessed Veronica's dry, crepe-like skin. "Did you exfoliate today?" She inspected Veronica's calves. "Or shave?"

What was this, the Tannish Inquisition? Veronica stiffened—escape impossible, homicide tempting—as her sponsor Paula's voice ricocheted through her mind with the old, familiar acronym: *HALT!*

Veronica forced herself to cycle through the questions.

Are you hungry? Obviously. It had been over a week since she'd eaten—and here was this dumb, succulent dimwit dangling right in front of her. *Yes. Patient intake is down, Ethel refuses to die and they boxed up Phil before I could get to him. I'm pretty fucking hungry, okay?*

"No," she said to Brittany with deliberate calm. "Was I supposed to?" She glanced down at the downy hair on her legs, her milk-colored skin road-mapped with thick blue veins and cottage cheese curves, and longed to shield the world from their awfulness.

Brittany didn't quite roll her eyes. "Um, yeah. It's like spray tanning 101. I'm not sure what's gonna happen, but I'm guessing that the hair will look darker than it already does. Do you want to shave real quick? We have razors." Brittany reached for the door handle. "You don't have to do your underarms, but it wouldn't hurt."

Are you angry? Veronica bit back her first unkind reply. *I'm menopausal. I've been fifty-one forever. I'm ALWAYS angry, and this isn't helping.*

"Let's just get this over with, shall we?" Veronica tucked her long, salt and pepper curls beneath the plastic bag, inserted the nose plugs and for once felt gratitude for the invisibility that middle age afforded.

"Are you sure?" Brittany's skepticism was writ large between her penciled eyebrows.

"Yes. It's a long dress. I assure you, no one will notice my hairy legs."

"Okay. There might be some darker areas and streaking but it will be way better than what's going on right now. Ready?"

"As I'll ever be." Veronica's arms dropped to her side as the sepia spray settled on her pale form, relieved to have finally finished the gauntlet of inanities and commenced the task at hand. Ten more minutes, she promised herself. And no more humiliating questions.

"Can you lift your boobs for just a quick sec so I can spray under them?"

"Oh, for Christ's—"

Are you lonely? Veronica forcefully interrupted herself and opened her eyes to maneuver her breasts out of the way. *To the pit of my soul.*

Brittany squatted to spray Veronica's legs and feet. "With your receipt from tonight's visit, you can get a half-price bikini wax at the place next door." She nodded in the direction of the paper panties. "You really need to do something about that."

Are you tired? Veronica wanted nothing more than to wrap her long fingers around the girl's neck and squeeze, but instead opted for a nice, deep, relaxing breath. *Are you kidding me? I've been awake for over a century. Hell yes, I'm tired.*

Brittany leaned over, exposing her perfect braless cleavage. An illegible tattooed name was scrolled over her heart.

She needed to humanize her. "How old are you, Brittany?"

"Nineteen." Brittany stood. Stepping back to assess her handiwork, her face couldn't hide the disappointment. "I think this is as good as it's gonna get."

Veronica removed the nose plugs and inhaled an intoxicating mix of coconut tanning spray with an undertone of Brittany's warm, flowing, morphine-free blood. God, she smelled *delicious.*

"Do you enjoy being nineteen?" Veronica stepped closer and tongued the increasing sharpness of her incisors. Like a teenage boy standing at the chalkboard with a boner, she tried to squelch her unnatural instincts with visions of her ten-year sobriety chip and the prospect of an ethical meal in her immediate future. Ethel at the hospice facility couldn't hold out forever. And Frank was waiting for her at home.

Ten years. Ten minutes. Hungry—lonely—angry—tired—but still working the program, dammit.

"Yeah, I guess so. But I'd rather be twenty-one, so I could party without all the hassle." Brittany bent over and flipped the power switch. "Aw, shit. I think my period just started. Do you by chance have a tampon?"

Veronica stifled a laugh. "I haven't had a period in years." Menstruating seemed like such an innocent, childish thing to do. Poor little girl.

Brittany all but pouted her agreement. "You're so lucky!"

"Yeah, it's such a relief." Veronica grinned, the tension draining from her shoulders. She was done with the tan, self-control and sobriety intact—and permanently excused from the need to plug up her privates.

"You should smile more, you know? It makes you look less angry." Brittany paused at the door. "Or there's always Botox."

Veronica's smile withered. Her stomach growled.

Fuck it.

"Wait a second. You have a little something there on your neck." With the single-minded purpose of a chocoholic prying the lid from a pint of Super-Fudge Chunk, Veronica brushed aside the immaculate curtain of Brittany's hair. "Here, let me get it."

As the paper towels fell off the mirror, Veronica caught a brief glimpse of Brittany's lone reflection as she leaned in and latched on to her jugular.

EVEN COLD, limp and lifeless under the ghastly lighting of a florescent bulb, Brittany somehow managed to still appear healthy and alive. It had to be the tan. Satiated, yet sickened by her own impulsive actions, Veronica inspected the girl's unblemished, but now rather bloodied face. This was the deciding moment. She could offer her own wrist, but why? The world was already brimming with enough youthful photoshopped beauty. Death was a far better option—less collateral damage. Veronica took a step backwards to justify her inaction. An awakened, blood-thirsty Brittany would more than likely target the middle-aged female population of North Texas and Veronica couldn't live with that. She felt for a pulse, then curiously pulled back the top of Brittany's bloodied tank to read the tattooed inscription above her breast. "Their real." Veronica rolled her eyes at the permanently inked grammatical error.

Yep, this was real alright. It had been decades since she'd killed someone on a whim, and now she had to deal with the pesky details of cleanup and disposal. Surveying the room, she wanted to kick herself for throwing away her hard-earned sobriety over an irritating teenage girl with weak, starvation diet blood. What a waste. The whole episode made Veronica feel as gross, shameful and dirty as the sticky spray tan that still hadn't managed to dry.

In nothing but paper panties, Veronica darted to the front desk, killed the lights, then locked the front door. The parking lot was empty except for two cars. Veronica found Brittany's purse and keys under the front counter. Returning to room four, she dragged Brittany's lithe body down the hall towards the front door. Sweat streamed from Veronica's forehead, under her arms and beneath her breasts. Even without a reflection to verify it, she knew her Tropi-Tan was toast and there probably wasn't enough foundation in the world to fix this epidermal nightmare in time for the wedding.

She wanted to let her skin dry, but she also wanted to reason things out with another human being. As a concession, she sat down on the cedar bench and pulled out her phone. Her sponsor, Paula, answered on the first ring.

"I fucked up. Like big time. And I don't know why." Veronica's voice quivered with self-pity. She stepped out of the paper panties and wiped up the errant drops of blood with them. "I don't know what came over me, but I drank. I drank a lot." Veronica patted her legs then slipped on her pants and shirt. "Well, of course I feel horrible." Zipping towards the front door, she popped the trunk of Brittany's car from inside the salon. "No, I'm not driving. Hold on a sec." Veronica set the phone down and hefted Brittany's body into the cramped trunk. "I'm back. Sorry, I made a huge mess and I want to clean it up before Frank gets home." She opened the driver's side door. It hit her then that her spray tanned prints were everywhere. *Do I still have prints?* "I am just as baffled as you are, Paula. I've been sober for years and now I'm going to have to re-establish a sobriety date. I feel like such an asshole." She sat down and clutched the steering wheel. "I know. I will. I'll call you tomorrow after I've slept it off. Good night."

At the edge of Grapevine Lake, sunburned stragglers wobbled through the skeletal parking lot towards their cars. Incensed that she would have to kill an extra hour or two as Brittany decayed in the trunk, she dug her ten-year chip out of her wallet and studied it by the blue light of her phone. "To thine own self be true." With resentment directed at her own impulsive actions, she stepped out of Brittany's sporty little car and flicked the coin into the placid water. What was ten years when she had an eternity?

AT 3 A.M., Veronica lifted the blanket to crawl into bed and was assaulted by her sleeping husband's exuberant digestive system. He rolled over onto his back, stopped breathing for a good thirty seconds, then exhaled like an outboard motor as she placed her head on his meaty chest. Despite the flatulence and sleep apnea, Frank was by far her favorite partner. She didn't need to sleep, but she went through the ritual anyway to make him happy.

"Roll over honey," she whispered into the warmth of his neck. She preferred spooning in silence, but there was rarely silence with Frank.

They'd met at an AA meeting in the fall of 2000. She couldn't drink alcohol even if she'd wanted to—and boy did she want to—but found in the 1950s that twelve step meetings were a fertile hunting ground. Newcomers were at the end of their rope, their brains were cloudy and wet, and they were more than willing to leave a meeting with a chatty, caring offer of sponsorship. Lucky for him, Frank received his ten-year sobriety chip the night they met.

Frank pulled her towards him. "You finally got to eat. Thank god." He opened his eyes and stared at the sepia splotches on her neck.

"I slipped, Frank." She sat up crossing her arms in front of her chest. "I don't know what came over me." She rubbed her temples. "I'm so tired of sucking down all that morphine. It's horrible. It would be like if I poured paint thinner all over your steak dinner."

Frank kicked off the covers and stood. "You're pretty good at justification, Ronnie. Have you called your sponsor?" He paced the room. "Or are you going to work this one out on your own?"

"Yes, I already called her, but it's not the same. I've never had to tell Paula I've been," she raised her hands to punctuate the word, "*drinking*. It's embarrassing. I feel like such a failure."

"We all fail, some of us more spectacularly than others. And FYI, alcoholism kills plenty of people." He clicked on the lamp next to their bed and sat down beside her. "Oh my god! What happened to your face? Are you hurt?"

"The only thing that hurts is my pride. I got one of those spray tans. I didn't exfoliate and apparently sweating isn't exactly conducive to its adhesion onto my old scaly skin. I look like a dirty old lady and that little twit at the Tropi-Tan was hell bent on making me feel pathetic."

"Oh, so it was her fault that you killed her?" Frank buried his head in his hands. "What did you do with her then, this twit?"

"Well, as far as the police are concerned, Brittany lost control of her car and is at the bottom of Grapevine Lake."

"You don't think they're going to notice that there's no blood? And what about the two little holes in her neck?"

"Listen Frank, they're not going to find her for a while and by that time, she will have bloated into such an unrecognizable mess that it won't matter. Don't worry," she said patting him on the knee. "It's handled." At least she thought it was, but the times and DNA tests had changed since the last time she'd killed someone who wasn't already dying.

His eyes widened. "It's handled, huh? You think your life is manageable right now?" His voice crept higher with each word.

"Oh, don't get all twelve-steppy on me. I made a huge mistake. It won't happen again. Okay?" Deep in the trenches of denial, she didn't believe her own words, even as they left her mouth.

He shook his head and flipped off the light. "I love you, Ronnie, but I'll never get used to this side of you."

"Join the club."

THE DALLAS COUNTRY CLUB was invite-only and Veronica was definitely not a member. She sprinted as quickly as she could through the artfully decorated hallways towards the bridal suite, but the full-body Spanx contraption was limiting her mobility. Rich, mostly white eyes stared at her at every turn. She was normally quite stunning, but her first attempt at warm glowing skin made her look as though she was suffering from that Michael Jackson disease, viti-something or other. The yellow dress only accentuated her dermatological disaster.

Julie waved her into the suite with a bemused expression.

"What happened?" she asked, shutting the door quickly behind her.

"Spray tan gone wrong."

"Oh, honey, I'm so sorry." Julie patted her on the shoulder. "Are you okay? You feel a little clammy."

"I'm fine. I just had the AC set to arctic on the drive over. I've been hot flashing all over the place. Fucking hormones." Veronica planted herself on the olive-green couch to avoid stepping in front of the large mirror. "Do you need me to do anything?"

"I need you to tell me the truth. How does this look?" Julie grabbed a brown wig with fringed bangs, waved it in front of Veronica, and then placed it carefully on her head.

Veronica stared from different angles to give the impression that she was carefully considering it. "I don't know. It looks kind of wrong for your face or something." She wanted to swallow the words as soon as she'd said them.

Julie removed the wig and dabbed at her eyes. "You're right."

"Aw, hell. Don't cry. It'll ruin your makeup." Veronica handed her a box of tissues. "Julie, everyone knows what you've been through in the last year. You don't normally wear a hair piece, so why start today? Did Marie put you up to this?"

"No, I just want this day to be perfect. Ya know? It's bad enough I'm going to be dead soon." Julie's lips quivered.

"Don't say that! I've worked in hospice long enough to know that you, my dear, are not at death's door." Veronica squeezed Julie's knee. She knew full well that her friend had two, maybe three months left, and that was if she were lucky.

"Okay. You're right." Julie stood up to study her reflection in the mirror. "Can I at least draw on some eyebrows?"

"Yes. Everyone looks better with eyebrows."

DESPITE THE BEAUTIFUL ROOM, the yellow dresses and the upbeat music promising everlasting love, the wedding was a forlorn affair with only forty people in attendance. Most of them were from the hospice facility. A fourth of them would be dead in less than six months. Six of them, the ones who chose to be cremated, would undoubtedly be Veronica's breakfast, lunch or dinner. She eyed them longingly as she pushed the lasagna around her plate. The last time she'd attempted a tiny nibble of food to fool a date, she dry-heaved for hours.

Once the bride and groom sealed the deal with a kiss, Mike never left his bride's side. Her house, her savings account and her life insurance policy would now all go to him. Veronica knew there was something a little off about his careful attentiveness and people pleasing behavior, but who was she to interfere with true love? She was just the nurse.

2
_____

Veronica glided into room 212 without a sound. She kept the light off, lifted the blanket and inspected Ethel's toes. They were blue.

"George? Is that you?" Ethel's voice creaked like old wooden stairs.

"Nope. It's just me. How are you feeling?" She gently tucked the blanket under Ethel's feet.

"George won't leave me alone. I'm so tired." Ethel stretched her arms like a cat, sinking deeper into the bed.

"Is George your husband?" Veronica lowered the railing and sat down next to her.

"Lover. He's right behind you." She raised a curved arthritic finger.

Veronica turned to look behind her. "Well, hello there, George," she said to the saline drip.

"I know you can't see him," Ethel coughed, choking on the phlegm.

"Would you like some water?" She reached for the pitcher.

"No." Ethel struggled to sit up. Her eyes were cataract gray but there was clarity within the cloudiness. "He says you can help."

Veronica stood. "Help?" Veronica nervously scanned Ethel's chart. "With what?" She knew the dark, back alley this conversation was headed towards, yet it always made her a bit jumpy when her reputation preceded her.

"Will it hurt?" Ethel pulled the blanket towards her neck.

Veronica exhaled. "No. You won't feel a thing."

"Really? Can we do this before my daughter gets here tomorrow?"

"If that is your wish."

"It is. Please help me."

Veronica nodded silently and upped the morphine drip.

"She wants my house." Ethel closed her eyes. "But she can't have it. She's meaner than a sack of rattlers, that one."

"Do you have that in your will, Ethel?"

"Yes. I sure do. Thank…" And she was out.

"Good, girl." Veronica stroked Ethel's cheek. She didn't anticipate an interruption, but she checked the hallway anyway. Empty. Marie and Kenneth were either chatting at the nurse's station or in with other patients. Silently, she closed Ethel's door and returned to her side. With just a slip of the IV, it was like eating a five-course liquid meal with the benefit of a straw. No muss, no fuss.

Veronica scrawled Ethel's time of death as 4:12 a.m. on the chart. She had people to notify and copious amounts of paperwork to fill out, but she had plenty of time and enough blood to carry her through the week. It was a peaceful, ethical, well-timed death, which equated to a good night.

They weren't always good. Left to their own circadian rhythms, most people died at 11 a.m. At Heartwood Hospice, most people flat lined between 4 and 5 a.m., the hour before shift change. To prevent the sun's rays from turning her into Texas toast, Veronica left right at six. The morning crew hated her for not pulling the occasional double, but she had what they didn't—seniority. In a pinch, she'd retreat to the trunk of her car, but now the morning shift knew not to expect her to sit around and chat. She wrote stellar notes, the patients liked her and so did their families. She was golden.

But after fifteen years, give or take a few, people began to question the fact that she never aged. Everything about her remained the same; the thick curly locks never grew an inch or grayed, the crow's feet never deepened, nor did she gain or lose an ounce of weight despite the fact that she never ingested food. Only the places changed. And after falling off the wagon, it was approaching departure time.

"ETHEL'S GONE," Veronica said as dryly as if she were reporting the weather. Marie and Kenneth's eyes were fixed on an iPad.

"Where did you get your spray tan?" Marie asked.

"Tropi-Tan. It was horrible. If I were you, I'd just bake in the sun before your trip, Marie."

"Holy shit!" exclaimed Kenneth. "That can't be real."

"She was eighty-three with stage four lung cancer, Kenneth. Did you expect her to live forever?" Veronica said and picked up the phone.

"Oh, my god, Veronica. You have to see this," Marie said like the town gossip in a sewing circle.

Veronica placed the receiver in its cradle and turned to look at the video. In grainy black and white, she saw Brittany's body being dragged down the hall of Tropi-Tan by a streaky blob. The newscasters hinted at demonic possession. The family pleaded with the viewing public about the whereabouts of their daughter, Brittany Anne Jameson, saying her name as clearly and as slowly as possible in an attempt to humanize her. At the end of the newscast, they hinted that the police discovered a second video taken by the pervy owner that took place in room four, but its contents wouldn't be available until the morning newscast. Stay tuned!

"Wow. Well that was certainly something you don't see every day," said Veronica and returned her attention to the phone.

"I know, right?" Kenneth slapped the desk. It was hard to shock a hospice nurse, but this video appeared to do the trick.

"I need to inform Ethel's family of her death, if you will excuse me," said Veronica, dialing the demon daughter's digits.

"Ethel's gone?" asked Marie.

Veronica nodded. "4:12. Is this Rebecca Edwards?" Veronica shifted her weight from side to side. "This is Veronica Bouchard from Heartwood. I'm sorry to inform you that your mother, Ethel Bernstein, passed away this morning." Veronica pressed her finger against her free ear and strained to understand Rebecca's slurred words. "Yes, I was with her when it happened. Will you be coming in?" She knew the answer but asked anyway. "Okay, we'll have her transferred to Davis. Once again, I'm very sorry. Good night."

Veronica rolled her eyes and placed the phone down. "Too drunk to drive."

"Hey, Veronica. Was it the tanning place by your house?" asked Marie.

"Yeah. Tropi something or other. It was horrible."

"That's the place!" interjected Kenneth.

"And that means what, exactly?" Veronica's mind raced for an appropriate slogan to calm her down. *How important is it? Easy does it. Think.* She picked up the phone and dialed Davis Funeral Home.

"You should talk to the police. That owner probably jacked off watching you prance around in your birthday suit," said Marie.

"You could totally sue that place," added Kenneth.

"First of all, I don't prance. Secondly, I assure you that nobody jacked off in response to my naked body. Oh, hello, this is Veronica at Heartwood. I have a patient that made pre-arrangements. She just passed. No, she wasn't an organ donor. Ethel Bernstein. Yes. Okay, then. Thank you."

Upon her return home, Frank followed Veronica into the dark room, closing the door behind him to seal out the light.

"Did you happen to catch the news tonight?" he asked.

"Yes." She settled into the recliner as Frank towered above her in the darkness.

"Well?"

"Will you turn the light on?"

Frank pulled the string. Warm pink light filled the small space.

"I'm afraid this unfortunate turn of events will hasten my departure." She closed her eyes and rubbed her temples. Her head was throbbing.

"But, what if…"

"What?" she interrupted.

"I came with you." Frank knelt next to her, taking her cold hands in his.

"And leave your group, your life? Don't be ridiculous."

Tears welled in his eyes. "You are my life."

"Oh, Frank. Please don't make this more difficult than it has to be. I love you. More deeply than any other person I've ever known, but..."

"Can't you just, you know..." His pale blue eyes pleaded with her.

"No, absolutely not. You don't want this, Frank. You're an addict. And let me tell you, those first few years are the worst. I've been as ethical as possible, well, with the exception of this latest debacle, but it took years to get to that point. You'd be like a toddler at an ice cream buffet and I don't have the patience to be anyone's mother. Not now."

She kissed him on the mouth. The salt from his tears lingered on her lips. "We'll talk more about this later."

He looked as if he'd aged ten years in the span of three minutes.

"That is, if you want to," she added.

"Of course I do."

Frank squeezed her hand and stepped out into the kitchen. From inside the room, she could hear the familiar voices of NPR and the clinking of dishes in the sink. She prayed she wouldn't have to leave, at least not yet. If it were possible, and she knew it wasn't, she wanted to live out the rest of her life and die with Frank, the only man to love and accept her exactly for who she was.

ON *DAY BREAK*, the newscaster warned of explicit content despite the early morning hour. It was horrifying to watch. Not because it was bloody or explicitly graphic, but because Veronica recognized the unmistakable shape of her fifty-one-year-old body. It was also in color. Long ago, she was told she would never reflect on film or in a mirrored surface because she had no soul. But the spray tan showed up, as did the paper panties. And for this tiny bit of reflection, she was grateful. She also thanked the God of her understanding for not revealing her face or the sagginess of her breasts. The world only bore witness to her perky behind and the piss poor paint job on her non-exfoliated flesh.

She ruminated on this tiny miracle all day until she stepped into the stand-alone building that held her twice weekly AA meeting. Cheaply framed slogans covered the walls, stains and cigarette burns littered the industrial carpet, while the constant hum of the dehumidifier kept the gray cinder block walls from crying. As always, the room was bustling with people, the smell of coffee and the sound of laughter, which always felt wrong. To her, addiction, in whatever form it manifested, wasn't all that funny. Although Frank wasn't actively drinking when they met, it was mutually decided that she would attend her own meetings. She initially showed up to appease him, but recently found she depended on them to get through the week.

Paula spotted her from across the room. "Ronnie!" she shouted and rushed to embrace Veronica with the enthusiasm of a parent greeting their child at the airport. Her sponsor, like herself, was an enthusiastic double winner, which made her doubly enthusiastic about working the program. Veronica hadn't called her since the night of Brittany's plunge.

"What's the story, morning glory?" Paula ran a hand through her short spiky hair.

"Oh, you know, the same old, same old." Veronica dropped her book bag on the jump seat by the door.

"How are you really doing?" Paula asked.

"Do you think maybe we could step out into the hall?" Veronica grabbed her purse form the back of the chair.

"Sure."

The lighting in the hallway was dimmer and more conducive to admitting failure. Veronica leaned against the cool cinderblock.

"It hasn't happened again. Okay? You don't need to worry."

"Why haven't you called me?" Paula placed a firm hand on Veronica's shoulder. She could smell bullshit from across a jampacked room.

"There was no need. I'm fine. I'm better than fine. Seriously, it all happened so quick," Veronica lowered her head. "I didn't even really want that drink, but I wanted to prove something, I guess."

Exasperated, Paula exhaled. "You know, Veronica, you always wind up back where you left off. You'll never be able to drink again.

Ever." Early in her own recovery, Paula had tried. One teeny-tiny sip of Merlot led to another DUI and a court ordered stint in rehab.

"I know, and I really messed things up with Frank. I also hurt someone else in the process."

"Bar fight?" Paula raised her eyebrows in disbelief.

"Something like that."

"Have you made amends?" Paula's phone beeped. She dug it out of her front pocket, briefly looked at it and shoved it back into her faded jeans.

"No."

Paula remained silent with a stern expression.

"Not yet," added Veronica.

"Get to work on that. Come on, the meeting's about to start and someone needs to re-establish their sobriety." Paula put her arm around Veronica's shoulder and led her to a chair in the far corner of the room.

AMENDS WERE TRICKY. Later that night, in front of her computer screen, Veronica stared at Brittany's public Facebook page. She contemplated posting "I'm sorry for your loss," but those words coming from her— an anonymous middle-aged woman, who also happened to be responsible for her death—seemed trivial, bordering on serial-killer type taunting. *Would one more 'I'm sorry' really lessen their grief?*

Brittany had nine hundred and seventy-six friends. At least half of them had offered condolences or posted pictures of themselves with Brittany to prove their connection to her. They missed her laugh, her smile and her fun-loving nature. They said they'd see her on the flip side or that she was in a better place. They proclaimed her an angel. They lamented with sad emoticons that she would forever rest in peace and for that they were eternally sorry—so, so sorry. How could this happen to such a young, vibrant, not to mention smoking hot woman? Why, they wailed into the ether.

Well, why not?

Brittany's mother posted her thoughts sporadically throughout the day, as if Facebook was a direct link to the mind and soul of her dead child. The Internet age was baffling to Veronica, but she did her best to keep up with the times.

If she posted to Brittany's wall as Veronica Bouchard, it could potentially cause problems or questions. She'd paid cash at Tropi-Tan, she was invisible on film, but you never knew. Marie had a big mouth. There could be a streaky spray-tanned print. Anything was possible after watching that god-awful video.

Veronica logged out and logged back in as Astrid Dahling—her original name. Unlike her current incarnation, Astrid had only one friend, a Swedish woman with the same name. Veronica took a deep breath and swore to herself that after these amends were made, she was done—for real this time. There would be no more slips. Eating would be an act of intention, not emotion. As she typed, "I'm sorry," on Brittany's timeline, she noticed a message in the upper right corner of her page. Her newfound friend was a young, scantily clad redhead named Anna Graham. Despite the fact that this message was most likely some kind of porn spam, Veronica clicked it open.

"Hi Mom."

3

Veronica hadn't seen or heard from her daughter since the winter of 1932. Those two simple words opened floodgates of tenderness, terror, and resentments as wide and cold as the Great Plains from which they'd both fled—and now, budding amazement. Veronica studied the photo with disbelief. *How had she done it?* There was no denying it was her daughter. Same blue gray eyes, red hair and porcelain skin with the tiniest sprinkling of freckles across the bridge of her nose. Ingrid was forever fifteen, but with the right makeup and clothes, she could easily pass for twenty. It was that desire to appear older and more sophisticated that landed them both knee-deep in this eternal mess.

With a quick punch of the keys, Veronica accepted Ingrid's friend request and typed a brief response.

"Hello Ingrid. I'm now residing in Texas. Where are you?"

Paula once told her that if she couldn't say what she needed to say in less than ten words, she would be wise to keep her trap shut. Paula was usually right.

MAKING amends to Brittany was tough. Not so with Frank. He hated grocery shopping about as much as Veronica hated not being able to stomach a slow cooked stew or a rhubarb pie fresh from the oven. At night while the house slept, she would binge cook casseroles, cookies and cakes for Frank to bring to his meetings. Since she couldn't even lick the spoon, she considered it service work. Frank called it love.

Picking up a block of Havarti cheese from the deli cooler, Veronica noticed Mike standing at the seafood counter with a bouquet of red roses in his hand. A pang of guilt hit her in the gut. She hadn't called Julie to inquire about the honeymoon, much less her health.

She pushed the recalcitrant cart towards the awful aroma of fish while scanning the area for Julie.

"Hey, Mike. How's it going?"

Mike jumped at the sound of her voice. "Good god. You scared me!"

Veronica slapped him on the shoulder and laughed. "I'm so sorry. I didn't mean to. Is Julie here?"

Mike flinched. "No. She's at home. I'm just getting us some dinner."

The acne covered deli clerk approached and handed Mike what looked like a cat carrier.

"Here's your lobsters, sir. Can I get you anything else?" Veronica froze. Mike had to know. There's no way Julie wouldn't have brought it up.

"That's it. Thank you."

Veronica played along—for now. "Aww, that's sweet. She'll love that. And flowers too." She lowered her head and took a whiff from the bouquet. "So how was the honeymoon?"

"Gorgeous, but not long enough. Italy is just so beautiful this time of year. I think getting away for the week did wonders for Julie's health."

"That's great. I'm so glad to hear it." Veronica stared at the white box with its clawing contents and clutched the cart handle. "Well, I better get going. My ice cream's gonna melt and your dinner looks like it's planning an escape. Tell Julie I said hello."

"I will. Have a good night."

Veronica seethed all the way through the checkout line. Anyone who knew Julie knew she was allergic to shellfish. She remembered it from Julie's chart at the hospital and she sure as shit remembered it from when they were strong-armed by the pushy caterer at the country club. Julie spelled it out in no uncertain terms; no crab legs, no lobster, and to be absolutely safe, no ocean, creek, pond, lake, swimming-hole dwellers at all at the reception. Nothing.

Veronica waited in the parking lot with the engine idling. Two rows over, Mike hopped into his brand new "race red" pony, revved the engine and peeled out of the lot. Veronica stayed two cars behind, her mind racing around and around the worst of all conclusions. Mike was planning a romantic dinner, all right—but not with his new bride.

When he reached Cherry Creek Estates, a McMansion community that had neither cherry trees nor a creek, Veronica practically kissed his back bumper with her own. Unaware or unconcerned by an aggressive tailgater, he punched in a code at an unmanned kiosk and the gate opened. Staying right on his bumper, she felt grateful that she wouldn't have to jump a fence or attempt to turn into a bat. That transformation hadn't worked since a hallucinogenic episode in the 60s.

The minute he turned into a driveway, Veronica parked a few houses down, hopped out of her car and sprinted towards him.

"Hey Mike!" she shouted, as he lifted the white box from the passenger seat.

"What are you doing here?" he asked, clutching the box to his chest.

"Oh, I just need to see Julie right quick. It concerns someone we both know, and I figured it would be best to tell her in person. It'll only take a minute. About as long as it will take you to boil those tasty little anaphylactic shock lobsters." She looked up towards the house as she attempted to catch her breath. "I like your new house. They have excellent security."

"Listen…"

"Yes, Mike?" She leaned in closer. The smell of fear emanated from his pores like a noxious perfume. If only she could bottle it, it could carry her through the lean times.

Mike's face flushed as tiny beads of sweat gathered at the edge of his receding hairline. "Oh, um. This is my sister's house." He wiped his forehead with the back of his hand. "It's her birthday, so it's not really a good time."

"Oh, terrific! She's a Leo. They're lots of fun. I'd love to meet her. Shall we?" Veronica stared with intent into the darkness of his brown, fully dilated, eyes. *Invite me in, invite me in, invite me in.* She believed vampires could bend the will of others—almost as surely as she knew that they couldn't enter a home uninvited.

"Give me a sec. Okay?" Mike rushed towards the door and held his arm out towards Veronica. "Let me just check with her."

"You do that." She planted herself on an artfully distressed bench on the front porch and tried to think of a plan. Paula's voice entered her head like a mantra. *What side of the street are you on? Is this your business?*

The door cracked open and Mike poked his head out. "She's in the shower."

Veronica stood. "Well, darn. I know this sounds crazy, Mike, but can I just take a quick peek inside? Frank and I are in the market for a new place and I really like the idea of a gated community. I promise, I just want to see what the living room and kitchen look like."

He sighed heavily and shook his head no.

"You're not going to invite me in?" She could feel her fangs straining against her gums.

"Why in the hell would I let you in? You need to mind your own fucking business and go away before I call the cops."

"I'm calling Julie." Veronica reached for her phone.

Mike smirked. "And ruin her last days of happiness? I thought you were her friend."

"And I thought you pledged to love, honor, and obey. Let me in or I swear to god, I will call her right now."

"Fuck off." He slammed the door.

ON THE DRIVE HOME, Veronica sobbed into her steering wheel. Men like Mike were everywhere. In her series of ill-fated relationships, she had dated and even married a serial philanderer. *Who did they think they were?* It was the most ridiculous fact of life to learn that she had no control over other people and their dumbass behaviors. Even more maddening was how easy it would be to eliminate Mike's presence from the rest of Julie's life—and his disappearance would bring Julie just as much heartache as telling her the truth. It was better for everyone involved to let the guilty bastard go free.

With that thought, Veronica's stomach grumbled. Inhaling a deep, cleansing breath, she imagined that Mike's chlamydia-ridden blood probably tasted like shit and it wasn't worth the trouble to kill him. There were multitudes of indiscretions in her own past, and she would never intentionally harm someone she loved. But like most codependents, there was always the possibility that she might love someone to death.

4

Marie stood in front of room 201, which was directly across from the nurse's station, chatting with an armed guard. She twirled her hair and laughed with the tall muscular man as if she were a smitten schoolgirl at a junior high dance.

Marie waved Veronica over. "You're never going to guess who just moved into room 201."

Veronica waited patiently.

"Bobby Lee Garrett!" The words spewed from her mouth with sneeze-like intensity.

"Who's that?" Veronica smiled up at the handsome guard.

"You've got to be kidding me. You call yourself a Texan and you don't know who Bobby Lee Garrett is?" Marie playfully jabbed Veronica in the ribs.

Veronica protectively crossed her arms and rolled her eyes. "Was he a quarterback for the Dallas Cowboys?"

Marie nudged the guard playfully with her elbow.

"Cattle rancher? Cowboy? Oil and gas magnate? I don't know, Marie. Why don't you just tell me?"

"Serial killer." Marie lowered her voice. "In the 80s, he murdered like twenty…" Marie looked towards the guard and raised her eyebrows.

"I believe it was twenty-seven, ma'am."

"Women! He killed twenty-seven women in Dallas. Can you believe that?"

Veronica stared blankly at Marie's animated face. *Amateur.*

"They were mostly prostitutes, but still, he cut them up and did all sorts of weird stuff with their body parts. It gives me the willies just thinking about it." Marie stared down at her feet, then looked up dramatically as if she were an actress in a daytime soap. "If you don't mind, Veronica, I just don't think I can care for him. It would be too difficult for me."

"He's on what they call compassionate release, ma'am," the guard said, and opened the door. Veronica stepped inside the darkened room. In the corner by the window sat another guard. His eyes were closed, as were Bobby Lee Garrett's.

"He's got pancreatic cancer and prolly don't have much time left. The warden felt kinda sorry for him, I s'pose." The guard lifted the blanket, revealing Bobby Lee's emaciated frame. "As you can see right here, he's chained up. Two guards will be here twenty-four seven to keep an eye on him, so you don't need to worry 'bout nothin'. He ain't going nowhere."

The cute, but painfully stupid guard patted Veronica on the back. It wasn't Bobby Lee she was worried about. He already had one foot in the grave. It was the extra supervision.

Bobby Lee opened his droopy basset hound eyes and focused on Veronica. "You my nurse?"

"Yes, sir. I'm Veronica. How's your pain level?"

"I'm doped up just fine, but I feel like I'm drowning in my own spit." He turned his head to the side and coughed violently into the pillow.

"How about we elevate you?" Veronica approached the bed and lifted the remote. "You can do this yourself with just a press of this button right here." She demonstrated the controls. His brown eyes fixated on the v-neck opening at the top of her scrubs.

"My arms are chained to the bed, Miss Veronica, so you're just going to have to help me get it up." He licked his lips. "Can you help me get it up, Veronica? Or do I need to call Betty?" He cackled, exposing a mouthful of decayed teeth.

Veronica felt the sharpness of her own teeth straining against her gums. *A world full of Mikes.* She took a deep breath and smiled with her lips firmly pressed together.

"Watch it, there," the guard said and stepped towards the bed with his arm stretched out in front of Veronica, like a parent shielding their child from hitting the dash.

"Oh, pipe down Patterson. Veronica here's cool. Aren't you, girl?"

"Oh, yes, I'm quite cool, Mr. Garrett." Veronica looked at the chart at the end of his bed. "It looks like Dr. Swanson has ordered a catheter for you. Would it make you more comfortable to have Kenneth perform this procedure?"

"What's a catheter?"

"It's a tube inserted into your penis to drain your bladder."

Bobby Lee grimaced. "I don't want no fag nurse touching my pecker. I want you to do it."

"Alright then. I'll be back in a jiff." Her heart resumed a slower beat as she turned to leave the room. Calmly. Professionally. Like someone who didn't have a phallic axe to grind.

Veronica figured Bobby Lee Garrett would exit this world just as he'd entered it—kicking, screaming and raising a fuss. "Live and let live" would have to get her through this one. Who was she to judge? In all her years, she had witnessed hundreds of deaths and not once was sainthood bestowed upon the dying. If Bobby Lee's behavior got too out of control, there was nothing like a little morphine to calm them both down.

She returned to the nurses' station and stared longingly at the computer. She desperately wanted to check and see if Ingrid had posted a response, but it was too risky to log into her account. No one had ever barged in on her during a patient's final moments, but when it came to computer use, there were always prying eyes.

Marie was on her bedazzled phone playing another round of Solitaire while simultaneously typing up a report. "So, did you ever talk to the police about that spray tan place?"

"No. I've been pretty busy and to tell you the truth, Marie, I'm not that concerned about the videotape." Maybe saying it out loud would make it true.

"Veronica!" Marie's jaw dropped. "Have you considered that maybe you saw the killer when you were there. You know, it wouldn't hurt to at least call them." Marie scrolled through her contacts. "I tell ya what. Bill's brother works for the Grapevine PD. I'll give him a call and see if he can come in here when you're on shift."

"Marie. Stop! Nobody else was there that night and if there was, I didn't see them." Veronica stood up. "I really don't want to get involved."

Marie set her phone down. "Well, alright then. Geez."

Patterson clomped over to the station and leaned on the counter. "Would you ladies be okay if I went and grabbed myself a cup of coffee?"

"I'll get it for you." Marie jumped from her chair and smiled. "Do you need cream or sugar?"

"Both, if it's not too much trouble."

Marie sashayed down the hall towards the lounge. Like many of the women Veronica met in her Al-Anon meetings, Marie was both a caretaker and a control freak.

"This must be very boring for you," Veronica said to fill the awkward silence. This guy looked like he was more into NASCAR than the news. She could only hope.

"Nah. This is like a vacation."

"Would you like something to read? We've got a ton of magazines back here." Veronica grabbed a stack from under the desk.

"No, ma'am. We ain't allowed to read or nothing while we're here. I'm just supposed to sit outside that room and make sure no one sneaks in." Flecks of smokeless tobacco littered his front teeth.

Veronica would have loved to sneak into Bobby Lee's room and rip his vocal cords out. "Does that happen a lot?"

"You'd be surprised. Sometimes it's family members bringing in stuff they shouldn't and sometimes a victim's family member catches wind of the release."

"And then what?" Veronica leaned forward.

"Well, some of 'em try to play executioner."

"Hmmm. Does Bobby Lee have any family?"

"Yeah, his mama should be here sometime tomorrow. And I think his wife is fixin' to fly in on Tuesday."

Marie sidled up next to Patterson. In her bright-pink Hello Kitty scrubs and ponytail, she looked like a forty-year-old toddler. "Whose wife?"

"Bobby Lee's." Veronica enjoyed toying with Marie's comfort level. "And she's going to come visit him. Probably on my night off."

"What kind of woman would marry a man like that? He's a killer for god's sakes!"

Patterson nodded at the room. "That man gets a ton of letters and visits from some very good lookin' women."

"That is just plain ridiculous. Why would a woman want to be romantically tangled with that monster?"

"Well, I reckon it's because he's famous, he's dangerous and they always know where he's at." Patterson laughed. "Thank you for the coffee, Marie. I best be getting back to my post."

"If you need anything, you just holler." Marie patted him on the shoulder, her hand lingering a little too long on his well-formed arms. He took a seat, spat into an empty cup and stared at the station.

Veronica eyed the empty hallways and Patterson's heavy stare. *This is going to be a long night.*

LATER THAT MORNING, Veronica tiptoed into the house, hoping to retreat into the seclusion of the darkroom without waking Frank. It wasn't safe to be around him when her unnatural instincts were aroused. Earlier that morning while inserting Bobby Lee's catheter, he had asked her for a hand job, whispering that he'd pay her for it. Either the guard was hard of hearing or he'd fallen asleep again. She had not been conscientious or kind or gentle during the procedure. She wanted to hurt men like him and Mike, men who hurt women either physically or emotionally. She drew blood in the process. If it hadn't been for the fact that Kenneth was required to be in the room during the insertion, she may have given Bobby Lee a different kind of blowjob. It wouldn't have been the first time. It never failed to surprise her that some men would go so far as to attempt to maneuver her head even as she was sucking the life out of them.

Kenneth remained silent and professional, even when Bobby Lee snapped, "What you looking at, fag?"

"Ronnie!" Frank's voice boomed from the bedroom. "Come here and give me some sugar."

Veronica poked her head into the bedroom. The sight of Frank's morning erection under the thin white sheet, normally so adorable, today brought nothing but bile-tinged memories of the hand-job Bobby Lee had asked her for when she inserted the catheter. "I'd love to, but not today. In fact, I want you to lock me in."

"Like that could stop you. I think I've replaced that door about..."

"Yeah, yeah, I know. Just do it. It's been a rough night. I'll see both of you later. I promise."

As soon as she escaped to the seclusion of her closet, Veronica immediately signed on to Facebook. Nothing. It was just like Ingrid to make a dramatic entrance and then slip out of the party while no one was looking. She wanted to call Paula and hash this out, but it was too early. Anger rose inside of her, white hot and directionless, and she wanted to take it out on something. Or someone.

The two locks slid into place outside the door. "Okay, Ronnie. You and the mailman are now safe. If you need anything, call me." She could hear his breath through the slit in the doorjamb. "Love you."

"Love you, too." Her voice dripped sweetness. "Frank?" *It would be so easy to lure him inside.*

"Yeah?"

From the desk, the computer beeped. A small box appeared at the bottom of the screen. Veronica pressed her open palm against the door.

"Thank you."

"You're welcome. We'll see you at 8:17 on the dot."

———

VERONICA STARED at the instant message box. Ingrid's picture had changed.

"I'm in San Francisco."

Of course you are. The grass was always greener somewhere else.

"How are you taking care of yourself?"

"Blood bank. I'm a phlebotomist at Western Blood Center."

"So, how in the world did you manage to take a picture of yourself?"

"You don't know?"

Veronica pounded the keys. "No, I don't. That's why I'm asking you, you ungrateful little bitch." A wave of heat rolled over her cool skin. She didn't know whether it was a hot flash or stress. Probably both. She reached for the fan. A bead of sweat trickled down the inside of her shirt, which oddly made her feel more human. She paused, took a deep breath and wiped her upper lip with the back of her hand. *Think. Is it thoughtful, helpful, intelligent, necessary or kind?*

Nope. Calling your fifteen-year-old daughter a bitch was none of these things. She erased the message.

"No, I don't know and I'm very curious." She pressed Send.

"I'll tell you."

Veronica tapped the desk in rhythm to her jiggling feet, then typed, "Yes?"

"But you have to come to San Francisco first."

Like that was going to happen. Despite her seniority, it would take a Christmas miracle to pull off a last-minute jaunt to San Francisco. Marie was headed to Maui for two weeks on Sunday and they'd never let two night-shifters leave at the same time, especially with Bobby Lee Garrett and his three-ring circus in full swing. Ingrid had waited this long to make contact; it wouldn't kill her to wait another month. The possibility of a reconciliation with her only living child filled her with hope and a certain amount of dread. Things might have turned out differently in their relationship if they hadn't both been stuck eternally in a battle of raging hormones.

It had been over eighty years, and yet the familiar two-word refrain of mothers everywhere sprang fresh and unbidden from Veronica's keyboard. "We'll see."

5

It had been eight days, fourteen hours and thirty-seven minutes since anyone croaked at Heartwood Hospice. Instead of peacefully expiring like they were supposed to, people were thriving in the midst of the resident serial killer drama. Two patients had gained weight. Four patients were now craving food. And almost all patients were requesting daily walks down the halls to get a gander at the security guard or maybe a peek at Bobby Lee Garrett and his six-foot tall Norwegian wife, Annika.

Veronica didn't bother chatting up Patterson when she first arrived on shift. She flashed him a quick smile and pushed right past him into Bobby Lee's room. It was 10:25 on a Tuesday night and she was hoping to find him fast asleep in a narcotic slumber. Instead she found Annika, his twenty-six year-old-bride, riding his now uncatheterized penis as if she were in a speed-screwing contest.

"What the...?" Veronica shouted over the grunts and groans.

"Privacy please," Annika panted, turning to look back at Veronica like an irritated and very winded jockey.

"Excuse me, but this, this, what you're doing right now is not allowed here! Do you understand me? Where is the guard?"

"He's... not... coming yet."

"The guard?"

"No, Bobby. Come on, Bobby." Annika thrust faster.

"Maybe he's dead," Veronica muttered to herself. "I mean, look at you. You've probably killed him with all that unbridled exuberance." She threw her hands up in the air and turned to leave.

"There I go. There I go. Yes! Yes! Awwwwwwww," Bobby Lee moaned. Annika collapsed on top of him and kissed his scrawny neck. He looked straight at Veronica. "Hey, Veronica."

She turned to look at him.

"You wanna get in on this? I could totally go again. Whadda ya say, Old Nelly? Want to take a ride on the Pony Express?"

"Um, I don't really know how to respond to that, seeing as how I just vomited a little right then." Veronica swiped Annika's skirt from the floor and tossed it to her. "You need to get dressed and get out of here. Visiting hours are officially over."

Annika stood and slipped on the jean mini-skirt that barely covered her ass. "I think we just made a baby."

"Well, that's just terrific. Really. You must be thrilled." Veronica surveyed the room and kicked a red lace thong towards Annika. "Listen, I don't know how you two orchestrated this completely disgusting episode, but it won't happen again. And if you thought the catheter hurt last time..." She looked towards the guard's empty chair. "Where's Sleepy?"

"He had to go jerk off from looking at my beautiful wife all day, didn't he?"

Annika giggled, straightened Bobby Lee's gown and tucked the blanket around him like a doting mother.

"Out!" Veronica demanded. It was then that she saw the laptop sitting on the window ledge. The little webcam light glowing green. Recording them.

Veronica burst out of the room, grabbed Patterson's arm and pulled him inside.

"What is going on here?" she roared, causing her fangs to shoot through her gums until they reached her bottom lip. She covered her mouth as if to sneeze, then fished for a surgical mask from her pocket.

Inhaling deeply through her nose, she attached the mask and looked towards Patterson for his response.

"Should I be wearing one of those? Is he contagious or somethin'?" He backpedaled towards the door.

"No, he's fine. Where's your partner?" she barked.

"He's on break. Listen…" Patterson's voice lowered to a whisper. "The man's dying, and he's never been, you know, alone with his wife. And just look at her. Jesus."

Patterson's gaze fell on Annika, who was now lying on the tile floor with her hips elevated by three pillows. "It helps the sperms to find the egg this way," she said dreamily.

"God. Damn," he murmured.

Veronica breathed heavily into the mask. "Listen. She has a computer in here and I don't know what she was doing with it, but it's probably illegal."

Annika propped herself up by her elbows. "It is not illegal to, what you call it, make a sex tape."

Bobby Lee chuckled. "And you're in it, naughty nurse!"

"No, we're erasing that right now. Where's the computer?" Frantic, Veronica scanned the room.

"You can't have it," Annika clutched the laptop to her chest. "It's mine so I can remember the moment our baby was made."

"Hand it over." Veronica thrust her arms at Annika.

"Why is she so mean, this nurse?" Annika fluffed her long blonde hair and smiled up at Patterson, whose eyes were fixated on the length of her legs.

"I think she needs to get laid," said Bobby Lee.

Veronica wanted nothing more than to take out the whole room, starting with Annika and her maddening, hippy-dippiness. She looked at Bobby Lee, who met her wild eyes with a smug grin. Veronica bit into her lip. A thin trickle of blood dripped from the corner of her mouth. She mumbled into the mask and fled before she could do anything truly stupid.

WHEN SHE RETURNED to Bobby Lee's room, Annika was gone. And so was the laptop. The guard sat in the darkness with his eyes fixated on the bed. Veronica picked up the chart and attempted to decipher Dr. Swanson's latest scribbling, but the whereabouts of the laptop consumed her thoughts. Where had she been standing? Maybe she wasn't in the frame after all. Annika wasn't the brightest crayon in the box—surely, she wouldn't notice or care about whether the grumpy bitch nurse showed up on the playback. Right?

Like a pit bull, it was hard for Veronica to let go of things. Having to subsist on Ethel for the past week had made her weak and, despite Paula's best efforts, she was still on edge.

She leaned on the chair beside the guard. "How are you tonight?" she cooed.

"Bored. So, when's he gonna die?" he whispered.

"Well, that's the million-dollar question, now isn't it? I think he's still got some life in him. Don't you?" Veronica moved towards the bed and messed with the IV bag, giving Bobby Lee an extra dose of morphine.

"I don't know about that, but he sure seems a lot happier here than when he was in solitary."

"I'm sure he had a ball with his wife earlier. Look at him, he's all tuckered out." Another Mike—so sure he'd gotten clean away with it. Another prick taunting the pit bull, knowing she was chained to the fence by rules he'd never bothered to follow.

"That wasn't my idea." The guard took a swig from his soda. "I should have never let that happen. You won't say anything will you? We could get in real big trouble."

"Of course not." She gently squeezed his shoulder and smiled as warmly as she could muster. "You look sleepy. Do you want me to turn out this light?" She raised her arm to flip the bedside lamp before he could answer. *Now go to sleep.*

"Yes, ma'am," he yawned and took another swig from his soda.

"He should be out for the night. If you need anything, don't hesitate to buzz me. Good night."

From all her time in darkness, she could see that the guard's eyes were now closed. When she stepped into the bathroom to wash her hands, she heard him snore.

And Patterson was in the lounge for more coffee, after which he'd hit the bathroom for a good five minutes after.

Which meant that right now, for this single rare moment, Bobby Lee was alone and unprotected... and the pit bull just might slip her chain.

Veronica sidled back over to his bedside. She upped the morphine dose again. Decisions, decisions.

Bobby Lee slowly opened his eyes and slurred, "What are you doing?" He struggled against the weight of sedation to lift his three-hundred-pound head from the pillow.

"Just making sure you don't experience any pain. Are you ready to go home now and meet your maker?" She patted him on the head.

"Get off uh me, bitch," he snarled, fighting against the restraints that pinned his emaciated arms.

Veronica leaned over his body and whispered in his ear. "Did you just ask me to off you, Bobby Lee?" She smiled, exposing her long sharp teeth.

As if bracing for a hit, he shuddered and squeezed his eyes shut.

"Don't tell me you're scared of a middle-aged woman?" Mockingly, she sniffed at his neck, inhaling a sickening mixture of Annika's cheap perfume, sweat and narcotics. "That was a question." She exhaled into his ear, to mess with him.

He opened his watery eyes. "Fuck you," his voice cracked. Frantic, he whipped his head in the direction of the snoozing guard. "Help me!" he rasped.

Veronica raised one slender finger in front of her lips. "Shhhhhh. If I were you, Mr. Garrett, I'd keep my voice down." She bit the edge of his ear, piercing it with her fang. "Did that hurt? To me, it looks like Annika gave you a little love bite this afternoon."

Tears of pain and self-pity streamed down the sides of his drained face.

"One more peep and you'll wish you'd been strapped to old Sparky. Just relax, I'm not going to hurt you. It will be just like falling asleep." *And never waking up.*

He nodded, closed his eyes and accepted his fate. He was either almost dead or he'd simply surrendered to the idea that death was near. Veronica felt he deserved more pain, but torture took time and tonight was not the night to play with her prey. She felt his neck for a pulse. He was barely alive.

As she padded out of the room, Patterson's sleepy Texas twang echoed from down the hall. Rounding the corner, he pointed in her direction. "There she is," he said to the uniformed officer by his side.

Veronica froze. *Marie*. Safe and sound in some Hawaiian condo, she had opened her big old gossip-loving pie-hole to her cop brother-in-law. Of all fucking nights.

"Veronica here is Garrett's nurse," Patterson bragged to the officer as they sidled up next to her. The portly, white-haired officer extended his arm towards her and she shook it limply, as if it were covered in excrement.

"Nice to meet you. I'm Officer Slater. I don't know if Patterson told you about me or not."

"No, he didn't. What's going on? It's awfully late to be visiting the hospital." Veronica's voice quavered.

"Officer Slater was Garrett's arresting officer," Patterson said.

Veronica raised her eyebrows. "Oh. Dallas PD?" The irritation she felt was at its tipping point.

"Used to be. I now work in good old Grapevine. One of your coworkers mentioned that you were at the tanning salon the night of Brittany Jameson's disappearance. When you have some time, I'd like to ask you a few questions, if that would be okay."

Veronica felt as if she were about to faint. "Is that why you're here at this ungodly hour?"

"I'm actually here for closure," he said with all seriousness.

"Closure?" she repeated.

"He wants to speak with him." Patterson interjected.

Fuck.

Patterson and Slater casually shuffled behind her into Bobby Lee's room. She flipped on the light, exposing two bodies that were either dead or dead asleep.

Slater stepped up to Bobby Lee's bed and inspected his face. "My word. He looks horrible."

Patterson joined him at the bedside. "He sure does. He looks dead. Oh my god, is he dead?" Patterson fumbled around Bobby Lee's neck in search of a pulse. "He's dead." Shocked surprise animated his face.

Veronica couldn't tell if it was a gasp of grief or glee coming from Patterson. She placed the stethoscope in her ears and joined them.

"Aren't you going to do something?" Patterson prodded.

"Like what?"

"I dunno. Like shock his heart with those things. What are they called?"

"A defibrillator," Slater offered.

"Yes, that's what they're called, but this is hospice. We don't do that here."

"But…"

"But, what? Anyone who enters hospice signs a DNR. It's standard procedure. We offer palliative care, not life-saving measures." Veronica placed her stethoscope on Bobby Lee's chest. "He's still alive, but his heart rate is really slow. I should probably call the family."

Patterson's jaw dropped. "So, you're just going to let him die?"

Veronica suppressed a flash of aggravation. "That's why he's here. Remember? Even if he wasn't on death row for the murder of over twenty women, he's terminal and he's here to die. That's what you do in hospice."

Patterson looked down at the floor and wiped his eyes. "I don't know. It just doesn't seem right."

Typical—one prick looking out for another. "Okay, how about this? Why don't we give the Governor a call and see if he wants you to give him mouth to mouth right now? Should we call him? What do you think, Officer Slater? Want to have a go at his chest?" Veronica forced a joking tone.

"Johnson!" Patterson shouted. "Jesus, we've got a shit ton of paper-work to fill out if he dies and that asshole's gonna sleep right through it." Patterson shook Johnson's shoulder. "Wake up!"

Bobby Lee coughed violently. Slater jumped and grabbed Bobby Lee's hand as if to greet him. He opened his eyes and mumbled, "She..."

Slater leaned in closer, gripping Bobby Lee's hand. "What? What was that?" Bobby Lee's eyes widened and focused on Veronica as if to clarify, then closed.

Veronica approached with her stethoscope and placed it on Bobby Lee's chest. "Dying patients often hallucinate. They see things that aren't there. They talk to people that aren't there. It's all very normal. For all we know, he could have seen his dearly departed granny calling him to the other side." She listened closely as the two men watched her every move. "He's gone."

As she dutifully noted the time of death and left the officers to begin the postmortem paperwork, Veronica was the very picture of professionalism—until she reached the solitude of the staff bathroom.

Stupid, stupid, stupid. She stared at the "I'm a Nurse, What's your Super Power" poster above the toilet. She didn't need her reflection in a mirror to confirm that she was physically ready to rip someone's throat out.

Paula had a "not after 10" calling rule, but she answered on the first ring. "Ronnie?"

Veronica pressed the phone to her ear and made her confession to the wet brown strand of hair in the sink. "I just did something totally stupid and I don't know how to stop myself."

Paula's voice deepened with concern. "Your voice sounds funny. How much have you had to drink?"

"Nothing. At least not yet."

VERONICA PULLED out of the parking garage of the hospital. Her time in Texas was officially over. The Grapevine Police might never have pegged her for Brittany's death at the Tropi-Tan, but with her non-appearance on Ingrid's laptop and the lethal dose of morphine they were sure to find in Bobby Lee's bloodstream, they might be able to suspend their supernatural disbelief and haul her in for something.

She'd starve or burn to death in a sunlit jail cell, and worse, they'd bring Frank in for questioning, and then… no, she couldn't do that to him. Not now. Not ever.

With a heavy heart, she drove to the airport and booked the next red-eye flight to San Francisco. She parked in the long-term garage and crawled into the roomy trunk. She doubted Frank would answer at this early hour, but she dialed his number anyway. It went straight to voicemail.

6

Frank pulled into the American Airline's passenger drop-off, killed the engine of his '65 Ford truck and hopped out to retrieve the brand new, navy-blue carry-on from the truck's bed. Veronica arose from a bench near the entrance to security.

"Come here," he said, extending his arms out towards Veronica. Hesitantly, she stepped towards him and allowed him a quick embrace. Any longer and she might never leave. She needed to be brave, but she felt as if she were about to embark on her first day of kindergarten. A security officer on his smoke break stepped out of the shadows, eyeing them as he stepped closer to the ashtray.

"You're going to be fine," Frank murmured into the mass of curls on top of her head.

"What if..."

"The plane crashes? Well, I imagine you'll be the lone survivor with one hell of a story to tell," he laughed.

"Don't say that. What if someone pisses me off?"

"Honey, you'll be fine. Like I said: I've packed boxes of chocolates to give to the gate agent and the flight attendants. Don't forget to request a window seat, and if your seatmate wants to talk about the weather in San Francisco, you have earphones and a new thriller in your bag. And if shit gets real, there's always the bathroom."

"Sir, there's a line of people waiting to get into this unloading zone. You're going to have to move your vehicle," the officer interrupted, pointing his lit menthol at the truck.

Frank pulled Veronica into his arms, dipped her body backward and kissed her hard on the mouth. "I love you, Ronnie. Call me as soon as you get in."

"I will." A flood of emotion hit her as the guard invaded their space. "Good…"

Frank placed a calloused finger on her lips and shook his head. "This isn't goodbye." He slapped her playfully on the rump, jiggled his keys and hopped into the truck. "Don't make me come to California to bring you back home. I don't think the truck will make it."

VERONICA LUGGED the blue carry-on towards the security checkpoint and handed over her boarding pass and fake ID to a young woman with a severe bun and overly gelled claw bangs. The woman greeted her with indifference. "Boo-chard? Is that like the lettuce?"

"No. It's French. Not that I'm French. I'm American, as you can see by my identification right there."

The woman looked back down at the card. Veronica's fingers tapped the podium. "Bouchard means big mouth. At least that's what I think it means. So, no, it has nothing to do with Swiss chard. Or lettuce." Beads of sweat began to collect at the band of her bra.

The woman handed back her items. "Interesting. Have a nice flight."

Veronica shuffled forward towards the conveyor belt, removed her black clogs and placed them gently into the plastic bin, along with her quart-sized baggie of toiletries and her phone. A geriatric man in front of her hobbled into the body scan machine, placed his thin, wobbly arms above his head and stood motionless like a clueless model. A young couple and three squawking children pulled up behind her with a luggage cart and two strollers.

In all their talks about the ins and outs of airports, Frank had never mentioned a full-body scan. Were those x-rays? Did she show up on x-rays? Seized with panic, she turned to question the family behind her, but they only pushed closer.

"Next." The TSA agent met her eyes and waved her over.

Her legs felt heavy and stiff as if she were trudging through thigh-level snow banks. "I've never done this before," she admitted, as if it wasn't painfully obvious by the way she had lugged her wheeled carry-on through the airport.

"Just put your feet on the floor where it's marked and lift your arms above your head."

Her body quivered slightly. Her light green shirt only accentuated the growing circles of armpit sweat. While the sound of her rapid heart rate thumped in her head, she watched the agent for any sign or signal to drop her arms and proceed forward. Instead, he picked up his radio and nodded. His eyes crinkled, and he motioned her forward.

"Ma'am, they're detecting something on your scan," he said in a lowered voice.

Veronica turned to look at her escape route. The line was crammed with angry, heavily sighing people. Instead of staring at their phones, all eyes were on her—the potential terrorist holding up the flow of traffic towards the nearest Starbucks.

"It's probably nothing. These millimeter wave machines are so sensitive," he said. "It's no big deal."

A brunette female agent with purple surgical gloves approached and collected Veronica's ID and boarding pass.

"Mrs. Bouchard, if you'll follow me, I'm going to take you to a private room for a quick pat down. You have plenty of time before your flight to San Francisco."

Fuck. I'm fucked. I'm so fucked. "Can I get my stuff?" Veronica took a step towards the bins, hoping to retrieve a box of chocolates.

"No, ma'am. We'll put it aside for you. Follow me."

A male agent, who thrived on the perceived power of his under-paid job, patted down a middle-aged Hispanic man, while random travelers tied their shoelaces and secured their trousers with belts.

"Can't we just do this out here?"

"I'm afraid not. We have to look under your clothes."

With no other options and very little hope, Veronica followed the agent, mentally surrendering herself to the will of fate and the Transportation Security Administration.

THE ROOM WAS SMALL, fluorescently lit and covered with posters regarding safety concerns and current travel regulations. Two young female agents stared at monitors, indifferent to Veronica's presence.

"We don't normally do the pat downs in this room, but because of the holiday, we're extra busy. Is that alright with you, Ms. Bouchard?"

"It's fine. I guess."

"Okay. I just need you to turn and face the wall and stand like this." The woman extended her arms out and widened her stance like a cheerleader.

Veronica turned and stared at the wall. As she lifted her arms, she calmed herself with thoughts of walking through the sunflower field behind her childhood home. The agent's gloved hands ran along the underside of her breasts, down her side and seemed to focus on the small of her back.

"Were you in the military?" asked one of the women at the desk.

"No."

The gloved hands moved down the inside of her legs.

"Would you lift your feet, please?"

"Have you ever been shot?"

"Excuse me?" Veronica turned to look at the seated woman.

"Shot. With a gun," she clarified.

"No."

"Well, according to this scan, it looks like you have two bullets near your lower rib cage and some very strange scarring."

"Would you please lift your shirt? We're almost done."

Veronica clutched the bottom of the green shirt that was now drenched in sweat.

"Just to your bra. I only need to see your stomach and back."

Although glaringly white and flabby from carrying six children, the skin of Veronica's stomach was flawless.

"There's no external scarring," said the gloved agent as she circled Veronica's body.

"That is so weird. Tattoos?"

"No."

"Are you done?" asked Veronica, her voice rising an octave.

"Yes. I'm sorry. You can put your shirt down. These scans are so sensitive. It could just be sweat it's picking up."

"Yeah, well, I'm super sweaty. The change of life and all that." Veronica smoothed her shirt and took a deep breath. Looking directly at the seated agent, she smiled. "Would you mind if I took a look? I'm a bit concerned that I may have a foreign object or a tumor floating around in my body." She stepped forward. "I'm a nurse."

"We're really not supposed to show anyone these images."

"I'll be quick. Please?" Unlike her typical professional monotone, her voice was now warm and syrupy. As the agent turned the monitor, Veronica's ego swelled with pride that she had somehow managed to use her vampire powers to actually get what she wanted.

"Wow. It kind of looks like people's faces." The brunette agent angled her head. "If you squint. Like right there." She pointed at the screen.

"Yeah. It's like Jesus on a piece of toast or something." The seated agent stood to look at the image again.

Veronica looked at the two floating bullets.

Detroit, 1978. "I'm Not in Love" played softly in the background as the bullets tore through her flesh. Kevin Black was not relieved or grateful to be brought back from the brink of death. Covered in their combined blood, he ran. The physical damage that had been inflicted had healed within seconds, but like the bullets still lodged within her body, the memory of his betrayal lingered.

The blonde pointed at the most prominent face on the screen. "That totally looks like a face."

Veronica's eyes widened with recognition. "Knud."

"Bless you!" The agent removed her gloves and threw them in the waste bin. "You're free to go, Ms. Bouchard."

As Veronica settled into her cramped window seat, she still couldn't believe it. Knud Jorgensen's face had appeared right above her belly button like an ugly tattoo. He was the first person she had ever turned. And like a tattoo that seems like a really good idea when you're young and slightly drunk, Knud changed from an affable fur trader with a kind word for everyone into a bitter recluse who lived solely on animal blood. In a moment of poor judgement, she thought he'd be a nice guy to spend eternity with, but then he managed to deplete the local beaver population within a year.

As Veronica studied the emergency card, a young woman with greasy black hair, torn jeans and a cat-hair-covered hoody stared down at her.

"You're in my seat," she shouted above the muffled music emanating from her ear buds.

Veronica looked at her ticket. 19 F. She showed it to the girl and smiled as if she were ashamed to be the winner. The girl plopped down, shoved her backpack under the seat and slammed down the armrest.

"My cheap parents can't even get me a decent seat on this lame ass flight. This blows," she huffed.

A large man looked down at his two strange flying companions and gingerly placed his laptop under the aisle seat. He smiled apologetically as he struggled to adjust his belt, then leaned his upper body forward so as not to invade their space.

"Great. I feel like I'm in a fat sandwich." The girl pounded the button on her iPod. A new song played, faster and louder than the first. Irritated, Veronica smiled and nodded at the man with her mouth closed. She tongued her front teeth to check their position and closed her eyes so as not to be further disturbed.

While she feigned sleep, her cramped seatmates remained quiet. Behind her, a fussy baby's cries increasingly reverberated in her eardrums. Irritated, Veronica opened her eyes and turned to look at the young, frustrated parents. They cooed, cajoled and jiggled the wriggling infant while their disgusted seatmate stared at the screen of his tablet. She mouthed, "Poor thing," to the child's mother. As she smiled reassuringly, the lights in the cabin darkened as if the plane had had enough. A collective gasp drowned the infant's cries.

"Ladies and gentlemen, we are experiencing some technical difficulty with the aircraft's generators. As a precautionary measure, we will be landing in New Mexico shortly. Please remain seated with your seatbelts securely fastened."

The exit lights lit up on the floor, but the cabin remained dark.

The greasy girl grabbed hold of Veronica's hand and rocked nervously back and forth.

"I don't want to die. Not now. This is totally not fucking cool." She turned to look at Veronica who was staring out at the dark sky.

The large man reached over and tapped her on the shoulder. "Are you okay, ma'am? You're really pale. You're not going to faint, are you?"

"I'm fine. My phone's dead. Do either of you know what time the sun rises in New Mexico?"

7

E veryone on the plane remained seated in a non-reclining position with their seatbelts securely fastened low and tight across their laps. Tray tables stayed upright. Peanuts and complimentary beverages were not served. No one complained. Prayers and pleas to God were whispered along with sweet, impassioned phone calls to loved ones. *I love you. I love you. No, I LOVE you. Oh my god. I love you.*

Veronica's phone was dead, so calling Frank was out of the question. It didn't matter. If the plane crashed, she'd walk home from the burning rubble without a scratch. Confronting the sun's rays was a different matter.

She'd never actually witnessed one of her kind burst into flames when the sun met undead skin, but she'd seen enough movies to know that daylight was not something to dabble in. Frank had warned her about delayed flights, aggressive seat recliners, and overly chatty passengers, but not about emergency landings in the middle of nowhere.

Greasy Girl finally let go of Veronica's hand to remove a cracked iPhone from her backpack. She scrolled through her contacts with shaky hands, then brought the phone to her ear. Her voice became that of a child's.

"It's Jenny. Yeah, so my plane is probably going to fucking crash. Yeah, seriously. Engine failure. You can probably Google it in about twenty minutes. So, um. I just wanted to call you and Mom and say I'm sorry for fucking up so epically."

Turbulence rocked the plane. Veronica gasped from the woozy feeling in her stomach. She didn't know if it was possible for her to vomit even though she hadn't eaten anything, but she felt the need just the same. Her seatmate's catastrophic disposition wasn't helping.

"Oh, my god! We just dropped like a thousand feet, Dad. Listen. Can you tell Jimmy I love him? I still think Julie's a bitch, but she's twelve so I forgive her. Dad? Are you there?" Jenny stared at her ancient phone and sighed. "It figures. I'm going to die and there are no fucking bars on this old ass phone." She stretched out her arm to take a selfie and turned to Veronica. "Well, when they're digging through the piles of wreckage they'll find this one final photo of Row 19. We'll be famous."

Click.

"Please don't take my picture." Veronica pressed closer to the window. "Are you high?"

"Not any more. Hey, even better, let's make a video. I'll keep filming as we're going down so people can see what it's really like to die."

Veronica unbuckled her belt and looked anxiously towards the aisle. The man on the end leaned forward and placed his head between his hands. Teardrops landed on his khakis.

Veronica leaned over. "Are you okay?"

The man sat upright and wiped his face with the sleeve of his plaid shirt. "I'm fine. Just stressed out like everyone else."

"I think we're going to be okay." Veronica stood. "I hate to do this to you, but I really need to use the restroom." She gazed into his watery eyes in an attempt to work her vampire magic.

No such luck. "Ma'am, the seatbelt sign is on and with all this turbulence, I don't think it's a good idea for you to be gallivanting around."

She hated that word and anyone who used it. "But," escaped her lips as the plane jolted to the right, slamming her into the seat and thumping her head against the window. "Ow!"

"Put your seatbelt on!" he yelled.

Veronica rubbed her head with one hand and fished for the belt beneath her with the other. Tightening it across her waist, she closed her eyes and prayed. "God, Grant me the serenity to accept the things I cannot change. Courage to change the things I can. And…"

"Wisdom to know the difference! Am I right?" The greasy girl—Jenny—smiled knowingly at Veronica. "NA. You?"

"Lots of people know the serenity prayer. It doesn't mean I'm an addict."

"I am. I just got my one-month chip, but I blew it on a three-day bender with some guy I met in Plano." Jenny retrieved the orange medallion from her jean pocket and rubbed it between her fingers.

"Are you sober right now?" asked Veronica.

"Nope, but I was on my way to some fancy ass rehab in Palm Springs. My parents were too cheap to get me on a direct flight, so I took that as an opportunity to fuck up again and now I'm going to die."

The pilot's voice boomed, startling them. "Ladies and gentlemen, we are beginning our descent into Cannon Air Force Base. We might experience some air pockets, so please make sure your seatbelts are securely fastened. Attendants, please prepare for landing."

"Sweet!" Jenny slapped Veronica on the arm with the back of her hand.

The second the plane's wheels touched the ground, the passengers erupted into wild cheers and clapping as if the pilot had performed a miracle, which maybe he had. Veronica quickly unbuckled herself and grabbed her purse. "What time is it?"

"It's fucking Miller Time!" Jenny pounded the armrest and slapped her other seatmate's khaki-clad knee.

"You're kidding, right?"

"Technically I'm not in rehab, so what are they going to do?" Jenny bounced in her seat.

Veronica chuckled at the ridiculousness of the situation. "Can you please, for the love of god, chill out for just a second and tell me what time it is?"

Jenny sighed dramatically and retrieved the phone from her backpack. "Three twenty-one in the AM. You got a date or something?"

"Yeah. Something along those lines." She gazed out the small window into the dark desert night.

"Good morning ladies and gentlemen and welcome to Clovis, New Mexico. I have good news and bad news. The good news is that we have landed safely. The bad news is that we are going to be parked here until they are able to repair the generator, which could take a while. So, sit back, relax and enjoy a complimentary beverage. You are now free to move about the cabin."

"Shit."

"What's the big deal? It's the middle of the night. How important is it? Even I know that. Chill."

Veronica removed her seatbelt, sank back into the seat and turned towards Jenny.

"How old are you?"

"Nineteen."

"Do you like being nineteen?"

"No. Why?"

"No reason." Veronica drummed the armrest with her fingers as if that would send a message to the ground crew and speed up the repairs.

When a flight attendant passed by, Veronica bolted upright. "Ma'am! I really need to stretch my legs."

The attendant stared blankly back at Veronica.

"What I meant to say was, can we get off the plane? I'm feeling sort of claustrophobic just sitting here."

"You're welcome to walk up and down the aisle, but we can't exit the air craft. We're at a military base."

"So, how long do they anticipate this generator thing taking?" She tried to keep her tone light and conversational.

"We don't have all the details yet, but it could be several hours. Can I get you something to drink?"

Yes, warm and red and preferably free from methamphetamine. "I'm fine. Thanks."

"I'll have a Bloody Mary with a side of Stoli," Jenny said and pushed in her ear buds. The attendant made her the drink, handed it to her without checking her ID and pushed the cart on down the aisle. "You're gonna pass up a free drink?" Jenny opened the tiny bottle and guzzled it. "You must be in AA, huh? That's cool."

As the booze kicked in, Jenny reclined the seat and closed her tired eyes. The man on the aisle clicked open his laptop. Veronica glared down at the armed military men milling around outside the plane. One stupid move and they'd probably shoot her. She closed the shade and attempted to control her breath. While everyone around her slept or busied themselves with electronic devices, she tried to accept the fact that she was powerless over her circumstances and that her life had become increasingly unmanageable. In the air or not, circumstances were going to get really real for the passengers of Flight 1297.

8

The plane remained motionless at six a.m., while the flight attendants busied themselves with the delivery of pillows, blankets and "It's five o'clock somewhere" cocktails. Veronica had filled the previous agonizing hours by penning a long letter to Frank. She hoped Jenny would drop it in the mail on her way to rehab. She also hoped that whatever happened in the next hour wouldn't hurt, but from her years spent working in hospice, she knew that that was not always the case. She'd witnessed gentle last breaths that looked like deep slumber, but she'd also witnessed folks who struggled against that white light with panic and fear in their eyes.

The sound of Bobby Lee's breathy cackle echoed in her head, filling her squirrel-cage mind with resentment and regret. If she hadn't fucked up, she could be home spooning Frank. Instead, she was forced to consume forkfuls of humble pie. With a trembling hand, she lifted the window shade. Still dark. It was not her choice to die on a flight to San Francisco surrounded by strangers, but she'd surrendered to the idea of sunlight and whatever that might bring. If anything, death would be like a good night's sleep, something she hadn't experienced in years. She shook Jenny's arm.

"Mom?" Jenny slurred and opened her raccoon eyes.

"It's Veronica. I need you to listen to me for just a minute. We don't have much time." Veronica looked towards Khaki Pants. He was fast asleep, his mouth gaping open.

Jenny sat up in her seat, exhaled into her cupped hands and winced. "My breath smells like ass. Got any gum?"

"No." Veronica handed her the letter. "I need you to mail this for me. I've written the address down on the first page. Here's ten bucks to buy some envelopes and a stamp. Will you do that?"

"What, you can't mail it?"

"No." She lowered her voice to a whisper. "Something really weird is probably going to happen in the next thirty minutes."

"I think something really weird is happening right now. What else?" Jenny lifted her backpack onto her lap.

"Listen, I don't know the specifics of what is going to happen, but it will be weird. Even for a girl like you." Veronica stood and squeezed her body towards the aisle. "That letter is an amends to my husband. Please don't read it. Okay?"

Jenny rolled her eyes and placed the letter in the outside pocket of her pack. "You have my word, but I'm an addict not a postal worker, so whatever."

"Thank you." Veronica trudged slowly towards the back of the plane as if her feet were shackled. She stepped inside the vacant bathroom for a quick peek, locking the door behind her. Like the closet where she spent her days, it was cramped and windowless. For a moment she entertained the thought of barricading herself inside till sundown. But people would inevitably complain, and the crew would be forced to pry the door open. It depressed her that her final resting place would be a bathroom. Even if she went out in a theatrical blaze of glory, there would be no dignity in dying on the toilet. She glanced briefly at the mirrored surface above the sink. For a split second, she thought she saw herself reflected, but she knew too well that the mind plays tricks when death is near.

She opened the door to find Khaki Pants picking his nose. "This is the flight from hell," he yawned, edging closer to the door like a dog marking its territory.

You have no idea. She smiled, nodded and entered the empty galley. There was a tiny window on the escape door. The sky was lightening. She wasn't sure if she needed direct contact with the sun or if peripheral exposure would do the trick. The last thing she wanted was to injure anyone or inflict emotional trauma during her demise, so she sat on the floor, brought her knees to her chest, and closed her eyes. She couldn't think of an appropriate prayer for the moment, so she recited the Lord's Prayer in a low voice.

"Our father, who art in Heaven. Hallowed be thy name. Thy kingdom come. Thy will be done, on earth as it is in Heaven. Give us this day, our daily bread. And forgive us our trespasses, as we forgive those who trespassed against us. And lead us not into temptation but deliver us from evil. For thine is the kingdom and the power and the glory. Forever and ever, Amen."

In a singsong voice, a male's voice added, "Keep coming back—it works if you work it."

She opened her eyes.

"I'm sorry to interrupt you, ma'am, but could you please make your way back to your seat?"

Veronica looked up at the young steward with perfectly gelled hair and pleaded with her best puppy dog eyes. "I don't think I can. My legs. It's probably a blood clot. Can I please just stay back here and exercise them until we take off?" Veronica rolled to her side and performed animated leg lifts. "I promise I won't bother anyone. I'm a nurse."

Probably exhausted and fed up with all the complaints he'd endured, he spoke down at her like she was a naughty child. "Okay, but don't call attention to yourself. I don't want this area to turn into an aerobics class."

"I'll do my best."

He turned his attention to the small window. "Wow. Look at that. I guess that's the reason they call New Mexico the land of enchantment."

"What do you mean?"

"The sunrise. It's enchanting."

Veronica inhaled deeply and braced herself for impact as streams of warm morning light touched the skin of her face. The attendant looked down at her with a furrowed brow.

"Are you okay?"

"I'm fine. I'm just crampy. Do I look okay?'

"You look fine. I mean, despite the fact that you're lying on this nasty floor." He loaded a variety of sodas onto his cart. "You were smart to stay out of the sun. My mom's face looks like an old Coach purse."

"So, I'm not changing?"

"Um, do you mean like the change of life, changing? I'm confused."

She nodded, and he stooped down to inspect her face. "Well, your upper lip is kind of sweaty. I hear those hot flashes can be a bitch. Do you want something cold to drink?"

Confused and vaguely agitated, Veronica pressed her face to the cold window, daring the sun to take the first swing.

"I'm ready, God," she murmured into the plexiglass, her breath steaming up the window, waiting through a ten-second eternity for…

…nothing. No bursting into flames, no crumbling into dust, no spewing of blood—nothing. Nothing but a god-damned glorious southwestern sunrise. In a huff, Veronica stood, dusted off her black pants and stared at the skin on her arms as if she were hallucinating.

The attendant pushed his cart into the aisle as if this kind of passenger behavior was par for the Dallas/San Francisco course.

"What. The. Fuck?" She exhaled and shuffled back to her seat. She touched her face in random places to make sure it was still there. As it said in fancy cross-stitch on the wall of her Al-Anon meeting, "An Expectation is a premeditated Resentment." *Fucking-A it is.*

Khaki Pants was MIA. Jenny flipped through the pages of the in-flight shopping catalogue and was now sipping from a can of Miller Lite.

"Move," Veronica said, and crawled over Jenny's extended legs.

"So, did the really weird thing happen yet?"

"No. False alarm. How do I look?" Veronica turned her head from side to side.

"Um, is this a trick question?"

"No, it's not a trick question. How do I look?"

Jenny sized her up. "You look like a middle-aged woman who doesn't try very hard."

Veronica lifted her brows. "Really?"

"Well you don't! If you put a little makeup on, did something with your hair and lost that muffin top, you could be a total cougar. You should see my mom. I don't think my dad has ever seen her without her face on. Last month she got that Botox shit all over her forehead and now she can't lift her eyebrows. Given the choice between looking old or weird, I'd take old."

"What the hell are you talking about?"

"Makeup, bitch. What do you want to know?"

"Oh, never mind. You know, you could use a little less makeup. That foundation makes you look like an Oompa-Loompa."

"I'm not wearing foundation." Jenny leaned forward and pulled off her hoody to reveal a black Ramones t-shirt. Her arms were as orange as her face and covered in track marks.

"Don't tell me you shoot meth?"

"No fucking way. Do I look that crazy?"

Veronica stared at the small orange girl covered in cat hair and nodded slowly. "Yes. Yes, you do."

"Well, I'm not. I have a blood condition." Jenny leaned back into her chair and swallowed the rest of her beer in one gulp. Crushing the can with one hand, she drew out a long, dramatic burp and leered at Veronica. "So, put that in your sanctimonious pipe and smoke it."

"A blood condition?" Veronica's eyes widened, and she moved closer to Jenny's face, hoping to catch a whiff. "Hemochromatosis? Is that it? Is that your blood condition?"

"Yeah. Take a chill pill, psycho." Jenny leaned away from her. "How did you know?"

"I'm a nurse." Veronica wasn't particularly hungry, but the mere thought of Jenny's medical condition took her mind off the sun. Some of her fondest meals were from hemochromatosis patients. Compared to the regular old skim milk of the general population, their iron-rich blood tasted like fresh, heavy cream.

Khaki Pants sat down and buckled his seat belt. "I suggest you ladies buckle up. We're going to be taking off any minute."

For the rest of the flight, they remained silent. Veronica closed her eyes and let the sun spill onto the exposed flesh of her arms and face, fantasizing about iron-rich blood, tanned skin and the possibility of sleeveless shirts.

9

The passengers of flight 1297 clapped half-heartedly as the wheels of the airliner touched the runway. The fear of death was quickly replaced by the minutiae of missed flights, dead batteries and morning hunger. Everyone was exhausted. The pilot's announcement that it was fifty-eight degrees and foggy outside didn't help.

"Can I use your phone?" Veronica tapped Jenny on the back as they waited to deplane.

"Sure." Jenny handed her the cracked iPhone from her back pocket.

Veronica stared at a crumpled piece of paper while pressing Ingrid's number onto the greasy screen. "Hey, Ingrid. We just landed. The sun is out and I'm still here. Anyway, I hope the plan is still the same. I'm a little worried you're not picking up." Veronica looked at the phone to make sure it was still connected. "As we discussed, I'll meet you at the baggage claim. In case you didn't know it, the sun thing is a lie. Okay, then. Bye."

Veronica handed the phone back to Jenny. "That's my daughter. She probably didn't pick up since she didn't recognize the number."

"Or she didn't pick up because she hates you and has no intention of picking you up at the airport."

"Are you always this negative?"

"Yes." Jenny slung her backpack over her shoulder and soldiered down the aisle. As she entered the terminal, Veronica tapped her on the arm again.

"I just wanted to wish you good luck with treatment. I don't know you very well, Jenny, but I do know that you can do it. One day at a time, okay?"

Jenny rolled her eyes and attempted to fist bump Veronica. "Later."

Veronica embraced her in a quick, awkward hug. She reeked of sweat and methamphetamine. "Take care of yourself."

Veronica was slammed by guilt as she walked away from this mess of a girl. If it were up to her and her codependent ways, she would accompany Jenny to her connecting flight and make damned sure that she checked into rehab within an hour of landing in Santa Barbara. But Jenny's recovery was none of her business. Jenny had to want sobriety, and Veronica wasn't convinced that she did.

Veronica scanned the crowd of people at baggage claim for Ingrid's red hair and fair skin. She wasn't there. She probably hadn't bothered to check that the flight was delayed. As an eternal teenager, there would inevitably be a million excuses.

To kill time until her daughter's arrival, Veronica crept out of the building through the automatic doors like a jittery cat. Feeling like an animal that had been caged for years, she wanted nothing more than to roll around on the grass in the sun. But with those first tenuous steps, doubt crept in. Maybe the sun wasn't strong enough in the plane or in the grey clouds that hovered above San Francisco. Maybe it would take an Arizona scorcher to burst her into flames. She didn't know if she'd been living a lie set forth by those before her, or if it was remotely possible that all the cancer drugs and narcotics she'd ingested had finally pickled her body into immunity. A fine mist settled on her skin as she reveled in the uncertainty of the moment.

"Taxi!" Jenny hollered into the street.

Bewildered, Veronica sprinted towards her. "What are you doing? What about your flight to Santa Barbara?"

"What? Are you my mom now?"

"No, but I could be."

"The next flight to Santa Barbara doesn't leave for another six hours and I'm not staying in this shithole airport for standby. Where are the fucking taxis?" She stomped her black, thick-soled boots on the pavement.

"There's a taxi stand over there. You see where all those people are lined up?"

"Oh." Jenny's phone jingled, and she peered down at the screen. "I think it's your daughter. Pizza slut," she answered with an impish grin, then stuttered. "Wait, wait, wait a second! You have the right number. She's right here. Here." She tossed the phone to Veronica like a hot plate she hadn't ordered.

"Where are you? Oh. Super Shuttle? Hold on a second. Let me get a pen." Veronica snapped her fingers at Jenny.

Jenny dug in the bowels of her tattered backpack and managed to produce a pen and a crinkled-up receipt.

"Three seven seven Sycamore Street. Like the tree? Okay. See you in a bit." Veronica handed the phone back to Jenny.

"Want to go to Western Blood Center with me? My daughter's a phlebotomist. She's working. That's why she isn't here."

Jenny looked at her as if she were crazy.

"Listen, I know it's not the most exciting of plans, but maybe you could make a donation and it would help with your coloring. After that, we'll get you something to eat and then back to the airport for your flight. What do you say?"

Jenny thought about it for a minute, then wiped her eyes with the sleeve of her sweatshirt. "Sure. Why not? It's not like I have anything better to do."

They shuffled towards the taxi stand.

"You're not going to kill me and dump me in the bay, are you?" Jenny's brows arched.

"What would give you that impression?"

Jenny pulled the letter from her pack. "This."

10

The faint aroma of vomit and stale cigarettes lingered in the vinyl-covered back seat, despite the lilac-scented air freshener that overwhelmed the tiny space. Veronica rolled down the window and leaned her head out to escape the olfactory assault, daring the sun to obliterate her. Jenny didn't seem to notice the smell. She was more concerned with the curious letter in her sweaty hands.

"So. Would you care to illuminate me on your deathbed scribbling? Or are you just going to plead the fifth?" Jenny unfolded the crumpled paper and read it aloud in a monotone voice. "'More than anything, I'm sorry for subjecting you to my strange ways, and yes, that includes all the people I've killed. I tried to be as ethical as possible in my pursuit of blood, but sometimes, as you know, it was beyond my control. If anything, I am so grateful that I never changed you. Unlike the life I've lived, yours will be so much happier in that one day it will end.'"

The driver slammed on the brakes. Jenny flew forward, crashing against the plastic window that divided the cab. "Idiot," the driver shouted at the dented white Prius in front of them.

"Put your seatbelt on," Veronica demanded above the wailing of the cab's horn.

"Mother fucker!" Jenny punched the window and flipped off the driver. Grabbing the greasy belt, she strapped it across her thin waist. "There. Are you satisfied?"

"Yes. The last thing we need is for you to die on your way to rehab," Veronica said and leaned back against the seat.

"I'm not going to rehab." Jenny folded the letter into a tiny square and stuffed it in her backpack. "So, um, are you like a serial killer or something? Or are you just mentally ill?"

Veronica rubbed her temples, contemplating her response. "Yes, something along those lines."

"Well, which one? An inquiring mind wants to know if she should walk down a dark alley with your ass."

"I'm a vampire. And yes, you are going to rehab." Veronica chuckled in a deep low voice at those strange words.

"No, I'm not. And if you really are a vampire, shouldn't you be sexier or something?" Jenny placed her boot-clad feet on the cab's plastic divider. The driver scowled at her in the rearview mirror.

"I just admitted to you that I'm a vampire and your main concern is what I look like? Who's the mentally ill one here?" Veronica swatted at Jenny's leg. "And get your feet off that. Were you raised in a barn?"

Jenny let her feet drop with a thud. "Okay, Dracula. If you really are a vampire, why did you fly on an airplane? Why didn't you just turn yourself into a bat and fly your shit for free to California?"

"Why? I'll tell you why. I never figured out shape shifting or whatever it's called. And the way things have been playing out lately, I'm going to assume that shape shifting is a myth. Kind of like that myth about the sun, which absolutely kills me, just not *literally*! Do you know how long I've been hiding in closets and basements and the trunks of cars?"

Jenny's eyes widened at the rising tide of anger in Veronica's voice.

"I'll tell you. A long fucking time. I've been hiding in dark places since the eighteen fucking hundreds! And now! Now! When I finally discover that it's a big, fat lie, I'm in a city that's covered by an enormous fog bank. Where is the fucking sunshine? Where?"

"That would be the Eastbay or Marin," the driver shouted over the radio.

"I think you're freaking him out, so you may want to keep your voice down and that vampire shit to yourself."

Veronica rolled her eyes. "What about you? You're not freaked out?"

"My sister is scarier than you. She's twelve." Jenny stared at her phone expectantly.

The driver pulled up to the curb, clicked off the meter and turned towards the back seat. "Forty-six."

AT THE ENTRANCE to the blood bank, Veronica brushed a few cat hairs from Jenny's hoody. "Whatever you do, don't talk too much. And try not to swear. You may think it's the groovy, cool, bitchin', or whatever thing to do, but let me tell you, it's really not becoming for a girl your age."

"Well, neither is your hair, but you don't see me pointing out that shit to you." Jenny smiled. She kicked at the brick building. "I get the feeling that you really don't want to go in there, do you?"

"It would be like you walking into a meth lab with free samples. Plus..." Veronica's voice trailed off as she popped her neck from side to side.

"What?"

"I haven't seen my daughter in a really long time." Veronica turned towards the front window of the blood bank and fluffed her hair. "I must look like hell."

Jenny looked towards their reflection, but the space beside her was empty. She spun around to face Veronica. "I can't see you in the window." Jenny's mouth gaped open as she turned back towards her reflection. "I can't believe it. Either I'm still totally high or..."

"Let's get this over with before I burst into flames." Veronica smiled and put her arm around her, pushing her towards the entrance.

"Oh my god. Wait till I tell my little sister." Jenny pulled away. "You're not going to kill me, are you?"

Only if I'm desperate. Veronica yanked open the glass door and stepped inside the fluorescent-lit building. Every bed was full. Pints of blood dangled below eye level so as not to disturb anyone's aesthetic sensibilities. The scent was an intoxicating mix of hope and ruin. "No, but I do want some of the blood you're donating," she whispered near Jenny's ear.

At the back of the room, Ingrid dropped her clipboard and ran towards Veronica with the unbridled enthusiasm of a child. "Mama!"

Veronica tensed like a body builder about to lift an enormous weight as Ingrid embraced her. The young woman buried her face in the crook of her mother's neck. Veronica patted her stiffly on the back as all eyes in the room focused on the awkward exchange.

Jenny took a step back from the pair. "You could hug her back, you know," she said and fiddled with her phone.

Ingrid looked at Jenny with a questioning look. "Is she with you?"

"Oh, I'm sorry. This is Jenny." Veronica cleared her throat and wiped at her damp forehead. Anger and resentment rose like bile, elevating the temperature of her body and pummeling her brain with images of the night Ingrid deserted her with Desmond. "The two of us bonded on the plane and she has a few hours to kill until her next flight. You don't mind, do you?"

"No, of course not. Nice to meet you, Jenny." Ingrid extended her pale, slender arm.

Jenny wiped her hands nervously on her jeans before limply shaking Ingrid's hand. "You too."

"As you can see by her coloring, this poor dear has hereditary hemochromatosis. Would it be possible while we're here for you to drain her of a pint?" Veronica smiled with a flash of her milk white-fangs and placed her arm protectively around Jenny.

"Um, I guess so. Why don't we go back to the special donations room, if that's okay?"

Ingrid quickly shuffled them back to a small room and opened the door.

"Have a seat." Ingrid grabbed a pair of purple surgical gloves. The door closed with a click.

"Does this door lock?" asked Veronica.

"Okay, I don't know what the hell is going on here, but I'm seriously getting freaked out." Jenny jutted her arms out, making the sign of the cross with her fingers. With her eyes fixated on Veronica, she slowly backed herself into a corner. "Is your daughter a blood sucker, too?"

"Yes. As a matter of fact, she is. Aren't you, dear?" Veronica sat in one of the plastic chairs lining the wall. A smug grin revealed that her teeth hadn't retracted.

"Jesus, Mom. You're scaring her. Jenny, first of all, you can put your fingers down. Doesn't work." Ingrid walked slowly towards her with her arms up as if she were surrendering. "Listen to me. I'm not going to hurt you. I'm going to help you." Ingrid gestured to the gurney. "Do you prefer your left or right arm?"

"She'd never hurt you, Jenny." Veronica crossed her arms firmly. "Well, at least not intentionally."

Jenny let her arms flop to her side and shuffled to the gurney. "Okay. Whatever. You two need to hug it out like for reals this time, because this room is tense." She hopped up on the gurney and eased her body back onto the crinkly paper. "Okay, Doogie. They usually have better luck with the left. And whatever you do, don't mention my veins or tell me they're wiggly. That shit makes me pass out. Speaking of which, do you have anything to drink?"

"Sure, I'll get you some juice. Mom?"

"Oh, gee, why don't you bring me a nice warm O positive with an AB negative chaser." Sarcasm didn't literally tear flesh, but it was her favorite defense.

Ingrid smiled nervously. "Sorry. I've been working among the living for so long, I sometimes forget." She tucked a red lock of hair behind her ear and bit her lip. "I can't wait to eat a bacon cheeseburger. Do you remember food, Mom?"

"What do you mean by that? We can't eat bacon and you can forget about cheeseburgers. Believe me, I've tried. Nonstop vomit for hours." Veronica stood with a jolt. Her purse fell to the floor with a loud thump. "Oh, god, no. Please don't tell me it's a myth. I will seriously go postal on every person in this place if it's a fucking myth."

"Calm down. Geez. What's wrong with you?" Ingrid rushed towards Veronica and placed her hand on her shoulder. "Sit. And keep your voice down."

Veronica plopped back down and wearily reached for the spilled contents of her purse.

"It's not a myth, Mama, but as God is my witness, after tonight, I'm never drinking blood again. Ever."

"And how's that going to work, Scarlett? You'll die."

Jenny swung her legs to the side of the gurney and sat up. "Technically, aren't both of you already dead? I mean, I don't know much about vampires, other than that they sparkle in the sun and they like baseball, but, wait a second." Jenny pointed at Veronica as if clarity had suddenly struck her drug-addled brain. "Never mind. That was just a movie my sister watched like five times a day and that's fiction. Right?"

"Who the hell knows what's real and what isn't? I certainly don't." Veronica leaned forward and placed her hand under her chin like a schoolgirl. "So, tell me, Ingrid, how are you going to eat bacon? And while you're at it, why don't you tell me how you managed to take a picture of yourself."

"Let me draw her blood before her organs fail. And then I'll tell you. Promise."

11

Like watching her favorite meal lovingly prepared, Veronica stared at the slowly filling bag of blood and licked her lips. "I want that when you're done, Ingrid."

"It's all yours, mom. They won't let us donate it, which is ridiculous. It's like super blood." Ingrid patted Jenny on the arm. "You're almost done, sweetheart. Keep squeezing the ball."

Veronica tapped her foot on the green linoleum. Ingrid's sugary sweet behavior towards Jenny was stirring the murky waters of jealousy. "So, let's talk about bacon, shall we?"

Ingrid motioned to Jenny with her head. "I would prefer to keep this between us," she whispered.

"I love bacon. I used to be a vegetarian, but I couldn't give up the bacon. It's like the gateway meat to a carnivorous lifestyle," Jenny mused louder than was necessary in the tiny room. "Hey, was bacon invented in the 1800s?"

"Yes, of course it was. Are you okay? You sound weird. I mean, weirder than usual."

"I haven't eaten in like three days. A BLT sounds really fucking good." Jenny's voice trailed off as her eyes closed.

"And she's out. Great. Mom, I need to go grab some cookies and some more juice from the front." Ingrid placed a pillow under Jenny's feet. "Make sure her legs stay elevated."

"Yeah, yeah, yeah. I am a nurse, you know." Veronica watched as her impossibly youthful daughter darted out the door, then turned to Jenny, who had seen better days. She looked like a typical meth addict —a meth addict on her way to a rehab facility—which made her the perfect victim. No one would bat an eye if she didn't make it to check-in. And even if she did make it through the thirty-day course of treatment, she was statistically doomed to relapse.

Prior to hospice work and the ethically convenient hastening of death in the terminally ill, Veronica picked her victims based on their untimely demise trajectory. Bars, particularly those opened before noon, were the perfect culling ground. Every town, no matter how small, had one, and by sundown, they were ripe with asthmatic smokers, urine-soaked alcoholics, delirious drug addicts and those chronically unhealthy folks who subsisted on bar food and microwave dinners. If she bought any one of them a drink, they'd follow her to the basement, to the next bar or to the bathroom without question. Most of them were lonely, off the radar and physically incapable of running fast enough to avert her homicidal advances. But instead of wanting to sink her razor-sharp incisors into Jenny's scrawny, strangely hued neck, Veronica felt the overwhelming desire to wash the girl's greasy black hair and brush the goo off her teeth. Making do with what was available to her, she wet a brown paper towel, doused it in antibacterial soap and wiped Jenny's face.

"How's she doing?" Ingrid dropped two packages of Nutter Butters on the gurney and punctured the juice box with a straw.

"She's still out. Look at her. She looks like she got a bad spray tan. It's mostly her condition, though." Veronica wiped behind Jenny's ear.

Ingrid paced the small room, then faced her mother with grim determination. "I need to tell you something, like right now."

"I'm all ears." Veronica wiped behind the other heavily pierced lobe, currently missing all its ornamentation. "Damn, she smells. Uck."

"Look at me. Please," Ingrid pleaded.

Veronica stopped the methodical wiping and looked directly into her daughter's eyes. "Yes?"

"I just wanted to tell you that I'm sorry."

Veronica raised her eyebrows. "Huh?"

"I'm sorry that I turned you into a vampire." Ingrid's pale blue eyes welled up with tears. She averted her gaze to the floor before facing her mother's knitted brow. "I was so scared of losing you, but in the process, I robbed you of a normal life and ended up losing you anyway."

"It's okay," Jenny murmured and flailed her free arm in the air. "I pass out all the time. Why are you licking me?"

"Ingrid, you were fifteen. You didn't know any better. It's okay. I forgive you."

Ingrid handed Jenny the juice box. "Drink this," she said and braced herself against the gurney with both hands. "You better sit down, Mom."

"Why?"

"You're going to feel strange."

As soon as those words left Ingrid's lips, Veronica felt a whoosh of energy hit her in the gut like a B-12 shot. She grabbed her fleshy midsection and sank into the plastic chair.

"What in the hell was that?"

Ingrid ripped open the package of Nutter Butters and shoved one in her mouth. "Oh my god. I knew these would be good." She leaned back against the counter and wiped the crumbs from her face. "That? That was your soul, Mom," she said with her eyes fixed on the other package of cookies. "Are you going to eat those?"

12

Veronica swallowed down an impossible rush of energy. "My what?"

"Your soul. Come here." Ingrid waved her mother over to the sink and pointed at the metal paper towel dispenser. "Look. There's your lovely face. Now you can take pictures of yourself and post them on Facebook." She wrapped her arm around her mother's waist and squeezed up next to her.

"Whatever you do, don't do that. Fucking old people ruined Facebook." Irritated, Jenny looked down at the full bag. "I think I'm done. Are you going to remove this needle, or should I?"

While Ingrid attended to Jenny, Veronica stared at her gauzy reflection with wonder. She touched her face gingerly, marveling in disbelief.

Then she leaned in closer and inspected her pores. "Have I always looked this bad?"

"What are you talking about? You look great. You're like a hundred and…"

"Shut it! I'm fifty-one."

"But how long have you been fifty-one?" Jenny held a cotton ball against the puncture wound and raised her arm.

"None of your business." Veronica snatched the bag of blood and brought it closer to her nose. Her grey eyes rolled back in ecstasy. "Can I get a straw?"

"No. That's not a good idea." Ingrid opened one of the grey cabinets above the sink and retrieved a kitschy Western Blood Center travel mug. "Let's get out of here. I'm starving."

Veronica held the warm, sloshing bag towards her daughter. "Here. We can share it."

Ingrid flashed her an "as if" look and placed a French manicured hand on her hip. "I want real food." She removed the bag from her mother's clenched fingers and carefully poured its contents into the mug. "Do you have any idea what just happened to us?"

"Actually, I don't. All I know is that now I can see myself and that you can ingest Nutter Butters without barfing. Why don't you just cut to the chase?"

"Well, let's start with the most important news. I am now mortal. Which means that all the souls I've taken over the years, including yours, are back to their original owners." Ingrid twirled and handed the mug to Veronica. "It's like the ultimate cleanse."

Veronica plopped down on the edge of the gurney and stared at the floor as if the answers were hidden in the swirly green linoleum. "Okay, so what does that mean? Exactly?"

"What it means is that from this moment forward, I will age, I can eat whatever I want, I can sleep, I can go to the bathroom, and one day —and the beauty of it is that I don't know when—I will die. Just like everyone else." Ingrid's voice reached such a fevered pitch that Veronica worried someone might be pressing their ear to the outside of the door.

"And you're excited about that? Why would you pick a boring ass life over being a vampire?" Jenny lifted her phone. "You know, I think this is a moment you're going to want to remember. Can I get a picture of you two?"

Excited by the possibility of a finite life filled with bacon, Ingrid rushed next to her mother. "Say cheese!" she squealed in the direction of Jenny's phone.

"Brie," Veronica retorted with a face as pale and immovable as a marble statue. As Jenny snapped another photo, she tried to recount the number of souls she had taken over the years. Fortunately, the people she'd killed didn't count in that calculation. For those unfortunates, she was just a bitch who had stopped their beating hearts in an act of self-preservation or menopausal madness—it all depended on the day.

On the rare occasion that she had turned someone, there was a little more consideration, kind of like picking a spouse without the *till death do you part* escape clause in the contract. Knud Jorgensen had been the first. JA the last. The others were still blurry.

"So, let me get this straight. You apologized to me and now you're mortal? That's it? That's all you have to do?" Veronica threw her arms up in the air as Ingrid nodded like the giddy teenager she was. "Say you're sorry, huh? That's so simple."

"Well, you have to mean it. You can't just say the words."

"It's not easy to say you're sorry, especially if you're not." Jenny scrolled through the pictures on her phone. "These photos are horrible. You need to work on that resting bitch face if you're going to start posting selfies."

"Aww, she's just mad that she can't eat a bacon double cheeseburger with us." Ingrid smiled smugly.

"Actually, I'm not mad, I'm thinking." She was thinking that she needed to head to North Dakota to get Knud Jorgenson out of her gut. "What changes with me, other than reflection?"

"You'll see. Come on, let's get out of here. Des is waiting."

13

D esmond Bodkin. Veronica despised the name almost as much as she despised the man.

When he first entered their lives, he was twenty-seven and fresh off the boat with a devilishly handsome face, alabaster skin and jet-black hair. But it was his handshake that first gave Veronica pause. His fingers were extraordinarily long, his nails free of dirt and his skin as soft as a rabbit's coat. Unheard of for a man in North Dakota in the 1800s, a land of brutish, leather-skinned farmhands who smelled of manure and sweat.

Desmond was so new and different, with his sophisticated manner and dress, that Veronica trusted him to give Ingrid piano lessons in the evenings after dinner. With six kids and a long-dead husband, she had little time and even less inclination to tickle the dust-dappled ivories of the old box grand.

Leaving Desmond alone with her boy-crazy, hormonal daughter would be Veronica's first fatal mistake.

WHILE VERONICA FIXATED on the waiter's physique beneath his faded jeans, Desmond slid into the booth beside Ingrid. Without a hint of recognition directed towards his heavily cologned presence, Veronica sipped slowly and carefully from her travel mug.

"Are you all ready to order?"

Veronica kept her eyes on the waiter's tattooed biceps and tried to squelch her feelings. "I'm on one of those weird cleanses so I'm good, but I think these girls are ready. Desmond?" Veronica did not smile, worried that Jenny's still-warm blood might be clinging to her teeth.

"I'll have the Philly cheesesteak with rings instead of fries," blurted Jenny, who then proceeded to gulp down half of her Coke. "And a refill when you get a chance."

"And for you, young lady?"

"I'll take the Grubstake with fries, please."

"For you?"

"I'm just here to enjoy the company, thank you." Desmond smiled wearily at Veronica.

She averted her gaze to the waiter's ass as he waded through a sea of empty chairs towards the kitchen. "Too bad he's not on the menu," she said to no one in particular.

"I had a feeling this was going to be awkward," Desmond exhaled, "so why don't I just get things started? Hello, Veronica. It's wonderful to see you. You're looking well, as always." He reached forward.

"Don't," she sneered, and dropped her arm from the table.

"Are you one of them?" Jenny burped.

"Yes, I'm one of them. I'm Ingrid's," he smiled, revealing crooked teeth.

"Boyfriend? Husband? Brother? What?" Jenny pulled the straw from her drink and rolled it around her finger.

"I think the more apropos question, my dear, is who are you?" Desmond replied with a hint of flirtation.

"Jenny. I'm just an innocent bystander to all this crazy shit. Y'all should get a TV show. 'Keeping Up with the Creeps' or something."

"Hmm. That would prove problematic for some. Isn't that right, dear?" Desmond grasped Ingrid's tiny hand and kissed it. "I'm Ingrid's maker."

"Maker, huh? I don't know what kind of pervy shit you're talking about, Edward, but I get the feeling that she's done making. Like vegan-bitch-eating-bacon done. I saw it happen."

Veronica tried to suppress a giggle, but it came out as a guffaw, splattering Desmond in Jenny's spectacularly tasty blood.

Desmond dabbed at the droplets on his face with a paper napkin. "Nice, Veronica. Classy."

"Oh, get over yourself, you pompous, arrogant..." Veronica's face contorted into pure hatred as she scrambled to find the words.

"Douchebag?" offered Jenny.

"Why are you even here? I came to visit my daughter. Not you." Veronica rose from the booth.

Ingrid bolted upright. "He needs your help!"

"Help? Him? And what exactly do you need me to help you with, Desmond? Erection difficulties?" Her eyes narrowed.

"I need you to kill me."

14

After secluding herself in the Grubstake's single-stall bathroom, Veronica tried both Paula and Frank. Both calls went straight to voicemail, leaving her with nothing to do but stare at her reflection in the bathroom mirror. It was both exciting and strangely calming to finally see her face, like reconnecting with a long-forgotten friend. For far too many years she had been living in the abstract, her sense of self comprising words and actions only. She knew she had a nose, she just couldn't see it.

As it turned out, she was surprisingly well-preserved. Even before becoming a vampire, she had never exposed her Scandinavian skin to the sun. On the rare summer day when the temperature had soared above ninety, she wore a wide-brimmed hat and tarped/draped herself in an unflattering piece of dark fabric masquerading as a dress. If there was anything that aged her, it was the sprinkling of white strands near the crown of her long curly hair.

To ground herself before returning to the table, she tried to think of something to be grateful for. Even though the most obvious thing was staring back at her in the mirror, she decided that today she would be grateful for the invention of stretchy pants.

Placing her hand on the door handle, she could hear Jenny's voice in the hall outside the bathroom. She paused.

"I only got twenty. Come on man. I'm totally good for it."

Veronica pressed her ear against the door.

"Come back here at three and we can work something out. Do me a solid and take a shower."

That greasy, conniving junkie. Veronica felt like busting through the door and pummeling them, but this transaction was none of her business. If Jenny was hell-bent on damaging the few brain cells that remained in her angry little head, that was her choice. In the years she'd spent sitting in the universally uncomfortable chairs of twelve-step programs, Veronica had learned that life was a lot less chaotic when she focused on herself. Paula's words echoed in her head. *Keep your mouth shut.* As a vampire, keeping her lips sealed had helped her in more ways than one.

Feeling calmer, Veronica shuffled back to the chrome sink, splashed cold water on her face and tried to convince herself that all these hot flashes were God's way of reminding her of her own humanity.

When she returned to the table, Jenny was disemboweling her backpack on the table while Ingrid and Desmond sat in stoic silence.

"Can I borrow some cash?" Jenny asked without looking in Veronica's direction.

Veronica forced herself to play it cool. "That depends on what you need it for."

"Cab fare to the airport." Jenny placed a stuffed Pikachu that had seen better days onto the table. All eyes were now focused on the odd paraphernalia of Jenny Pearson's life. "What?" She met their gaze. "He's my traveling companion."

"You don't need to get a cab; we'll take you." Veronica glanced at Ingrid to confirm they were on the same page. "You two have a car, right?"

"We sure do, and we'd be happy to take you, Jenny. What time's your flight?" asked Ingrid.

Jenny stared at the dirty table top. "I don't know. Something like six or seven. I can't remember."

"She's on her way to a rehab facility in Santa Barbara." Veronica scooted Jenny's hair-filled brush towards her.

"Good for you. Treatment is a wonderful first step towards a happier, more serene life." Desmond patted her on the hand. "I remember—"

"Dude, you want to kill yourself. Save the rainbows and unicorn speech for someone else." Jenny dug deep into her backpack with both hands and let out a sigh. "So, are you going to kill him?" She nudged Veronica with her elbow like a tween teasing a friend about her latest crush.

After an awkward pause interrupted by the delivery of their meal, Veronica gulped down what was left of her drink. "I worry about you, Jenny. To be honest, I wouldn't even know where to begin. Do I have to procure a wooden stake? Holy water? A silver bullet? What?"

"No. None of that. Arm and leg restraints and a very sharp knife should do it." Desmond leaned forward, rested his elbows on the table and intertwined his fingers as if in prayer.

"Is she gonna have to cut off your head?" Jenny took a bite of the cheesesteak and wiped the grease from her mouth.

"I'm sorry to interrupt this oh so pleasant conversation, but this is my first real meal in almost a hundred and fifty years. Do you mind?" Ingrid brought the bacon cheeseburger to her lips. "Oh. My. God. This smells divine. Would you take a picture of me, Jenny?"

"Gladly," Jenny said as Ingrid posed with her cheeseburger.

"You have to remove my heart and dispose of it as far away from my body as you can." Desmond pantomimed grabbing his own heart with his long slender fingers and tossed it out into the empty restaurant. "And when I say, 'dispose of,' what I really mean is 'destroy.'"

"Kind of like in *Dumb and Dumber* when Jim Carrey rips that guy's heart out and puts it in a doggy bag?" Jenny squeezed a flatulent ketchup bottle over her onion rings. "Like that?"

"Yes, but don't feed my heart to a dog. A crematorium would be ideal for disposal because of the incineration. I know someone who will accommodate you."

Jenny nodded with enthusiasm as if this was the most normal

conversation she had ever engaged in. Ingrid ignored them and wolfed down half of her burger in three successive bites.

"Slow down. You're going to choke," Veronica scolded with a bitter mix of motherly concern and jealousy. Her last meal had been roast rabbit with potatoes, something she did not feel a sentimental fondness for. Food used to sustain life. These days, it was its own addiction—one Veronica resented being denied.

"I can't help it. It's so good. I think I want dessert too."

"Whatever you'd like, dear." Desmond stroked her hair and turned to face Veronica. Tears welled in his eyes. "I realize you want nothing to do with me, Veronica, and you have every right to feel that way, but I would very much appreciate your help in this matter."

"I don't understand. Why now? Don't you want to be mortal with Ingrid?"

"I would, but that's not a possibility. I've taken too many souls. Some of the physical bodies are dead, which leaves them stuck inside me to fester like a cancer." He wiped his eyes with his shirt sleeve and returned his gaze to meet hers. "I'm ready to die. And I want you to be the one to do it."

Veronica had ushered many people to their deaths, but this felt vastly different. Unlike most of her patients at Heartwood, this was personal—and she *wanted* him dead. "I head back to Texas in five days. When exactly do you envision this happening?"

"Today."

"This is so cool! Can I be there?" Jenny bounced in her seat like an excited toddler.

Veronica rubbed her face and dabbed at the perspiration forming on her upper lip with a balled-up napkin. Desmond and Ingrid remained silently hopeful, as if speaking another word might change her mind. Her phone vibrated, and she looked to see a text from an unknown number.

It's Frank. The cops are looking for you. Don't come home.

15

In Veronica's experience, vampires were not an especially helpful or caring group of people. It absolutely sickened her that the few blood suckers she had encountered over the years had kept insightful tips and debunked myths solely to themselves—including her own daughter.

Veronica rationalized that this stinginess of spirit was common in the undead, since most of them self-isolated, including herself. It was hard enough to score even a semi-ethical blood supply without some just-turned plasma addict breathing down her neck, trying to edge their way in. Veronica imagined it would be like Jenny trailing Keith Richards in the hopes that he would show her the ins and outs of scoring medical-grade heroin. It wasn't going to happen. Vampires, like most addicts, were selfish and self-centered, especially when it came to their stash.

And right now, the closest thing Veronica had to a stash was the greasy runaway squished up next to her in the painfully small back seat of Ingrid's Mini Cooper. Like a true caregiving codependent, she refused to drop Jenny off at the airport. They both knew she had no intention of getting on a plane and Veronica wanted her around, if only for the fact that her bi-weekly blood draws could sustain her until she returned to Texas, whenever that was. She didn't know when to spring this half-baked idea on Jenny, or if she even needed to. So far, it appeared to all concerned that Jenny had no intention of going anywhere. She was just happy to be wherever there was a remote chance of scoring drugs.

"We're here," Desmond said and pulled into the small parking lot of a brick building with tinted windows, whose yellowed sign proclaimed it Cook's Funeral Home.

"Aren't we going to your house? Why are we at a funeral home?" Veronica stared at the sign.

Ingrid turned to face her mother in the back seat. "This is where it's going to happen. It'll make the cleanup and disposal much easier."

Disposal? Veronica was bothered by Ingrid's matter-of-factness. Planning a loved one's death should require a little more tact, not to mention gravitas when discussing the details. While Ingrid and Desmond had probably orchestrated this crazy plan for the last few weeks, it was new to Veronica, and she felt that they should behave accordingly. If the love of her daughter's life was truly going to die today, she should at least act like it bothered her.

"This is where I work." Desmond exited the car in one graceful, fluid motion. "I'm one of their embalmers. Ready?" He waved her forward like a parent coaxing a reluctant child.

"Are you kidding me? I think the more pertinent question right now is, are *you* ready?" Veronica opened the door and struggled to exit the tiny vehicle with her dignity intact. Jenny darted after her like a puppy.

"I've been ready for decades." Desmond grasped Ingrid's hand on their way in, Veronica and Jenny trailing behind.

A piped-in hymn greeted them at the door. Veronica couldn't place it, but she hadn't been in a church in over fifty years.

"Follow me." Desmond descended the stairs to the lower level of the funeral home. Unlike the ground floor with all its "avoid the pink elephant" accoutrements, there were no quaint couches, tissue boxes or comforting music here. There was nothing but a long, chilly hallway, stained concrete floors and three doors marked "Employees Only." Veronica shivered.

As Desmond led them through the middle door, Veronica glanced at the clipboard medical chart hung beside it. *Eye donation, Lori Grant, 35.*

Veronica peered inside the fluorescently lit room. "Is anyone here?"

"I am." A middle-aged man dressed in khakis and a rumpled denim shirt stepped forward. "Maynard Dirks. Veronica, I take it. It's a pleasure to finally meet you." He extended his hand.

She didn't know what she expected when she agreed to remove Desmond's heart, but it didn't involve limply shaking hands with a disheveled librarian-type in the middle of a torture chamber. Splayed out in the middle of the room was a black bench with leather-strapped appendages sticking out in the form of an x, and a tray full of surgical tools. Some Veronica had seen before, while others looked grimly archaic.

"And may I ask who this is?" Maynard eyed Jenny with a disapproving glare.

"I'm your worst fucking nightmare, Maynard." Jenny shook his hand with the confidence of someone with a drug score in her near future. "What kind of name is that anyway? May-Nard."

Holding her hand longer than necessary, he squeezed. "It means *strength.*"

"Nice firm handshake you got there, Bruce Banner. I'm Jenny. It means *fair one*, since you seem to care about that kind of shit." She pulled her hand away and plopped down on the leather bench.

"Well, isn't that interesting." Maynard smoothed his shirt and rubbed his clammy hands together. "I suppose we should all suit up in Tyvek, as I imagine this could get very messy."

Veronica glanced at Ingrid out of the corner of her eye. Her daughter stared calmly at her phone, seemingly immune to the reality of what was about to transpire. Her own heart raced, and she wanted nothing more than to run screaming from Maynard and the prefabricated ghastliness of this room.

If there was ever a myth about vampires that truly bothered her, it was that they were dramatic, evil, universally untidy creatures. She prided herself in the clean and clinical nature with which she could suck a person dry without spilling a drop. Everywhere she turned, though, from book covers to TV shows or movies, vampires were always pictured with blood dribbling down their chin or some other such nonsense. The last thing she wanted was to splatter someone's blood on her eighty-five-dollar yoga pants or even on her hospital scrubs. It was difficult to get out in the wash.

"Yes, I'll take a Tyvek suit. Extra-large. But before we begin, I need to use the little girl's room. Ingrid, would you care to join me?" Veronica slung her purse over her shoulder.

"Can I go?" Jenny rose from the bench.

"Of course, you can." Veronica sighed. The last thing Jenny needed was to be stuck in a room with Desmond the despot and Maynard the masochist.

The third door on the lower level was a unisex restroom with an adjoining lounge, the two seat-up stall toilets suggesting a dearth of self-respecting women employed at Cook's Funeral Home.

"Okay, Ingrid. We need to talk." Veronica leaned against the faux granite countertop.

Ingrid plopped down on an over-loved loveseat and drew her skinny knees up to her chest. "Yes?"

"What do you mean, yes? Listen, I'm about to end Desmond's life. Any thoughts or feelings you might want to express before I commit this final act?"

She paused to look up at the ceiling. "I thank you for agreeing to it. You are doing him a huge solid, Mom."

Veronica had heard this expression but couldn't place it. It made her wince.

Ingrid chewed her manicured nails. "He's tired and bored and he just wants to die. He's like really old. Like he won't even tell me how old he is."

"Okay, enough about Desmond and his geriatric anxiety. How long have you known about how to reflect or becoming mortal? Because to tell you the truth, the fact that you kept it to yourself really bothers me."

"I've known for a while."

Veronica inhaled deeply. The lines between her brows grew more prominent as her eyes squinted shut.

Ingrid jutted her arms out in front of her as if to shield herself from an assault. "I'm sorry! I didn't know how to get in contact with you. Once you left Detroit, I couldn't find you. It never dawned on me to look you up on Facebook. It just didn't seem like something you would even do."

"You're on Facebook? Dude, I'm totally going to friend you. What's your last name?" Jenny's hand flew into her back pocket to retrieve her phone. Her fingers hovered above the screen.

Veronica wanted to snap at Jenny, but it was easier to just surrender. "Bouchard. B-o-u-c..."

"I'm not stupid. I can spell." Jenny rolled her eyes. "So, let's upload one of your new pictures to replace that lame-o default icon."

Ingrid jumped up from the couch with a jolt. "Oh em gee, I have to pee!" Ingrid danced into one of the empty stalls. "I made a rhyme!"

Veronica had willingly corralled herself in a mortuary restroom with two hopelessly immature little girls. Abandoning all hope of having any kind of rational conversation about Desmond, she decided to take what she could get. "No, don't post any pictures or friend me. It's not a good idea right now. I need to stay off Facebook till some things blow over."

"Do you wipe back to front or front to back?" Ingrid's voice echoed in the small stall.

"Front to back," Veronica yelled back at her. "Do you need to go? Now would be a good time," she told Jenny.

"Not really. You?"

"I haven't pissed in years." Veronica turned to stare at herself in the mirror. "So, Ingrid. How did you learn about getting your soul back?"

Ingrid swung the door open and sauntered over to the sink as if she had really accomplished something. "It happened by accident. I hadn't had sex with Des in like a year and one night he offered me a rather heartfelt apology for stealing my life and taking me away from you. I know this is TMI, but we had amazing makeup sex and later when I got out of the shower, I could see myself in the bathroom mirror. I almost had a heart attack. I couldn't remember what I looked like."

"And?"

"He knew about it all along, but he never told me. His maker is dead, so..."

"Hmmm. Well, that changes things." Veronica felt lighter somehow in knowing that it was simply a happy accident and not a grand conspiracy. She returned to her own reflection, the one thing she could now count on. "Do you have any lipstick? I look so washed out." Veronica pinched her cheeks.

Ingrid handed her a tube of Mac from her purse. Both young women stared at Veronica's reflection in the mirror as she carefully applied Russian Red to her full lips. Her calm face projected pure detachment, but her mind was pondering the easiest way to remove a man's heart without having to break his ribcage.

16

Veronica strutted through the second door sporting a sensible bun, fierce lipstick and a renewed sense of purpose. "I'm going to need gloves. Long ones," she demanded.

Maynard nodded officiously and dug through one of the many cabinets. He retrieved a pair of industrial strength blue gloves and handed them to her. "Anything else?"

"Now that you mention it, yes. I need all three of you to get out of here. I am perfectly capable of doing this by myself, and for your own protection, I don't want witnesses or accomplices. This is technically an act of murder, so I suggest you all go busy yourselves elsewhere. Is that okay with you, Desmond? Or do you want to turn this into performance art? Never mind. Don't answer that. This is my circus and I'm the mother-fucking monkey." Veronica grabbed the Tyvek suit and stepped inside of it.

"But—" Maynard began.

"Listen—anything you say after *but* is simply justification for your own behavior or thoughts. And judging that you want to witness this, I seriously question both."

"My duty is to dispose of his heart." Maynard crossed his arms and squared his shoulders.

"I'm perfectly capable of opening the door, throwing it in that machine and pressing a button. It's not rocket science." She motioned towards the crematory. "Is it fired up and ready to go?"

"Yes, but—"

"There you go again. Try saying whatever you need to say without *but*. Preferably in ten words or less." Veronica zipped up the blinding white suit and placed the hood over her hair.

Maynard glared at her. "While I appreciate that you are undertaking the more difficult task, this is my room. Not yours."

"Excellent use of brevity, Maynard, but you don't have a compelling enough argument to change my mind."

"You just said *but*," he stammered.

"I'm also the one who will be holding a very sharp instrument, so you may want to drop the proverbial rope." Veronica grabbed the most menacing knife from the tray and held it up for inspection.

"You don't scare me," he mumbled under his breath.

"I'm not trying to," she replied and set the knife back down. She rolled her head from side to side. Audible cracking sounds emanated from her neck as she advanced towards Maynard. "All I'm asking is that you respect my wishes. It's for your own good."

"You can strap me down," Desmond reassured him, patting him on the shoulder. "I guess I should take this off, huh?" He sat down on the bench and lifted the grey cashmere sweater over his head, exposing his ripped abs. Jenny's jaw dropped.

"Damn. You're just gonna let that shit go?" Jenny whispered to Ingrid.

"I can hear you, Jenny. What the hell is going on with my hearing?" Veronica tapped at her ear and shook her head.

"You have your soul back. Something I never got to experience." Colder and less confident with his shirt off, Desmond rubbed his muscular arms. "I only got to live it vicariously through Ingrid. Right now, you are more alive than you've ever been. All six of your senses have been awakened."

"Awakened by what?" She widened her stance as if to plant herself. There was too much change in the past forty-eight hours.

"Hope. A world filtered through the eyes of possibility is a lot brighter than one filled with endless days of monotonous nothing." Desmond's eyes pleaded with her. *Do it quick before I change my mind.* His voice was clear and insistent in her head.

She nodded in understanding. "Would you please strap him down, Maynard?"

Ingrid glided towards Desmond and knelt beside him with confident grace. She smoothed his dark hair and kissed his lips. "This isn't the end. You and I both know that. I love you."

"I love you too. Be good, Ingrid." He stroked her pale face and whispered into her neck. "Listen to your mother. I don't want you to see this."

Jenny stepped forward as Ingrid rose. "I really don't know what to say so, see ya." She meekly waved in his direction and turned towards Veronica. *Wouldn't want to be ya.* Jenny's sing-songy thought echoed in Veronica's head.

"Good luck with your recovery, Jenny." Desmond laid back and Maynard stooped down to secure the first strap across his left leg.

"Where should we go?" asked Ingrid, looking somehow even more childlike than before.

"There's a nice quiet room off the main chapel if you want to wait there," said Desmond as Maynard moved on to the right leg. "Tighter," he instructed, lifting his leg to demonstrate.

"I really think I should be here. Don't you?" Maynard strapped Desmond's arms down to the bench with more force.

"You can wait in the next room, but I think it's wise if you adhere to her wishes."

"Fine." Maynard finished tightening the last strap and stood. "But —" He threw his arms up. "Jesus, I can't stop saying *but.*" He sneered in Veronica's direction and lowered his voice. "It just won't be the same here without you. Goodbye, my friend. Are you sure you won't...?" He raised his brows.

"Yes, I'm sure. You don't want this." Desmond smiled wearily, and Veronica didn't know whether to be touched at Desmond's eagerness to spare his friend the trauma of witnessing the dirty work to come or disgusted at his willingness to foist it off on Veronica instead.

"Has everyone said what they need to say?" Veronica scanned the room and lingered on Ingrid, who nodded solemnly.

"I think we're good to go." Desmond closed his eyes. A single tear streamed down the side of his face. Veronica hoped her daughter saw it.

"Alright, ladies and gentlemen, time to skedaddle. I'll come upstairs when I'm..." Veronica hesitated.

"Done," Desmond offered.

Jenny and Ingrid couldn't leave fast enough, but Maynard shuffled around the periphery of the room like a hungry raccoon at a Boy Scout campsite.

"I'll holler if I need anything from you, Mr. Dirks." Veronica grabbed one of the knives and walked towards the exit. She cleared her throat and opened the door.

Maynard's pace slowed, and he glowered at her like a pouty child. She attempted to read his thoughts as he passed, but nothing came. Incensed, she slammed the lockless metal door after him.

Up until this point, she had tried to behave as if she were a bad ass who knew what she was doing. Ending someone's life was never easy, even when they begged and pleaded for it. Veronica returned to Desmond, jittery and unsure. She inhaled deeply to steady her nerves.

"I don't know if I can do this," she exhaled and lowered the knife to her side.

"I know what you're going through and if my words can make it any easier for you, I want you to know this—I have a high tolerance for pain."

Veronica laughed at his admission. "This is different. It's final."

"I've been clubbed, stoned, hung, shot, stabbed, and eviscerated on more occasions than I would really care to remember." He raised his head as far as the restraints would allow. "And like yours, my body keeps coming back for further abuse. It's a crazy way to live and I'm truly sorry for my part in your creation. I don't know about you, but I'm done." He dropped his head and sighed. "Ingrid needs to have a life, and it will be much easier for her to do that if I'm gone. That's why I want you to do it. I owe that to you."

"I understand, Desmond. I do. I'm going to help you. I'll do my best to make it quick." Veronica stepped between his legs and grabbed a pair of goggles from the tray. She lowered the knife to his abdomen, pricking the soft flesh with the sharp tip. A stream of blood appeared, and her teeth pushed hungrily through her gums. If she held back now, it would only prolong his suffering.

Veronica went for it, thrusting the blade up and into his abdomen with surprising speed and precision. Desmond's naked chest rose and fell as he attempted to control his breathing through the excruciating pain.

"Okay, I'm going to do this, Desmond. Are you ready?" she asked.

"Do it," he growled between clenched teeth.

She shoved her arm elbow deep into his rib cage, groping until she could feel his pounding heart at the tip of her trembling fingers. She reached, grasped, seized the pulsating thing—and then gave it a violent full-body yank.

Desmond arched in mortal agony. Veronica stumbled back, clutched the horrible, spurting prize to her chest, drenching the front of her suit in his blood.

And that was it, apparently. It didn't turn to dust, or burst into flames, or even turn to stone. It just flopped weakly in her grasp like a gory trout. Tearing herself away from the sight of Desmond's gruesome half-pound anticlimax, she leaned over his gutted body, peering into his still opened eyes.

"Done," she said.

His eyes widened in recognition. "Behind you," he moaned.

The first blow hit the back of her head. Veronica collapsed. Desmond's heart slipped from her grasp and slid across the floor in a crimson slick.

Maynard scrambled after it, grunting like an animal.

Veronica struggled to focus her heavy, doubled gaze as wisps of gray smoke rose from Desmond's gaping wound. Accompanied by a strange cacophony of high-pitched screams and low bellows, the newly freed army of smoke swirled around the room, as if searching for an exit.

"It's mine!" Maynard scooped up Desmond's heart, brought it to his gaping mouth, and took a ravenous bite.

Veronica staggered to her feet and lunged. "Give it to me! It has to be destroyed!"

Maynard kicked Veronica to the floor and took another greedy bite, brandishing a wicked-looking dissection knife. "I'll cut your heart out too if you don't stay back!"

With the size and dexterity of a rabid squirrel, Jenny leapt onto Maynard's back and wrapped her left arm around his neck. Forcing his chin back, she plunged one of the archaic blades into his throat. Bucking her off, he fell face first onto the floor.

"Die, douchebag!" Jenny spit, kicking his head with her heavy boot.

"Where's the heart?" Veronica rose to her knees, frantically searching the floor.

"There," Jenny pointed.

"Pick it up, open the hatch door thingy and throw it in the crematory. Now!" Veronica heaved Maynard over onto his back.

Eyes wide, blood and air bubbling from his new tracheotomy, he gasped like a fish in an empty tank. "I'm—it's—why isn't it working?"

Veronica didn't have to know what he was talking about to be sure she didn't care. After hours of watching other people wax orgasmic over cookies and cheeseburgers, it was finally her turn. In one smooth motion, she yanked the knife from Maynard's throat and sunk her face into the bloody pool of his neck.

17

"Dude, you totally look like a used tampon." Jenny lifted Maynard's legs as Veronica hefted his upper body towards the crematory.

"That was exactly the look I was going for, thanks for noticing." Veronica spied her reflection in the gargantuan machine's shiny chrome and winced. Jenny was right—and they both needed a shower and a change of clothes. "Where's Ingrid?"

"Probably still upstairs. I hate to break it to you, but your daughter is kind of a wimp. She wouldn't even come back down here with me."

Veronica opened the door and pulled out the slab. "It's perfectly normal that she didn't want to witness a loved one's death." Veronica lifted her brows. "Do you think you can lift him with me or should we get a gurney?"

"We don't need no gurney." Jenny grabbed his calves. "Why do you think he wanted to eat Desmond's heart? That's pretty fucking out there, even for you guys. Right?"

"I haven't the slightest idea. Lift with your knees, not your back. On the count of three."

Veronica managed to heave the upper part of Maynard's body onto the slab as Jenny struggled with the lower half. "Stand right here and make sure he doesn't fall off. I'll get his legs." She pushed his butt up and over. His legs followed. "Would you like to do the honors, killer?"

"Gladly." Jenny pushed his body into the crematory, closed the door and clapped her hands. "Easy peasy lemon squeezy." Sauntering over to Desmond's body with the swagger of an assassin, she assessed the giant gash in his abdomen. "Is he next?"

"Yeah, we can't just leave him here. The last thing I need is more police." Veronica unbuckled the leather straps. "I think we should use a gurney. He's heavy."

"Yeah, because he's totally ripped. What a waste." Jenny touched his bare bicep with the tip of her finger, as if she'd been dared.

Veronica rolled her eyes at Jenny's callous treatment of the dead. "He lived a very long time, despite his appearance. You're young, but I'd like to let you in on a little secret. What gives life meaning is that one day it will be over. Which is exactly what makes being a vampire suck. It's like that movie *Groundhog Day*, except there's no Bill Murray and it never ends. Ever." Veronica wheeled the gurney next to Desmond and lowered it to his level. "Grab his legs."

"But it can end, right? Why don't you just apologize, like Ingrid?" Jenny lifted his legs and dropped them. "Holy shit! Talk about dead weight."

For a brief moment, Veronica entertained the thought. Then Kevin Black entered her mind and negated all possibility. "That would mean I would have to find every person I'd ever turned into a vampire. Do you know how difficult that would be?"

Ingrid entered the room and began collecting the various blades gingerly into a large purple gym bag. "Listen, the owner is going to be here any minute, so we have to..." She looked towards Desmond's body and gasped. "Oh my god. He looks so horrible."

"He's dead. What did you expect?" Jenny pushed up the sleeves of her bloodstained hoody. "Shit got real when that dick tried to kill your mom."

Ingrid's mouth gaped open.

"And then he tried to eat your boyfriend's heart. You totally missed it." Jenny attempted to lift his legs again.

"Why don't you go upstairs, Ingrid? We'll get this handled." Veronica strategically placed herself in front of Desmond's ravaged body. Ingrid had never been good at handling a mess.

"Wait, what happened?"

"Mr. Dirks clubbed me on the back of the head and then proceeded to stab me…"

"And I took him out. Bam! Right in the jugular." Jenny pantomimed stabbing Maynard in the throat.

"This isn't good. Where is he?"

"He's in the slow cooker." Jenny reached for the handle of the crematory with a wicked grin. "Wanna see?"

Ingrid wiped at her eyes in disbelief. "This is so not good. Maynard is…" Her voice trailed off. She assessed the state of the room and rubbed at her temples. "We need to get out of here. There's no way that bench is going to fit in my car, but it has to go."

"We'll deal with it," Veronica assured her. The last thing she needed was Ingrid going to pieces now. "Don't worry. Why don't you wait for the owner and if he comes in, you can stall for time? You know him, right?"

Ingrid nodded.

"Okay. Just call me when he arrives."

"Mom, I don't think you understand. We need to get out of here, maybe even the city. She'll know, and she won't stop till she finds the person that killed her familiar."

"What are you talking about? Who is this 'she' and what the hell is a familiar?" Veronica leaned against the counter and removed the blood-splattered hood from her hair. "Damn, these fucking hot flashes. I feel like I'm in hell."

"It's really hot in here, mom. It's not just you. A familiar is a vampire's bitch, for lack of a better word."

"I don't get it. If vampires can get out in the sun and do pretty much everything that a normal person can do, why would they need a lackey?"

"Power. And, well," Ingrid took a deep breath. "Not every vampire knows about the sun thing, or garlic or being invited in. It's a way to keep the poor and uninformed in check."

Great. More weaponized ignorance. "Kind of like me, huh?" Veronica clenched her fists. "So, who's this woman that's going to murder Jenny?"

"Beatrice Prendergast. But everyone just calls her Betty."

"Oooh, Betty. I'm scared." Jenny pranced around the room like a shadow boxer. "I'll take that bitch out."

"Really? Who are you? And why are you still here?" Ingrid dumped the rest of the knives into the bag and forcefully zipped it up.

Jenny tossed her a look. "I thought we'd already gone over this, Ingrid, but here goes. My name is Jenny Anne Pearson. I'm originally from Mineral Wells, Texas, but my ultra-conservative, politically-motivated father moved our family to Fort Worth when I was ten. I'm currently a college dropout with drug dependency issues; you may have heard about my shenanigans in the liberal-leaning press. And the reason I'm here is because I have nothing better to do."

"Oh, Jenny. Please don't tell me your dad is Jimbo Pearson." Veronica unzipped the Tyvek suit, ripped it from her body and handed it to Ingrid.

"Bingo. Two points for you, Count Chocula." Jenny cracked her knuckles and swung at the air.

Great. If Ingrid didn't fall apart over this Maynard thing, half of Texas was going to be up in arms over Jenny. Veronica tightened her grip on sensibility. "We need to get you to that rehab facility before your dad sends out a search party."

"Are you fucking kidding me? I just killed that dude. I may have had issues before today, but now I've got some serious trauma shit to deal with. No way am I going to spa-la-land to sit around with a bunch of losers whining about their wounded inner child. Fuck that. Take me back to that restaurant and we'll call it good."

"Mom, we've got to go," Ingrid pleaded. "Maynard disposed of Betty's, you know." Her voice dropped. "He served a very important role, and since he's not coming home or checking in with her, she could show up here any minute."

Veronica dug through her purse and removed her phone. She opened the crematory door and threw it in with Maynard's body. "I need to get one of those disposable phones tonight. Maybe after we have a chat with Betty."

"You've got to be kidding me. Telling Betty that you killed her familiar is suicide."

Veronica did her best to look unmoved by the fear in her daughter's voice. "No, Ingrid, that's not suicide. It's the ninth step."

18

Veronica's desire to decompress was superseded by Ingrid's need to purchase every available flavor of Ben & Jerry's at the Safeway. While wandering the aisles, she attempted to make conscious contact with her higher power. Two days without Paula, Frank or a measly twelve-step meeting and she felt the overwhelming urge to pummel the next person who looked at her funny in the freezer section. Her inner voice screamed *Texas*, but North Dakota and the promise of mortality played in the background of her mind like a catchy pop song that she couldn't tune out.

Knud. She could definitely find Knud—probably still hiding in his dank cellar, gnawing on squirrel carcasses. As for the others, though...

And then there was Jenny. She would be an excellent and ethical food source on the drive to North Dakota, but driving cross country with a withdrawing meth addict could bring about homicidal impulses that Veronica wasn't convinced she could control. The last thing she needed was Jenny's Bible-quoting, death-penalty-loving father hot on their trail. Jimbo Pearson loved the idea of executing people who messed with his state, and Veronica pondered what he'd do to someone he caught absconding with his embarrassment of a daughter.

A wave of fire rose the length of her back and burned through her neck. Veronica opened one of the freezer doors, leaned in, and shuffled around a few bags of vegetables to cool her scorching skin. From the corner of her eye, she could see herself reflected in the glass door. The haggard-looking woman glancing back at her had flakes of dried blood speckling the bridge of her nose like chocolate freckles as she stuffed two bags of corn under her arms.

Jesus Christ. Veronica was hitting bottom, to be witnessed by every random shopper shuffling along to the instrumental version of "I Want to Be Sedated" on their way to the pizza rolls. She needed help.

"SEAMUS SANSBURY." Ingrid handed her mother a blood red business card from her Louis Vuitton wallet. "He's the man." Relaxing into the pillows of her couch, she grabbed the unopened pint of Chunky Monkey from the coffee table. For a hundred-year-old case of arrested development, Ingrid certainly had developed mature home decorating tastes.

"And who is this Seamus Sansbury?" Fresh out of the shower, Veronica secured the belt of Ingrid's plaid bathrobe and sat carefully on the edge of the leather recliner.

"I don't know much about him, other than he's one of us. He locates people. He changes identities. He's helped me lots of times and he's pretty reasonable." She scooped a large spoonful of ice cream into her mouth. "Holy shit, this is good."

"Language," Veronica reprimanded.

Ingrid rolled her eyes. "Oh, please. Your little addict friend swears like a sailor."

"I'm not her mother."

"You haven't been my mother for a long time, so I would appreciate it if you would back off." She brought the pint closer to her face and taunted Veronica with one heavenly mouthful after another.

Veronica held her ground in the face of her daughter's double-churned immaturity. "Okay, as an equal, you may want to back off that ice cream. I realize you're nervous because this Betty lady is coming over, but trust me, food won't fix what ails you."

"You're just jealous that you can't have any." Ingrid took another bite and purred.

Veronica's mouth flattened to a hard line. "Well there's that and the fact that I am perpetually emotional, sweaty and dependent on other people's blood to sustain my pathetic life." Veronica stood. "And yes, I am jealous, Ingrid. I want some fucking ice cream. Is that too much to ask?"

"Geez, take a chill pill." Jenny sauntered into the living room with a towel around her head and plopped on the sofa next to Ingrid. "Oooh, can I have some?"

Ingrid stabbed the pint with her spoon and handed it to Jenny. "No, it isn't too much to ask for. I know how you can eat all the fucking ice cream you want, but you're too stubborn and angry to listen. God, it's maddening!" She threw one of the couch pillows onto the floor and screamed.

"Oh, take it easy on the pillows. I'll call him, Ingrid." Veronica placed the card in the empty phone slot of her purse. "I'm sorry for what I said. This has been a rather stressful day and I don't mean to take it out on you."

"So, what time's that bitch gonna be here?" Jenny asked around a mouth full of ice cream.

"Any minute. Mom, you might want to put some clothes on."

"Do I have to?"

"You're the one who wanted to go all twelve-steppy with this and invite her over. Her being here is an epically bad idea, but whatever." Ingrid bit her manicured nail. "You could at least have the decency to wear a bra when you tell her that you killed Maynard."

Veronica grabbed her suitcase and wheeled it into Ingrid's bedroom, which looked straight out of a Pottery Barn catalogue. Everything was crisp, clean, and disturbingly tidy… just like Ingrid herself.

Or so it seemed.

Veronica locked the door and pulled open the top drawer of the mid-century modern dresser, hunting for a vibrator, a bag of weed—anything dark or embarrassing at all.

Panties. Nothing but rows and rows of expensive underwear,

neatly folded and coordinated by color and cut. The five pairs Frank packed were ill-fitting, made of cotton and sold in a plastic bag at Target.

And as for the body they belonged to...

Veronica removed Ingrid's robe and stood in front of the full-length mirror. Turning from side to side, she attempted to examine every possible angle of her foreign figure.

Well, it wasn't as bad as all that. Certainly not the tragic-looking bag-lady she'd glimpsed in the freezer door. Maybe Veronica just hadn't found the right angle yet. As she lowered herself to the floor to take a gander at her vagina, something she'd never actually seen, Ingrid pounded on the door. "Mom? Let me in!"

Fine, fine. Veronica crawled towards the mirror like a long-lost lover and quickly kissed her own face. A remnant of the Russian Red remained.

"Mom! She just texted me. Hurry!"

Stark naked, Veronica swung open the door. The cool breeze from the open window felt good on her skin.

"What have you been doing?" Ingrid shielded her eyes and fast-walked it towards the closet.

"Snooping, obviously." Veronica opened her suitcase, grabbed a pair of white granny panties and stepped into them. "You sure have some fancy underwear."

"Des had a thing. Never mind. What are you wearing?"

"Yoga pants with this shirt." Veronica held up a purple A-line shirt. "Why?"

Jenny came bounding into the room, ramped up and breathless. "I think the bitch is here. Does she drive a black Mercedes?"

"Would you please stop calling her a bitch?" Ingrid stepped into a pair of ballet flats and peered out the window. "Yep, that's her. She's still on her phone. Oh god. She is going to go beyond ballistic when you tell her."

"Don't be such a worry wart, Ingrid." Veronica threw on the rest of her clothes, bent over and fluffed her still wet hair. "Sufficient?"

"You look like a soccer mom." Jenny zipped up her clean hoody and ran her fingers through her jet-black hair.

"That's exactly the look I was going for. I want to look like the innocent flower…"

"But be the serpent underneath it." Jenny added. "Macbeth, bitch! Am I right? I love me some Shakespeare." Jenny peered out the window. "Oooooh, Betty looks like an old timey pin-up bitch. I'm scared."

"You should be. And stop calling her bitch." Ingrid sprinted from the room and made her way to the front door.

Veronica wasn't scared of telling Betty that Maynard was dead. Vampires were well acquainted with the Grim Reaper. People died every day. Most of them didn't deserve it, if there was truly an all-knowing score keeper in the sky bestowing a "stay" for numerous prayer requests or rewards for past good deeds, but Maynard did deserve it. Veronica expected that Betty would understand, maybe even envy the fact that death was the most natural and dependable milestone of the human experience and let it go.

19

Veronica cracked open the bedroom door to take a quick peek at the woman who instilled fear in her daughter, something she had never quite accomplished in their artificially extended time together. Beatrice Prendergast strode into Ingrid's apartment dressed like a pin-up girl from the 1950s, which in pop culture had become the uniform for the morbidly-inclined female of the twenty-first century. From her tight angora sweater, skin-tight pencil-skirt and leopard-print heels, it was glaringly apparent that she was not the type of vampire to hide in the shadows or isolate herself in a makeshift closet. She wanted to be seen.

Veronica, catching her own sensibly clad reflection in Ingrid's full-length mirror, rolled her eyes with a resolved surrender to do the best she could with the outfit she was given. In her mind, she looked like she was headed into a job interview for which she was regrettably underdressed. But there was nothing she could do about it now. In vampire age, Veronica had t-shirts older than Betty. She closed the door and pinched her cheeks to bring about some needed color to her face.

"Ingrid, darling! It's been forever. Look at you!" Betty beamed and kissed Ingrid's face, imprinting a brick-red "o" on the apple of her cheek. She paused briefly before pulling away. Raising an artfully arched brow, she clutched Ingrid's narrow shoulders with her long, slender fingers. "You smell different. Like…" She moved in closer and inhaled deeply. "Dinner," she whispered. Never letting her eyes drop from Ingrid's frightened gaze, she gracefully sat her hourglass figure onto the leather recliner and crossed her long legs.

"It's the Chunky Monkey. I only got like two bites." Jenny jumped over the arm of the sofa, crossed her legs and removed the phone from her back pocket in one fluid movement.

"And you are?" Betty opened her purse and pulled out her super-sized smartphone.

"I'm Jenny." Jenny's eyes remained on the glowing screen of her own cracked phone.

"Mom," Ingrid bellowed towards the bedroom.

"I'm Betty…"

"Yeah, I know who you are. I got the full debriefing before you pulled up in the Batmobile." Jenny looked up from her phone. A thin trail of blood trickled from her right nostril. She dabbed at it with the sleeve of her sweatshirt.

"Well, then." Betty straightened in her chair and looked directly up at Ingrid. "I'm very curious as to why you've invited me over. Is this some sort of party?" She looked back down at her vibrating phone and frowned. "Hmmm. I do hope that Desmond will be joining us."

"No, he won't." Ingrid nervously tucked a lock of hair behind her ear and crossed her arms firmly in front of her chest to steady herself.

"Have a seat, darling. You're making me nervous. And please get that awful girl a tissue before she uses her sleeve again." Betty stroked the phone's screen one last time and placed it back in her purse. "Well?" She tapped her talon-like nails on the armrest of the chair.

"My name is Jenny. Jenny. Ann. Pearson. And I can get my own fucking tissue." Jenny bolted up from the couch. "Let me guess, vampires don't use tissues because they're too fucking sexy to produce boogers. Am I right?"

"Bathroom," Ingrid pointed her shaking hand towards the hall.

Veronica stumbled into the living room bumping shoulders with Jenny as she stormed out.

"There you are. Mom, this is…"

Veronica extended her hand. "It's a pleasure. Ingrid's told me so much about you."

"That's funny. In all the time I've known your daughter, I don't believe Ingrid has ever mentioned you." Betty watched Veronica's eyes. "To me, that is."

Veronica forced a smile. *Bitch.* The last thing she wanted was for her freshly applied mascara to run. It took too damn long to apply. "Well, there's not much to say. I'm just a hospice nurse from Texas."

"Well, I guess the apple doesn't fall far from the tree, now does it? Noble and ethical to a fault, your Ingrid. Yawn. Doesn't all that morphine make you sick? Personally, I can't stand the taste of junkies. If they only knew how horrific they tasted."

"Apparently, I taste pretty good." Jenny offered Betty a whiff of the bloody tissue she held against her nostril.

Forcefully pushing Jenny's hand away, she barked, "Sit, before I rip the vocal cords out of your pathetic, little throat."

"You and what army, bitch?" Jenny ambled over to the sofa, plopped down among the ample pillows and slowly raised the middle finger of her right hand.

"Don't mind Jenny. She's apparently flying very high on meth right now. Ingrid, take a seat. Jenny, shut your pie hole and don't open it until I say it's okay. *Capiche?*"

"If you say so," Jenny mumbled.

Veronica sat in the matching recliner next to Betty and casually crossed her legs, accentuating the fact that she wasn't wearing any shoes. Her feet looked horrifically in need of a pedicure. *Was a pedicure even possible now?* With her best amicable expression, she turned to Betty. "The reason we've asked you to come here, Beatrice, is because we've been involved in an unfortunate incident that you need to be aware of."

"Incident?" Betty leaned forward.

"Yes. At the funeral home. You see, Ingrid brought me to San Francisco to end Desmond's life."

"What?" Betty gasped, gripping the arms of the chair for support. "Desmond's dead?"

"Yes, as of today. He'd been wanting to end his life for a while now," Ingrid offered in her most upbeat, hopeful voice. "Yep. He's gone."

"And since he took my life, it only seemed fitting that I take his." Veronica laced her fingers together and leaned back in the chair. She was trying her best to convey sincerity with her apologetic tone, but she was pathetic at lying through her fangs. "But here's the thing. We had an issue during the actual event that involves your familiar."

Betty grabbed the phone from her purse and scrolled through her messages. "That dimwit hasn't texted me all day. Where is he?"

"He's in the crematory at Cook's." Veronica said.

"Yes, I know where he works. Did you duct tape his arms to a chair or something? Why won't he answer my texts?"

Jenny rolled back onto the couch and laughed. "You've got to be kidding me. Are you that daft? He's *inside* the crematory. It's pretty hard to text someone when you've been reduced to kitty litter."

"You killed Maynard?" Rising from her chair, almost to the point of levitating, Betty's fangs jutted between her heavily stained lips.

Veronica flinched at the threat of violence. "Yes, and I wanted to apologize to you in person for taking his life. Maynard stabbed me and then..." She lowered her voice. "He attempted to ingest Desmond's heart. I don't tolerate violence very well, as I'm sure you can understand." Veronica signaled towards the other chair. "Please sit. I know you're a reasonable woman, Beatrice, so please, let's try and work this out." Veronica's voice began with the peaceful cadence of Ghandi but shifted to Gonzo when she addressed Jenny. "I'm not going to say it again, Ms. Pearson. Shut the fuck up."

"Mom!" Ingrid gasped.

"That stupid, insipid little man. I can just see his disappointed face when he took that first bite." Beatrice smiled wickedly. "Did he cry when he learned the truth?"

Confused, Veronica looked to Ingrid for clarification. "What truth?"

Ingrid shrugged.

"You don't know anything do you?" Betty sat back in the chair. "I pity your ignorance, but I don't pity the position you are now in. You killed one of mine. Now I get to kill one of yours."

"Bitch is lying. She didn't kill Maynard." Jenny tossed the bloody tissue onto the coffee table and looked Betty square in the eye. "I killed him. And if you've got a problem with that, I suggest you take it up with me, not her, bitch."

"Stop calling people bitches," Ingrid yelped, her voice rising an octave as she paced the living room. "It's so disrespectful, and you're just escalating the situation with your nonsense."

Jenny rolled her eyes. "Bitch has dual meanings, Ingrid. It can be used in a derogatory sense but also as a term of endearment, at least in its modern-day usage. But if you crazy bitches can't comprehend the nuances of language, whatever." She stood and waved her arms as if she were attempting to swim through a crowded room. "I'm out of here."

"Not so fast." Betty lunged, lifting Jenny by the neck and slamming her head first against the wall. "I am not a reasonable woman. Nor do I take kindly to being called a bitch in any sense of the word." She squeezed Jenny's neck harder, then let her fragile body fall to the floor.

Aghast, Veronica and Ingrid stood back, watching the events unfold yet unable to move. Frozen by fear and guilt, Veronica knew she could never take on Betty in a physical match. All she wanted was to be home with Frank, but that possibility didn't seem to exist anymore.

"As payment for Maynard, this one's mine." Betty dragged Jenny to her feet. "Perhaps I'll let her detox in my basement for a few days before I drain her."

"No!" Veronica grabbed Jenny's track-marked arm and pulled. "She's my familiar and you can't have her."

Betty roared with laughter. "What could this rude, ugly little runt possibly offer you?"

Veronica thought hard as Jenny's nose continued to trickle more blood. It smelled heavenly. Jenny's droll voice resonated inside her head. *Bitch thinks she's Betty Page. Take a swing. Do it. I'll hold her down.*

"She makes me laugh," Veronica offered sheepishly.

"If I was eternally your age, I'd need something to laugh about too." Betty smiled and drew Jenny closer.

I know you can hear me, Veronica. Let go of my arm and hit the bitch. Knock her teeth out with your walker, Grandma! Veronica dropped Jenny's arm and giggled. Nervously, she rubbed her nose and flashed Jenny a look. What if Betty could read her thoughts too?

"See, there she goes making you laugh again. I'm so glad you find this situation humorous, but here's the deal: I'm not leaving empty handed," Betty snarled. "You need to make a choice: Ingrid or this piece of funny-smelling trash." She sniffed Jenny's jet-black hair and placed her in a choke hold.

Ingrid darted over to Betty's side and dropped to her knees. "Please don't hurt her. She's just a stupid addict. We can make this situation right. Can't we Mom?" Ingrid's gaze darted frantically to her mother's.

Veronica remained as silent and frozen as the Northern Plains.

Betty released her grip on Jenny's neck.

"If you take me. I'll do anything you need. Do you need someone to take over Maynard's duties? I can do that. Mr. Cook knows me and I'm sure he wouldn't have a problem with me working the crematory. I mean, if you spoke to him first, of course." Ingrid nearly kissed Betty's bejeweled hand.

Veronica had never seen this side of her daughter. Either she had become a total kiss-ass, or she was deathly afraid for Jenny's life.

Make your choice, Sophie. Your daughter thinks she's Katniss Everdeen, but I'm cool with whatever you choose. It's better than rehab.

"You can have Ingrid, but only for a year. I'm sure you'll find someone more suitable to your particular needs in that time. Is that okay with you, Ingrid?" Veronica pushed up her sleeves as if she were going to start a fight, or maybe wash the dishes.

Ingrid nodded, but could not hide the shock of rejection.

Veronica reasoned that a year was nothing to a vampire or at least someone who used to be a vampire. "You'll have to work around her school schedule, of course. She recently enrolled in high school. Isn't that right, Ingrid? Prom, football games, pimples and all that fun teenage stuff," Veronica lied.

"Yes, that's right. I start George Washington High on Monday." Ingrid rose and brushed off her knees, going along with it. Betty wouldn't own every hour.

"Why in the world would you want to go back to high school?" Betty sniffed, pushing Jenny back onto the couch.

"Because I've never been. I missed out on a lot of things because of Desmond. So did my Mom."

"The only thing your mom missed out on was incontinence and a nursing home. Am I right?" Betty smiled smugly.

"When would you like for me to start?" Ingrid grabbed her phone from the end table.

"Give me a week with Mr. Cook to figure out a schedule. Truth is, I only really need you for my deliveries on Saturdays. No exceptions. There will be no sick days or homecoming dances. If you're not there, I have to push people off of the Golden Gate and that's just a giant pain in my ass. Are we good?"

"Yep." Ingrid flashed her mom a look that indicated they were one step closer to becoming even.

"Now that that's resolved, I have a question for you." The truth, or lack of the truth, was gnawing away at Veronica's insides. "Why did Maynard want to eat Desmond's heart?"

"Mom," Ingrid rolled her eyes.

Betty stood. "Because he was stupid and gullible. Kind of like you." She caressed Veronica's cheek. "He wanted to be one of us so badly, he could taste it. I just can't believe he was dumb enough to actually do it." She slid her leather clutch onto her arm. "I tell you, ignorance is one thing, but desperate and dumb is a lethal combination. It's probably a good thing you killed him."

"So, you lied to him?" Veronica clutched her hand into a fist. "What is it with you people? All you do is lie." She straightened her fingers and smoothed them on her pants.

"If you spot it, you got it," Jenny interjected.

"Shut it, Jenny, before I rip your thorax out and shit down your neck." Veronica's nostril's flared.

"Well, this has been fun, but I have people to eat." Betty strode across the room.

"Aren't you tired of it?" Veronica called after her. "I know I sure as fuck am. I'm tired of the hiding and the running and the lying. We could have avoided this whole bullshit situation if you hadn't lied to Maynard."

"Yes, dear. I lied to him. But that's all in the past now. Let's move forward, shall we?" She pulled out her phone and swiped at the screen, keeping her eyes fixed on Veronica. "Would you like to know how to tell when I'm lying to you, Ms. Bouchard?" She raised the phone above her head and smiled. "My lips are moving."

After Betty and her Chanel No. 5 departed the apartment, the three women remained silent. Veronica didn't know what to say to her daughter. They'd been estranged for so long. While she was grateful for her sacrifice, she was simultaneously resentful of the withholding of information. Her life would have been so much more pleasant had she known about the sun.

"Are you going to be okay?" Veronica scooched closer to Ingrid on the sofa. "Because..."

"Mom. I'll do it. It's no big deal."

But it was, and Veronica knew it. There wasn't time to ruminate on regrets and personal debts. Veronica wanted to get to North Dakota before she changed her mind.

20

"So where on earth did you get the drugs, Jenny? You didn't get them at the airport, did you?" Veronica adjusted the seat of Desmond's meticulously maintained vehicle and glanced at her reflection in the rearview mirror. It was both satisfying and surprising to see her own eyes again.

"They were on me, but now they're all gone. All gone." Jenny's voice trailed off into a yawn. She reclined her seat.

"If they were on you, how did you get them through airport security? Those machines can see everything, and if I were a TSA agent, you would be the first person I would pat down." Veronica didn't really care about the origin of the drugs; she was just trying to kill some time on the drive to North Dakota. After checking the GPS on the car's dash for the third time, it was apparently going to be at least a thirty-hour haul to Pembina at the tip of the Canadian border.

"Okay officer, you got me. My rehab stash was in a hollowed-out tampon in my vajiggles. Can I go to sleep now?" Jenny stuffed her balled-up sweatshirt under her head, curled into a fetal position and closed her eyes.

Veronica had been desperate for Jenny to shut up earlier, but now all she wanted to do was keep her talking. Anything to keep from being alone with her thoughts. "How can you possibly sleep after snorting amphetamines? I'd be awake for days. I take that back, I'm always awake. Maybe that stuff would make me sleep."

"Ya know, crazy shit might happen to you every day in vampire land, but yesterday was pretty fucking bonkers." With half-closed, bloodshot eyes, Jenny peered up at Veronica. "Do you think I'm going to go to hell for killing that dude?"

"No, I don't." Her voice softened. "Jenny, you were defending me, and I think anyone would agree that he deserved it." She tapped her short nails on the steering wheel. "And If I were you, I wouldn't worry too much about the afterlife. Judging by the traffic on this bridge, I think we're already in hell." Veronica turned on the radio and hit the scanner.

"Summer of 69" blared from the stereo. The tempting image of bleeding fingers like little warm popsicles popped into Veronica's mind.

"God, I wish I had some weed." Jenny stretched in her seat like a cat in the sun.

Before she could bite one of Jenny's fingers, the station changed. "Young Blood" played by some dastardly DJ. *Oh my god. Yes!* Jenny's blood was young and iron rich and she was right there! It would be so easy. And she would taste so good. "I don't think God assists in the procurement of drugs. And since you're clean out of money, you're kind of SOL if you're planning to do any shopping at the doobie department store."

"This song is gross." Jenny pressed the scan button.

It landed on the opening of Foreigner's "Hot Blooded," its pounding rhythm pulsing from the car's speakers.

"Don't call it doobie. You sound like my health science teacher, and he was beyond stupid. And just so you know, God, Buddha, Allah, or whatever star you wish on, works in mysterious ways. I've seen like five different cars with people smoking chronic in the past ten minutes. I'm a young chick with low standards and even lower self-esteem. I don't need money to score weed."

The scanner switched to a distant, scratchy "Sunday Bloody Sunday." *What day of the week was it?*

"Eh, please don't go there. I don't want to hear about it." Veronica flipped off the radio, looked up at the sprawling bridge and the cars that sandwiched her. "Burning Man or Bust" was scrawled in pink paint on the back window of the dented junker in front of them. "Why aren't we moving? It's noon on a Friday. Don't people work in this town?"

"I think it might be Labor Day or something." Jenny grabbed the worn Pikachu from her backpack and snuggled it to her chest.

Veronica looked down at Jenny's tiny body; a rush of maternal protectiveness came over her. "Get some sleep. I'll wake you when we stop for gas." She reached over and rubbed her arm, wishing it were Ingrid's.

"How long will that be?"

"If you want to stay alive, don't even start with that line of questioning." Out of curiosity, Veronica peered down at the gas level. Full tank. "It will be about three hours, maybe more." Eyeing the bumper to bumper cars and the jovial passengers they contained wasn't helping her state of mind. She wanted to remain somewhat hopeful and positive, but the enormity of the task ahead and the humility it would require weighed on her. She sighed heavily, hoping to arouse Jenny's sympathy. But the young woman she chose over her own flesh and blood simply snored her indifference into the worn upholstery of her seat.

TRAFFIC INCHED ALL the way from San Francisco to Nevada. As Jenny lay comatose in her seat, a parade of odd cars and odder people were making their way to something called "Burning Man." Veronica had never heard of such a thing, but almost every person at every gas station was either part of the strange gridlock pilgrimage or else complaining about it. Standing in line at the 76, she selected random items for Jenny, guessing according to what Frank usually asked her to smuggle into the movies: Twinkies, beef jerky, Raisinettes, Gatorade, spearmint gum and a jumbo box of Hot Tamales. But Jenny never roused from her slumber.

Without anyone to talk to, Veronica blazed through Idaho and Montana with the cruise control set to 82. Jenny managed to zombie walk into a few gas stations to relieve her bladder but returned to her comatose state in the car. Not even her ringing phone could arouse her.

Don't wanna be an American idiot
  Don't want a nation under the new mania...

Veronica didn't feel compelled to grope around the passenger seat to find and silence the annoying ringtone. More than likely, it was the rehab facility, and neither of them was in any state to address Jenny's "no show" status.

Don't wanna be an American idiot
  Don't want a nation under the new mania...

And that was the irregular, gratingly repetitive soundtrack to Veronica's drive, all through the flat expanse of North Dakota.

Don't wanna be an American idiot
  Don't want a nation under the new mania...

Feeling like quite the martyr for all the miles she'd travelled in the last twenty-nine hours, Veronica pulled into the lot of the Pembina Motor Lodge Motel.

Don't wanna be an American—

Veronica had had enough. She dug in the side pocket of Jenny's backpack to mute the damn thing—and accidentally thumbed the green button.

Senator Jimbo Pearson's bloated face and shellacked hair appeared on its screen. "Jennifer Ann Pearson, where in the world are you?" His thick Texas twang boomed in Veronica's ear.

"I'm sorry, but you have the wrong number." Veronica turned the power off and dropped the phone in her own purse. She'd seen enough true crime shows to know that the surrounding cellphone towers would eventually give Jenny's location away. But only if they were looking.

21

With a blue ballpoint and a nervous hand, Veronica penned a letter to Jenny on the motel's stationary. Unsure of where to place the scribbled explanation of her whereabouts, she chose the lid of the toilet. The girl would have to pee at some point.

"Wakey, wakey, eggs and bakey!" Veronica gently jostled Jenny's body, hoping that by some miracle of the universe, she'd have companionship for the grim task ahead, or better yet, a reason not to go at all. It was so much easier to focus on someone else's problems, and Jenny had them in abundance, especially now that the meth was all gone and Pembina, North Dakota was not going to be the easiest place to score another fix.

"Stop it." Jenny groaned, burrowing her face deeper into the bleach-scented sheets. With one brusque move, she pulled the flowered coverlet over her head. "I have a fucking headache. Leave me alone."

"Okay, sunshine. I've got to go apologize to a paranoid Norwegian. I'll be back as quickly as I possibly can, so please don't do anything stupid or illegal while I'm gone." Veronica gathered her purse and the keys to the car. "There's food on the desk if you're hungry."

She let herself out quietly, even though a bomb could have detonated in the ice machine next door, and Jenny would simply flinch or maybe tell it to fuck off. Veronica didn't understand it, considering the checkered history she had with her own daughter, but she found a lovability in this young woman despite her abundant faults. If anything, Veronica appreciated the fact that Jenny was at least honest about her defects of character. Almost every person she encountered was pretending to be someone else. And as was often said in the rooms of Al-Anon, "If you spot it, you got it." Veronica had been pretending to be something she wasn't for almost a century. But that was all about to change. Today was the day she would change that.

EVEN WITHOUT THE GPS to guide her, Veronica instinctively knew how to find the old stretch of Jorgenson land. It had been imprinted on her memory like a red wine stain on a honey-colored table. The only novelty would be discovering just how decrepit the place had become in the hundred years since.

But when she turned into the drive, Veronica was startled to find the small A-frame house freshly painted pale yellow with planters of flowers on the teak wood porch. The surrounding fields of the property still flowing with flax and sunflowers. Someone was tending them.

Beams of sun warmed her exposed skin as she exited the vehicle. If she hadn't been on a ninth step mission with time constraints, she would have sat down for a spell on the porch swing before announcing her arrival. A warm day in Dakota needed to be appreciated when it happened—especially in September, when every pleasant day might be the last of the year—but dragging a scared, reluctant vampire to sit with her in the daylight would be about as easy as winning the Power Ball. She could still envision Knud cloistered in his candlelit basement, working on some whittling or sucking the life out of some poor animal that he'd named and grown to love.

In a soft, tentative manner, Veronica knocked on the front door. There was either going to be an awkward exchange with the new owners or a harder knock he would be able to hear from the basement. As nervous sweat trickled down the inside of her shirt, she visualized ripping a bandage from a reluctant patient. With a renewed fervor to just get it over with, she pounded on the thick oak door.

"Just a moment, please," a female voice with a Russian accent called out.

Disheartened by the excuses she'd have to make to this stranger, Veronica stepped back from the door. As it swung open, a young woman holding a tiny, trembling dog greeted her with a weary smile.

"Yes?" The ball of fluff yapped at Veronica, while the woman murmured foreign words into its furry ear.

"Hello, um…" The dog's insistent barking wasn't helping her nerves. "I was wondering if, by any chance, Knud Jorgenson still lived here, or if you knew where I could find him."

The woman's eyes narrowed with suspicion. "Yes. And you are with?" She set the dog down. It sniffed Veronica's ankles, then darted down the steps and into the yard.

"I'm not with anyone. I'm an old friend. A very old friend. And you are?"

"Nataliya." She stepped out onto the front porch. Her bare feet and pedicured toes announced that she wasn't from these rustic parts. "Igor, stop with the digging. Why must you be so naughty?"

"Dogs." Veronica smiled, trying to convince this strange woman that she was totally down with yippy canines and reclusive vampires. Looking towards Igor, who was now pooping in the flower bed, she hoped he wasn't slated for breakfast. "Is he here? Possibly in the basement?"

"Yes. I will tell him of your arrival. We so rarely get visitors other than the UPS man. Who may I say is calling?"

"Astrid Dahling."

"Igor!" Nataliya screamed. "Would you like a cookie?" The dog sprinted towards the house and through the front door, stopping at her feet. "Astrid. I will be back in a moment. Would you like something to drink?" Nataliya chuckled to herself in a low voice and scooped up the dog, hugging him tightly to her slight frame.

"No, thank you. I'm fine."

"Of course. My mistake. Please have a seat." She motioned towards a worn leather sofa in the living area.

The darkened room was nothing like Veronica remembered. Taxidermied animals were scattered about. A grizzly, who was the obvious centerpiece, reared up with wild eyes and exposed fangs while the other animals looked peacefully alive, frozen in their tracks by his terrifying magnificence. An obscenely large flat screen TV covered the two front windows, and on the corner desk sat an expensive laptop. From the living room, she spied new stainless-steel appliances in the kitchen.

Nataliya peeked her head out from the cellar staircase. "You may come down. He says it is okay. Come, Igor." She shuffled towards the kitchen with the dog on her heels. "Who is a good boy? You are, you are," she cooed, somehow sounding more like an evil dictator than a doting dog owner.

Fearful, Veronica rose from the sofa. Heat bloomed from her skin with beads of sweat as if she'd just entered a sauna. It never failed. Emotion equaled hot flash. As if guided by a power greater than herself, she padded down the old wooden steps into the basement. The last time she'd seen her second husband, he was covered in a motley collection of animal hides that he'd fashioned to honor their blood sacrifice. If anything, he was creative. She hoped that Knud would greet her at the bottom of the stairs to soften her entry into the past.

"Hello? Knud?" Her voice cracked.

"Hold on. This auction's about to end." In the corner of the room, Knud Jorgenson's ruggedly good-looking face was illuminated by the blue light of a computer screen. Looking like a hipster lumberjack in black framed glasses, a plaid flannel shirt, worn denim, and thick wool socks, he was physically the same as the day she'd turned him. His full beard hadn't grown or receded nor had his thick mop of unruly curls. He was a man frozen in time, like one of the woodland creatures upstairs—a mannequin changing with the seasons. Veronica felt a pang of jealousy that he'd endured the years so well.

"I won, I won!" He pounded the table and hopped up to his feet. Opening his arms like a bear about to maul its prey, he bounded towards her. "Astrid! It's so good to see you." He grabbed her towards him, squeezing his muscular body against hers. Stroking her back with his strong, calloused hands, he sniffed her hair. "By golly, I love a woman with some meat on her bones. You just feel so much better than those skinny ladies they keep hooking me up with on that dating app."

Veronica could feel the heat rise in her face. Knud was eternally forty-two and dripping with his own kind of heat—from the top of his 6'4" solid frame down to his wool-clad toes. When they first began courting, she felt unworthy of his attention—he was that good looking —and yet he didn't seem to be aware of the effect it had on those around him. His first wife, along with their only child, had died in labor, cementing her as a saint within his mind. He never got over the loss but found comfort in Veronica's own widowed arms. As he sized every inch of her up with his blue eyes, Veronica giggled from the crazy thought that if they'd gotten together today, she would have been considered a cougar.

"Thank you, Knud. I appreciate that." She squeezed his arm as if to say *that's enough touching, unless you want to lock that cellar door*, and backed away.

"Have a seat and tell me what you've been doing with yourself since 1932." He plopped down in a chair and leaned towards her, resting his chin on the knuckle of his right hand, like The Thinker.

She laughed and sat in one of the oversized recliners, placing her purse carefully on the wooden floor. This room used to crawl with spiders, the one thing on this earth she would never get used to.

Nataliya's voice called from upstairs. "The UPS man is here with that flying thing."

"Thank you, honey, just put it in my office," he yelled towards the ceiling. "I ordered a drone. Can you believe that? It is absolutely crazy the amount of progress we've witnessed in our lifetime. Granted, I've seen most of it only at night or on a television screen, but still. It's pretty amazing." He leaned back in the chair. "It was thirty-two, right?" His tone changed, teetering on accusatory.

Veronica nodded, feeling a sudden surge of shame. After forty years, she'd slipped out of his life in the winter of '32 without a good-bye, a note or any sort of explanation. While he was in the barn draining one of their dairy cows, she hopped the Northern Pacific, heading for Fargo, the divorce capital of the Midwest. At the time, she simply wanted to meet her great-granddaughter, Millie.

"So, what's been going on? What's your story?" He seemed genuinely interested, leaning forward in his chair again.

"Well, I went to Fargo, the big city, don't you know, and stayed there till..." Veronica looked up at the ceiling as if the answer was written on one of the wooden beams. "Thirty-nine. And then I just traveled around from there. First to Massachusetts then to Michigan. Along the way, I just tried to figure out how best to survive. Right now, I live in Texas."

"Yee haw! I bet they love you down there with your big hair. You are so brave to travel and see all these places. I've lived here my whole life. I'd love to see the ocean." His gaze drifted towards the stairs. "If you don't mind me asking, how are you surviving?"

She looked down at her trembling hands. "Ethically, for the most part. I continue to have slip ups every now and then, but I'm working on it, with the help of AA."

Knud slapped his knee and chuckled as if that was the craziest thing he'd ever heard. "The program for drunks?"

"Yes. We prefer the term *alcoholic*." She could feel her teeth gently nudging at her gums. "I don't know about you, but I suffer from a drinking problem that has gotten me into a lot of trouble." She had always hated his dismissive, holier-than-thou attitude. It reminded her of why she left. *Animals don't have souls. It's the only way. How could you kill another person, Astrid?* "The program has helped me in ways you couldn't understand right now. Anyway, currently I'm working in a hospice facility as a nurse. Many people want my help to pass on, so I help them. It's all nicey, nicey and nobody is screaming bloody murder. They're grateful."

"Well, I'll be! That's great that you found a calling. Did you ever find Ingrid?"

Veronica nodded, guiltily.

"Is she still with that young man, what's his name? Draco? Drago?"

"Desmond. Not anymore. She's doing very well, out in San Francisco. She's been working as a phlebotomist but recently got hired in a funeral home. She's mortal now."

Knud frowned and sat back in his chair. "What do you mean, 'she's mortal now'? What does that even mean?"

"Before we move on to the meaning of mortality and its implications on the modern-day vampire, I'd like to hear what you've been up to, between online dating and buying things off the internet." Just a hint of snark peppered her voice. Veronica felt the power shift back into her corner. It was all in her mind, but it made her pulse slow and her teeth recede.

For his part, Knud remained oblivious; his shoulders relaxed at this more agreeable subject. "Well, for a good long stretch, I was alone. I continued to hunt at night but as the years progressed, I found I didn't need as much blood to get by. Then the internet happened, and I found that the whole world opened up to me. I could order anything I could ever want or desire, including companionship, on the world-wide-web, and it could be delivered right to my door without a signature. It was magnificent."

"Did you order Nataliya from the internet?" Veronica shifted in her chair, fairly certain of his answer.

Knud took no apparent offense. "As a matter of fact, I did. You wouldn't believe the things you can find on the internet. It's crazy. Heck," he lowered his voice and leaned in closer. "There's this thing called the dark web."

Veronica raised her brows as a warning to tread carefully. She could tolerate a lot from her years in the ER, but if this conversation veered anywhere near child pornography, she was out. "Mmmhmmm." She glared at the blinking lights of computer equipment behind him.

"And I found a group for people like us."

Veronica sat up. "What do you mean?"

"Like vampires from around the world and their lineage or some such nonsense. I could only access that thread and I ended up getting malware from it, so I never went back. It was probably just a couple of bored teenagers who'd just read Anne Rice."

Veronica rolled her eyes. He loved the sound of his own voice, and she didn't imagine Nataliya did much talking to anyone besides the dog. "How have you survived?" Her gaze darted around what once used to be a dank, depressing cellar. It was now a digital wonderland. "And thrived?"

"It's helped that my father's land in Western Dakota struck oil. I'm loaded, and with the help of a few unethical attorneys, I've managed to forge birth and death records to keep me as the sole inheritor of the estate. The fur trade died, as you can imagine, and now I just do taxidermy as a side project to keep my hands busy."

"Are you happy?"

Knud looked down at his empty hands, then met Veronica's gaze. "As happy as one can be without an expiration date."

Veronica crossed her legs and uncrossed her arms, anxious not to let her chronic case of resting bitch face sabotage her kind intentions. "The reason I came here, in case you were wondering..." She took a deep breath and smiled on the exhale.

Knud nodded enthusiastically, as if he'd been waiting all his life to hear what she had to say.

"...is to apologize. I took advantage of you. You were sad and lonely, and I was desperate to cling to someone after Ingrid turned me. You just happened to be that person. Which wasn't that bad, now that I think about it. I could just as easily have sucked the life out of Einar Halvorson, but he wasn't as enigmatic or attractive as you. Knud, what I'm really trying to say is that I robbed you of a normal life—and for that I'm truly sorry."

Knud rose from his chair with his arms extended and a big, goofy smile on his face.

Veronica raised her hand defensively. "Sit back down. You're going to feel a bit funny here in a sec and I don't want you getting hurt." She felt completely in control, even as her own body shuddered from his soul's exit.

He fell back into the chair, grasping his chest. "I think I'm having a heart attack," he gasped. "What's happening?"

"Don't worry, you're not having a heart attack." She stood and rubbed her stomach. "Dang, I suddenly feel a ton lighter." She offered her hand to him, which he took as if it were a lifeline. "Up, Simba. Let's head upstairs."

"The sun's out, and Nataliya is upstairs watching TV. Why don't we just stay down here?" He pulled her onto his lap, as if he were suddenly healthy as a horse and the last thirty seconds hadn't happened. "Ya know, Astrid, technically we're still married." He buried his face in her neck.

She could feel through her yoga pants that he wasn't joking about the offer. For a fraction of a second, she entertained the thought of surrendering, but all she could think about was Frank. She had every intention of returning to him at the end of this journey with a clear conscience and a retirement plan that involved the two of them getting frisky in the back of a Winnebago.

"I'm flattered. Truly, I am." She freed herself from his grip and hopped from his lap. "But I'm a married woman. And I go by Veronica now. Or as my husband Frank likes to call me, Ronnie."

"I respect that." He stood, grasping one of the ceiling beams and stretched towards her like a preening Marlon Brando. His blue flannel shirt revealed a small slice of his pale, muscled stomach. He wanted to make sure he still had it. "So, are you going to tell me what just happened?"

"I want to show you. Let's go upstairs before I do something I'll regret. Jesus, man." She stopped gazing at his stomach and began to climb the rickety stairs. Stopping midway up, she turned and waved him up. "Come on. I promise that everything is going to be okay. How do you think I was able to arrive here at eleven in the morning and not burst into flames?"

"I don't know." He took a step forward, then stopped. "I don't think I can do this. Seriously, I…" He blinked and wiped at his eyes.

"I, what?"

His face crumpled, as if Paul Bunyan had just found fifty tons of blue roadkill at the top of the stairs. "I—I'm scared."

"Knud Jorgenson, I got you into this mess and I intend to get you out of it. Get up here right now," she demanded and held her hand out to him.

"I fear change." He walked towards her, sliding his feet into a pair of worn Birkenstocks at the bottom of the stairs.

"Don't we all? But what's the worst thing that could happen?" She laced her fingers through his and tugged him towards her.

"I'll die."

"Believe me, that's not the worst thing that could happen to you. It might bother Nataliya and Igor for a little while, but they'll get over it."

The thought of annoying his mail-order bride seemed to shake Knud out of his fearful daze. He slapped Veronica playfully on the butt. "Okay, let's go, woman."

FROM THE CELLAR DOOR, Veronica spied Nataliya standing over the stove frying something in a skillet. Beams of sun illuminated her slender frame from the kitchen's southern-facing window. The room smelled of bacon, toast and old leather. As Igor darted towards her in a spastic greeting, she turned towards Knud. "Ready?"

"Damn that smells good."

"Are you talking about my ass or the bacon?"

Veronica let go of his hand and leapt into the room to demonstrate her superior bravery in the face of the sun. Knud shuffled behind with his hand now clinging to the back of her shirt. "Stop touching me. Go kiss your girl or something. Do you have a mirror in this man cave?"

Nataliya turned her attention from the frying pan. "What are you doing? Oh, my goodness. Knud! It's the daytime. What are you thinking?"

Knud rushed to the kitchen and kissed her on the cheek, as if making the final leap of faith on the strength of love and bacon grease. "Don't burn that. What is it?" He looked down at the pan and inhaled deeply.

"Knud, did you ever turn anyone? Like a person? Or did you just stick to animals?" Veronica leaned against the granite counter. It occurred to her that she hadn't thought everything through. Not everyone lived as she did.

"No, just animals. Why?"

"Figures. Oh, those soulless creatures have just changed your life irrevocably," she muttered under her breath. "Well, I've got some good news and some bad news for you."

"Okay." He crossed his arms and hopped up on the counter. "Let's start with the good news."

"The good news is that you can now eat bacon. Nataliya, what are you making? BLTs, perhaps? Do me a solid and make one up for your old man."

"What is she talking about? The bacon will make you sick. Won't it?"

"No, it will actually make him fat and happy. Now for the bad news, or maybe good news. It all depends on how you look at it." Veronica pushed off from the counter and began pacing the kitchen with Igor following behind. "Make some more toast, Nataliya." She snapped her fingers to stop the woman from gawking.

"I'm waiting. Am I going to die? Is that what you're trying to tell me?"

"Yes. You are going to die, just like a normal person. As a forty-two-year old man, you are now at the midpoint of your life. Hair loss, flatulence and erectile dysfunction await you."

Knud stared blankly. "I'm forty-one."

"Really? I was ten years older than you? Rawwr!" She clawed at the air and slapped her hands on his knees. "Knud, the extra special sauce news is that what happened down stairs was a gift. I gave you your soul back."

His face remained expressionless as he stared at her nervously ticking cheek.

"But here's the rub; you had more self-control than me in the blood-letting department, so you became mortal in like a millisecond. Unlike me who still depends on the kindness of dying people to sup, you can now eat all the bacon and ice cream you could possibly ever want, sleep till noon on a Monday, and die like Elvis on the toilet if you so wish. I, on the other hand, have to traipse around this god-forsaken country in search of people that I never want to see again and apologize to them just to get where you are at this exact moment. Am I making any sense?" She exhaled and moved back to the other counter in case he lost it.

"Here's the sandwich." Nataliya handed it to him on a dainty, ancient plate. "I put the mayo on it the way I like it and I cut the tomato very thin, so it doesn't make the toast wet and squishy. You try. Stand over the sink for the crumbs. I just cleaned."

Knud glanced over at Nataliya, as if just then noticing her. "You're a fantastic cook. Thank you." He walked over to the sink and sniffed the sandwich. "Last time I tried to eat, I dry heaved for an hour. Are you sure about this?"

Veronica nodded. "You'll be fine. More than fine. Go ahead. I dare you."

He opened his mouth and took a bite. Chewing longer than was necessary, he struggled to swallow it.

"How do you feel? Are you going to throw up the bacon?" Nataliya rubbed his back as if he were sick.

Knud's unfocused gaze lingered on the kitchen cabinets as the first tentative toast crumbs dusted his beard like whole-wheat snow. "No, I don't think so. It just takes a little getting used to." He looked back down at the mayonnaised miracle on his plate. "I think I want another one. I'm so hungry."

Unlike Ingrid, Knud ate slowly and cautiously. It took him over an hour to finish three sandwiches, but Veronica was in no hurry. He seemed to be enjoying himself, like an infant discovering solid foods for the first time.

While petting Igor, who seemed to have taken a shine to her, her mind wandered back to Jenny. How were the next few days going to play out? Meth withdrawal wasn't as bad as heroin but, depending on her level of use and the dopamine receptors she had destroyed, she would be unable to feel anything close to joy. That is, unless she used again, which was what made the march to relapse so inevitable.

"Ready for your next adventure?" Veronica placed a squirming Igor onto the couch, as Knud wiped the crumbs from his beard.

"Sure."

"Let's go outside. I'd love some sunflowers to cheer up my motel room." She skipped towards the door.

"When did you become Mary Poppins?" Knud grabbed a sweater from the coat rack.

"When I stopped spending my days in a basement. There's an amazing world out there, Knud, and the Internet doesn't do it justice."

Veronica felt awfully proud of herself and the ease in which Knud accepted his new reality. She reasoned that sudden and unexpected change was easiest when the shine of possibility overshadowed the dust bunnies and dirt that hid in the corners. Tomorrow would be trickier.

22

On the way back to the motel, Veronica stopped at a gas station and picked up a turkey and Swiss for Jenny. Tiptoeing back into the room, she found the girl just where she'd left her hours before, buried under a sea of sheets. Labored breathing assured her that Jenny wasn't dead, just dead tired, and a possible candidate for deviated septum surgery.

It had been a good day. She'd set Knud free to enjoy a lifetime of TLC and BLTs with Nataliya. Taken care of Jenny, in as much as a three-day-old gas station hoagie counted as care.

But that left nobody to make Veronica a sandwich, and she couldn't have eaten it even if they had. Where was her TLC?

Veronica glanced back over at her comatose companion. If she stuck around watching Jenny sleep in this tiny room, there was the distinct possibility that she would end up doing something she'd regret.

Veronica needed a healthier kind of fix—one that had nothing to do with blood or appetite. She pulled Jenny's iPhone out of her purse, but it was too risky to switch it on even for the length of a Google search.

With no one and nothing else left to go on, Veronica let her fragile moral compass guide her out of the room, through the parking lot, into the car, and south—towards Fargo and a phone book.

AFTER A QUICK STOP at the local Walmart to purchase a disposable phone and peruse a local directory, Veronica had just enough time to make the seven-thirty Big Book Study in a church basement.

On her way there, she tried to remember Frank's cell number. After six wrong numbers, she wanted to flip out for throwing her phone into the crematory. She could remember the faces and fashion sense of people who had been dead for a hundred years, but apparently a simple, seven-digit number was beyond her. Like other menopausal women, she suffered from brain fog—but in her case, it was terminal. Her hormones, no matter what she did, were never going to level out.

Our Father, who art in heaven, she prayed at each successive red light, *give me this day my husband's cell number, and deliver me from temptation, evil, and senior moments, for yours is the power and the glory...*

But of course, such a specific "Dear Santa" request was wasted air. God didn't grant wishes like a genie in a bottle.

But that didn't mean there was no divine order to her predicament. It could be that she wasn't supposed to speak with Frank at this exact moment, that this separation without communication was somehow a good thing—absence making the heart grow fonder and all that.

Feeling a tad more optimistic, Veronica prayed for patience and the strength of character to keep from killing Jenny.

FORTUNATELY FOR HER SOBRIETY EFFORT, Veronica had long since discovered that that whole "no setting foot on sacred ground" thing was complete bunk. After heading into the empty vestibule of the Hope Lutheran Church, she followed her nose towards the basement. AA meetings rarely had identifying signage, but if Veronica could smell coffee, she knew she would find at least three recovering alcoholics, a Big Book and an overflowing ashtray.

This meeting met the mark. Barely. Four men and one woman sat in timelessly uncomfortable folding chairs under the yellow fluorescent light—and staggered up to greet her the minute she stepped through the door. The undivided attention unnerved her, as if they were in cahoots to hog-tie her to a chair as soon as she crossed the threshold. Veronica reflexively clutched her purse in front of her as a shield.

The elderly woman, who still looked like she could win a wrestling match with a home invader, was encased in a pale blue polyester ensemble that matched her short crop of tightly set hair. "Hello, sweetheart. Are you here for the Serenity Seekers Al-Anon meeting or the Twelve Steppers AA group?" The woman's voice dripped sincerity like a dipped cone from the neighboring Dairy Queen.

"The AA meeting?" Veronica could have attended either, since she was a double winner, both an alcoholic and a friend or family member of one, but it wasn't any of the woman's business to know that.

"Well, take a seat, missy, cuz you're in the right place. My name's Barb. I'm the hospitality director, as well as the treasurer of the Twelve Steppers. Is this your first meeting?"

"Hi Barb, I'm Veronica." She offered her hand to Barb and was met with a clammy, limp jiggle of her fingers. "I'm just visiting a friend for a few days and thought I'd catch a local meeting. My home group is in Texas."

"You got family around here, Veronica? You look awful familiar." Barb studied Veronica's face. "Real familiar."

"Nope, just a friend." Veronica's thoughts turned to her great-granddaughter.

"We'll get started here in a jiff, but we're waiting on Marge Anderson. She's bringing the lemon bars. She don't walk real good since she had her leg amputated from the diabetes. It's a real bitch, that disease, especially when you're still active in the cunning clutches of alcoholism like she is." Barb plopped down in one of the metal chairs and made the sign of the cross over her chest. "One day at a time, though, right?"

So much for anonymity. Veronica took a seat a few chairs away. The three men remained silent. One flipped through his book, the other closed his eyes, but the third, a man in his eighties, stared at Veronica as if he'd seen a ghost.

I know you. His deep, raspy voice resonated over and over in her head like a skipping record. *I know you.*

But that was impossible. She hadn't been in Fargo since the 30s.

Checking the clock compulsively, Veronica was tempted to feign a headache or a digestive issue to excuse herself from the worst meeting she'd ever attended. The Twelve Steppers had no experience, strength or hope to speak of, just country-song-inspired drunkalogues, stale baked goods and funny-smelling coffee. The old man with his filmy eyes kept looking over at her every time he mentioned one of his old haunts, the Empire Cafe.

"Are you talking about the Empire Tavern on Broadway?" One of the others interrupted, adjusting his hearing aid.

Veronica rolled her eyes at the cross talk. She vaguely remembered the place. After prohibition ended, bars were her favorite place to hunt, and Fargo had quite a few: The Bismarck Tavern, the Silver Trey, and the Flame. The Empire Café later became the Empire Tavern when the owners wanted to emphasize the fact that they sold bourbon instead of biscuits.

As they stood to recite the Lord's Prayer, the old man grasped Veronica's hand and squeezed it as if he were trying to extract juice from her fingertips. Knowing she'd be leaving immediately after "Forever and Ever, Amen," she allowed him this indiscretion.

"Keep coming back—it works if you work it," they said in unison, and unclasped their sweaty palms.

The old man turned to Veronica and cleared his throat. "1940, Empire Tavern. You, or someone who looks a lot like you, walked out the door with my pop. Haven't heard from him since."

"Vernon's crazy, don't listen to him," Barb interrupted. "Last week he swore he saw Buddy Holly over in Moorehead ordering a caramel macchiato at the Starbucks."

Marge limped over and put her arm around Vernon's shoulder. "When's the VA doing your cataract surgery, old man? This young lady wasn't even born in 1940. You need your eyes fixed."

Vernon scowled at Veronica, undeterred. "I know what I saw."

"You were probably three sheets to the wind," Barb laughed.

"I was eight." He pulled away from Marge. "And those lemon bars you made tasted like furniture polish. Who taught you how to cook?"

Marge's waxy fuchsia lips pursed into a hard line. "Your dad. Right after he ran off to Niagara Falls with her."

Everyone remained silent.

"Well, I best be on my way." Veronica grabbed her purse from the back of the chair and slung it over her shoulder. "Vern, I was born in 1964, but I'm flattered that all my doppelgangers seem to be alive and thriving in Fargo."

Barb wiped her hands on her sweater, as if eager to smooth out the conversation likewise. "Well, if you want to go see one for yourself, there's a young woman who looks a lot like you on 25th Avenue North. She's probably walking one of her yappy dogs and yelling dirty words like some kind of lunatic."

Veronica blinked, hardly able to trust her ears.

Millie.

"Thank you—I may just do that." Veronica felt the weight of her keys as keenly as the passing of time. She needed to find out if her great-granddaughter had returned. Jenny would have to wait a few more hours without her beloved phone.

23

MASSACHUSETTS – 1939

illicent Ganelle Albrecht was twenty-seven, the expiration date of many a modern-day rock star, when Veronica first laid eyes on her. Millie wasn't musically inclined or inclined towards anything in particular, other than flailing her arms and shouting obscenities at the most inopportune moments. Her well-to-do parents were dumbfounded as to how they were going to manage their daughter's animated physical tics and foul language. At first, they quietly consulted a priest to exorcise her of the demons that spewed forth from her wicked tongue, but when God failed to manage her maniacal mouth, they relinquished her at the age of sixteen to the Danvers State Insane Asylum in rural Massachusetts. Like her upbringing up until that point, she was discreetly placed far away from the easily offended and kept subdued with a heaping helping of psychotropic medications. Compared to the various schizophrenics that inhabited every corner of the overcrowded facility, the nurses found Millie's naughty verbal antics amusing. They concluded that she was definitely sane; she just tended to swear like an Elizabethan sailor.

In 1939, when Veronica fled Fargo to find her one remaining family member in the east wing of the loony bin, she had to wade through a sea of psych patients to find someone who looked somewhat official, or at least not crazy, to point her in the right direction. There was barely a nurse in sight. When she finally spotted one who had just dragged a very reluctant patient into her bed, the exhausted woman rubbed her eyes and asked if she was there to relieve her for the night.

Without thinking, Veronica nodded in affirmation.

The woman handed her a clipboard. "Thank the Lord. Is this your first night?"

"Yes, ma'am, it is."

"Where's your uniform?" The nurse scanned Veronica's ensemble with narrowed eyes.

"My luggage was misplaced in transit, but I should have a replacement by tomorrow. Should I leave?"

"Oh, no. We're so short on hands tonight, you could be wearing a potato sack for all I care."

Veronica tried to act as prim and professional as possible, despite the fact that she was wearing a full-length burgundy dress ripe with train travel and her hair was pulled into an unruly bun. The inability to look in a mirror proved extremely problematic when she had to dress herself and venture out in public.

"Thank your lucky stars that you got assigned to this wing. I started out in the snake pit and after a week, I felt like I was ready for a lobotomy myself."

Veronica didn't know what a lobotomy was, but she gathered from the woman's pained expression that it wasn't something she wanted to line up for.

"This floor has had their evening meds, but all doors need to be locked to keep the other wing from wandering in. I think Miss Jenkins is doing that now if you want to follow her and see how it's done."

Veronica looked around at all the blank faces passing her in the hall and felt as if she had just been invited to a smorgasbord. She'd never considered it before, but working in an overcrowded hospital was perfect for her needs. Patients wouldn't be missed, nor would they be believed if she happened to relieve them of a pint or two in the middle of the night.

According to the chart on the clipboard, Millie's bed was at the end of the row.

Veronica knew the minute she saw the pale face and dark curly hair that she was gazing at kin. Staring down at the sleeping woman was like looking at a reflection of her younger self. She gingerly positioned herself at the end of the bed, careful not to disturb her.

Millie opened her eyes and growled. "Be gone, thou rank, heavy headed malkin!"

"Easy now. I'm not going to hurt you." Veronica patted her on the leg.

Millie bolted upright, clutching the worn blanket to her chin. "Are you the nurse?"

"Yes. My uniform became a bit messy, so I'm wearing this for tonight. I hope you don't mind."

"Infection ridden hugger-mugger! Eeeeeeeeeeeeeeeeeeeeeeeeeeeeeep!" Millie's pale skinny arms flew out from beneath the thin blanket and shot towards the ceiling. Her head flopped from side to side as if a spastic puppeteer was controlling her movements. "Why won't you people just let me die?" she moaned.

Veronica winced from the emotional pain of witnessing misery. "Are you sick?"

"No, but I grow oh, so weary of living like this. Eeeeeeeeeeeeeeeeeeeeeeeeep! Be gone, cantankerous cunt!"

Veronica had never heard a woman speak such dangerous words before.

"Just kill me," Millie pleaded.

Veronica could do that. Maybe she should do that. She was alone. Millie was alone.

Maybe an all blood diet would offer a cure that no lobotomy could. There was only one way to find out.

Veronica's incisors reacted before her brain could intercept. "Shhh-hh," she whispered near Millie's neck. "This will be quick."

24

THE PRESENT

Veronica scanned the darkened suburban street where her granddaughter once resided in hopes that Millie would miraculously appear. They hadn't spoken in years, although Veronica had faithfully supplied her with a monthly stipend to sustain the mess she'd created. If all went according to this last-minute magical plan, there would be a quick apology, an even quicker hug, and before the clock struck midnight, she could drive back to Pembina before Jenny did something illegal. It was a million to one chance, but on occasion, God did work in mysterious ways. She pulled over beneath a street lamp, lowered her window and opened a dog-eared copy of the *Big Book* that she had swiped from the Twelve Steppers. Scrolled on the front page, a long-ago member had written, "Don't just do something, sit there." She took it as a sign.

Veronica was barely into Bill's Story when she spotted a motley pack of canines pulling a long, slender woman down the street. Like an oddly dressed water skier on an asphalt lake, the woman's upper body leaned back against the forward momentum of multiple, multi-colored leashes that fanned out from her clutched hands. Sporting a trucker hat, aviator sunglasses and faded overalls, she looked as if she were trying, but ultimately failing at remaining incognito.

Inevitably, the pack of recalcitrant canines led her towards the most well-manicured and meticulously maintained lawn to do their business. A limping Husky fussily circled in place, then squatted in the plush St. Augustine grass. While reaching for a bag from her back pocket, Millie's arms flailed upwards as she eeeeeped into the quiet street. In unison, the leashed dogs barked, bellowed and howled to match their master's rising wail. Lights flickered on in the neighboring houses. A man in a blue terry robe stepped out onto his porch and exhaled a heavy sigh.

"You gonna clean up your dog's doody there, Miss Millie?" he asked politely.

"Yes, sir, I'm on it, you cock-sucking, crotch muncher eeeeeeeeeeeeeeeeeeeeeeeep!!!" The dogs tilted their heads as Millie's screeching howl approached the upper octaves.

Veronica flinched at the sound of Millie's unmistakable voice. She set the worn, blue book down on the passenger seat and grabbed her purse from the floorboard.

"Ya know, it's real great what you're doing for those there dogs, but we're all getting pretty darn tired of this eleven-o-clock ritual you got going on. I don't know about you, Missy, but there's people on this here block that are trying to get some sleep. Don't you think you could take em out a little earlier?" He kicked at some leaves on his porch. "Sometime before supper might be good."

"No, sir, I can't." She placed a black bag on her open hand and stooped to retrieve the Husky's poop. "Who gave you ice cream, Clyde? Your poop looks like pudding and smells even worse than usual. It was Judy, wasn't it?" The Husky licked her face and barked at the middle-aged man. "Can I put this in your trash can, Mr. Anderson? As you can see—dog shit, dick face eeeeeeeeeeeeeeeeeeeeeeeeeeeep— my hands are full."

The dogs barked, straining at their leashes towards the robed man. He refastened the belt around his waist and chuckled despite the stern expression he was trying to maintain.

Veronica exited the car with urgency as if she might have to rescue her odd great-granddaughter from an altercation. She slammed the car's door. All eyes—human, animal and vampire—turned to look at her. "Excuse me. I don't mean to interrupt." She stepped onto the lawn. "Millie? Is that you?" Veronica knelt to scratch a wiggly Boston Terrier's chin.

Millie removed her glasses, dropped the leashes from her hands and bolted towards Veronica. "Gigi!" She yelped and wrapped her skinny body around Veronica. The dogs joined in on the excitement, toppling both women in a tangled mess onto the damp grass.

"Okay, ladies. That's enough. I'm pulling a double tomorrow and if I don't get some shut eye, I'm gonna be in a world of hurt." He coughed. "I might not be so kind tomorrow night. Go on now." He waved at the air.

Several dogs rolled onto their backs as Veronica struggled to rise up among the tangle of limbs and leashes. A black Lab sniffed at her ankle and lifted its arthritic leg, relieving himself on her sensible shoes.

"Bart!" Millie exclaimed, "We don't pee on Gigi. She's family."

"It's alright, Bart. I'm a very bad Gigi. I'd pee on me too." Veronica managed to stand. To appease the man who stared at their every move, she gathered several leashes. "I imagine you live somewhere around here?"

"Next block down."

MILLIE'S HOUSE looked as if Boo Radley might make an appearance at any moment. The gray paint was faded, the front windows were boarded up, and what should have been a lawn was simply a mound of dirt sprinkled with the detritus of dog shit and dandelions. All the yard needed was a rusted-out jalopy on cinderblocks to complete the picture of abject poverty. If the noisy late-night walks didn't inflame her neighbors, then the condition of her house probably did.

As Veronica attempted to balance herself on the weathered boards of the front porch, Millie fumbled for a ring of keys in the equally weathered pocket of her overalls. Locking the front door of this fixer upper seemed like overkill to Veronica, but she tried not to judge the contents based on the dilapidated exterior.

Millie pushed the door open. The dogs scampered inside, leashes dangling behind them. "Sorry about the mess. I just...."

"Didn't clean your house for the last fifty years?" Veronica interjected from the doorway. It was a tornado of crates, carriers, fur, chewed toys and one very brave calico perched atop an ancient entertainment center. More than anything, it was an olfactory assault of ammonia-smelling awfulness.

"So how have you, you know, been able to survive all these years?" Veronica leaned against a wall, trying not to touch anything. "Is it them?"

Millie sat down on the floor. She methodically removed each dog's harness and kissed them on the forehead. "Yeah, it's them. I know it's not very sexy or dangerous, but it's easy. Nobody wants them. Either they've lost their new-puppy sheen or they're old and sick. If I didn't take them, they'd be euthanized anyway. I give them a good month or two of steak dinners, unconditional love and t-r-e-a-t-s and I just end their lives a little differently. They love me."

"That's obvious."

"I take the sick ones first." She exclaimed proudly, as if she had to justify her actions. She cradled a three-legged chihuahua to her chest and murmured into its ear.

"Me too. I'm now working as a hospice nurse."

"I just work at the inhumane society. My shift starts in an hour— dumb ass, dingleberry, douchebagger eeeeeeeeeeeep—would you like to come with me?"

"I love that your swearing has advanced with the times." She laughed and brushed tufts of fur off her shirt. "I'll definitely come with you, but there's something I need to talk to you about first." Veronica tiptoed through the living room to what was left of the couch and sat down.

"Uh, oh. Gigi's gonna get serious." Millie brought her knees to her chest and removed her sunglasses.

"I want you to be honest with me, Millie. Do you enjoy the way you're living?"

"It's better than Dan..." Millie's face contorted. She hugged her skinny arms firmly to her chest. "...vers. I don't enjoy these tics."

The Husky climbed onto the couch and placed its head on Veronica's lap. "There's medication that can help, you know."

"Yeah, for normal people that can go out into the light of day. I tried going to the ER to get a prescription. As you can probably guess, swearing and spazzing out wasn't exactly considered an emergency. They just thought I was drunk—drunk spunk, twat face, eeeeeeeeeeeeeeeeeeeeeeeeeeeep!" Millie laid back on the floor, exasperated. The Husky whimpered, jumped off the couch and scooted towards her. "They called the cops."

"I'm sorry. ERs are the worst. I've worked in a few, and you get some real whackos who just want pain meds."

Millie sat back up and pulled a plastic baggie out of her pocket. "Who wants a treat?" At the word *treat*, the dogs went spastic. "What I like about dogs is they don't mind that I'm a nut job. They probably think I just bark a lot." She handed each dog a strip of bacon from the bag.

"You're not a nut job. I think what you have is Tourette's." Veronica leaned back on the couch. "Okay, here goes. I don't know how to say this other than that the sun thing is a myth."

"It's not a myth. I remember seeing it." She threw the empty bag on the littered floor. "All gone." She showed her empty hands like a blackjack dealer leaving the table. They sniffed at her pockets and licked her fingers.

Veronica continued. "Yes, I'm perfectly aware that it exists. But it's a myth that it will kill you. If you want, you can walk those dogs tomorrow morning and you'll be fine. You could even go to a doctor's office tomorrow at noon and you'd be fine."

Millie's head jerked from shoulder to shoulder. "You've got to be kidding me."

Bart picked up his leash and set it on Veronica's lap. She pet his graying head and turned back to Millie. "I'm afraid I'm not. Have you ever turned another person into a vampire?"

Millie rocked back and forth as tears filled her eyes. Her voice became a whisper. "You said w-a-l-k. He thinks you're going to take him, you know, on a w-a-l-k."

"I'm sorry, Bart. I didn't mean to mislead you." Veronica got down on the floor and placed her arm around Millie's shoulder. "Are you okay?"

"No. I'm pretty fucking far from okay. Okay?" She brushed Veronica's arm away. "And no, I've never turned another person. Besides Doctor Bridwell and a couple of other rapist psychos at Danvers, I've never even killed anyone. I don't know about you, but for me, it's really fucking hard to sneak up on somebody when you can't stop shouting obscenities at them. I've tried."

"You know what? Human blood is not all it's cracked up to be. Believe me."

"Whatever. You've had plenty and you're probably on husband number nine or something. I've never even been on a date." Millie buried her head in her hands and sobbed like a hungry baby whose mother had just left the room. "I'm a total loser."

"No, you're not. Listen, if you had the choice, would you like to be mortal again?" Veronica rubbed Millie's back.

"I don't know. I never really thought about it." She wiped her eyes on the sleeve of her shirt. "I think I'd rather win the lotto, so I could get a housekeeper. I really don't like cleaning." She forced a smile.

"I've noticed." Veronica gazed around the room and sighed. After she'd made the terrible decision to turn Millie, the girl almost seemed happy with the novelty of life outside of Danvers, but it didn't take long for her to discover the unfortunate truth that wherever she went, there she was. "Okay, Millie, I realize this sounds crazy, but I know how to make you mortal again."

Millie raised an incredulous eyebrow as her arms shot out in front of her. "What difference would it make if I was mortal?"

"Well, for one, you'd be able to ingest medicine that might help with your condition. Wouldn't that be worth it?" Veronica knew by her own pleading tone that her own desperation was settling in. Millie had to consent.

"Will it hurt?"

"No." That was a lie. "Not really." Closer to the truth. "Actually, it feels more surprising than painful." Veronica gazed into Millie's eyes hoping to work her vampire magic. "But as a mortal, your life will eventually end. Would you be okay with that?" *Please God, let her be okay with that.*

Millie nodded. "Yeah, of course. I mean, I guess so."

"Okay." Veronica stood, sat back on the couch, and impatiently patted the seat next to her. "Come here."

Millie rolled her eyes and quickly complied.

Veronica cleared her throat. "Millicent, what I did to you that night at Danvers and the weeks that followed was a mistake. I thought I could save you, but in the long run, I just prolonged your isolation and misery. I robbed you of a normal life and for that, I am eternally sorry." Veronica braced herself for Millie's bodily response, which she secretly hoped might be spectacular.

"I was in a mental hospital, Gigi. It was never going to get normal. Ever. Fuck, fuck, fuckity fuck duck goose, eeeeeeeeeeeeeeeeeeeeeeeeeeeeeeeeeep! What the hell was that??" She grasped at her stomach and curled into a fetal position on the floor. The dogs rushed towards her and worriedly sniffed her body.

"It's okay," Veronica reassured them. "She's fine. Your mama is now going to have to take you to the vet like a normal person. And when she gets herself up off this dirty ass floor, she is going to research the best doctor to deal with her condition and then she's going to make an appointment. At her appointment, she's going to ask that doctor to help her find a support group so that she feels less alone in the world. And then, she's going to clean this shit hole up."

Veronica stood and stretched. "Who wants a bacon cheeseburger? I'm buying."

25

To kill the hours till sunrise so she could prove the existence of a benevolent sun, Veronica dragged Millie to the local Walmart to purchase an industrial-strength vacuum cleaner. On the way back home from this terrifying midnight jaunt, they hit up the only open fast food restaurant in town to purchase ten cheeseburgers with a side of fries. While Millie fretted over her French fries and the catastrophic possibilities of a morning walk, Veronica spent the remaining night-time hours attempting to rid the house of as much dog fur as possible. It was the worst kind of service work, but as the weeping wall back home promised, "When you get busy, you get better." It helped that she felt lighter on her feet without Millie's soul eeeping and swearing in the caverns of her core. With the flick of an on switch, Veronica approached the task of hair removal with the fervor of an Olympic athlete. It wasn't always easy to measure serenity, but today, it was a reassuringly symmetrical pattern of vacuum tracks in the carpet.

"I think that thing is scaring them." Millie shouted over the vacuum's whir.

Veronica looked at the dogs. Most of them peered at her from the stairs, grateful for the greasy fast food and probably wondering when it might happen again. She pushed the vacuum harder in a different direction and marveled at the strip of Persian rug that revealed itself.

"They're fine. They'll get used to it, as will you. Why don't you tackle the bathroom?"

"I feel really tired. Is this normal?" She stretched her long body and yawned.

"From here on out it will be. But you're young and good looking." Veronica patted her playfully on the butt. "Oh shit, I forgot about the mirror." Veronica turned off the vacuum. "Where's the little girl's room?"

"Huh?"

"The bathroom? You know that room that contains a toilet, a shower and hopefully a litter box."

"It's down the hall and on the right. Do you need to use the restroom?" Millie's face contorted in confusion.

"No, but you need to come with me. This is what women do. They go to the bathroom together in packs. I want to show you something." Veronica grabbed Millie's hand.

"The last time someone said that to me, I got locked in a supply closet with a paranoid schizophrenic. He was convinced that I was his mother—fucker, cock sucker, wooooop!"

"Hey, your vocal tics are progressing from an eeep to a woop. You're already changing. Come on," Veronica tugged. "I want to show you something."

In the bathroom, they found Bart clawing at the cat box to unearth a treat. With lips sprinkled in litter, he bowed his head in shame and scampered from the room. Veronica placed her hands on Millie's shoulders and led her towards the mirror.

"Look." She removed Millie's trucker hat. Long black curls cascaded down her shoulders. "Look at yourself. You're gorgeous."

Millie gasped at the sight of her reflection yet edged closer to the poorly lit mirror. In stunned silence, she touched her face and hair with the transfixed intensity of someone flying high on LSD. This tender, yet somewhat awkward moment, ended with a stream of obscenities and spittle spewing from her mouth and sprinkling the mirror. When Millie's vocal gymnastics ended, she took a deep breath and stepped back to take in more of her reflected image. Turning around, she looked over her shoulder to gaze at her backside.

"Oh my god. Have you noticed? My butt? It's like perfect! I had no idea. Why didn't you tell me?"

"For one, I assumed you knew—but now that I think of it, Danvers kept mirrors to a minimum."

"I need to get laid. Seriously. For years I thought I was a living, breathing Quasimodo but I look like one of those chicks you see in a beer commercial." Millie growled at her reflection, baring her white teeth. "And I've got killer teeth too!"

"Speaking of killer choppers, Millie. Those days are done." Veronica wrapped her arm around Millie's shoulder. "From now on, you shall forgo the blood of Fido and eat heavily processed food like a normal American."

IT WASN'T easy to leave the next morning, but once Veronica witnessed the joy and enthusiasm with which Millie strutted down the street in the presence of her shocked neighbors, she knew that her great-grand-daughter would be okay.

She would be better than okay. Millie could now reside in the pleasure of possibility instead of the usual monotony of slang-laden survival. Veronica wondered what it would be like to be young again as the two-lane blacktop stretched out before her. "Back in Black" boomed from the car's speakers as the sun kissed the exposed skin of her forearms. The world and all it had to offer felt as if it were streaming through her open hand. Smiling, she glanced at her reflection in the rearview mirror. She was still fifty-one. Wiping the beads of sweat from her upper lip, she turned down the stereo.

THE LOT of the motel was empty with the exception of a lone police cruiser hidden behind its prominent red sign. Veronica looked up at the room she'd rented. The curtains were still drawn. As she stepped out of the car, Veronica told herself that Jenny was probably happily ingesting the gas station smorgasbord while binge watching a *Golden Girls* marathon. She was definitely not lying stiff and cold on a vomit stained mattress. Inserting her card in the door's reader, the light flashed red. She turned it around and inserted it again.

"Jenny? Let me in. My card's not working," she whispered into the door frame.

Silence.

Veronica took a deep breath and stepped back, approaching the door as if to reason with it. She wiped the card on her shirt, studied the printed instructions as if there were a special secret to make it work, and tried again.

Red.

Irritated, she clomped down the stairs to the front office. An elderly woman in a lavender pant suit smiled at her from the desk. "Can I help you?"

"My key isn't working." Veronica placed it on the counter. "Astrid Dahling. Room 23."

The woman typed something and stared at the computer screen. "Looks like your daughter checked you all out of the room yesterday, Ms. Dahling. Bart's notes said we refunded her the cash deposit, since there wasn't a credit card on file."

Veronica felt like screaming a Millie-esque stream of profanities at the elderly woman. Instead, she forced a closed-mouth smile. "Oh, that's right. I forgot she was going to check us out early. Would you mind pointing me in the direction of the nearest bar?"

26

Despite the early hour, the local watering hole was hopping with a motley assortment of alcoholics drinking their way towards sanity or at least steadier hands. Veronica scanned the mostly middle-aged crowd, looking for Jenny's jet-black hair and grimy clothes. Everyone in the dim, cavernous space eyed her expectantly, as if she might be the one stranger to buy the house a round or liven the place up by feeding the jukebox.

Veronica maneuvered herself between a ripe old man and a middle-aged woman with her head resting on the bar. The bartender winked in her direction and pounded his fist beside the sleeping woman's open mouth. "Wake up, Marge! You can't sleep in here!" His voice startled the sleeping woman. He smiled at Veronica as if he couldn't believe the audacity of the drunks in his care. His front teeth were missing, but he didn't seem to mind. "Get you something to drink, sweetheart?"

"I wanna another one," the woman slurred and slowly raised her head, as if an invisible hand was pushing it back towards the sticky surface of the bar. "And I'm not sleeping, Richard, I'm thinking."

Veronica took a deep breath and tried to reciprocate the bartender's eager smile. "I'm looking for a young woman. She's petite, dark hair and probably wearing black."

"Hey, me too!" The man beside her cackled. "If you find her, send her to this side of the bar." The old man elbowed Veronica's ribs. His laugh morphed into a phlegmy, uncontrollable cough. She pressed her lips together to ward off his spewing germs. She hadn't been sick since she was mortal, but lately, anything was possible.

As the bartender contemplated Veronica's question, the opening notes of "Dream On" began to play on the yellowed Wurlitzer. "Yeah, she was in here yesterday. Had a real mouth on her."

"Sounds like the girl I'm looking for. Was she with anyone?" Veronica leaned away from the coughing man and moved towards the waitress station, clutching her purse tightly as if it were Jenny's tiny head. The bartender followed.

"You a cop or something?" He eyes narrowed.

"Actually, I'm her aunt. She's not supposed to be drinking. She's in recovery." And leaving her alone for so long was irresponsible on bad old Auntie V's part. She wanted to kick herself, and everyone in this bar, for being so stupid.

"Well, she was drinking alright. Wild Turkey and Miller Lite. And she was with a guy I ain't never seen before."

"What did he look like?"

"Like most of them oil guys do. Young, dirty hands, wearing Wranglers and some old flannel shirt." He wiped at a spot on the bar with a damp gray towel. "We get all sorts coming through here ever since the oil boom. Some are a bit seedier than others, if you catch my drift."

"They weren't on drugs, were they?" She leaned in to the bar, flashing him a smile as if it didn't matter one way or the other.

"Well, they was awfully amped up considering all the beers they was drinking. They were dancing everywhere and as you can see, this ain't exactly the kinda place to cut a rug."

"I see. Well, thanks for the information." Veronica pushed away from the bar and rolled her shoulders. She was ravenous, and it was way too easy to slip in a place like this.

"Can I get you something to drink?"

She flashed him an inquisitive look. *Don't tempt me.* "Do you have anything fresh and warm, Richard?" The question was ripe with sarcasm, which was more to feed her need to tear flesh than an honest inquiry of his liquid wares.

"Sorry, the coffee machine's out. Tequila makes you warm." He lifted a bottle of rot-gut from the well and smiled his toothless grin. When she didn't bite, he plopped the half-empty bottle back into its slot and continued to wipe at the invisible spot on the bar.

"Yes, it does. It also makes my clothes come off, which defeats the original purpose. I need to go. Thanks for your help." Veronica fished in her purse for the car keys and practically sprinted out of the dank bar. For the first time in decades, she felt the overwhelming need to burst into tears. The last place she wanted that to happen was in a crappy bar in North Dakota. She didn't know if it was the depressing Aerosmith song or the fact that Jenny, her only ethical food source, had abandoned her for a few free beers and a roughneck stranger.

She pulled the atlas from under the seat and studied it. Although Jenny certainly wasn't inside its pages, she felt overwhelmed that the people she'd turned could be anywhere. Her best bet was to look in the place she'd left them, as that was her pattern. Turn and burn. She was resolved to search the streets of Pembina for Jenny, but from there, it would most likely be I-94 towards Detroit. The thought of being in the same town with Kevin Black turned her stomach, but whether she liked it or not, eventually she'd have to meet up with him. But first she needed to find Mary Katherine. Of all the people she'd turned, Mary was the only one who forced her hand.

SHE WAS ONLY a mile out of town when she spotted Jenny sitting on the side of the road. Her orange arm was resting on her knees, but it was extended out towards the road with a tiny, tentative thumb in the air. Veronica pulled over and Jenny leapt to her feet.

"Where the hell were you?" Jenny yelled into the open passenger window. "When you didn't come back to the room, I thought you'd been killed or..."

Veronica gasped. "What happened to your eye?"

Jenny leaned into the window, giving Veronica a better look at the black and blue shiner. "Some douchebag bought me a couple of drinks last night and thought he could fuck me in his truck."

"And your neck. Oh my god, Jenny. Are you alright?" Jenny's neck was covered in angry, deep, finger-shaped bruises.

She opened the door and slid into the passenger seat, throwing her bag behind her. "I'm fine. You should see him." Jenny forced a laugh.

"Oh god. Let's get out of here." Veronica shifted the car into drive and peeled out from the shoulder in a halo of dust, her empathy for Jenny's battered face fast rising into rage.

Jenny secured the belt and pulled down the visor. Inspecting her ravaged face, she touched her split lip. "I look absolutely fucking horrible. No wonder no one gave me a lift."

"Listen, Jenny. I need to eat. And it's either going to be him or you."

Jenny rolled up her window. "You don't need to find him."

"Why not? Don't you think he should pay for this? I certainly do." She clawed her nails into the steering wheel.

"I seriously doubt there's an ounce of blood left in his body." Jenny rested her face against the window.

"What do you mean by that? What did you do?" Veronica's gaze darted between the rearview mirror and the speedometer.

"Gee, well, while he was busy raping me, I managed to grab the gun from his holster. He didn't like that very much. But he stopped." Jenny picked at the grime beneath her nails.

"Why would you leave the bar with him?" Veronica looked towards Jenny.

"What? Are you saying I deserved it?"

"No. Absolutely not, but come on. What were you thinking?"

"I wasn't thinking, alright," Jenny snapped. "I was high. And I don't know if you've ever snorted coke, but when you're coming down and it's two o'clock in the morning, it's pretty fucking depressing. All you want is more." Jenny's voice cracked. "He said he had some more in his truck, so I followed him outside."

"So, you shot him?" Veronica placed her hand on Jenny's trembling shoulder.

Jenny sobbed. "Yes." She buried her face in her hands and winced. "First Maynard and now this. I'm like a fucking serial killer."

"You are not a serial killer, but we should probably get out of here." Veronica floored the gas pedal.

An ambulance screamed by with its lights flashing. Jenny turned to look and grabbed her bag from the back seat. "So, where to now?" Her voice was flat and lifeless.

"You didn't steal his phone, did you? The police can find us with that."

Jenny removed a 9mm revolver from her bag and stared at it. "No. Just this."

Veronica hated guns even more than she hated North Dakota. "We're going to Massachusetts. And please put that thing away. They make me nervous."

"They make me feel safe." Jenny returned the gun to the backpack but clutched it closely against her chest.

Veronica didn't know what to do. The nurse in her wanted to rush Jenny to the ER for a rape kit and some good old-fashioned retribution, but the man was already dead. What more could anybody do? If anything, Jenny would be questioned and possibly convicted of murder.

"I am so sorry that this happened to you, Jenny. It's my fault. I should never have brought you along on this stupid trip. You could have been safe and unharmed in California if it wasn't for me and my selfishness." Veronica's eyes welled with tears. "Can you ever forgive me?"

"It's not your fault."

"Do you want me to take you back home to Texas? I will. You just say the word and we'll go."

Jenny straightened in her chair and set the bag in front of her. "Let's just keep going where you're headed. You're getting pretty good at this apologizing shit."

27

MASSACHUSETTS - 1949

Veronica felt that her time was drawing to a close at Danvers. Even though the overcrowded, mentally unstable population was perfect for her needs, the old-timers on staff began to question the fact that her appearance never changed. While their hair greyed, and their faces became roadmaps of increasing age and disappointment, Veronica remained forever frozen in middle age. Despite that, they never questioned her about the many patients who swore that she visited them in the middle of the night to poke them with needles and suck their blood through metal catheters. That was, until the night Mary Katherine Malone, a fellow nurse, caught her in the act.

Mr. Jones had undergone a lobotomy earlier in the day and was heavily sedated. In the darkness of the room, Veronica palpated his inner thigh until she found the steady pulse of his femoral artery. Blindly, she inserted the needle, carefully straddling his lower body for the best angle. She was starving. As his O positive blood saturated the inside of her mouth and ran dreamily down her throat, she moaned with pleasure.

It was at this point that Mary Katherine Malone entered the room. Mary averted her eyes and gasped at the impropriety. Veronica turned and waved her away as a dribble of blood escaped her tightened lips.

"It's not what you think, Mary." Veronica pulled the needle and applied pressure to the puncture wound.

With a clipboard clutched tightly to her chest, Mary shuffled towards the bed, her eyebrows raised in disbelief. Veronica quickly placed a large bandage on the man's thigh and hopped off the bed.

"You've been drinking his blood, haven't you?" she whispered, as if the man might be listening. "I knew it. Is that how you stay so young?"

"Don't be silly. I wasn't drinking his blood. I was inspecting his leg for clots. He underwent a surgical procedure earlier today." Veronica wiped her mouth with the back of her hand, then smoothed her smock.

Mary wrinkled her upturned nose. She was in her early thirties, single and Catholic. Despite her parent's needling suggestions, she avoided marrying Jesus. On her knees every night before work, she prayed that one day she might have sexual relations with another human being. Those unclean thoughts were specifically directed at Dr. Dan, who also worked the graveyard shift at Danvers. She mostly avoided the other nurses. They were competition for Dan's affection.

She bravely took one step closer. "I saw what you were doing. Plain as day. And by the way, there's still a little smidge of it...just there." Mary moved in closer and inspected Veronica's face. "Do you need a hanky, dear? Blood on your face could raise suspicion."

Veronica didn't know whether to run, reveal the truth, or slug Mary in her pouty little kisser. "No, but thank you for the offer." With a heavy sigh, Veronica wiped at her face and walked towards the door with rounded shoulders.

"No need to worry, dear. I won't tell a soul." Mary flashed Veronica an impish grin and tucked the covers around the sleeping man. "Well, I might tell Father Patrick."

For weeks, Veronica tiptoed around Danvers, while Mary stayed tight on her heels. Each night, the fledgling detective attempted to catch the elusive vampire in the blood-letting act. If Mary had a purpose in mind, it didn't involve getting her coworker fired or hung in the town square. After a while, the chase became their own private joke. Mary would peek into a darkened room and blurt out, "Drinking the blood of psychotics will do nothing for your crow's feet, dear."

The first time it happened, it felt menacing, but with each successive occurrence, the teasing became frivolous and fun. It became friendship—something Veronica hadn't experienced in years.

When Mary was diagnosed with breast cancer at 34, Veronica dreaded having to watch her friend suffer. She knew how quickly a person's priorities changed when their last day was no longer an ephemeral future ending, but foreseeable. There would be no more days of cat and mouse or camaraderie. Instead, Veronica was forced to bear witness to the slow, sad death march, accompanied by a rehashing of all the things Mary failed to accomplish or do in her short life, including Dr. Dan.

The day before Mary's heavily dimpled right breast was scheduled to be removed, Veronica snuck into her hospital room in the middle of the night. "Wakey, wakey, Mary. I'm here for a collection." She tapped her lightly on the shoulder and inched slowly towards her face. "Hey, lady, can you spare a pint or two for a good Lutheran?"

Mary slowly opened her eyes and smiled. "What are you, Astrid?"

"I'm a Norwegian from the north." Veronica knelt beside her bed as if she were about to pray. "Why do you ask?"

"No. I mean, what are you? Are you some sort of female Dracula? I really think you owe me this information before I die." Mary rubbed her tired eyes and struggled to sit upright in the twin bed.

"You're not going to die, Mary. You're going to be fine." Veronica forced a smile. She could smell impending death.

"I should have just become a nun and maybe this wouldn't have happened." She peered inside her hospital gown. "You know what irony is, Astrid? I am going to die a virgin, just like a nun. No man will ever want to see, let alone touch what's left of my Franken-boobs."

"Sure they will. Men don't care what they look like. They just want to be able to touch them." Veronica rested her chin on her entwined hands. "Franken-boobs. I like that."

"I don't like it. My cleavage was my best feature and now one of them is going to be buried along with my hopes of ever having a husband. It's not fair."

"You know what your problem is, Mary? You go after completely unattainable men." Veronica leaned in closer. "I have news for you. Dr. Dan doesn't even like women."

"What are you talking about? He's been very kind, I might even call it flirtatious, towards me. He's not that way with all the nurses."

"Dr. Dan is forty-two years old and a confirmed bachelor for a reason."

"I see what you're doing. You're just trying to change the subject. I'm a dying woman and I deserve to know the truth, the whole truth and nothing but the truth, so help you god, Astrid." Mary scooted over and playfully patted the bed. "Come sit up here and keep me warm." She shivered, pulling the blanket up to her chin.

Veronica removed her shoes and sat gingerly next to her friend.

Mary laced her arm into Veronica's. "I hate to break it to you, Astrid, but you're about as cuddly as a corpse. Would you be a dear and hand me my Bible?"

Veronica lifted the worn black book from the nightstand and placed it on Mary's lap. "I am a corpse, but a friendly, helpful corpse. Who else would talk to you about your boobs at three o'clock in the morning?" She brushed a stray hair out of her eyes. "Do you think I look dead? I can't see myself in a mirror, you know."

"No, you look nothing at all like the dearly departed. In fact, you look very natural and alive. Very alive." Mary thumbed through the book in the darkness. "I know this sounds crazy, but I think I want to be dead too, but only your kind of dead. Not the permanent kind. I don't want Dan crying as my body is placed in a coffin or sealed away in a crypt." She leaned her head on Astrid's shoulder. "When you're dead like you, do you have to sleep in a coffin?"

"No, that would be overkill. Just a very dark room."

"Good." Mary lifted a tiny razor from the pages of Genesis and dug the blade vertically into her wrist. Warm blood gushed from the cut and pooled onto the bedsheet. "Help me," she gasped and lifted her arm towards Veronica's mouth.

The smell, feel and urgency of her friend's forced hand was too intoxicating. Veronica latched on to Mary's wrist like a hungry baby.

"Please don't let me die," Mary whispered and patted Veronica's head.

Veronica nodded frantically. The last thing she needed was spillage or a nosy nurse barging into the room and spoiling her dinner. As Mary's pulse dimmed, she had to decide which type of death to deliver.

28

PRESENT

After six hours of silence, Veronica lowered the volume of the annoying Top 40 station and placed her hand on Jenny's knee. "I'm pretty sure I already know the answer to this question, but would it make you feel any better to talk about what happened?"

Jenny remained motionless, her eyes fixed on something in the distance. "No, not really. Can we stop somewhere? I need a shower. I smell and my vagina's bleeding."

"Do you need some pads?"

"I don't know. Do I need pads for this?"

"What do you mean you don't know? Have you never had a period?" Veronica wanted to swallow the words as soon as she'd said them.

Jenny's voice remained low and robotic. "It's not my period."

"Oh." Veronica didn't want to deepen an already seeping wound by inquiring further. Either the bleeding was a result of the rape or it was due to the slight chance that Jenny was still a virgin, at least in the intact hymen sense.

"Why don't I find us a motel so you can clean up and get some rest." Her voice sounded as if she were in control, but inside, her nerves were as shot as the gun in Jenny's backpack. At the first sight of a cheap motel, she turned into the lot, hopped out of the car, and bolted through the door as sweat streamed down the back of her shirt.

"Can I help you?" The desk clerk eyed Veronica as if she were covered in fire ants. Her gaze moved towards the jingling door.

Veronica turned to find Jenny standing behind her. In the glaring fluorescent light, her face looked like an old bruised pear. Veronica turned back to the clerk. "Poor girl was in a car accident yesterday."

"You don't need to lie about what happened to me." Jenny sauntered up to the counter and rested her battered head in her cupped hands. "I got punched in the face by an asshole."

The clerk's eyes widened. Veronica nudged Jenny with her foot.

"He thought buying me a couple of drinks…"

Veronica coughed "shut up" into her upper arm and shot Jenny a look that could melt a glacier.

"So, anyway. Can we get a room? I need a shower like yesterday." Jenny smiled at the lady behind the counter, revealing a chipped front tooth, but the clerk's eyes were fixed on the computer screen.

As soon as the green entry light flashed, Jenny pushed through the door and sprinted towards the bathroom. The click of the lock resounded in the small room. Veronica collapsed onto the heavily patterned bedspread as catastrophic thoughts pierced her mind like bullets. Jenny. Rape. Jim Pearson. Ingrid. The cops. Frank. Blood. Hunger. *Money.*

At last count, Veronica had less than a thousand dollars and was driving half way across the country on a sliver of hope that Mary might still be hanging around Danvers. Despite these wishful thoughts, she knew from experience that the undead didn't stick around a place for too long. And Mary's messy foray into vampirism was riddled with mistakes.

As Veronica knew too well, it was easy to get away with killing a prostitute, an addict or a homeless person—but when you offed ten of them in a three-week period, the townsfolk became a little more cautious about where they walked at night and with whom. Veronica remembered cringing in horror as her former friend decided to carpe-diem all over the local population. After Dr. Dan made the fatal mistake of refusing her advances, Mary left a blood-spattered trail of carnally motivated consumption. Irritated and disgusted by her friend's obnoxious behavior, Veronica fled the comfort of Massachusetts for Michigan, leaving Mary to recreate the vampire wheel on her own. She never said goodbye.

"HELLO?" Jenny peeked her head out of the bathroom. "Do you think you could go get me something to wear? I can't put these things back on."

Alarmed by the vulnerability in Jenny's voice, Veronica rose from the bed and grabbed her purse. "Sure, there was a Target down the road a couple miles. What size?"

"I don't know. I'm like a four in jeans. Small t-shirt. Maybe a hoodie and some new underwear."

"Do you need anything else? Shampoo, cleanser, pads?"

"No. I'm good. There's some free shit in the bathroom." She closed the door and opened it back up. "On second thought. Would you get me some hair dye? I want to go red."

PICKING out clothes for Jenny was simple enough. But without a phone number, a last-sighting, or any idea of what alias she might be using these days, finding Mary Katherine was going to be all but impossible. As Veronica perused aisle six and the multitude of red-hued coloring options, she stuck her hand in the depths of her purse to retrieve her wallet. Although credit would be convenient, it was too risky. She thumbed through the crisp twenties. Nestled in the stacks of Jackson was the glossy crimson card from Ingrid. In black print was simply a name—Seamus Sansbury—and a phone number with a 539 area code. Without much contemplation or care, she grabbed a box of Vidal Sassoon "Runway Red" from the shelf, dropped it in her cart and dialed the number with paranoid precision. He answered on the first ring.

"This is Seamus. What can I possibly do for you today?" His voice rose and fell like a teenage boy in the throes of puberty.

"Um, hi. My daughter gave me your card a few weeks ago. She said you might be able to help me." Veronica pushed her cart towards checkout, feeling dumb and unsure of how to proceed with this irritating man. "My daughter's name is Ingrid."

"Is this Veronica?" His voice cracked at the *I* in her name.

"Yes." Suspicious, she looked at the phone, then placed it back to her ear.

"What took you so long? I was beginning to worry."

"I didn't need your help." Irritated by the familiarity in his tone, she parked the cart next to a DVD display and wiped her upper lip. "But now I do. So, how do we do this? And before you answer that, how did you know it was me?"

"I have my ways. Nice flip phone by the way. Ingrid said you were old, but I didn't expect geriatric."

Veronica scanned the store to see if anyone was watching her. "Mr. Sansbury, I don't have time for this. Can you help me find someone or not?"

"Of course, I can. Who exactly are you looking for?"

"Mary Katherine Malone. She's from Massachusetts."

"Hmmmm. Very interesting. Ms. Malone has been frantically searching for you as well. This type of synchronicity generally happens when one of our kind becomes hip to the way things really are." He sighed into the phone. "Anyway, long story short, Ms. Malone wants her soul back. Like today. But if you ask me, I think she really just wants to reconnect with an old friend."

Veronica resisted the urge to roll her eyes. "So, how do we do this?"

"I take cash or plasma. Whatever's easiest for you."

Veronica lowered her voice. "How in the world am I supposed to get blood to you?"

"You're not. I'm joking, Veronica. It's five-hundred. I prefer PayPal. I'll text you the particulars. You do know how to text, right?"

Veronica wanted to rip his throat out. "I'm a little cash poor right now. Is Mary paying you to find me?"

He laughed. "She is now. Stay where you are. Not at the Target, but at your motel. She's on her way."

"How is that possible?" Veronica stuttered.

The line went dead. A text appeared. "There are others looking for you too. Bye."

29

Veronica felt the weight of dread as she drove back to the motel. Mary would be pounding on their door any minute expecting an apology—and neither she nor Jenny were in any state for company. Some plans were much easier to work out in the realm of possibility rather than in the harsh ticking clock that was now her reality. There was nothing worse than having to make amends to a person when you weren't that sorry for the things you'd done. It was in these confounding moments that Veronica needed a meeting, but leaving Jenny alone for more than forty-five minutes was not in the plan.

With the squirrel cage spinning in her head, Veronica sat in the motel's parking lot searching for a quick fix. On the end page of *Courage to Change,* she found it. The words were scrawled decades ago in blue ballpoint. "HALT! Are you hungry? Are you angry? Are you lonely? Are you tired?" In the detritus of the dirty car, Veronica nodded. She was starving, she was livid, she was yearning for Frank, and even though she hadn't felt tired in ages, she still felt a weariness that was akin to exhaustion. The only thing she could control at this exact moment was her hunger... and that in itself produced a sick combination of shame and guilt in the pit of her empty stomach.

With awareness and acceptance crossed off her mental list, she opted for action. Quietly she crept into room 133 and bolted the lock behind her. Jenny, her only food source, was still cloistered in the locked bathroom. An erectile dysfunction commercial blared from the ancient TV. Veronica knocked gently and placed the new bag of clothes on the floor.

"I got you the hair dye, a couple of outfits and some pajamas."

"I'm almost done," Jenny shouted.

Veronica picked up the germ-riddled remote and scanned the local stations. The evening news was in full swing. A picture of Jenny's father riding a horse appeared on the screen. Veronica cringed and braced herself for breaking news about his missing daughter.

"Jimbo Pearson, the Governor of Texas, announced today that he is throwing his Stetson into the presidential ring. Pearson, known for his staunch support of the death penalty..." Veronica powered off the TV and collapsed onto the bed.

Jenny, clutching a skimpy towel around her equally scrawny orange body, grabbed the bag from the floor. "Did I just hear that my dad is running for president?"

"I think that's what the TV said, so it must be true. Are you hungry? There's a couple of restaurants that deliver. How about pizza?" Veronica was fully aware that she was forcing her will. The hopeful insistence in her tone was a dead giveaway.

"I'm not really hungry." Jenny stepped back into the bathroom.

"Well, I am. And you're beginning to look like a wilted carrot," Veronica muttered under her breath. The way things were going, she could either quickly sneak into a hospital and drain a patient or maybe just relieve Jenny of a pint while she slept. Neither option was ideal: Mary could arrive any minute, and god only knew what Jenny would do if she woke up in the middle of a second, more surreptitious assault.

Jenny reemerged in pink pajamas looking like a wet cat. "These are absolutely ridiculous. Why would you pick these?"

"You look good in pink. Besides, they were plum out of black pajamas covered in skulls and cat hair." Veronica sighed and reached for a menu from the nightstand. "Are you sure you don't want something? I know this is really bad timing on my part, but I'm starving and either I need to take a pint from you or I need to go find a willing victim to tide me over."

"My blood is the only reason you're keeping me around. Isn't it?" Jenny hopped up on the bed as if a monster might take a swipe at her ankles. She hugged a thin white pillow to her chest. "Are you good with a needle?"

"Are you kidding me? I'm like the Michael Jordan of phlebotomy." Veronica handed Jenny the menu. "And no, I'm not just keeping you around for your blood. I find you highly entertaining." She patted Jenny on the leg and sat up. "Let's get you something to eat. If we're going to do this, I don't want you to pass out on me."

"Are you kidding me? Passing out sounds awesome." She scanned one of the menus, her lips moving slightly as she read. "I think I'll get the meat lover's pizza with a Coke. Wait. Can I get a couple of beers?"

"Not only no"—the two lines between Veronica's brows deepened as her gray eyes narrowed into angry slits—"but, hell no. If you want to buy your own beer with your own hard-earned money, that's one thing, but I won't enable your behavior with my own dwindling resources."

Nervously, she returned her gaze to the safety of the extensive menu. "Whatever. I don't really want one anyway. I just wanted to see how quickly you'd cave to my whims."

Jenny jumped at the sound of three knocks.

"Simmer down, girl. It's just one of those people I have to suck up to. I can't believe she got here so fast." Veronica stood in front of the mirror and fluffed her hair. "She's a little on the odd side, but I have to talk with her and apologize and blah, blah, blah. Hopefully this won't take too long. Why don't you order the pizza?" Veronica took a deep breath and walked towards the door as if she were on her way to the gas chamber.

She hadn't even turned the knob before the breathy, perfumed whisper seeped around the deadbolt. "Can you spare a pint for a very naughty Catholic?"

Veronica unbolted the lock and braced herself.

"I can hear you breathing, Astrid. Are you going to open the door or am I…?"

Veronica attempted a look more welcoming than resting bitch face as she swung open the door. "Mary! Oh, my goodness. Look at you in that outfit."

Timid good-girl nurse Mary Katherine Malone now leaned into the door-frame, flaunting a tiny black skirt, fishnet stockings and five-inch fuck-me pumps. She pursed her oil-slick cherry lips. "I know, right. Pretty damn hot for one hundred." She moved in towards Veronica and kissed her on the cheek. "You look pretty good too, old lady." She glided into the tacky room as if it were her second home. Her drugstore perfume followed, overwhelming the small space as much as her outfit. She cast a glance toward Jenny. "And who have we here? Is this your daughter?"

"No. That's Jenny. It's a long story better saved for another time." Veronica wiped at the thick remnant of lipstick on her cheek and turned towards Jenny. "Are you going to order the pizza?"

"Yeah." Jenny stared at the painted lady who was a lot more interesting than the Pizza Shack's menu.

Mary stuck out her bejeweled hand. "Hello there, little lady. I'm Porsche."

"For real?" Jenny grinned as her eyes narrowed in disbelief.

"Of course not. Who in their right mind would name their kid after a sports car?" Mary plopped down on the bed and kicked off her shoes.

"So, is that like your stripper name?" Jenny moved closer to the edge of the bed, letting her feet dangle off the side.

"Close, but no cigar, sweetie. Stripping is too much work with all that dancing. Plus, who wants to touch all those nasty dollar bills?"

"So, you'd rather touch all those nasty—"

"How was your flight?" Veronica interjected.

"Fabulous. One of my favorite clients purchased the ticket for me. He's a pilot. And a masochist. All I had to do was yell at him, make him wear these shoes and *voila*, an upgrade to first class."

"Nice. You must be very pleased with yourself." Veronica sat down at the dilapidated desk and attempted to control her increasingly rapid breathing. "So, do you know this Seamus character?"

"I don't know him personally, but I've used his services a few times. He's a peach and very helpful in a pinch." Mary rummaged through her purse, removed a tube of gloss and applied a thick coat to her lips. "He helped me find you, which I'd never been able to do after you changed your name."

"Yeah, so, about that. Why exactly did you want to find me after all these years?"

"You don't know?" Mary uncrossed her legs, flashing a strip of neon green underwear.

"Let's just pretend I don't." Veronica reciprocated the smile and leaned back in the chair. She was done talking. Beneath her calm façade, pangs of jealousy seethed beneath the surface, agitated by every fresh glimpse of Mary Katherine's impossibly glamorous physique. She felt like they had both bought the same dress for the junior high dance, but only Mary looked good in it.

"I want my soul back." Mary said as if she were simply ordering a hamburger.

Veronica strove to keep her voice neutral. "Really? And you're ready to become mortal?"

"Who said anything about becoming mortal? I just want to be able to see myself. I don't know about you, but putting mascara on without the aid of a mirror is a nightmare. I'm not sure if I look like a clown, Alice Cooper or what."

Veronica leaned forward, her hands clutching the arms of the chair. Mary Katherine obviously needed no help putting on makeup. She was here for the apology. For the sheer pleasure of watching Veronica grovel, when they both knew that Mary was the sole architect of her own misery. "You can stop the cutesy act. I know why you're here. But just so you know, you brought this all on yourself."

Mary rubbed her feet and inspected her toenails, as if Veronica didn't even merit a sideways glance. "Oh, I did, did I? Just because I slit my wrist? You could have easily killed me. Sounds to me like you suffer from a big, fat god complex."

Jenny rose from the bed and tiptoed towards the bathroom with the box of hair dye.

It was all Veronica could do not to pick up one of those pumps and beat Mary with it. "So, it's all my fault you are the way you are? I distinctly remember you killing off a good portion of the population and having a pretty fantastic time while you were doing it. And now, for all appearances, you still seem to be having a grand old time with the way things are, so what's the big problem?"

Mary treated her to a pouty frown. "I already told you, Astrid. Mascara. That's the big problem."

"You've got to be kidding me. You want your soul back so that you can apply makeup? That's it? That's all you really care about?" Veronica rose along with the volume of her voice and slowly paced from the now closed bathroom to the front door. The fact that she needed Mary more than Mary needed her fed the seed of rage building in her core. "You used me, Mary. And because of your behavior, I was forced to leave Massachusetts."

"You were going to leave anyway. That's what you do—you leave. And if you think I'm going to apologize to you for what you did, you are delusional. That's not how it works. You're supposed to apologize to me." Mary examined her chipped nails, but her lips had begun to tremble.

"You know what? You're fucking ridiculous and I can't deal with this kind of idiocy right now." Veronica stomped towards the door and grabbed the handle. "Get out. I've got bigger problems than you right now."

"No! I'm not leaving until you say you're sorry." Her eyes were shimmering wet.

"Oh, for crying out loud. Don't start crying." Veronica let go of the handle and placed her hands defensively on her hips. "I'm sorry. There. I said it. Are you happy now?"

Mary bolted from the bed towards the mirror. "I still can't see myself. Shouldn't I feel something? I was told I would feel something." Mary pounded her tiny fist on the dresser and bowed her head as a solitary tear spattered onto the stained varnish.

Typical. Even in the midst of anger and sadness, she took care not to smudge anything. Even at her tacky, tawdry worst, Mary was more a beauty than Veronica ever could be.

Not that Mary would ever think of that. "I thought you were my friend." She turned towards Veronica. "Do you think maybe you could try saying it again?"

"I'm sorry." Veronica softened the way she spoke the words, but she knew without looking at the mirror that it would remain free of Mary's reflection.

"She doesn't mean it. That's why it's not working." Jenny shuffled out of the bathroom with wet hair. Red dye dripped down her face and splattered her pink pajama top. "And I wasn't a twelve-stepper for very long, but I do know that apologies have a way of setting you free. So maybe you two need to hug it out or something."

The two women eyed each other like boxers in the ring. Veronica didn't want to fight Mary—she just wanted her to leave so she could eat. "Are you in a hurry to get back to Vegas? Maybe you could check into the motel. Hell, you could probably make a few bucks while you're here."

Mary plopped back down on the bed with a sigh. "Why can't I just stay here with you? There's two beds. Maybe we could try and work this out? It's not like we're going to go to sleep."

No. Absolutely not. But out loud, all Veronica said was, "We don't need to sleep, but Jenny does. And I really need to eat before I kill the pizza delivery guy."

There was a light, almost tentative knock at the door. "There he is," Jenny chirped.

"How much is it?" Veronica grabbed her wallet.

"Nineteen and some change. Before you pay, make sure they brought the parmigiana and peppers. They always forget that shit."

Veronica pulled out a twenty and a five—but as she opened the door, it was impossible to notice that the pizza guy, a short, husky man in an over-starched western shirt, was not carrying a greasy cardboard box. He flashed a badge by way of apology.

"Did you forget the pizza?" Veronica eyed the man and his holstered gun.

"No, ma'am. Carl Grandy, private investigator. May I have a word with you?"

Veronica stepped outside and closed the door. "Yes, sir. What can I do for you?"

"I'm here to retrieve that young lady you've got in there, Jenny Ann Pearson. She was on her way to a, um, medical facility, and she failed to show up. Her family is very concerned."

"Isn't she an adult?" Veronica didn't know what else to say.

Carl stepped in closer and inhaled through his nose near Veronica's shoulders. "Are you all doing drugs in there? I'm not an officer of the law, but..."

Veronica had had plenty of close calls in her long nursing career. She smiled as old instinct kicked in. "Of course not. Listen, you'll be doing me a favor by taking her. She's all yours, Mr. Grandy. I'd be thrilled to see her safely returned to her father. I hear he's running for president." Veronica smiled and touched Carl lightly on his arm. He smelled delicious. "Why don't you come on in. We just ordered a bite to eat."

"Don't mind if I do." Carl removed his black cowboy hat and followed Veronica inside.

"Jenny?" Veronica called out. "There's someone here to see you."

The bathroom door swung open and Jenny shuffled out with a towel on her head. Mary followed, favoring Carl with a shit-eating grin.

"Jenny, this here is Carl. Carl is a private investigator who's been hired to bring you home."

"Actually, ma'am, I've been hired to transport Ms. Pearson to Serenity of the West. How are you doing, Miss Jenny? Your dad's been very worried about you."

Jenny smirked and nodded knowingly. "Hey, Carl."

"You two know each other?" Veronica's fangs attempted to push through her pursed lips. She flinched at the insistent pounding at the motel's door.

"There's the pizza," Mary said. "You want me to answer it? You look a little peaked." They were the first welcome words out of her mouth all evening.

Veronica handed her the cash and flashed a look of desperation. Mary stepped outside and closed the door quietly behind her.

"Yeah, me and Carl go way back. Don't we Carl?" Jenny pulled the towel from her head and blotted her bright red hair.

"Yes, we do, Miss Jenny." Carl sat on the edge of the bed, drumming his short, stubby fingers on the thigh of his starched jeans. "I see you've dyed your hair an unnatural color again. Your daddy don't like it much when you do that."

"You know what, Carl? I really don't care that he doesn't like it. And FYI, I'm not going with you for another round of rock climbing and hot yoga with a bunch of rich assholes. The only person who benefits from me being out of the presidential family photo is my father."

"Who wants pizza and a Coke?" Mary dropped the pizza box on the desk and dished up two slices on a paper plate. "Jenny, here you go, hon. Sir, can I interest you in anything?" Mary bent over to pick up a napkin that dropped onto the heavily patterned carpet.

Carl's gaze traveled the length of her curves. He licked his lips. "A slice and a cold beverage sounds heavenly, Miss."

"It's Porsche, but you can call me Mary." Like a dutiful waitress, she brought him his food with a smile.

"Well, thank you, Mary. I've had a long day of traveling and I can't tell you how grateful I am for the kindness." Carl gulped the beverage and placed the empty cup between his knees.

Mary skittered back to the table, grabbed the two-liter bottle and poured a refill, allowing him a quick peek down her low-cut sweater. "You're not married, Carl?"

"No, ma'am."

"A man like you? What's wrong with those women in Texas? Why, if you lived in Vegas, you'd be snatched up in a second." She winked.

Jenny rolled her eyes and shuffled over to the desk for another slice. "You're not going to have any?" Jenny nudged Veronica's shoulder.

"No, I'm lactose and gluten intolerant, but thanks for asking." Veronica intertwined her hands, unsure of what to do with them. Mary was up to something, and Veronica dimly hoped that it didn't involve seducing Carl right there on the bed. One never knew with Mary.

Carl ate half the slice in one greedy bite as grease dribbled down his chin.

"Napkin?" Mary settled close to Carl on the bed and dabbed at the grease. "Is it hot in here or is it just me?"

And that was how it went for the next twenty minutes—Mary cooing and fawning over Carl, Jenny and Veronica giving each other the side-eye. But when the pizza was gone, he wiped his mouth in gentlemanly fashion and nodded at Mary. "Thank you kindly, ma'am. But Miss Jenny, your daddy's gonna be real mad at me if I don't get you to that treatment center."

"I really don't care, Carl. It's none of my business what my dad thinks about you." Jenny wiped her mouth on her pajama sleeve and crumpled up the plate.

"He loves you and only wants what's..."

"Best for me, right?" Jenny stared at Carl, whose eyes were slowly closing. "What's a matter, cat got your tongue, Carl?"

Carl laid back on the bed and rubbed at his eyes. "I feel really sleepy all of a sudden. Would y'all mind if I just closed my..."

"Eyes?" Mary rumpled Carl's hair and kissed him on the cheek. "Would you like to duct tape him to the bed, or should I?"

For the second time in an hour, Mary had made herself invaluably useful. And for the second time in a day, Veronica found herself reciting the Serenity Prayer as she abetted yet another absurd felony.

30

After Carl was securely fastened to the double bed—fully clothed with two pillows beneath his head—the three women tiptoed through the motel room to gather their belongings. Mary thoughtfully grabbed Carl's keys from his front pocket and proceeded to remove all items from his car that might be of use to him once the maid found him in the morning. The roofies would knock him out for a good six, if not eight hours. They hoped he wouldn't remember a thing in the morning, and if he did, they'd be two states away.

With adrenaline pumping, Veronica jumped behind the wheel. Mary called shotgun and Jenny hurled herself into the backseat. In a cloud of dust and gravel, they peeled out of the lot.

"Where's your phone?" Veronica boomed at Jenny from the front seat. "You turned it on, didn't you?" She raised her right hand with splayed fingers. "Give it to me."

Jenny pulled the cracked phone from her backpack, along with the charger and tossed it into the front seat like it was on fire. "I was just checking my email. Geez. I didn't call or text anyone."

"Doesn't matter. That's how he found us." Veronica unrolled the driver's side window and tossed the phone into oncoming traffic.

"What the fuck, man!"

"Does your dad have any more private investigators on his payroll or was Carl-the-fucking-genius it?"

Veronica glared at Jenny from the rearview mirror. She was so accustomed to not seeing herself that once she caught a glimpse of her own reflection, she couldn't help but stare at her old face. Two thick lines etched between her furrowed brows. Disgusted, she jutted her chin towards the mirror and fingered the lone prickly hair. Even in the dimming light, the black stubble stood out against the whiteness of her skin. She pinched it between her fingers and forcibly yanked it free from her flesh. An identical hair sprouted within seconds. There was nothing she could do about it now other than forgetting it existed. A plucked hair or a shaved leg would return to its former state almost instantaneously. This regenerative power was great for bullet wounds; not so great for vanity. Reflection, at least in the physical sense, made matters worse.

Jenny deflated into her seat and pressed her face against the cool window. "I should have just gone with Carl. It would be way better than road-raging Count Chocula and her crazy prostitute side-kick. Seriously, what kind of woman carries roofies and duct tape in her purse?"

"I can turn this car around right now. Is that what you want? Just say the word, missy, and I will bring your ungrateful ass right back to that motel and you can go climb rocks with the hollyweirdos."

"Take a chill pill." Jenny leaned into the front seat. "Speaking of chill pills, Porsche, you got any Valium? I was just kidding about the duct tape. It's actually a very handy item to have around."

"How about a Xanax?" Mary lifted her knockoff Luis Vuitton purse onto her lap.

"Don't you dare." Veronica pushed the cheap bag back onto the floor. "She's a recovering addict."

"Yes, ma'am." Mary turned and half-smiled at Jenny. "Hugs not drugs, okay?"

Veronica couldn't take it anymore. She needed to connect with someone sane, someone who loved her unconditionally. She held out her hand to Mary. "Give me your phone."

Mary leaned away. "Not if you're going to throw it out the window."

"I'm not going to throw it out the window." Veronica pawed the space between them. "Give it to me. Is it a smart phone?"

"Well, duh."

"Hand it over! Hurry!" Veronica pounded the steering wheel.

Mary grabbed a pair of readers from the spilled contents of her purse and swiped the screen. "Jesus, calm down! You need to keep your eyes on the road. What do you need?"

"Serenity Seekers in Fort Worth, Texas." Veronica barked.

"Okay. Now what?"

"Call that number and leave a message. Tell them Frank R. needs to call Astrid. It's urgent. And don't forget to leave your number." Veronica placed both hands on the steering wheel and gripped till her knuckles whitened.

Mary's voice was as chipper and bright as a caffeinated telemarketer's. "Oh, hello. Is this Frank? Oh, okay. Would you be a dear and take an important message for him? Go right ahead." Mary turned towards Veronica and placed her hand over the phone. "It's Bob J. He needs to find a pen and some paper. Yes, I'm here, Bob. Please tell Frank to call Astrid at 702-555-1234. It's very important. Thank you. You, too."

"Now I need you to call that little Seamus shit and see if he ratted me out to Carl. He said someone else was looking for me, so you know what, he probably did." Veronica leaned forward and hugged the steering wheel.

"Carl isn't one of our kind, so I wouldn't worry about that. If you ask me, it was the phone that led him to the motel."

"You hear that, Jenny? It's all your fault," Veronica shouted. "I swear. People can't wipe their ass without an electronic companion in their germy little hands."

"Would you stop yelling?" Jenny snapped. "You sound just like my grandpa and nobody likes my grandpa. Why don't you pull over and get something to eat before I jump out of this car?"

"That sounds like a marvelous idea," Mary exclaimed. "Not the jumping out of the car part. What's the plan, ladies?"

Jenny rolled her eyes. "I'm the plan."

Mary directed her gaze towards the backseat. "Really?" She smiled, revealing her protruding fangs.

"Back off, Porsche. I'm a happy meal, not an all-you-can-eat buffet."

"She has a blood condition that requires donating a pint now and then. That's why she's so orange," Veronica said.

"I was beginning to question her spray tan choices, but who am I to judge?" Mary looked at Veronica. "Have you ever tried spray tanning? I got an Ooompa Loompa the first time I ever did it and let me tell you, orange skin doesn't flatter anyone."

"Gee thanks." Jenny sighed heavily. "Can we just get this over with, so my skin doesn't offend anyone?"

"Yes, I would be more than happy to get this over with." Veronica glanced at Mary. "I did try a spray-tan once. It didn't go well. For anyone."

Veronica sandwiched the car between two giant SUVs in a packed parking lot. With renewed pep, she grabbed the coffee mug from the console, opened her door and slid into the backseat.

"You're going to draw my blood out here?" Jenny's gaze darted around the lot and its pedestrian traffic.

"Nobody pays attention in parking lots. If we pulled over behind a building or on the side of the road, then we'd probably have every cop and looky-loo within a twenty-mile radius checking in on us. Poor gals can't change their own tire. But here, everyone is staring at their phone or thinking about what processed food they're going to stuff their carts with."

"I heard on the news that someone died in a grocery store parking lot and they weren't discovered for weeks!" Mary peeked around her seat and smiled. "I'm starving. Can I watch?"

"See? Nobody notices or cares here, except for her and her fucking mascara. Left or right?"

"Left." Jenny removed her new red hoody. "Or right. I really don't care. You're the expert." She held out both of her skinny bruised arms.

Mary's phone jingled. She pushed her glasses up the bridge of her nose and read a text. "Seamus said he doesn't know this Carl person.

He says that the person that is looking for you is Eddie Riordan—and he's paying a pretty penny to find you."

Veronica inserted the needle into Jenny's arm. "See, I told you I was good. I bet you didn't even feel that." Veronica patted Jenny's slender shoulder. "I'm sorry I yelled. I was a little freaked out about that whole thing back at the motel. I think we all were." Jenny's iron rich blood flowed from the tube into the dirty travel mug. Veronica instantly felt calmer knowing a meal was in her future. "Do you feel alright?"

"I'm okay, but can we stop at that Dairy Queen across the street when you're done? I want a Blizzard."

"Sure." Veronica leaned towards the front seat. "What did you say about Seamus?"

"Eddie Riordan is looking for you. That's what Seamus said, anyway."

"When did you talk to him?"

"I didn't. I texted him. That's his preferred method of communication."

"Like most people," Jenny added.

Eddie Riordan's name didn't ring a bell. Was it someone whose soul was stuck inside her? Was he somehow involved in the Jenny situation? Was he a cop from the Grapevine PD? "Who is this Eddie Riordan?"

"Apparently he's someone you turned. You don't remember doing that? Hmm." Mary studied her phone's screen to avoid Veronica's reaction.

"No." Veronica's memory was foggy, but she figured it had to have happened in the fifties when she couldn't find a job. He was either a drunk or an AA member. Maybe both.

In '52, Veronica had become a fixture at the downtown Detroit AA meeting, which wasn't exactly keen on letting a lone woman into the fellowship of their male-dominated group. At the time, a female member was considered a distraction that might potentially lead to hanky-panky. Unbeknownst to them, Veronica had no intention of sleeping with any of the reformed drunks. All she wanted was a meal. Like a lion surveying the Serengeti, she laid low in the back of the room, kept her mouth shut and zeroed in on the particularly wobbly, forgettable newcomers that she could follow home after the meeting.

"I have no idea who this Eddie Riordan is but ask Seamus to arrange a meeting with him." Veronica withdrew the needle and stuck a crumpled napkin on Jenny's arm.

"So you can make amends for something you don't remember doing? That should go well." Mary's voice sang with sarcasm. "Hell, if it didn't work with an old friend, how is it going to work with a stranger?"

"You are NOT my friend."

"Who wants ice cream?" Jenny pressed the napkin to her tiny wound and raised her arm above her head.

THE DAIRY QUEEN was cold and empty inside, but the drive thru was packed with a line of cars. Jenny sidled up to the red Formica counter and stared at the menu. Veronica and Mary slid into a booth near the freezers.

"Do you have any other clothes you could put on?" Veronica said in a low voice. Her gaze darted around the room to avoid looking at Mary.

Mary frowned. "Why?"

"People are staring."

"What people? I don't see any people." Mary looked around the empty restaurant. The lone counter person was leaning half way out the drive thru window.

"Well, if there were, they would be. Do you always dress like this? Or is this ensemble reserved for special occasions?"

Mary rested her head on her clasped hands. "Astrid, I'm a lady of the evening. This outfit is my billboard."

"Jesus." Veronica shrunk down into her seat and rubbed her forehead. "So, are you killing all of your customers?"

"You wish. Why would I do that?" Mary stretched, and her tiny shirt became a tube top.

"I don't know. To survive?"

Mary leaned forward exposing her ample breasts. "Do you want to know how I survive?"

"I imagine you're going to tell me whether I want you to or not. Go for it." Her voice dripped with resentment, fueled by the ever-increasing pressure that Mary wasn't going to leave until she could reflect.

"Well, you know that old saying, whatever happens in Vegas stays in Vegas? I apply that philosophy to those customers that are visiting for the weekend. After we've done our business, I fetch them a glass of water or whatever with a little something extra in it. While they're zonked out, I take a pint, sometimes two, and then I simply slip out of the room. No harm, no foul. I learned that from you at the hospital. They have no idea what hit them and if they do, it's not like they're going to call the police to rat out the prostitute that slipped them a roofie."

"And that's working for you?"

"They don't call it the oldest profession in the world for nothing. I don't know if you've realized it yet or not," Mary looked up at Veronica's dour expression. "I'm guessing not. But our bodies are amazing. Nasty case of the clap? Gone in six seconds. Listen, I'm very ethical. I don't steal from my Johns. I do exactly what they pay me to do."

"But you do steal their blood."

"And?" Mary rubbed her arms. "Blood regenerates. It's not like I'm removing one of their kidneys and selling it on the black market. What happened to you? You're such a sour puss."

"I've always been a sour puss." Veronica's lip beaded with sweat despite the chilly temperature.

Mary dropped her bangled arm on the table. "Bullshit. You used to be fun."

"This is so not bullshit." Jenny plopped down next to Veronica. "Bullshit is best served warm. Blizzards not so much." She turned the cup upside down. "Would you look at that? It's ice cream magic."

Veronica couldn't remember the last time she'd had fun. Monotony? Yes. Resentment? Yes. Fun? No. She brought the travel mug to her lips to swallow her feelings. "It's not very fun to live as a fifty-one-year-old menopausal woman. You're all about seeing yourself, Mary, but let me tell you—now that I can finally see myself, I just want to disappear. Fifty will never be the new forty. It's not even the old forty."

Mary reached across the table and grasped Veronica's arm. "Do you need a hug?"

Just a tiny bit of compassion from someone filled Veronica's grey blue eyes with tears. Unsure of what to say, Jenny handed her a wad of napkins and dug into her ice cream. Veronica buried her face in the mound of stiff paper.

Mary slid out of the booth, waved Jenny towards her with a playful wink, and scooched towards Veronica. "I'm sorry my lack of clothes hurt your feelings. I'm also sorry that you're having a tough time of it." Mary's voice teetered between playfulness and sincerity.

Veronica patted the tears from her naked face. Mary's face was still smudged from her bout of tears at the motel, but she didn't want to tell her.

"It's a good thing you don't wear mascara, even though you totally could if you wanted to. Come here." Mary pulled Veronica's stiff body into an awkward embrace.

"No offense, but I need out." Veronica pushed her way out of the booth, stood and fanned her shirt. "I'm so freaking hot. I can't take it." She scanned the restaurant, opened one of the doors to the freezer in the dining area and lifted her shirt.

"And I'm the embarrassing one? She's flashing the Dilly Bars." Mary rolled her eyes at Jenny, then looked down at her buzzing phone. "You have a date with Eddie at the Field Museum in Chicago tomorrow at 2 p.m. sharp. Meet him at Sue. What does he mean by Sue?"

"Sue? She's a T-Rex. How far is Chicago?" asked Jenny.

"Probably about six or seven hours. We're going to have police hot on our trail as soon as Carl wakes up." Veronica said.

As Mary's phone played the opening notes to *Sexual Healing*, she laughed nervously and looked at the incoming call's number. "It's an 817 number. I think it's for you."

31

In their room on the thirty-third floor, Veronica attempted to relay the craziness of the last few weeks to Frank in coded snippets. Despite the posh surroundings, her voice trembled, registering between a low whisper and a full-blown panic attack. Jenny and Mary were within earshot, but she didn't care if they heard or not. Frank's end of the line stayed mostly silent. Every few minutes, he would simply say, "I'm sorry, Astrid." Her real name uttered in his deep, resonant voice felt like a cozy blanket.

She could have listened to the sound of his voice all night, but the phone beeped steadily, causing Mary to scamper over like a treat-starved dog to peek at the screen. Vegas was texting. A lot.

Veronica tried to pay no mind to the intrusion. She was beyond grateful to reconnect with Frank.

"Any chance you'll be making it back to Texas any time soon, Astrid?" Frank's voice sounded hopeful.

"No. This ninth step work is going to take longer than I expected. Call me tomorrow when you're at the group." She hoped he'd get the hint and call her from someone else's phone.

He said he would. With the phone still pressed to her ear, she watched Jenny sneak several bottles of Ketel One and a Diet Coke from the mini-bar into the bathroom. She wanted to throw her shoe at the girl but opted instead to admit her own powerlessness over alcohol—well, Jenny's craving for it, anyway—and do nothing. She chuckled to herself. It was much easier to admit powerlessness over Jenny when Mary was footing the bill for the room.

———

LATER THAT NIGHT, Veronica studied Mary painting her toenails by the light of the desk lamp, while Jenny restlessly tossed and turned in a tangle of sheets.

"I love nail polish." Mary extended her leg and examined the paint job. "Pretty, huh?"

Veronica picked up the dark red bottle of polish and squinted to examine the name. "Fussy Hussy?"

"It's just a name. Want me to do yours?" Mary reached out for Veronica's hand and inspected her nails. "Nice nails, but geez, your hands are cold."

"I hate to break it to you, Mary, but I imagine that yours are too. Do your clients ever wonder why your body feels refrigerated?" Veronica let her hand linger inside Mary's.

"They don't ask too many questions." Mary shook the bottle and placed the hotel magazine under Veronica's hand. "Between nerves and desire, they usually have enough heat for the both of us." She unscrewed the top and brushed a line of crimson on Veronica's thumbnail.

"Have they ever tried to hurt you?" She knew the answer but needed to drum up some sort of compassion.

"Who hasn't?" Mary leaned back in her chair and studied the ceiling. "Actually, this one creep kept me chained to the hotel bed for three days while he experimented on my body with a utility knife. As soon as he'd slice something off, he'd attempt to take a picture with his phone, but as you know, it didn't take long for my amazing body to be good as new. He thought he was going crazy. Well, he was crazy, but you know what I mean."

"I don't know how you do it."

"It wasn't a totally bad experience. I learned about the sun."

"I just learned about the sun like two weeks ago." Veronica rolled her eyes.

"Didn't that piss you off? All that planning and hiding? I felt so cheated when he opened the curtain and I didn't burst into flames." Mary moved the brush to Veronica's other hand.

"So, what happened to the guy? What did you do?"

"Once he realized he couldn't kill me, I convinced him to loosen the restraints. I told him I was a vampire and that I promised to turn him into one, too. That sounded awfully exciting to him."

Veronica leaned forward, genuinely curious. "Did you turn him?"

"Hell no. I ripped his dick off and shoved it down his throat."

So much for compassion. "That's overkill, don't you think?"

"He tortured me for days! He deserved it and it's not like I could have him screaming at the top of his lungs. It was the classiest place in Vegas with the fountains and all that colorful glass on the ceiling. I had to shut him up."

"Weren't you afraid the police would find you?"

"Not really. I scrolled through that asshole's phone. I wasn't the first woman he dissected. I figured the police would let me slide since I did them a favor."

"You sure did." Veronica held out her hands. "Hey, this looks pretty good."

"Well, you want to look your best for your date with that Eddie guy tomorrow." She screwed the top back on the bottle and gave it another shake. "Now don't go touching anything or you'll mess them up."

"I don't even know if I should go. Hell, he could be a psycho killer."

"He can't kill you. But maybe he'll be able to help you." Mary smiled.

"I don't know. It didn't work with you, so what's the point? I just want to go home to Texas."

"What's stopping you?"

Veronica blew on her nails. "Well, let's see. I kidnapped the future president's daughter and, according to my husband, I'm wanted for questioning by the Fort Worth PD for two separate murders."

Jenny snored loudly and rolled over to her stomach.

"You're married?" Skepticism enveloped Mary's tone.

"Yep. I'm actually on husband number five because I believe in the sanctity of two paychecks and a roof over my head. Did you ever marry Dr. Dan?"

"No." Mary smiled wistfully. "I totally forgot about Dr. Dan. I think I killed him, but at one time, I was thoroughly convinced we were going to live happily ever after and have six ridiculously good-looking kids."

"You could still have that, you know."

"Dr. Dan is dead, and I have breast cancer, remember?" Mary lifted her shirt. Her right breast was still swollen, red and dimpled like the skin of an orange. "If I ever became mortal, I'd be dead in six months, tops."

"Oh, shit. I'm sorry. That's right." Veronica hit her forehead with her hand.

"Nails!"

"You were dying of cancer. Oh, god. I'm sorry. I thought eternal menopause was bad, but that must be horrible. Does it hurt? Oh, Mary. I'm such a shit." Veronica looked down at her nails. Three of them had smudged. Instant karma.

"Ow!" Mary doubled over and fell off the chair. "I think I'm dying right now." She clutched her stomach. "Shit. And I just ruined my fucking toes."

Veronica stood and stared down at Mary lying in a fetal position on the plush carpeting. "How many people have you turned?"

"Too many to count. Why?" She rolled over onto her back.

"I have good news for you." Veronica reached down and pulled Mary to her feet. "Your mascara nightmares are over."

Mary bolted from the floor and jumped from side to side like an amped-up go-go dancer upon seeing herself in the mirror. She eyed herself from several angles while sucking in her stomach, sticking out her chest and fiddling with her long auburn hair. She leaned in closer to her heavily made-up face and licked her lips. "I lied about the mascara thing. My vanity runs much deeper. What I really want is to do video."

"Video?"

"There's more money to be made and less physical contact with ugly men." Never breaking contact with her reflection, she made a duck face as if she'd been posing in front of a bathroom mirror with her cell phone for years and smiled. "I'm going to make a killing."

32

DETROIT 1954

E ddie Riordan was a bouncer at Detroit's Stonehouse when he was plucked by "Black Bill" Tocco to be one of his featured enforcers. Ready Eddie was a man of few words with a hulking body and a deep red scar accentuating his right cheekbone. If some chump didn't pay back a loan or make good on their bet, his job was to show up with a bat clutched in his giant hands. His intimidating presence was all it took, making the bat more of an accoutrement, like a man purse, rather than an actual weapon. The first time he swung it with the intention of breaking a bone, he was overwhelmed by feelings of guilt and shame. Throwing someone out of a bar or breaking up a fight was far different than breaking someone's kneecaps. To drown his uncomfortable thoughts, he began a relationship with illegally imported Crown Royal—a regular gift from his boss.

When bats were replaced by bullets, Eddie wanted out. He figured it didn't matter who was holding the gun, as long as their hands didn't shake. And Eddie's hands shook, especially when he woke up. After his wife left him, taking their two young children and the stash of cash he hid in the cellar, he'd hit his bottom. One of the bartenders at the local dive, tired of dragging his drunken ass off the dirty floor every other night, suggested he might try this thing called AA.

It was at his first meeting that Eddie and Veronica's paths crossed. He was drunk on cheap whiskey when he entered the door and was even more drunk by the time he stumbled out into the cold January night. Veronica, intimidated by his size, but desperate with hunger, followed him anyway. Two blocks down, he slipped on a patch of ice and clonked his enormous head on the chrome bumper of a '52 Bel Air. Shrouded by two vehicles and the darkened street, she seized the serendipity of the moment and dove mouth first into his thick neck.

"What the hell?" He slurred, attempting to focus his gaze. "Stop doing that, Linda. It hurts."

"I'm almost done," Veronica said cheerily, as if she were reassuring a child.

"I don't feel so good." He rolled over with Veronica still latched onto his neck. His stomach heaved, drenching her dark hair in bourbon and bile. Blood gushed from his gaping wound as he collapsed on top of her.

She thought she'd drained him, but his chest still pressed and recessed against her. With as much strength as she could muster, she attempted to push him off, but his heft was immoveable. Trapped, she inhaled the cold night air through her mouth to avoid smelling the stench of his stomach contents. As she exhaled, her hot breath shrouded their bodies in fog. Lying helpless with vomit-cicles forming in the tendrils of her curls, she imagined that if hell existed, this was probably it.

"God, please help me," he whispered into the icy pavement. "I'll never drink and I won't never kill nobody. I'll be a good daddy to Shirley and…"

Veronica raised her right wrist to her mouth and ripped it open. She'd only done this a few times, but if it would get him off her, it was worth the effort. She shoved her bloody wrist into his face. "Drink this. Trust me. You'll die on top of me if you don't."

Without further prodding, he drank.

33

PRESENT

I n a sea of children with eagle-eyed teachers watching their every sticky-handed move, Veronica spotted Eddie Riordan on a bench staring up at the Field Museum's skeletal thirty-one-dollar attraction. The vomit, the cold, and the feeling of utter helplessness came back in an instant. Her legs felt dipped in concrete. She inched in his direction, fretting over what to say to atone for her reckless actions that night. There had to be a secret combination of words that would get this over with as quickly as possible, if she could only find them in the muddy menopausal recesses of her brain. *I'm sorry? I'm sorry I took your soul? I'm sorry I ruined your life?* Unlike the others she'd turned, Veronica didn't stick around to tutor him on the pesky details of surviving as a vampire.

But by all appearances, he had survived, maybe even thrived thus far. He looked gainfully employed as a mechanic, dressed in steel-toed boots, black pants and a Dickies work shirt that clung to his heavily muscled body. Apart from his size, the only thing remarkable about his appearance was his thick brown hair slicked back in a pompadour. If he hadn't been clutching a smart phone in one of his giant grease-stained hands, he could have recently stepped out of the fifties. It would certainly be easier on Veronica if he had. Outside of meetings, almost everyone she encountered in the twenty-first century was cynical, entitled and in a giant hurry for the next stupid thing to click, press or swipe. Unlike the people swarming around him, he didn't look like he was in a rush to go anywhere.

Veronica nodded in his direction. Mary followed, navigating through the maze of bustling, sugar-buzzed children.

"Is that him on the bench? Dear, Lord, I hope so. Why didn't you tell me he was a hunk?" Mary whispered, as if she had to keep her voice low.

"I'm old and I can't remember shit. The only thing I remember about the man is that I turned him to avoid being trapped under his body." Veronica laughed at her old fear. The sun's rays held no power over her or anyone else in the same undead predicament.

"Who in their right mind would want that man off their body?" Mary stuck out her chest and smiled. "Do I look okay?"

"Yes. In my clothes, you look like a nice respectable woman. Now just try and act like one. I want to get this over with as quickly as inhumanly possible."

A crowd of children darted in front of their path. Parents and teachers directed their movements, clicking endless pictures with phones in front of their faces. Mary stopped and clutched Veronica's arm to avoid an awkward photobomb.

Jenny tapped Mary's shoulder. "Will you take a picture of me in front of Sue?"

Mary reflexively pulled out her phone, eyeing Jenny through its lens. "Okay, move a little to the left and smile."

Veronica used this opportunity to meet Eddie Riordan without an entourage. *Here goes nothing.*

Eddie rose from his seat and smiled at her, revealing that his front right tooth was missing. Extending his arm, he shook Veronica's hand with a mixture of vigor and reverence, placing his other hand on top of hers.

"It's a pleasure to finally meet you after all these years," he said. His dark brown eyes welled with tears.

Veronica didn't know how to respond.

Fortunately, she didn't have to. Above the rapid pounding of her own heart, Jenny's unmistakable voice boomed a string of obscenities that echoed in the museum's grand entrance. Veronica whipped around in an instant. Carl, duct tape still stuck to yesterday's shirt, dragged Jenny by the arm towards the exit.

"Oh, shit." Veronica took off at a sprint.

"What's going on? Is she with you?" Eddie called out. He weaved through the crowd as frantic teachers pulled their students towards the periphery of the room.

"Get away from me, motherfucker! Help! Rape! Fire! I don't know this redneck douchebag!" Jenny kicked and screamed at Carl like an angry toddler.

Children, even a few teachers, pulled out their phones and started recording.

Veronica grabbed Jenny's free arm and tried to pull her from Carl's clutches. "Let go of her!" she growled.

Carl kept Jenny's right arm firmly in his grasp. "After what you pulled yesterday, you and your little slutty friend, I'm about one step away from calling the police." Carl squeezed one of the bruises on Jenny's arm. "Is that what you want? You want to embarrass your father even more than you already have?"

"Do it," Jenny spat. "I dare you."

"Is there a problem here?" Eddie edged between Jenny and Carl, dwarfing them both in the process.

"Yes, this asshole won't let go of me." Jenny yanked her arm from Veronica's.

Surrounded, Carl released Jenny's arm with grudging respect. "Her dad hired me to escort her to a rehab facility, sir."

"That's all well and good, dipshit, but I'm an adult," Jenny snarled. "You can't make me go anywhere, so fuck off." She sidled up to Eddie. "And by the way, Carl, this is my new boyfriend. We're moving to Nebraska to raise chickens. Aren't we, honey?"

"That's the plan, sugar-buns." Eddie pulled her tiny body close with his meaty arm. "Is this guy bothering you, baby-cakes?"

"What's going on here?" Armed with radios and stern expressions, two young security guards approached Carl, sandwiching him in chambray and khaki.

"It was just a little misunderstanding between me and this young lady. It's over now, and we're very sorry." Carl wiped the sweat from his brow.

One of the guards spoke into his radio as the other guard moved in closer. Carl narrowed his eyes at Jenny, shaking his head. "Does he know who your daddy is?"

"Yeah, he knows. He also knows where you live, so you best be skedaddling, Carl Junior."

"I think we should all be leaving. Once again I seem to be causing other people problems." Veronica looked up at Eddie, who was dutifully playing along, and mouthed *I'm sorry*. They'd been reacquainted for all of a minute and a half and already the poor guy was hip-deep in Veroni-drama. "Maybe we could all walk Carl to his car. Would that be okay?"

"That might be a good idea." Eddie released his arm from Jenny's shoulder and clutched his stomach. With a slight grimace, as if he had a bit of indigestion, he stepped behind Carl. "After you, sir."

Veronica felt a slight stirring in her own core, but it barely registered. *It couldn't be that easy.*

VERONICA HELD her breath until they were clear of the museum. Miraculously, everyone remained calm as they shuffled down the sidewalk. The air was cool, whispering a steady promise of winter. Veronica planted her arms firmly across her chest and attempted a directionless smile to keep herself from uttering words that would only stir the placid pot. Three paces in front of the group, Carl tugged at his shirt, removing the last remnant of tape. He crumpled the sticky wad and tossed it into the gutter.

"Hey, man. Pick that up," Eddie demanded, pointing at the grey ball. "The world is not your trash can. Have some respect."

A number six bus lurched beside the curb, exhaling a dark plume of exhaust. Passengers with downcast eyes spilled from the rear door. Veronica caught a glimpse of herself in the darkened window. Beside her, still pointing into the street was Eddie's reflection. No one else had witnessed this tiny miracle as all eyes were focused on Carl, who was rapidly turning a darker shade of red. Outwitted and outnumbered, Carl dashed into the street behind the bus and retrieved the orb of tape.

"Now deposit that in a proper trash receptacle." Eddie said.

Carl surveyed the street for a trashcan and shoved the ball into his front pocket. "Yes, sir."

"Where's your car?" Eddie's voice lowered.

"Same lot as them, down the block."

"Well, isn't that convenient?" Mary applied a fresh coat of lip gloss. "I'm curious. How were you able to find us at this museum? Was it Seamus?"

Carl plunged his hands into the front pockets of his Wranglers. "I don't know anyone by the name of Seamus."

"Did Seamus tell you how to find these ladies?" Eddie moved in closer.

"As I said, I don't know anyone by the name of Seamus and if I did, I'd surely remember a name like that. I used a GPS tracker, which is pretty much private investigation 101." Lowering his head in defeat, Carl trudged towards the garage.

Veronica looked at Mary. "Let me handle this." She caught up with Carl, while the others lagged behind. "We can't have you following us, Carl. I know you have a job to do, but Jenny has no intention of going to rehab. Trust me on this." She tried to sound confident, but even she couldn't predict Jenny's erratic behavior. "But I assure you, she's in good hands." Veronica smiled hopefully.

Carl stopped and turned to face her. "You drugged me, stole my gun and detained me against my will. Not only that, the car y'all are driving is registered to a man in San Francisco who appears to have gone missing, at least that's what his landlord said." Carl squinted in the sunlight. "I'm not feeling real good about Jenny being in your particular hands."

"I understand how you could feel that way." She dug in her purse for the keys. "And I apologize for what we did to you, but she's not going. Either you let her go or you'll be dragged into something you don't need to be a part of, Carl."

"Are you threatening me?"

The wind picked up, blowing long strands of Veronica's hair into her face. "Of course not. I'm just trying to talk some sense into you. Trust me, life is a lot easier when you drop the rope and let people like Jenny live their own lives." She gathered the long, unruly strands as if to secure them into a ponytail and forced a smile.

"I need to talk to her before I head back to Texas."

The word "Texas" in Carl's twang elicited the feeling of a homesick sucker punch. Irritated by the situation and her distance from home, she stabbed the air above her shoulder with a raised thumb. "She's right back there."

"Yeah, next to the Hulk. She ain't going to talk to me unless you tell her to. So, I would appreciate it if you got her over here. I'll be quick."

Veronica eyed him up and down. Despite his actions at the museum, he looked like a disheveled, broken man whose dog had just died. She couldn't sense imminent danger in his demeanor; just the agony of defeat. "Jenny," she called out. "Come here for a minute."

Jenny zipped up her hoody and shuffled forward. Mary and Eddie followed. "Alone," Veronica said.

"What?" Jenny said.

"He needs to talk to you and he'll be on his way. I'll be right over here." She walked backwards to lean against a street sign. She wanted to give Carl the impression that she was a badass.

The exchange between Jenny and Carl was quick. He handed her something small that Veronica couldn't see. Jenny shoved the item into her front jean's pocket, crossed her arms and nodded. He patted her on the shoulder and walked into the garage. Watching their interaction gave her an uneasy feeling in her considerably less crowded core. She had a feeling this wasn't the last time she'd see Carl if Jenny remained in her company.

34

M ary and Eddie were entangled in a deep eye-to-eye conversation when Jenny and Veronica rejoined them.

"He's hungry," Mary exclaimed, as if he were deathly ill.

"Well, don't look at me." Jenny crossed her arms and rolled her raccoon-tired eyes. "I'm hungry too, not that any of you bloodsuckers give a shit."

"Of course we give a shit. What are you hungry for?" Veronica tousled Jenny's red hair.

"Pizza. We should try and find a Chicago-style place. I mean, that's what they're known for here, right?"

They all stared blankly back at Jenny as if she'd suggested they venture to Toys R Us to pick out a car seat for a newborn baby. None of them had ever ingested a pizza, let alone understood the complexities of a deep-dish pie.

"Sounds good to me." Eddie's stomach grumbled audibly as he swiped at his phone. "Looks like there's a place right down the block. It says they've got pizza, salads and there's a ton of Yelp reviews. Looks good."

A FEW STRAGGLERS from the lunch crowd remained in the Italian restaurant. A chipper hostess led them to a corner table, covered in a vinyl red and white checked tablecloth. The second Eddie pulled out a chair, Mary clamored for the seat beside him. Veronica felt grateful that in her abnormally long life, she had experienced reciprocal love. She wasn't entirely sure that Mary had.

Jenny opened the menu and studied its contents. "Am I the only one ordering? If so, I'm just going to get a small."

"I'll share something with you." Eddie looked to Mary and Veronica with raised brows. "Do either of you have any experience with this? I'm not going to throw up, am I?"

"I can't believe you never turned anyone." Mary leaned in closer. For a dead person, she was radiating heat. "I love a man who is in control."

From the looks of their body language, Veronica figured Mary and Eddie were headed to a no-tell motel in the very near future. "I felt your soul leave my body. I'm pretty sure you felt it too. You're going to be okay. I was with my daughter when she became mortal and she wolfed down a giant burger half an hour later."

"So, what's it going to be, big guy? Cheese, meat, veggie, both?" Jenny asked.

"I really don't know." Eddie raised his open hands and shrugged his shoulders.

"What's the last thing you remember eating?" Mary asked.

Eddie looked down, as if he couldn't bear to meet her gaze. "Bourbon. And whatever was at the bar that night. Probably olives or a pickled egg. I wasn't too concerned with eating at that point."

"We should probably go with a vegetarian. It's healthier." Jenny closed her menu.

"But he needs protein. Look at him." Mary touched his bicep, biting her lip.

Eddie flashed a smile. "Whatever you're having is fine, little lady, but you better order an extra-large. I'm starving."

The waitress appeared with four water glasses, setting them down on the table with a thump. "Are you ready to order, or do you need a few minutes?"

"We'll have the veggie. Extra-large, please." Veronica felt a glimmer of normalcy ordering their food, as if she were the matriarch of the misfits.

"Sure thing." The waitress gathered the menus. "Anything to drink?"

"I'll take a Virgin Bloody Mary, and hold the garlic on that pizza," Jenny said, looking to Veronica for a reaction. "We don't want bad breath. Right?"

The table remained silent.

"I'll be right back with your drink." The waitress sashayed towards a neighboring table.

"Isn't garlic a thing? Or is that just another big lie to keep you kids in check?" Jenny stuck her hand in her front pocket, and then stuffed something in her backpack.

"It's a total myth. The only thing it repels is kissing." Mary placed her manicured hand on Eddie's forearm. "Speaking of kissing, you got any big plans?"

"Big plans? Not really. I'll keep doing what I've always done, with a few adjustments, of course." He brought the glass of water to his nose, swirled it gently and sniffed, as if tasting a forty-dollar glass of wine.

"You should probably just get it over with. I'm pretty sure it's easier that way," Jenny said.

"Have you done this before?" He took a sip and leaned back in his chair.

"Hell no. I'm human." She tucked her hair behind her ear. "I mean, last time I checked I was."

"Hmmmm." He lifted and inspected the glass. "This is pretty refreshing."

"It's water, dude. If you really want refreshment, you should order an ice-cold beer." Jenny pushed the beer placard towards him. "Bud on tap, can't get any more refreshing than that."

"I gave it up years ago, and it took that lady right there to help me do it." Eddie beamed at Veronica as if she were a saint. "She saved my life."

With incredulous faces, Mary and Jenny turned towards Veronica.

Mary winked at Eddie. "She saved your life? That's cute. Is that really what you think?"

"Yes, ma'am." He pulled his arm from under hers and massaged his massive hands together as if prepping for prayer.

"Please. Call me Mary."

"I thought you went by Porsche," Jenny quipped.

Mary shot her a warning glare. "Don't be ridiculous. I was just joking about that name."

Jenny sank into her chair and scanned the restaurant.

"I didn't save your life, Eddie. I took it." Veronica was thankful for Eddie's expression of gratitude, even if it was misplaced.

Eddie turned and looked her square in the eye. "Whatever you want to think about that night is your deal—but if it hadn't been for you showing up and doing whatever you did, I'd have never quit drinking. After that, I convinced my wife to give me another chance. I got my kids back. I even started my own business. For the first time in my life, I could walk down the street with my head held high."

Veronica leaned towards him and whispered. "But, didn't you have to..."

"Kill people?" Eddie smiled and smoothed back his hair. "I was already in that line of work. After my encounter with you, I just felt the need to clean up the mess before I left the room, if you know what I mean. That's what gave me the idea for my business, The Clean Team."

"So, were you some big tough guy for the mob or something?" Mary rested her head on her clasped hands like a school girl.

"Yeah, something like that. I'm not real proud of my affiliation, but yeah. I'm out now. Obviously."

"Let me get this straight. You're a vampire and you clean up murder scenes?" Jenny laughed. "This shit just keeps getting weirder."

Eddie shrugged. "It's not weird. Bio-hazard cleaning is practical. Detroit was the murder capital of the world for a good stretch, and you'd be surprised by how many people kill themselves at home. Someone needs to clean it up. Might as well be me."

"I could never do that," Mary sniffed.

The waitress approached, depositing a thick, deep-dish pie in the middle of the table. "If you need anything else, including breath mints, just let me know. Enjoy!"

"What do you mean?" Eddie dished out a slice and handed it to Jenny.

"Old smelly blood. I don't know. For me, it has to be fresh, like with the person's heart still beating. I used to, um, you know, but I've learned how to get my food without decimating the local population."

Eddie chuckled. "After I encountered Veronica, I had no idea what was going on. All I knew was that after I killed someone, I wanted to drink their blood."

"Dude, we're about to eat. This is so not a dinner conversation." Jenny scrunched up her face. "It's disgusting."

"I know, right?" He laughed and leaned back in his chair. "The people I worked for caught me lapping up some poor guy's blood after I'd shot him. They started calling me 'The Licker.' I had quite the reputation after that. Can you imagine? Not only would I kill you, but I'd lick up your blood afterwards."

"Ooh, The Licker. I like it," Mary cooed.

"Get a fucking room," Jenny said, and inhaled a slice.

Eddie picked up his fork, speared a dainty morsel of pizza, and carefully brought it to his lips. "Here goes nothing."

"So, after I turned you, did you go out during the day?" Veronica leaned forward, resting her elbows on the table.

"Yeah, of course. I didn't know it was a thing." He brought a forkful of cheese to his lips. "By the look on your face, I'm guessing for you it was a thing." Eddie smiled and shoveled a mound of deep dish into his mouth.

"Oh, it was definitely a thing. I orchestrated my entire life around avoiding the sun." Veronica felt that old familiar desire to punch Desmond in the face.

"That must have been a pain in the ass to live like that. Honestly, I had no idea what had happened or what I'd become, so I kind of figured out what I could and couldn't do by trial and error." He wiped his lips. "Damn, this pizza is so good!"

"I'm sorry about that. I was such a horrible person to just leave you there and not explain anything."

"How could you? I wouldn't have remembered. I was drunk off my ass and laying in the gutter. That next morning, I woke with a wicked hangover and a thirst for blood, but honestly, it wasn't that much of a change for me. It wasn't until Linda…"

"Who's Linda?" Mary frowned.

"Linda was my wife. She was diagnosed with Parkinson's in the 70s and I took care of her until her passing in…" He looked up at the ceiling, tonguing the space where his front tooth should have been. "83, I think it was. That's when I tried to end my life."

"Oh." Veronica cringed. "Shit."

Jenny belched. "You guys are so emo. It's giving me Hot Topic flashbacks."

Veronica rolled her eyes. "I don't even know what that means." Her gaze drifted back to Eddie. "How did you do it?"

"The first time I used a thirty-aught-six under the chin, but as you know, it didn't take long to put my pieces back together."

"Is this a thing? I've never tried to end my life. I love my life!" Mary exclaimed.

"Have you ever loved someone, Mary?" Eddie's voice cracked.

Mary shifted in her chair. "You mean the kind of love when somebody loves you back in the same way that you love them?" Her eyes welled with tears.

"Yeah. Like that." He swallowed hard and met her eyes with his own.

"No, but I keep hoping I'll find them."

"So, you said 'the first time.' You mean you tried again?" Jenny interrupted.

"Yeah." He cleared his throat. "The next time, I jumped from the roof of a ten-story building. I figured, I had to go really big to go home. That one hurt."

"And?" Jenny tapped the table with her fingers.

"And then, one night, I parked my car in the garage and kept the engine running. I played "The Sound of Silence" over and over again. I kept dying and coming back, but I liked the song so much, I didn't mind."

"That's weird."

"I had no one to ask for help. I thought I was some rare, one-of-a-kind creature. And then this guy Seamus showed up."

"That night? In your garage?" Veronica yelped.

"No. About a week later."

35

NEW ORLEANS 1974

S eamus Sansbury was a recruit for the Central Intelligence Agency
when he was attacked by a stranger in New Orleans. Peeling
himself up from the vile Sunday morning pavement, his head
pounded from dehydration, the heat of the morning sun and the
stifling humidity. As he staggered down Bourbon Street trying to recall
his hotel's location, drunk tourists parted like the Red Sea upon his
approach. Looking down to assess the damage, he found that his polyester suit was soaked with blood. He immediately checked his coat
pocket—his watch and wallet remained untouched—their presence
miraculously reassuring, considering he'd been passed out for hours
on a high traffic street corner. As much as he tried, he couldn't
remember any specifics of the attack. All he knew was that he was
alive. At least he thought he was.

When he couldn't see his own reflection in the hotel's bathroom
mirror, troubling thoughts bubbled to the surface. According to the
maid who interrupted his nervous breakdown, his bloodied throat was
neither cut nor bruised. With a horrified expression, she backed out of
his room clutching a handful of bloodied towels. Closing and bolting
the door with a thud behind her, he palpated every inch of his neck in
disbelief. There had to be a logical explanation. He vaguely remem-

bered a knife, the initial pain of sliced flesh and a gush of blood that rushed down the front of his shirt—but what transpired afterwards remained a blur. There was the distinct possibility that the blood was not his own. He had been drinking. A lot.

EVEN THOUGH HE wore his increasing uncertainty and shame like a cheaply made suit, back at work, his coworkers treated him as they always had—by largely ignoring him. When they did manage to acknowledge his presence with a passing glance or a nod in the hall, he fretted over the possibility that he looked different. It would only be a matter of time before they would take note of that imagined scar on his neck, his consistently crooked tie, or his messy hair. When they failed to notice, he figured it had to be his staggering IQ and faultless work ethic that kept them blinded to what he had surely become, even though he wasn't quite sure what that looked like.

Each morning as he walked past the carved Biblical quote on the lobby wall—*And ye shall know the truth, and the truth shall make you free* —it fueled his internal fire for fact. But as the seemingly endless days drew into worrisome weeks without any concrete answers, his caution and control began to wane. Whenever a secretary or librarian would pass by his tiny office, he could tell by the tiniest whiff of stirred air whether they were menstruating. Even cloaked in the sickeningly sweet smell of Charlie perfume, they were never able to mask the aroma of their wasted blood. He obsessed about the one thing he wanted, the thing he could no longer live without. It was everywhere, pulsing warm and steady below a thin layer of skin, yet it was nowhere readily accessible.

On the third floor, a cleaning lady discovered him sucking the hours-old contents of a sanitary pad in an unlocked bathroom stall. The following day, he was called in for a private lunchtime meeting with William Colby, the director of the CIA. He debated about just leaving and disappearing somewhere, but he worried they'd locate his whereabouts and ship him off to some private hell that only they could concoct. As God, and Juanita, were his witnesses, he had hit bottom in the ladies' room and there was nowhere to go but up.

The minute he sat down, Mr. Colby pushed a metal thermos towards him. Seamus didn't know the protocol or at least the etiquette for this kind of indoor picnic scenario.

"That's for you, Mr. Sansbury. It should still be warm."

"That's very thoughtful of you, Mr. Colby, but I've already eaten." Self-consciously, he folded his hands on his lap.

"Yes. I heard about your incident in the restroom." He pointed at the thermos. "Go ahead and open it." He smiled. "I'm surprised that your senses haven't awakened by now. They still seem rather dull."

Seamus looked around the sparsely decorated room, feeling as if someone were watching and recording his every movement. "I'm not quite sure what you're talking about, sir."

"Open it."

With trembling hands, Seamus unscrewed the lid from the thermos. When the intoxicating aroma reached his nose, his teeth shot from his gums, stabbing the back of his slightly opened lips.

"They tell me it's O positive, which apparently is the preferred type. Not that I'd know the difference." Colby leaned forward with a wicked grin on his heavily lined face. "Well look at that. You got your teeth, young man."

Seamus worried over his pointy canines with the tip of his salivating tongue. "What ith thith?" He wiped the drool with the back of his hand.

"It's your lunch, Mr. Sansbury." Colby leaned back in his chair, stretching his arms behind his head. "I was wondering how long it would take before you broke. You've got some willpower, young man, and I appreciate that you're ethical. I value that above all else, but I can't have you sneaking around sucking on used tampons. It makes us all look bad."

"You knew about this?" The smell of fresh blood was making him giddy, despite the admonishment from his superior.

"Mr. Sansbury, I'm the director of the CIA. Of course I knew. But the question I really want answered is, do you know?"

"Do I know what?"

He clasped his hands on the desk and pointed at the thermos once again. "What you are or what that is."

Seamus brought the thermos to his lips, sipping tentatively at first, as if his ingestion of this liquid gold were a test of his self-control. A feeling of euphoria washed over his senses and he greedily gulped the remainder of the warm, red fluid.

"I have no idea what I am, Mr. Colby, but I do know that I want more of this."

"Don't you worry, Seamus." He reached across his mahogany desk to retrieve the thermos. "May I call you Seamus?"

"Yes, sir. You can call me whatever you want, just don't call me late for dinner." Seamus guffawed, exposing flecks of coagulated blood clinging to his poorly brushed teeth.

"There's plenty more where that came from. You'll be well supplied if you keep your nose clean. No more tampons, Seamus. Are we clear?"

Seamus closed his mouth and nodded as sincerely as he could.

Colby opened a folder, removed a sheet of paper and pushed it across the desk. "Due to your fortuitous incident in Louisiana you are now the head of a very elite unit of the CIA. We've been following people like yourself since 1947 and we're very close to deciphering a document found in…"

"Let me guess. Transylvania?" Seamus chuckled, licking the remnants from his teeth.

"Albania. Sign that, Mr. Sansbury. I've got a twelve-thirty." Colby flicked his Montblanc pen across the desk.

Seamus quickly scanned the document. "This just looks like a standard non-disclosure agreement. Didn't I already sign one of these?"

"Yes, but now you're different. You've changed a bit. Go on. We haven't got all day." Colby pushed his glasses up the bridge of his nose.

"Different, huh?" Seamus smiled and carefully positioned the pen beside his typed name on the document.

"Very different. Your job from now on will be to locate the North American undead."

"Am I dead? How is that possible?" Seamus slowly studied the movement of his hand as muscle memory kicked in. The pen seemed to remember every flourish and flare as red ink soaked the thin paper.

"That, I'm afraid is top secret information."

"And how am I going to find these undead if what I am is a secret?"

"That is the conundrum, Mr. Sansbury. People like yourselves tend to be lone wolf types, prone to isolating due to fear and ignorance of what they are and what their bodies are capable of. Remember Brad Jameson, that kid back in sixty-six? It was all over the papers."

Seamus nodded enthusiastically. "Who doesn't remember that freak?"

"Undead. Just like you. Confessed to his priest that he'd killed his neighbor and her dog and then drank their blood. Four weeks at the county lock up and he died from dehydration. They force fed him, and you'll discover if you haven't already, that food will make you vomit. Those kinds of incidents drive the undead back into their hidey holes. And we need you to bring them out."

"Why me?" Seamus feared incarceration more than anything, especially now.

"Who better to find others like yourself than someone who is living the same secret? I say go to where the blood is, young man. Make us proud." Colby smiled, lifted the paper and slipped it back into the manila folder.

Seamus had a million and one questions trilling around his brain, but none that seemed as compelling or important as where his next warm meal would come from.

36

PRESENT

"I don't know what else to do." Veronica drummed the table with her chipping nails. She knew that the likelihood of finding her fourth husband—a John Smith needle in the haystack of white-bread Nebraska—would be next to impossible without Seamus's help.

"You're already on his radar, you might as well call him." Eddie wiped his mouth with a napkin and stacked his empty plate on top of Jenny's. "But just be aware: now that he knows what you know, you've moved up a level."

"What do you mean?"

"You're more of a threat." Eddie stretched his arms out and exhaled. "Most people, when they become like us, have no idea what they're doing, what they're capable of, or even what they are. They just figure out how to exist. I did."

Mary sat up straight; a look of concern wrinkled her unlined face. "Well, what are we? I mean, I've always kind of imagined that I was some kind of vampire or something. You know. The blood and all that, but maybe I'm way off the mark here." Mary's worried gaze darted between Eddie and Veronica. "Didn't you immediately think you were a vampire? Okay. Maybe I'm crazy. What are we?"

"I don't know. We're either nothing, candidates for the special forces, or terrorists—depending on who's looking at the data." Eddie rubbed his stomach.

"I'm nothing?" Mary wilted in her chair.

"What I mean is, when you don't know anything and you're hiding in a darkened room during the day because you've been told by a book, a Hollywood movie or an uninformed person that that's what you're supposed to do, you pose no threat to national security. There's thousands of people just like us sprinkled throughout the world. We're existing and thriving among the living and they don't have a clue."

"I bet my ninth-grade algebra teacher was a vampire. He was totally pissed off all the time and I never saw him eat." Jenny said.

"How do you know all this?" Veronica looked around the now-empty restaurant. The waitress had given up checking on them.

"Seamus tried to recruit me for Operation Undead. He's CIA."

All three women looked at Eddie with a mixture of awe, disbelief and amusement.

Jenny smirked and cracked her knuckles. "Dude, you've got to be kidding me. Operation Undead? That's ridiculous. What is it? Like *Walking Dead* without the zombies?" Jenny rubbed her forehead. "Wait a second. Are zombies real?"

"No. At least not that I'm aware of. I don't know about you guys, but zombies don't seem very plausible. Rotting flesh, eating brains. Anyway, OU is more like *The A-Team*," Eddie said without a hint of irony.

"She's too young to get the reference and I'm too old and set in my ways to fully grasp the magnitude of what you're saying. The CIA knows about us? We're weapons?" Veronica's pitch grew higher with each word. "It all seems too fantastical to be true." She reached into her purse and pulled two twenties from her wallet. "I've got lunch."

"Why wasn't I approached by Seamus? I could totally be a weapon of mass destruction. I mean, in the right hands." Mary flipped the thick strands of hair from her shoulder.

Veronica felt the same as Mary. All this time she thought she was one in a million, but it was becoming abundantly clear that there were probably eight, or maybe even eight-hundred, of her in New York alone.

"You as individuals don't raise any red flags, and if you do happen to take someone out before cancer or heart disease gets them, it's usually an undesirable that the government wants gone anyway. Nobody cares about the addicts or the runaways or the prostitutes that go missing." Eddie stood. "I do, but they don't."

Mary sighed, as if relieved to hear that Eddie was a good guy. They exchanged numbers and Facebook accounts and promised to stay in touch.

In spite of the immortal matchmaking, Veronica was itching to go. She had a call to make.

37

"Are you still up for this?" Veronica tapped Jenny on the arm. They had been driving for four hours and her butt had fallen asleep even as her mind kept churning. For the first time in ages, she wanted to close her eyes and rest—to escape the guilt from dragging this damaged young woman along for her selfish, self-centered ride. Jenny needed help, much more help than she could offer.

"Yes," Jenny yawned and stretched like a cat in a sliver of sun. "But can we please stay in a decent hotel when we get there? I'll pay."

"You'll pay, huh? Where, may I ask, did you get the money to pay for a hotel room?"

"Carl hooked me up with a debit card if I solemnly swore to disappear."

"He what?" Veronica whipped her head in Jenny's direction. The thought of Carl and what he tried to pull at the museum made her angrier than her ex-husband's infidelities.

"It's just a debit card, and knowing my cheap ass dad, it's probably got a three-hundred-dollar limit."

"Well, that's just great. They can track you with that, you know."

"Yeah, so." Jenny adjusted the seat and sat up. "Let them track me.

They don't give a shit where I am or what I'm doing as long as I don't do anything stupid that might get leaked to the press."

Veronica stared out at the vast expanse of green surrounding the highway. It felt like she was on a road to nowhere. JA would not be thrilled to see her face on his doorstep. "You know, maybe we could go to a meeting when we get to Lincoln. I don't know about you, but I could really use one."

Jenny rolled down the window and let her arm ride through waves of cool air. The bruises were fading from her skin, but the psychological wounds would remain. "Sure, whatever. For all the press knows, I'm at a rehab facility. It's not like they can check on that shit, right?"

"I doubt it because of HIPAA, but you never know. Your dad is running for president."

"So, I know it's none of my business, but in a way it kind of is. Who are we going to Nebraska for?"

"My ex-husband, Jonathan Allen Smith—or JA, as he insists."

"Is he a douchebag?"

"Yes, I'm afraid so." Overwhelmed by her upcoming confrontation with a person she wanted to intentionally harm, Veronica slowed the car and pulled over to the side of the road. She flipped her hazards on and reclined the seat.

"What are you doing?" Jenny rifled through her backpack.

"Meditating. Be quiet." Veronica slowly opened her eyes and spied the revolver on Jenny's lap. "I think the more pressing question is, what are you doing with that gun?"

"I just want it for protection."

"Do you even know how to shoot a…" Veronica stopped, realizing her question was redundant. "Is that thing loaded?"

Jenny inspected the cylinder. "Three shots left. One's all I need, though."

"You know, Jenny, you don't need to protect me. I'm pretty much invincible when it comes to guns, knives, or whatever someone wants to use. You could shoot me right now and I'd be good as new in less than a minute. It's my one and only super power."

"Yeah, well, I don't have any superpowers. The gun's for me. I don't know if you've noticed, but you run with a really strange crowd." Jenny placed the revolver back on her lap.

Veronica closed her eyes and tried to focus on the words *keep it simple*, but the word *gun* ricocheted through her mind like a live-fire round. She hated the idea of guns, even more than the cockiness of those who brandished them. As a weapon, they were too loud and impersonal. If she really wanted to kill someone, whether in a fit of rage or for merciful relief, she preferred to be close enough to feel their last breath on her face. "I get it, just be careful and don't point that thing in my direction."

"You don't need to worry. I'm a trick shot. Hell, I was raised in Texas. I knew how to shoot a gun before I knew how to ride a bike." Jenny clicked the cylinder back in place. "Maybe we should get some more ammo. Just in case."

"You planning on killing someone?" Veronica sat back up. Meditation, like everything else in her life, would have to wait.

"Not yet."

A red, dirt-caked pickup pulled up behind them, kicking up gravel. The faint sound of Patsy Cline's voice cut off with the engine. A middle-aged man with belted Wranglers and a western button-down stretched across the bulk of his belly hopped down from the cab and strode over to the driver's side window. Unfazed by the cars careening by, he leaned his face near the open window and removed his sunglasses. A sweat-stained "Make America Great Again" hat engulfed his large head.

"You ladies need a jump?"

Jenny picked up the gun and scratched her scalp with the barrel. "We're just sitting here. She's, like, trying, like, really fucking hard to meditate and you just interrupted that shit." Jenny blew into the barrel and smiled, revealing her chipped front tooth.

The man's nostrils twitched at the sight of the weapon. "I didn't mean to interrupt nothing. I was trying to be helpful's all. I'll be on my way."

"Not so fast." Jenny aimed the revolver at Veronica's temple. "I have a question I want to ask you. If you lie, I'm going to blow her brains out." She cocked the gun. "Ready?"

"Don't worry," Veronica assured him. "She's not going to blow my brains out." She turned toward Jenny. It would be so easy to snatch the gun away, as the barrel pointed between her eyes, but she decided it would be best if she didn't try to control the situation.

The man lifted his arms in the air, as if to show that he wasn't armed. "I, I," he stuttered, stepping backwards onto the highway.

Veronica turned and smiled reassuringly at the man, but she wasn't really sure of anything at this point. "You're going to get hit by a car. Come back here."

The man stepped closer to the car, eyeing his truck as if trying to figure out how quickly he could escape into the safety of the cab.

Veronica continued in a slow, even tone as if she were trying to calm a frightened animal. "Sir, she seems to be having a moment. She's had a rough week. Just humor her and you'll be on your way. I'm very sorry." The words that were becoming her salvation felt like her ruin as her teeth strained against her gums. The smell of the man's fear was intoxicating. The gun at her head wasn't helping. She pressed her lips together and inhaled deeply through her nose.

Jenny leaned towards the steering wheel. "Nice hat. When exactly was America great? Was it when we screwed the Native Americans?" Jenny gestured with the gun. "Or how about when we nuked Japan? Was that when we were great?"

"This ain't my hat, ma'am. It's my brother's. I'm just wearing it 'cause I got treated for melanoma a few days ago. Doc says I'm supposed to keep my head covered. The sun'll kill you."

"No. Actually it won't. Ask her." Jenny pointed the gun back at Veronica's head. "So, here's my question." Jenny leaned closer to the window and looked up at the man. "What's your name?"

"My name's Don Henderson, ma'am." He braced the door of the car. Scabs covered the knuckles of his weathered hands. "Can I go now?"

"That's not my question. Here's my question and don't you go lying to me, Donald, or she'll get it right in the noggin."

"Yes, ma'am." Sweat beaded his upper lip.

"Do you like the smell of your own farts, Donald Henderson?"

"Excuse me?" He cupped his sunburned ear and leaned forward.

Jenny raised her voice. "When you fart. Do you like how it smells or do you not like how it smells?"

"I really don't know how to answer that kind of question." He shifted his weight and wiped the sweat with the back of his hand. His gaze darted from Veronica's furrowed brow to Jenny's unsteady arm.

"*I don't know* is not the answer I'm looking for. Either you do or you don't, Donald." Jenny leaned back and clutched her knees to her chest. Her arm steadied. "Think back to the last time you farted, which I'm guessing was probably less than five minutes ago. Did you enjoy how it smelled?"

"No, ma'am. I can't say that I did."

"Bingo! So, your answer is no?" She nodded her head maniacally.

He returned her enthusiasm and smiled with quivering lips.

"Liar." Jenny roared and pulled the trigger.

38

"That was fucking awesome! Did you see his face?" Jenny laughed. "He totally shit his pants too." She wiped her eyes and the spittle from her lips.

Veronica sped down the highway as if her hair were on fire. Both she and Jenny were high on adrenaline, and if she didn't find an exit quick, Nebraska's finest were going to pull them over and throw them in the slammer. She looked at Jenny and flashed her razor-sharp canines. "If you ever do something like that again, I will rip your throat out. I don't care who your dad is. You will be dead. Got it?"

"Whatever. Why are you driving so fast? If I were you, I'd slow down before I got a speeding ticket." She bit at what remained of her nails. "Just saying."

"Are you fucking kidding me, Jenny? You just blew half of my head onto that poor man's shirt. I think the police will be a little more concerned with that. And then," her voice rose to a furious level, "*then*, they will be really concerned that you got that fucker's gun!"

"First of all, it was not murder. It was self-defense. And second, that redneck saw that you were okay when you were giving him that mouth to mouth shit. He's not going to call the police. He's going to go home, take a shower and probably wash his clothes. That's what he's going to do. Chill the fuck out." Jenny gingerly placed the gun into the glovebox and slammed the reluctant door shut. "You have to admit, that shit was crazy. For a minute there, I thought you were lying about your superpower, but you weren't. If we could film that, we'd be fucking rich, richer than my dad. You'd have like advertisers busting down your door and a million YouTube followers."

"What if I had been lying? What then? Jesus!" Veronica exited the highway and zipped into the darkened bay of a truck wash. As the engine idled, she angrily violated the nooks and crannies at the bottom of her purse. "Here," she handed Jenny a handful of quarters. "Wash off the evidence and whatever you do, don't do a half-assed job of it." Veronica hopped out of the car, inspected the door and shook her head in disbelief. In the window, she caught sight of her own reflection. No blood lingered on her body, but her cardigan was soaked. She peeled it from her skin and threw it in the trash bin. "I need to go do something about this." She waved her arms over the length of her body. "Don't say a word to anyone. Got it?" She grabbed the keys from the ignition and Serenity-prayed her way into the Flying J.

As the automatic doors whooshed open, she was assaulted by a blast of air conditioning and the chorus of George Strait's "All My Exes Live in Texas." Wishing for invisibility, she lowered her head and navigated the fluorescent maze of candy bars, chips and energy drinks to the safety and seclusion of the women's restroom. Passing a rack of t-shirts and hoodies, she briefly entertained the idea of grabbing one to cover her bare arms, but good sense and dwindling funds interrupted that plan. Forget the shirt—she needed a phone. Turning the corner of the restroom hall, she exhaled like a runner crossing the finish line. A lone trucker with ripe clothes and two-day stubble leaned against the wall as if waiting for her. He tried to meet her gaze with hungry, bloodshot eyes. She quickly darted through the door marked with a "W" and mentally dared him to follow.

At the littered counter, she wet a wad of rough brown paper towels and scrubbed the drops of drying blood. Flicking a bit of brain matter from her purple camisole, she turned to see her back in the mirror. Sweat soaked the back of her shirt. She pressed the hand dryer. The noise it made when ignited was angry and excessive, but it managed to dry her shirt.

Feeling confident that she could slip back to the car unnoticed, she tiptoed out of the restroom. Jenny was at the counter paying for a mound of unhealthy snacks and a soda twice the size of her head. The cashier handed her some bills, which she stuffed in her back pocket, along with the newly acquired debit card.

"Let's go," Veronica demanded.

"I've got to pee." Jenny handed Veronica the bag and the sweating soda. "Take this. I'll be right out."

"On your way out, get a prepaid phone. Got it?"

As Veronica steamrolled through the automatic doors, a Highway Patrol vehicle pulled into the lot directly in front of her. Two officers sat stone-faced in the front seat.

And sat.

And sat.

Veronica's pulse quickened as she looked for the easiest path between the parked cars. If someone dared to look close enough, they would be able to tell that she was a walking crime scene. All they needed was a black light.

Menopausal invisibility, don't fail me now. As nonchalantly as she could, Veronica walked directly past them. With her car in sight, her pace increased. She didn't know if it was fear or hope that fueled her forward… but she knew it would be all too easy to take off and leave Jenny behind.

The car was dried and spotless. Even the interior dash and seats were wiped down. A vanilla-scented air freshener dangled from the rearview mirror. Jenny wasn't good for much more than a laugh, but as a meth addict, she sure knew how to clean. As Veronica buckled her seatbelt, Jenny plopped down beside her, perhaps sensing that her days in Veronica's protective custody were numbered. She placed the phone on the dash.

"I got one too. Let's roll," Jenny dug into her bag of treats and ripped open a Snickers bar. "So, how long till we get to Lincoln?"

"Now that we have to take the back roads, I have no idea. In fact, I'm not quite sure we should even stay in this stupid flat-ass state."

"But Seamus hooked you up and your ex is expecting you. Come on, woman. We've already come this far. What's the problem?" As soon as the words left her lips, Jenny's face flashed in recognition—*she* was the problem.

Jenny dumped the half-eaten candy bar back in the bag and tapped her foot against the floorboard. "So, if we don't go to Lincoln, what's your plan B?"

"Detroit." Veronica pulled out of the bay as the two officers sauntered into the store. "I don't think I'm ready for that yet. I don't know if I'll ever be ready."

"Another ex?"

"Yes."

"Oh, come on. How bad can he be?"

She pulled cautiously onto the service road. "He tried to kill me. We were at his place and some guy just walks in and shoots me in the head. Kinda like what you did twenty minutes ago."

"No shit? I bet that fucker got a big surprise when you came back."

"Yeah, he was surprised alright. And then he shot Kevin. I was so stupid. I had no idea it had been planned. I didn't want to lose the man I loved, so..." Veronica's voice trailed off. "I'm too tired for this."

39

NEBRASKA 1978

With the accumulated crumbs of her abnormally long life crammed into boxes in the back of a crappy cargo van, Veronica fled Detroit towards the anonymous plains of Nebraska. In the last twenty-four hours, she had been drained by Kevin and shot several times. Being repeatedly shot and having to reassemble into her former physical-self took a psychic toll. Not only was she hungry, angry, lonely and tired, she was heartbroken. The man she loved was not who she thought he was... but neither was she. In the two years she'd known him, he was never privy to her secret. Not only did this make her a pretty damn good liar, it made her realize that she was part of her own problem. She had been to enough AA meetings to know that she was only as sick as her secrets. For her own serenity, it was time to tell the truth.

Determined to remain as ethical as possible in pursuit of a meal, she wandered into St. John's Regional Medical Center in the middle of a cold, cloudless night. The halls were empty, the lights were lowered, but she held out the hope that someone on one of these dimly lit floors was dying and might need a little help to get there. The first order of business was to procure a new outfit, so she wouldn't look like a bedraggled visitor in her brown cords and turtleneck sweater. She followed the numerous signs through empty halls to the OR. Trying the handle of a supply closet, she was relieved to find it unlocked. Several pairs of surgical scrubs in her size were neatly folded on one of the shelves. She changed into the blue, loose fitting fabric with "St. John's" embroidered on the front pocket and stuffed an extra pair in her purse. In her experience, it was surprisingly easy to walk the halls of a hospital when she dressed the part. No one ever seemed to question her sudden appearance. Most of the time, other employees were relieved to see her face, especially in the wee hours of the dreaded night shift. She stowed her clothes and purse behind a stack of surgical glove boxes and peeked her head out the door to make sure the coast was clear. It was.

Walking with a sense of purpose, she located the ICU on the hospital map and strode the bleach-scented halls. At each door, she studied the patient's chart. She wanted dire—hours or even days to live with no chance of recovery—and geriatric. Old folks were the least resistant. Most had already surrendered to the idea of death and many welcomed it.

In room 339, she found her midnight snack. She gently stepped through the cracked door of Lily Shelton, an eighty-seven-year-old with advanced leukemia. The room was dark, but she sensed movement at the bed. Quietly she crept into the open bathroom.

"Thank you, Johnathan," the woman gurgled. "It won't hurt, will it?"

"No, ma'am," the figure at her bedside replied. "You'll be fast asleep, and you won't feel a thing. I'll let your son know as soon as it happens."

Being competitive and petty were two of her character defects and they kicked in as if recovery had never happened.

The man, tall and plump with short brown hair combed forward to mask his receding hairline, stepped out of the room and closed the door behind him. Veronica froze in place, worried that he might interrupt and spoil her obvious superiority in killing a patient.

She listened to the familiar beeps and blips of the monitor. The woman's heart rate slowed along with her respiration. She was on the pharmaceutical expressway to meet her maker. Veronica stepped out of her hiding place and padded towards the bed. The woman's eyes were closed, and it looked as if her body had been swallowed beneath a layer of blankets. Crouched on the side of the bed, she lifted the woman's slender wrist to her mouth. In addition to hunger, she was also feeding her feelings. She didn't care if she left a mark or made a bloody mess. The woman didn't stir as she drained the remaining life from her failing body.

As the monitor flat lined, the burly nurse announced his on-the-dot presence with a flick of the light switch. Startled, Veronica wiped her mouth with the sheet and stood.

"What are you doing to my patient?" He rubbed his eyes, as if he could wipe this image and what it implied from his vision.

"I was simply finishing what you started." Veronica threw her shoulders back and lifted her chin. Honesty felt good.

"Excuse me?" He folded his pale, fleshy arms across his chest.

She strode past him, placing her hand on the door handle and turned. "I collected a blood sample from her and you should be hearing from your superior very, very soon, young man."

"Where do you think you're going? You were drinking her blood. I saw you."

"Really? Well I heard you agree to kill her about ten minutes ago. Which story do you think the administration of this fine institution is going to believe?" She opened the door.

"I can't believe this. You're sick."

"I was simply taking a blood sample, and it was delicious." She pulled the woman's chart and wrote the time of death. "3:23. We both got the desired end—we just used different means to get there. You ever heard of bloodletting, there, Johnathan? It's old. It's very old. Way before your time."

"You're crazy. I'm calling security." He reached for the call button.

Veronica stepped back into the room. "Listen. I've done exactly what you just did hundreds of times. Your angel-of-death secret is safe with me." Smiling, she could smell his fear.

"What are you implying?" He bit his thumb nail.

"Johnathan, I've been there, and I've done that. In fact, my t-shirt's older than you. Maybe you used a large dose of morphine to slow her respiration? Or perhaps you injected her with insulin?"

"Who are you?" He looked as if he were on the verge of crying, which was perfect for her self-confidence.

"I'm either your worst nightmare or your best friend, depending on how you want to play this next hand." She smiled, revealing her menacing teeth.

"We're really short staffed right now and I've got three other patients I need to check on. Are you going to kill me too?" He pulled the blanket over his patient's face.

She was losing him. "Don't be ridiculous. Would you like some help?" She moved to help him with the blanket.

He crossed his fingers at her approach. "I think you've done enough. Be gone, demon."

"Oh, please. Johnathan, I'm a nurse. Worked ER at General in Detroit until two days ago. I'm sure my boss would send over glowing reviews of my work ethic."

He dropped his arms and squeezed past her. As he reached for the door handle, she placed her hand on his. "If you don't help me, I'll make your life a living hell. I have a sneaking suspicion that this wasn't your first time at the Grim Reaper rodeo. Am I right?"

He looked back at the bed and lowered his voice. "She wanted to die. What exactly do you want from me?"

"She can't hear you, by the way. I want a job. I'm a good worker, I've never been late or called out sick and I never take breaks. I'm a work horse, Johnathan, and I've got the references to back that up. If you hire me, I'll give St. John's the best fifteen years of my life."

"I don't make hiring decisions. You'll have to apply and speak to Dean Williams in the morning."

"I'm afraid that is not a possibility. I don't do daytime. I work nights and I suggest you do whatever it takes to make it happen. And another thing, Johnathan—"

"It's JA," he interrupted.

"Okay, JA. I've been around hospitals a long time and litigation in matters such as these are a nightmare. They'll dig and they'll dig until they find exactly what they need to put you away. I'm afraid you're a little too, how do I say this nicely?" She rubbed her chin. "You're a little too soft to survive in prison. Despite what you may think, what you just did to Ms. Shelton is okay with me, but there are those who will be deeply—and I'm talking to the depths of their soul—offended. I hate to break it to you, JA, but there is a god and you're not him." She smiled, and her fangs were gone. "So, are you going to work with me or not?"

He stared at her with a mixture of hate and awe and nodded slightly in the affirmative. Veronica tailed his every move till 5 a.m., promising to return later that night. With a sweaty, suspicious handshake, their strange partnership was forged. Their foundation was built on a secret but solidified with an unappetizing truth.

40

PRESENT

Veronica's eyes felt as if they'd been glued shut. When she opened them, the car was parked at a dilapidated strip mall. Jenny was in the driver's seat, busying herself with the complexities of her new phone.

"Where are we? I feel like I fell asleep, but that's not possible."

"Well, your eyes were closed for like an hour. It sure looked like sleeping to me."

"Are we in Lincoln?" Her voice dripped dread.

"Yep, but look." Jenny pointed excitedly at the window in front of them. Two rough-looking men smoked short cigarettes on a wooden bench. Each held a Styrofoam cup, while flicking their ashes in a Folger's can. Printed in blue on the glass above their heads was "The Last Stop."

"Do you know them?"

"No, dude. It's an AA meeting. Didn't you say you wanted to go to a meeting when we got to Lincoln? Well here we are. It's almost time to let go and let God!" Jenny sounded as hyped up as a kid who'd just eaten two bowls of sugar cereal.

"Why are you so happy?" Veronica unbelted herself and lugged her purse up from the floor.

"I called the number on the back of my new debit card and, according to Bev at the Wells Fargo, I've got fifteen grand with a three-thousand-dollar daily spending limit. For once, my cheap-ass dad totally hooked me up."

"I have a feeling he is going to regret that." Veronica rolled her eyes and stepped out of the car. She wanted to get as far away from Jenny's mirth as she could. Even though their immediate money worries were over, she was pretty sure that Jenny was high and holding. "Are you coming?"

The two men rose from the bench as Veronica stepped up from the curb. The older of the two, a man with yellow teeth and a road-mapped face, rushed to open the door for her.

"Right on time. You our speaker tonight?" he asked.

"No, sir." Veronica smiled. "But thank you. I'm Veronica." She held out her hand, raising her eyebrows.

"Bill." He met her hand and shook it vigorously.

"Nice to meet you." She stepped into a room as well-traveled as Bill's face. Scratched folding chairs lined the scuffed walls and a yellowed Twelve Step banner hung for dear life behind the podium.

"Is she?"

Veronica glanced back towards Jenny, who hoisted her overstuffed backpack over her shoulder and slammed the car door. "Am I what?" Jenny shouted.

The younger man, pock-marked and tattooed, held out a crumpled piece of paper. "Will you sign this for me?"

Jenny waved it off. "Nice try, dude, but you have to sit through the meeting first."

"Where are you all visiting from?" Bill asked and took a seat near the coffee maker.

All eyes followed Veronica and Jenny as they settled into two empty seats near the front.

"California," Veronica lied. She wanted to kick herself for using her real name, even though half of this room would nod in silent understanding if they knew the shit she and Jenny were in.

Bill looked towards the clock. "Well, doesn't look like our speaker is going to show, so we better get started."

"I'll speak," Jenny raised her arm and bolted from the chair.

"Well, let's start with our opening and then you can have the floor after that, young lady."

Veronica planted her feet firmly on the dirty, industrial-grade carpet, bracing herself for the verbal vomit that would surely spew from Jenny's mouth. The pock-marked kid took the seat closest to the door and slouched back in his chair. The 'nudge from the judge' attendees rarely got anything from these rooms. They had to want recovery more than that next drink, but most of them were simply on their first DWI and hadn't hit bottom yet. She looked up at Bill, whose face had softened as he read the introduction and the steps. Gratitude radiated from his oversized pores, and Veronica was pre-emptively pissed that Jenny was going to ruin it.

"All right young lady, is this your first time telling your story?"

"No, sir. And it's Jenny." She looked out at the crowd and took a deep breath. "Hi, my name is Jenny P and I'm an alcoholic."

In unison, the twenty or so attendees said, "Hi, Jenny."

She placed her quivering hands on the podium to steady them. That was Veronica's first surprise. Was Jenny about to get real?

"I'm also an addict," Jenny continued, "but I'll leave the drug talk for NA. So, um, I grew up in Texas. I had a pretty regular childhood. Neither of my parents had a drinking problem, or at least not one that I was aware of. We went to church, my mom was in the PTA, although I think she belonged to the PNA, or Parent Nazi Association. She hovered over me and my brother and sister twenty-four-seven. She was crazy like that. Maybe untreated Al-Anon, I don't know, but she was kind of a control freak." Jenny paused and looked at Veronica's familiar face. Veronica smiled and nodded her encouragement.

"Anyway, so from the time I was like six years old, I knew I was different. I think my parents suspected as much and sent me off to one of those crazy camps where you are supposed to pray away the gay. At camp, two things happened. One, I met my first girlfriend, which was awesome, but I don't think we prayed hard enough or something because we made out every chance we got."

Several members in the group laughed, and Jenny laughed along with them. "Okay. And the second thing, which was even bigger and better than kissing a girl, was that I had my first drink. Those counselors were so worried about our sinful thoughts that they didn't notice that one of the kids had smuggled in this giant bottle of cheap vodka. We mixed it with our morning orange juice. I loved it. I loved the taste. I loved how it made me feel, different and confident. Needless to say, vodka made conversion camp a hell of a lot more tolerable."

Veronica couldn't believe her sincerity. It was both refreshing and disconcerting to hear this side of her.

A flash of headlights from the window caught Veronica's attention —and then froze her thoughts. A police car was pulling up behind their car.

Her mind raced, Jenny's voice drowned out by the blood whooshing and whirring in her ears. She turned her face from the window. They were probably running the California plates, which would lead them to Desmond, who was now a missing person. They would also be looking for a middle-aged woman with long dark hair accompanied by a foul-mouthed, gun-toting girl with hair the color of a fire hydrant. She coughed loudly and rose to use the bathroom.

"I spent my sixteenth birthday in rehab. It was awesome. Not." Jenny laughed.

Veronica quietly slipped into the bathroom and flipped on the light. Beads of sweat collected on her upper lip and a steady stream dribbled down the back of her neck. She lifted her thick hair and dabbed the sweat with a paper towel. Was there a back exit for this place? Too late to look now.

Unsure of what to do, she braided her hair, applied a thick coat of red lipstick and brushed several coats of Ingrid's mascara onto her lashes. In the tiny mirror's reflection, an overgrown toddler with Pippy Longstocking hair greeted her. *Jenny will need a hat. Hopefully there's one in that damn backpack of hers.* As she placed her hand on the door knob, she whispered "God, help me," and opened the door.

"I'll be honest with you," Jenny continued. "I have really yet to master this recovery, but I keep trying. My sponsor right there, she helps. Man, can she be a bitch, but I think I need that from someone. Plus, she understands about having to hide parts of herself from the world."

The officers walked in. Veronica froze, trapped. The female officer glanced at Jenny. "I'm sorry to interrupt your meeting, but I need to have a word with Dylan Przybylski."

The pock-marked kid rose from the jump seat and left the room, still clutching his crumpled piece of paper.

"Bummer, dude. Well, that's about all I got for now. Thanks for letting me share my story." Jenny bowed and plopped back in her chair as the room filled with applause.

"Who wants to follow that?" Bill said.

Veronica felt as if her heart was going to shoot out of her throat. She didn't know if she could take much more of this. She hugged Jenny and whispered in her ear. "Are you high?"

"No, just happy," she whispered back.

AFTER THE MEETING, Veronica jumped back in the driver's seat. "Do you have a hat or a bandana that you can cover your hair with?"

"No, why?" Jenny touched her red hair.

"We're too noticeable and it's making me nervous. After what you pulled, I'm afraid the police are looking for us. The last thing either of us need is to go to jail. With your mouth, you'll get killed and once they figure out who I am, I'll be shipped back to Texas for killing Bobby Lee Garrett."

"The serial killer? Dude, that's huge." Jenny bounced in her seat.

"He was my patient. Anyway, I want to go to JA's house tonight so we can get out of here as soon as possible. In the meantime, we either need to get a new car or new plates. Would you rather spend your daddy's money or commit a felony?"

AFTER PURCHASING black hair dye and a matching bandana to cover her tresses, Jenny opted for option two, removing the front and rear plates from an '84 Olds Cutlass in a darkened church parking lot. Veronica had learned a valuable lesson tonight: *Jenny Pearson* was a dangerous pain in the ass, but *Jenny P* just might be the "lower power" she needed to get through her final two amends.

41

As the GPS announced that they'd reached their destination, Veronica rechecked the address she'd been given for JA. The address brought them to a strip club. "Two-dollar beers till 8 and Topless Dancers" flashed across the building's sign. She removed Seamus's card from her wallet and dialed his number in the new phone, saving it as a contact.

"Yes, dear?" Seamus's voice dripped condescension as if her call was an expected annoyance.

"I must have the wrong address, unless JA has given up nursing and taken up bartending." Veronica clicked her pen, ready to write the new address on Jenny's receipt.

"You're in the right place. Give the doorman JA's name. They'll escort you to his VIP room." Seamus spoke above the faint sound of pulsing music.

She turned off the ignition and grabbed her purse. Something was up, and she didn't like it. "Apparently he's inside in one of the VIP rooms. I'd tell you to wait here, but I think I'd feel safer if you were with me."

Jenny opened the glove box to retrieve the gun.

"No. That stays here. They'll probably check your bag. Just stick close to me and keep your mouth shut. Can I trust you to do that?" Veronica placed her hand on Jenny's shoulder, giving it a firm squeeze.

"Yes, you can trust me. You got any dollar bills?"

"That's funny."

They trudged through the packed parking lot to the entrance. A burly bouncer with a black t-shirt clinging to his heavily muscled frame greeted them. In his right hand, he wielded a large chrome flash light.

"Good evening ladies. I just need to see some ID." He shone the light on their faces.

Veronica rolled her eyes and dug out her wallet. "Is this really necessary? I'm fifty-one." She handed over her wallet without removing the driver's license.

"According to your license, ma'am, you're sixty-five." He flashed his light back to her face. "Most people with a fake ID want to be a little older than they really are. No one wants to be retirement age." He handed her back the flowered wallet. "What about you, pipsqueak?"

Jenny reached into her overstuffed backpack and pulled out her ID. She held it next to her face.

The bouncer leaned in and shook his head. "Got to be twenty-one to enter, sweetheart."

"You've got to be kidding me. What if I told you I wanted to apply for a job as a dancer. How old would I have to be?"

"Eighteen." He eyed her up and down.

"That doesn't make sense. Come on, dude, let me in. I need a job like yesterday."

"You're the right shade of spray tan, but unless you've got a pair of magic inflatable tits under that t-shirt, you ain't gonna get one here."

"Listen, I'm her mother. We're just going to meet someone really quick. JA? Perhaps you know him. He's in the VIP room."

The bouncer's demeanor shifted immediately. "Why didn't you say so? Step right in, ladies. Up the stairs and to the right." He unlatched the velvet rope and they shuffled inside clutching their bags like shields. The room was dark with plush chairs and pulsing lights. Three bikini-clad dancers gyrated on the stage as "Pour Some Sugar on Me" blared from the sound system. Veronica felt like she'd stepped back into the 80s.

Veronica placed an unsteady hand on Jenny's back as they climbed the stairs. A bottle-blonde waitress with a tray of orange gelatin shots sidled up next to them when they reached the top of the stairs.

"Can I get you ladies a drink?"

"No, um, we're here to meet JA. I think he's in one of these rooms." Veronica scanned the empty hallway, hoping JA was anxiously awaiting her arrival.

"Right this way," the waitress wiggled to the third room on the right, knocked and opened the door. "I think this is who you're looking for."

Veronica braced herself for his shocked surprise upon seeing her. She hadn't changed physically, but she had grown emotionally since they'd parted ways.

In the center of the small room was a lone stripper pole with a zebra striped couch encircling it. A small man in a navy tailored suit closed his laptop and leaned back with a grin.

"Oh, sorry. I think we're in the wrong room." Veronica stepped backwards.

He smirked at her discomfort. "Took you long enough."

Veronica recognized the young voice. It was Seamus. She cautiously stepped back in, pulling Jenny along with her. "Where's JA?"

"Have a seat. Can I get you something to drink?"

"She doesn't drink. And I don't think they serve O positive here." Veronica sat down on the couch, while Jenny ran her hand up and down the pole.

Seamus leaned over a large legal briefcase and pulled out a thermos. "Jenny, would you be a dear and fetch Ms. Bouchard a glass from the bar. It's right back there."

"Well, isn't that convenient? Where's JA?" Her tone darkened.

"Patience." Seamus took the rocks glass from Jenny and carefully filled it with blood. He leaned across the couch, holding it out. "Have a drink, Ms. Bouchard. I prefer to speak with my clients over a meal. I find everyone is much more amenable when they've been fed."

Veronica took the glass and sniffed. "Please call me Veronica. Where did you get this?"

"I have my ways." He tightened the lid of the thermos and placed it carefully back into the case. "Don't worry, dear. It's not poisoned, if that's what you're worried about."

Jenny squeezed next to Veronica. "That is so fucking gross."

Veronica took a sip from the warm, fresh beverage while eyeing the contours of the room. She felt as anxious and expectant as a child cranking a jack-in-the-box handle. "Will he be joining us?"

"I'm afraid he won't." He clasped his hands together. "Mary and Eddie, your first two tastes of my services, were free. If you would like my help going forward to locate Johnathan, there is a fee."

"I already told you, I don't have a pot to piss in right now, but as soon as this whole thing is over, I will pay you the five-hundred. That's what it is, right? Five-hundred?"

"No, I'm afraid not." He inspected his neatly manicured nails.

"What is it, then? Blood?"

Jenny nudged Veronica with her arm. "Don't look at me."

"It's not cash or blood I'm after. I am in need of something only you can deliver. If you still want to locate your friend, that is." He straightened his tie and stood. "I'm afraid he goes by a different name now, which will make locating him rather difficult for you."

"What exactly do you want me to do? Join the CIA?"

"Oh, I see you've already spoken with Eddie. I don't need you to necessarily join the CIA. I just need you to help us turn a few men that will be leaving for Afghanistan next week."

Veronica stood. "Absolutely not. I'm on my way out of this, God willing. The last thing I need is more souls that I have to locate and apologize to, and if they're all the way in the Middle East that makes it rather difficult to reach them." She moved in his direction, towering almost a foot above him. "Why don't you just do it yourself?"

"That's an excellent question—and for the sake of brevity, my answer is that we like to keep the bloodlines diverse."

"That's bullshit. Come on, Jenny. I'm not stupid. I'll find him on my own."

Jenny rose from the couch and hefted her bag across her shoulder. "She's menopausal, dude. I wouldn't fuck with her."

"Why make this more difficult than it has to be?" He walked to the bar and retrieved a glass for himself. "If you agree to work with me, you're only committed for six months. At the end of that time, the young men will return from their mission, you do your thing, and mortality will be yours. I say the word and the illustrious JA with his eternal hair plugs and six pack abs will appear in twenty minutes." Seamus smiled, unblinking. "All you have to do is agree."

"Why me? Aren't there thousands of us out there?"

"Twelve hundred and thirty-seven to be exact. Those that don't reflect are more difficult to track and very few want to be mortal again. Most people would kill for eternal youth and, as you know, they do. You're a special case." He filled his glass and lifted it to his lips. "You're close, aren't you? Can you taste that medium rare steak with loaded baked potato yet?"

Veronica refused to let herself even picture it. "That wouldn't be my meal of choice. And I still have one more person beyond JA."

"You are close." He pursed his lip and narrowed his eyes. "And who would that final person be?"

Veronica stared down at the thickening crimson beverage in her trembling hands. She shouldn't tell him. If he knew, he could use it against her.

But finding Kevin wasn't going to be the hard part. Making amends and meaning it, on the other hand…

Veronica glanced back up at the only man who had been any help at all on this mad quest and tried not to notice the cockiness in his stare. "Kevin Black. Detroit. 1977."

Seamus favored her with one lifted eyebrow. "Oh, dear." He sipped from his glass, then wiped his lips with a cloth napkin.

"What?" Veronica sat back down with a huff, clutching the crusted armrest of the couch. She pulled her hand away, setting it in her lap. "Well?"

"I don't think you'd be able to get in the same room with him. He takes himself very seriously, if you know what I mean, and with reflection, he'd be vulnerable. He very much likes his life now."

"Do you know where he is?" Veronica blurted.

"Of course." His blue eyes sparkled as his lips parted with promise.

"Well?"

"Seriously, woman. Do you think I'm going to tell you?" He chuckled and picked up his giant phone. "Well? Do we have a deal?"

Veronica's face remained immobile, but she could feel her fangs pushing against her gums. A deal was the last thing she wanted. If anything, she wanted to beat the shit out of the little twerp. She lifted the coagulating drink and guzzled it greedily. "I'll do one for one. One for JA and one for Kevin."

He clapped his hands together. "Perfect. But before you sign your name in blood on the dotted line, I want you to be aware of the risk involved. There is always the chance that one or both of these men may die. IEDs are everywhere, and I'm sure you can imagine the mess those make."

Veronica couldn't quite picture it, but the memory of vivisecting Desmond on the mortuary table was all too fresh. "What do you mean?"

"Well, if a man's heart is blown from his body and burned, his soul will remain within you forever. There won't be anything left of him to apologize to. These casualties are rare, but they do happen. Do you understand what I'm saying?"

"Yes, I understand. Can't I just pay you? I could have my husband wire you the money."

"You're in a bit of trouble back in Texas, Veronica, and it wouldn't be wise to drag him into this. The authorities have video of your spray tanned body killing the girl. It's not just the hall footage. Every room had a camera. The owner sold those images on the black market. And let's not forget about Bobby Lee Garrett. He deserved what you did to him, but I'm afraid the state of Texas frowns on vigilante justice." Seamus licked his lips. "But here's the good news. I can erase all of it for you. And if you want, you can return home and be in your cozy bed by Friday."

"I need to think about it. Can you give me twenty-four hours?"

Anger flashed over Seamus's weasel-like face—the first she'd seen from him. "Are you seriously going to make me stay in this god-awful city another night?"

But Veronica had bought real estate more than once in her long lifetime, and more than her share of used cars, and she knew how to hold fast in the face of a pushy salesman. "Yes. I'm afraid so. This is a big decision and I need to meditate on it."

"Go." He swooshed his arm through the air dismissively. "But I expect an answer by seven tomorrow night. You have my number."

Veronica nodded. She couldn't get out of the room and down the black-lit stairs fast enough. The air was thick with desperation, the kind that wanted to dominate and destroy everything in its path, and that didn't include the men staring at the stage with bloodshot eyes and sweaty bills.

42

"I know it's really none of your business, but what do you think I should do?" Veronica pulled the patterned coverlet up around her neck and flipped through the channels on the muted flat screen.

From the smoke-stained table beside the bathroom door, Jenny snorted. "Yeah, it actually is kind of my business, since my ass is keeping you fed. If it were up to me, I wouldn't take the deal. Something tells me that that little douche needs you a lot more than you need him. If Eddie was right and there are a ton of you bloodsuckers out there, why would he pick you, out of all the people in the world, to turn these dudes?" She ripped open a bag of Doritos and chomped on one loudly as she talked. "You're like a soccer mom. He needs someone violent and ruthless. Someone like that Betty chick." She pointed a chip at Veronica as if she were about to make another insulting point.

"I can be ruthless too," Veronica said defensively. "Maybe he only wants my blood to turn these men because I've got the hormonal craziness of a menopausal woman pulsing through my veins. My soldiers could call themselves the Hot Flashes and take out every person who even looks at them funny. If it were Betty, they'd just be called the Bitches, and no man wants that."

"The Hot Flashes? Now that's funny, but I think you're more like a warm blanket, fresh out of the dryer." She crunched another chip.

"That's probably why he wants me. I'm passive and predictable and I've got the blood lust under control. Well, for the most part I do." Not even she was convinced of this statement. It wasn't about the quest for blood anymore. It was more about feeling powerful and in control, even in the most uncontrollable situations. Part of her would miss that.

"Yeah, well, he'll have more control over you, and you might not get what you want. I don't trust him. He's got a Napoleon complex, but he thinks he's all badass because he knows some things you don't. We can find your ex on our own. It's called Google." Jenny flopped onto her own bed and clutched a pillow to her chest. "I still don't get it. You really want to be mortal again?"

Veronica hadn't given mortality much thought but maybe she should have. After all, even if she became mortal tomorrow, she would never be able to resume her life back in Texas. Even if Seamus made all the trouble disappear, she would have to start over again somewhere else. "You're young. One day you'll understand."

"But once you become mortal, you're going to start aging again and then the next thing you know, you'll be dead."

Veronica glared at her. "So will you and everyone you know. It's called life, and aging is a part of that. I'm not particularly worried about getting older if it means this menopause shit will end. That's the joke of it all. I'm stuck in this well-worn body, but I feel like I'm a hormonal teenager again. Forever. It's horrifying."

"Yeah, I hear what you're saying. My forty-five-year old mother would kill to be frozen in time. Her face is halfway there. She can barely move her lips."

"She should relax. Fifty is the new forty." Veronica stopped clicking the remote and placed it on the nightstand.

"Don't you think you'll be bored when all this vampire glamour is over?"

Veronica laughed. "Glamour? There is nothing glamorous about living in a hyper-alert state for over one hundred years. I want to settle down somewhere and never have to move to another location or find a new job ever again. I also want ice cream, like every night after dinner."

"You're going to get fat if you do that." Jenny glanced at the television. "What the hell are you watching?"

"Knight Rider. I haven't seen this show since..." Veronica sat upright as if she'd seen a ghost.

"What?"

"Is there a phonebook in here?"

Jenny opened the nightstand drawer and pulled out the yellow pages. She tossed it carelessly on Veronica's bed as if it were the dumbest, most cumbersome thing she'd ever seen. "Your phone can do that, you know."

"I would prefer not to use this phone unless it is absolutely necessary." She grabbed the book and thumbed through the pages. Excited, she stopped and scrambled to the side of the bed. She lifted the receiver and dialed the number for the first hospice listing. "Hi, my name is Veronica and I am looking for the nurse who was with my mother when she died. I was out of town at the time and I want to give him something. His name is Michael Knight." She twirled her hair and waited as the woman checked to see if there was a nurse by that name. "Oh, well thank you for checking." She clicked the phone back in its cradle.

She continued down the list of places until she found him. A nurse by the name of Michael Knight was working in a hospice facility outside of Lincoln. His shift started in two hours.

"I found him! I knew it was either going to be Michael Knight or Thomas Magnum." Veronica squealed. "Get dressed, unless you want to stay here."

"Who is Michael Knight? I thought we were looking for a guy named JA?"

"JA is Michael Knight, at least I think he is. God, he's so freaking predictable. He did exactly what I always told him to do. Change his name, work in hospice and he'd be set for life. Except he was stupid to stay here in Nebraska. He's too close to those who might know him."

Jenny slid her jeans back on. "I want to go. That Seamus guy." She bent over to lace up her Converse. "And what the fuck kind of name is Seamus, anyway? He gives me the creeps. I think we need to stay as far away from that douche as possible."

Veronica bounded to her feet, firmly resolved at last. "If I'm right, we may never have to see him again."

43

The Hospice House was exactly what it promised in its half-page color ad—"Quality end of life care in the comfort of our home." It amazed Veronica how far removed people were from the site of death. Family members no longer died in their own homes, at least not by choice. The dying, depending on their expected expiration date, were shuttled off to a hospital, a nursing home or a hospice facility. Old age used to be revered; now it was simply an embarrassment for those in its clutches. *How dare you grow old and feeble where I can see you?*

"I can't believe I was able to remember that stupid name. I am going to shit a brick if it's him." Veronica darted from the car, practically skipping through the darkened parking lot to the front door. Winded, she turned to Jenny. "Please don't say anything, okay? I don't want to scare him. If you think I'm a warm blanket, wait till you get a load of him. He's a little on the sensitive side."

Inside, a young woman in an official-looking blue blazer and a security badge snoozed at the reception desk. The empty lobby was tastefully decorated with overstuffed furniture, cozy blankets and the newest magazines. The only signs of life were the rainbow assortment of tropical fish in the aquarium. They swam and swayed, serving as the stress-reducing focal point of the room.

"Good security." Veronica stopped at the desk, but as the woman let out a snore, she took it as a sign from her higher power. Maybe it would be better to surprise Michael Knight. The longer she lingered at the desk, the more her heart pounded. She had no idea how she would be received. She looked around the lobby and the two hallways that led in opposite directions. "He's got to be lurking around here somewhere." She waved Jenny to follow her to the right.

"Are people dying here? Like right now?" Jenny shivered, zipping up her red hoodie.

"I don't know about right now, but this is where some people go to die. I work at a place like this in Fort Worth. It's not quite as homey, more like a hospital."

The dimly lit hallways were empty. There were no voices, only monitors and oxygen tanks beeping and hissing at each other. A few doors were ajar. As they passed each one, Veronica took a quick peek inside. Most rooms contained skinny old people wrestling with the siren song of long-forgotten voices calling them home. Occasionally she encountered a worried family member at the bed side. If they were awake, she apologized for intruding. At the third to the last door, a handsome orderly appeared in the door frame, writing notes on his clipboard.

He looked exactly the same as the day she turned him. In the year proceeding their very clinical ceremony, JA had worked hard to achieve a gym sculpted body, along with suffering through a painful surgical procedure to produce a full head of hair. His aim was permanent perfection, but he'd only managed to date himself in a stylistically undesirable decade.

Veronica dashed in his direction, as Jenny shuffled behind like a jumpy cat.

"Michael? Michael Knight? Is that really you?" Veronica called out to him. Startled, he looked in her direction and rubbed his eyes. He walked slowly towards her with a questioning look. She ran up to him and wrapped her arms around his taut midsection.

She thought she'd feel something, as she'd loved him once. Instead, it was like seeing her brother. She kissed him quickly on the cheek and playfully ran her fingers through his hair. "Look at you! Those plugs lasted. Well, I'll be damned." She tugged at a lock. "You look good, JA. As good as the day I left you. Where's Kit?" She punched him on the arm, a little harder than she meant to.

JA stiffened and pushed her away. "What are you doing here? Is this about last night?"

Veronica didn't have to try hard to feign ignorance. "What happened last night?"

JA shook his head. "There was some strange man here. He tried to get me to eat a cookie in front of him and then he cornered me in the bathroom."

So maybe Veronica wasn't the only one who'd gotten an audience with Seamus. "Maybe he thought you were cute."

JA scowled at her affected nonchalance. "He was trying to prove something. He whipped out his phone and took a photo of us standing in front of the mirror. Neither of us reflected. Did you send him here or something?"

"No." She knew it had to be Seamus, but JA was a simple man, and talk of the CIA would complicate things. "Is there somewhere we could talk?" She looked around the empty halls.

She could feel his impatience as he glanced over his shoulder. "The last room on the right is free, but you need to make it quick. I'm the only one here tonight."

"Jenny, you stay out here." Veronica leaned closer. "If you see Seamus, scream. Okay?"

"Whatever." She clutched her phone and slid down the wall to sit on the floor.

JA flipped on the light and closed the door behind them. Like the first night she met him, he was irritated and on edge. "Okay, what's going on? I haven't heard from you since I can't even remember. What year was it?"

"Ninety-four." The year she moved to Texas.

"You didn't even have the decency to say goodbye to me. I came home from my shift and you were gone. No note, no nothing." He gnawed at the edge of his thumb nail.

"But look at you. You survived. I'm sure the lady at the twenty-four-hour fitness helped. Or was it ladies? I forget." She couldn't help but dig up some dirt to justify herself.

"You're still bitter about that?" He sat down on the bed and jiggled his right leg. "What do you want from me? A job? Or are you here to apologize for your cruelty and beg for my forgiveness?" His voice cracked with emotion. He scowled and pressed both feet firmly onto the floor.

Veronica was surprised that her absence, or even her presence, meant anything to him. He was always distant, unless she'd hurt his pride. "Actually, I am." She sat down next to him and gently rested her hand on his leg. "What I did to you was stupid. I robbed you of the possibility of a normal life."

"And then you left me to do all this by myself," he stammered.

It wasn't easy to conjure up sincerity—theirs had been a marriage of convenience from the start. But Veronica tried to imagine the better person that JA might have someday become, if she hadn't left him with a permanent case of arrested development. *That* man deserved more of an apology than she could ever give. "Listen, I know you thought you wanted to be immortal at the time, but I turned you for the wrong reasons. I wanted to continue our companionship and you pressed the issue, when I knew that the life I was bringing you into was lonely and filled with death. I'm truly sorry for the pain I've caused you. All of it."

His eyes widened in fear as his body betrayed him. Grasping at his stomach, he fell dramatically onto the tile floor as if he'd been shot, squirming and whimpering like a child. "What is going on?" He simpered and belched. "I think I'm going to be sick."

"You're not." She extended her arm. "Get up. That floor is a germ fest and you really will get sick if you stay down there."

He remained immobile. She didn't want to force the issue as the deed was definitely done. Veronica could feel his soul leave her body, but it barely registered, like the faint fluttering of fourth-month fetal movement. She rubbed at her own stomach, to see if it was somehow miraculously flattened. It wasn't. There was only one soul renting space now and it was a big one. Seamus had already confirmed her fears—Kevin Black's soul might be there awhile. Relieved at the relative ease of JA's transition, whimpering aside, she looked down at him and smiled maternally. "Come on now, let's get up before you get a nasty case of old age."

He pushed himself up from the floor and brushed off his scrubs. Veronica patted his back. "There, there," she cooed.

She led him into the bathroom like a child. The bathroom light was dim with a pink undertone, producing a much more flattering reflection than the fluorescent bulbs that made everyone look sickly.

"There you are," she said.

Startled by his reflection, he slammed his hands on the counter to steady himself. "Holy mother of Jesus. What have you done, Veronica?" He leaned in closer to the mirror, inspecting his face. "Oh great. Why didn't you tell me my nose was covered in blackheads? I've looked like this the whole time! No wonder I can't keep a girlfriend."

"I don't think you can blame your blackheads on that one. Your work schedule sucks, you're cold all the time and I imagine you don't wine and dine these girlfriends of yours. But now you can." Distracted by her own reflection, she wished the entire world could be lit like this.

"What do you mean?" He turned on the water and splashed his face.

"Have you turned someone else?" Frustrated by his show of vanity, she turned off the water.

"No, of course not. I had no desire or need for that. And after what happened with you, I didn't think it was a good idea to trap someone else into this lifestyle." He dried his face with a towel and flattened his hair. "Look at that mullet. Dear Lord. I've been kidnapped by the 80s."

"All you need is a Member's Only jacket and you'd be good to go." She tousled his hair again. "You can now cut your hair or grow it out however you want. At least I think you can. Do hair transplants grow?"

"Stop touching me!" He backed away from her and returned to his reflection. "How would I able to do that?" He inspected his teeth. "And my teeth. They're so yellow. I should have had them whitened when I had the chance."

"Listen to me. You are no longer what you were. You are now free to live your life during the day with the rest of the world. You can sleep at night and eat whatever you want. Actually, JA, you've always been free to walk outside during the day. That was just a giant lie perpetuated by some novelist a long, long time ago."

"Are you saying I'm not a…?" He whipped around to face her.

"No. You're not. You're mortal again."

"Wait a second. What did you just do?" His eyes narrowed and his nostril's flared, like a bull about to charge.

"I gave you your soul back."

"Well, undo it! You didn't even ask me if I wanted my soul back. You just went ahead and did whatever you wanted, like you always do." He kicked the trashcan. It flew into the shower stall. "I was perfectly fucking happy the way I was. You need…" His face reddened as he grabbed her by the shoulders.

"I can't." Her teeth shot out in fear. She tried to loosen herself from his grip.

"Of course, you can! You better turn me again, or I'll…" He tightened his grip, pressing his thumbs into her neck.

"Or you'll what? Kill me? Let me go before I do something I'll regret." She dug in her nails.

He pushed her away and stormed out of the room. Overwhelmed by heat and the desire to strike out against him, she splashed her face and checked her teeth in the mirror. They weren't moving. Outside the room, Jenny leaned against the wall.

"Where did he go?"

"Down that way." She pointed down the hall. "You sure pissed him off. Did it work?"

"Yes. Just give me another minute." She trotted towards the lounge and found him staring at the glowing vending machine. She walked up behind him. "I don't want us to part this way."

JA stared straight ahead, boring virtual holes into the Cheez-Its behind the glass. "Fuck you."

"Look, they've got Snickers. That was always your favorite."

He pulled out his wallet and slid a bill into the cash slot. "A9," he murmured and carefully pressed the buttons.

"Dove huh?"

"Go away. I've never had one, and I want to try it. I can, can't I?"
He reached into the slot and retrieved the candy bar. Veronica looked
him in the eye and nodded silently. He tore it open with care and
nibbled like a rodent tasting the outside edge of baited cheese.

A stoop-shouldered janitor pushed his cart past the lounge and
stopped. "You eating a candy bar, Michael?"

"Yeah, the diet's over." He popped it in his mouth, devouring it in
one bite.

"I was starting to worry about you. Have two." The man chuckled
and wheeled his cart away.

Veronica leaned against the back of a couch. "Please. It was never
my intention to hurt you. I left that night because I thought your life
would be better off without me."

"It wasn't." He took another bite of the candy bar.

"You can start over, you know. Do something new. Get your teeth
whitened. Date lots of women. Get fat. Whatever. The world is a whole
new place again."

"Get out of here before I call security." He glared at her with an
intensity she'd never seen before. "Something I should have done
years ago."

THE WORDS "except when to do so would injure them or others"
repeated in her head fifteen minutes too late. Her words had injured
JA, but there was no way she could take them back or return him to his
previous state. She could, but she didn't want to. With adrenaline
fueling each step, she dashed down the hall to find Jenny. They needed
to get as far away from this place as soon as possible.

She didn't trust Seamus, nor did she trust JA. Hurt people hurt
people and she didn't want to be present when the proverbial bomb
dropped. She'd lit the fuse ages ago by using people for her own benefit. Even in making direct amends to those she'd injured, she remained
selfish and self-centered. It was now merely a game of crossing people
off her list in order to achieve something she hadn't given much

thought to. Her words could have sentenced Mary to death and she'd be facing the same question she confronted the night she turned her—what kind of death do I deliver?

Only now did she realize that it wasn't her choice to make.

44

DETROIT—THE SEVENTIES

On a typical night, the Emergency Room at St. John's was understaffed and out of control. Tonight was no different. Veronica disliked the hectic pace, but with it came easy access to the bleeding—a lick here, a sip there, and it would sustain her until she could find a suitable meal. The full moon promised and usually delivered a nonstop night of chaos, which was both bad and good for the citizens of Detroit. Its luminous presence taunted her from the front window of the packed emergency room. There were no bleeders yet, only flu-ridden feverish folks, bruised and battered slip-and-falls and the drunken men who'd lost their midnight brawl.

She was deep into her shift, working triage, when she spotted the first man she'd ever truly desired. Dressed in black from head to toe, he staggered through the front door of the packed waiting room. Blood oozed from his shoulder, coloring the ends of his long salt and pepper ponytail. His angular face was tanned and weathered. What struck her initially about him, besides his crystal blue eyes, was his demeanor. He was calm, almost too calm, as he strode towards her, his large black work boots thudding heavily with each step. She grabbed his arm to steady his large frame, but he was the one who seemed to lead her to the examination room, as if he'd performed this waltz before. Closing the curtain, he edged his way onto the paper-covered cot and laid back with a heavy sigh.

"Left shoulder," he said.

She quickly cut the sopping shirt, revealing a scrambled mass of intertwining tattoos in various shades of red, black and blue. "Devil Hogs" was scrolled prominently across his muscular chest in solid black ink. As she rolled him on his side to inspect his back, he groaned.

"Fuck, that hurts," he said.

"Hunting accident, I take it?" She inspected the wound hungrily, her breath hot on his neck.

Rolling onto his back, he smiled up at her. "I love a woman who can handle the sight of a little blood." He looked down at his shoulder. "Is it still in there?"

"The bullet?"

He nodded, holding her gaze.

"The bullet's gone, but there might be some fragments left behind. I'll need to irrigate it, which won't be the most fun you've ever had. If you want pain relief, I've got to call the doctor." She shifted slightly. "But I get the feeling you don't want that to happen, do you?" She pressed a sterile bandage against his torn flesh.

"Yes, let's just keep this moment between us. You're a smart lady. I like that about you."

She could feel a wave of heat rising from her chest. Soon her pit sweat would soak through her shirt, increasing the anxiety. "I'm smart, but I'm not gullible. I could get into a lot of trouble for this. You are a trauma call, but I'm going to let you slide this one time if you promise never to come back. Let's make this quick."

"Now why would I promise that? I like it here. A pretty woman tending to my tiny little BB gun wound." He smiled, but only one corner of his mouth lifted... as if he were hiding something.

"BB gun, huh? Looks to me like a .22. A few inches to the left and your family would be picking out a coffin right now."

He laughed, then grimaced in pain. "I'm lucky that way. The Night Reapers sent Elmer Fudd to deliver their message."

"The Night Reapers? Sounds menacing. Is Elmer your hunting buddy?" Veronica raised her eyebrows.

"Yeah, we were shooting rabbits." He attempted to sit up.

"Uh, uh, uh. You need to lay back down there, Bugs."

"It's Mr. Black." He collapsed back down on the cot with a sigh. "But you can call me Kevin."

"Alright, Kevin." She placed her fingers on his wrist. Inhaling deeply, she counted the beats of his pulse. The flow of his blood was slow but strong, while hers accelerated from the heady mix of attraction and blood. From his constricted pupils and tolerance of pain, she gathered he was high on heroin. She inspected his thick arms for track marks, but if he was shooting it, it wasn't in his skull-and-flame-covered arms.

"I'm going to get some fluids into you. We can skip the catheter if you promise to stay still. Are you high on anything? Alcohol, drugs?"

"No, ma'am."

Veronica winced at the formality and implications of being called ma'am. He was no Southerner with good manners. "You can call me Veronica."

"I think I'll just call you V. Some of my favorite things begin with the letter V. Venison, violets, vodka, va...."

"Vagina? Or were you going for Valium? Now, now, Kevin Black. If I weren't an old, wise woman, I'd think you were trying to flirt with me. I'm smart, remember? I'm pretty sure you've had enough drugs for the evening." He watched her every move with interest, as she prepped his arm and inserted the IV.

"You're good with a needle too, there, V. Ever been on a bike?" His expression softened.

"Are we talking ten-speed or Harley?" She removed the bloody bandage, tossed it in the trash can to savor later, and placed a fresh pad against his shoulder. "I'm just going to press down a little bit to stop the bleeding."

"Cold hands." He smiled his crooked smile, engulfing her frigid hands with his own. "Let me warm them up a bit."

She kept her hand under his as the whimpering cries and painful shouts from other rooms faded into the distance. "Warm heart," she said under her breath, as if to remind herself of that long-forgotten fact.

"I bet you do."

———————

IN ALL HER YEARS, Veronica had never encountered a man who emanated danger equal to her own. Unwisely, she found it intoxicating. Kevin Black left her emergency room as unceremoniously as he'd entered. Red warning flags were everywhere, but it didn't matter, Veronica was already hooked.

45

PRESENT

As they crossed the border into Iowa, Veronica felt desperate to call Frank, if only to hear the sound of his voice. Surely, somehow, in a fifteen-minute conversation they could solve the Kevin Black problem and plan the rest of their lives together.

But she knew better. At one time, Frank had been willing to let her change him, but she wondered if he'd be open to leaving his life behind and starting over somewhere new. Immortality sounded infinitely more exciting and sexier than relocating their belongings in a rented U-Haul to the suburbs of a new state. Not only were Frank's familial roots deeply embedded in his home state, Texas pride dripped from his pores. He wouldn't go easily.

Veronica stared at the phone, running her long fingers over the keypad. She placed it back in the cup holder with a sigh. Sometimes it was easier not to know the answer.

"Do you by any chance still have that letter I wrote on the plane?" Veronica stared down at Jenny's backpack, nestled near her own feet.

"I don't know. Maybe. I'm tired. Can you take over?" Jenny's jet-black hair glistened in the sun, whipping around her face from the open window. Against the black Ramones t-shirt, the orange coloring of her skin had faded to what must have been her normal color. If

Veronica hadn't known her story, Jenny simply looked like a normal, healthy teenager on a Sunday drive with her strange aunt.

"Sure. I'm going to drive straight through to Detroit, though. I don't know how that Seamus guy can track us, but he can."

"I bet he's totally pissed that you blew him off, too." Jenny pulled over to the side of the road.

"Thanks for reminding me." Veronica hopped out of the car and stretched in the sun. She felt lighter, even though that was impossible. The weight of a few souls didn't amount to much, if anything. *28 grams times five?* Math was not her forte. A semi cab without its trailer slowed down and pulled to the side of the road in front of them. Veronica panicked.

"Get in!" She shouted and dove into the driver's seat.

Jenny scrambled for the passenger seat and slammed the door. "Who is it?"

"I don't fucking know, but I don't want to find out." Checking the side mirror, she gunned the car onto the interstate. "Where's the gun?"

"Glove box." Jenny patted the door like an old trusty friend.

Veronica checked the rearview mirror as the truck faded in the distance. "They're not following us, whoever they were."

"I think you're just being paranoid." Jenny picked up Veronica's phone. "The internet on these things sucks."

"What do you need to see on the internet?"

"I don't know. I could check my Facebook, look at Instagram, watch a few YouTube videos." The phone vibrated in her hand. Mary's name and face illuminated the screen. "How did Mary get your number?"

"I texted it to her. Put it on speakerphone."

Jenny swiped at the screen and placed the phone on the middle console.

"Hey, Mary," Veronica said. "Are you making a killing yet?"

"She's making a killing, alright." Seamus sounded as if he were at the bottom of a well. "Aren't you dear?" Mary's muffled voice echoed in the background. "Since you wouldn't play nice, we're using one of your former recruits. She reflects. We like that about her. It's more trackable."

"Let her go, Seamus!" Veronica roared at the tiny phone.

"You're on the naughty list, Ms. Bouchard. I don't appreciate being stood up. We're on our way to see Beatrice Prendergast. Does that name ring any bells?"

Veronica remained silent, hands on the wheel, running her tongue along the sharpness of her teeth.

"You have three days. Two recruits for your daughter. It will be a nice, tidy, even exchange. Don't worry about finding us. We'll find you."

The line went dead.

Jenny picked up the phone before Veronica could hurl it out the window. "Dude, he's psycho. You need to take his tiny ass out."

Veronica sped past the blue "Welcome to Michigan" sign as if being dared. It wasn't the police or the CIA she was worried about inside its state lines.

"I need to find Kevin Black first."

46

DETROIT – 1978

Veronica pretended to sip a rum and Coke while staring at the random album covers that plastered the nicotine-stained walls of Chuck's Wagon. Behind the horseshoe-shaped bar, Kevin ignored her familiar presence, playing a game of dice with Henry, an old timer with a fresh check from the state burning a hole in his pocket. The opening notes of "Night Fever" boomed from the jukebox.

Kevin twitched. "Which one of you dicks played that fucking song?" He scanned the sparse crowd with a menacing glare.

"Hey, I paid for that song. I don't know what you're complaining about. You're the asshole that put it on there in the first place." Henry slammed his cup on the wooden counter. He peeked at his roll, then set his cup to the side, revealing three sixes. "It's a good song. Something you can dance to. Not that you would know anything about dancing."

Kevin took a long swig from his beer. "Who are you planning on dancing with, Henry?" He waved his arm at the bedraggled regulars, shook his cup and pounded it on the bar. Lifting the cup with dramatic flourish, he glared down at his unfortunate roll.

"Your woman looks like she could cut a rug." Henry laughed and gulped the remnants of his gin and tonic. "If I had a gal like that, I wouldn't let her sit around in this dump." Henry held out his arthritic hand, waving his swollen fingers.

Veronica stared steadfastly down at the last feebly popping soda bubbles in her black glass. She had long since learned to keep her mouth shut.

Kevin grabbed a wad of cash from his tip jar, counted out ten ones and placed them in Henry's palm. "You're a lucky bastard." He swept the dice back into the cup and placed it on the back bar. Henry ambled out the door with a smile on his heavily lined face.

Kevin surveyed the remaining stragglers, while quieting "Lay Down Sally" on the jukebox. "Okay, assholes. You don't have to go home, but you can't stay here." He began herding the slowpokes to the exit. With a drunken moan, they reluctantly peeled themselves from their chairs as he flipped the lights off over the pool table. A Miller High Life neon illuminated the darkened bar with a soft glow.

Veronica grabbed a wet bar towel from the drip rail. *When you get busy, you get better.* "What's your hurry? You got a date or something?" The hurry made her worry.

"I figured we might do a little dancing, but I gotta shut this place down first. Wouldn't want to attract any pigs to our party." Three teenage pool players wobbled to the exit with key chains jangling from their limp fingers. Kevin opened the door and followed them outside into the frigid night.

"I'm Not in Love" played low on the jukebox. Veronica hummed along as she wiped down the sticky tables and dumped the overflowing ashtrays into the trash bin. Kevin returned from the parking lot, rubbing his arms. Hoping his promise of a dance wasn't just an empty threat, she dropped the towel and shimmied in his direction.

"Just going to check the restrooms." He passed without meeting her hopeful gaze, disappearing into the back rooms of the bar.

The bell over the door jingled. Veronica resumed her cleaning duties. "We're closed."

Randy Rogers, a squat, muscular kid with a buzz cut and a swastika tattoo on the inside of his wrist, pushed through the front door as if he owned the place. "Kevin here?"

"He's in back," Veronica said, averting her eyes to the beer covered table. She didn't dare look up. Last time she saw Randy, she'd walked in on him with a scale and a pound of heroin in the storage room.

He strode towards her with a swagger in his step, radiating coked-up confidence. "You don't drink, you don't smoke and you sure as shit don't shoot up. So, what exactly are you doing here at three in the morning? Are you the new janitor or something?"

Intimidated, she backed up slowly into the wall as sweat streamed down the inside of her shirt. She zipped her lips shut, causing her nostrils to flare. She needed to slow her breath and appear unthreatened, but drugs made her jumpy.

"Cat got your tongue? I asked you a question, bitch." With one meaty hand, he grabbed her face, squeezing her mouth open. "Answer me!" Spittle spewed her pale face. With his free hand, he lifted her shirt, exposing her fleshy stomach. Leaning into her, he reached around to molest the fiery skin of her back. "The narc's not wearing a wire," he shouted towards the back of the bar. "Unfortunate decision, I'm afraid." He reached behind his back and lifted his revolver to her temple.

Her teeth strained through her gums. "I'm not a narc, Randy. I'm a nurse," she whimpered. "Please don't do this."

"Not my decision." Without hesitation, he fired. The blast echoed through the empty bar.

The impact forced her exploding head backwards into the wall as her body slid slowly to the floor, leaving a trail of crimson-tinged brain matter in her wake. She closed her eyes for dramatic effect. She figured he'd expect that. Prone and panicked from the betrayal, she couldn't stop her eyes from twitching.

"Cunt's dead," he shouted.

Jingling his keyring, Kevin stomped from the back of the bar, stopping between Veronica's sprawled legs. "Jesus. I told you to do it out back. Now you're gonna have to patch that wall." He peered out the front window. "Where's Eddie? I need this cleaned up by morning and I sure as hell ain't gonna be the one to do it."

He knew.

"Busy, I guess." Randy kicked Veronica's foot. "I hate rats."

Kevin knew.

"Take the van and get her out of here." He tossed Randy his keys. "Usual place. Got it?"

Knew, hell. Kevin was the one who ordered Randy to kill her.

Shocked to her core, Veronica remained motionless, silently regenerating in a pool of her own coagulating blood.

"I don't know if she's a rat or not, but she never did anything, even when I offered. Hell, she didn't even drink. Crazy bitch pretended. What kind of person does that?"

"A narc."

"You know what? You're probably right. I caught her dumping her drinks in the trash." Kevin sighed as he kneeled at her side. "She's still breathing." He felt her neck. "I told you one shot through the head, Randy. I swear, if you want something done right, you've got to do the goddamn thing yourself."

As the gun's barrel entered her mouth, she opened her grey eyes. With rage and adrenaline fueling her, she wrestled him on top of her body and latched onto his neck with a ferocity she'd never expressed before. The gun slid from his reach.

"What the fuck?" Randy aimed in their direction.

"Shoot her!" Kevin screamed, struggling with her rabid body.

As they tangled on the blood-streaked floor, Randy pulled the trigger without aim or purpose. The first shot exploded in her shoulder. With Kevin's blood fortifying her, she shielded herself with his weakening frame. Randy emptied the chamber. Two bullets tore through Kevin's abdomen and into hers. The other two ricocheted off the yellowed wall. As Randy leapt forward, she released herself from Kevin's neck and pushed his broken body off hers.

"You can't kill me, so don't even think about it." She spat. "He's dead and I swear to god, if you shoot me again, you're next." She wiped Kevin's blood from her chin.

"I'll get you for this, bitch!" With a pained expression, he bolted from the bar.

"Yeah, you and what army," she mumbled as the low rumble of his chopper grew fainter by the second.

Through tears of pain and anger, she assessed what was left of Kevin. Palpating his bloodied neck, she found a faint pulse. She pushed herself up from the floor and surveyed the horrific scene. "I did not deserve this," she muttered to the silent bar.

She gazed down at Kevin's body, a body she once relished and enjoyed. Her voice rose. "I did not deserve any of this. Death is easy, motherfucker. But this? The shit that I've had to endure isn't for weak men like you."

Veronica stared down at the pulpy mess. "But now you're going to know what it feels like."

47

PRESENT

I n the morning sun, the city of Detroit looked as used and casually discarded as a twenty-dollar hooker. People, places and things often looked considerably different in the light of day, but this was beyond that. The city she once loved was now a fallen empire with decay on display in every boarded window. Every corner she turned appeared worse than the last. Abandoned buildings, crumbling pavement and an impending sense of doom seemed to pervade the streets. In the not-so-distant past, this city had flourished, but now it looked like the players had spitefully taken their ball and gone home.

Jenny was fast asleep in the reclined passenger seat as Veronica cruised past one of Kevin's old haunts, the Stonehouse. A solid line of Harleys sat sentry-like in front of the old farmhouse bar. As she had decades ago, Veronica quickly skimmed over each bike's detail work, hoping to find a black tank with a blue-eyed devil painted on the side. Nothing. She gunned her car's middle-aged engine and sputtered down the block.

INSIDE THE SAFETY of their chain hotel Veronica locked herself in the bathroom, dialing Frank's number with paranoid precision. He'd be at work, but he usually picked up calls from strange numbers. He was a more than willing sponsor to any man who requested his help. Some of these relationships lasted years, while others only days or weeks. Sobriety was a lot easier to imagine than practice day in and day out.

"Frank, it's me," she whispered into the phone.

"This isn't a good idea." His voice sounded as distant as the miles between them.

She was painfully aware that calling him wasn't a smart move, but somehow it didn't matter anymore. She was at her bottom, ready to accept the consequences of her actions, whatever that might be— prison, death, or running scared towards a future that would only echo her past.

Numb from the cold reception, she sat on the edge of the tub and planted both feet firmly on the floor. "Listen, I know it's stupid to call you, but you deserve a goodbye. You've probably realized it by now, but I can never come back home. Hell, I don't even know if I'm going to make it out of here alive." She was trying to come across as tough, but her voice was shaking. She swallowed hard and licked her parched lips. "But if I do, Frank, I give you my word that you'll be the first person I'll call. I love you."

His voice was gruff and firm in her ear. "Don't call this number again."

She snapped the cheap device in two as a tsunami of tears and snot ran down her face. Desperate to muffle the hurt animal sounds of her sadness, she grabbed a bleach-scented towel from above the toilet and buried her face in its stiffness. There was no way to stuff her feelings back down, so she wallowed in them.

Compared to what she would soon be facing, this was nothing, but it hurt more than bullet wounds or the boring monotony of her endless days. At this exact moment, she couldn't face knowing whether he was protecting or rejecting her with his curt and callous response. She didn't have the will to find out. At least not yet.

As Jenny studied the giant room service menu, Veronica flipped through the pages of the phone book. Her face hurt from crying. As much as she hated to admit it, she needed help beyond Jenny's bravado. She wasn't accustomed to asking for it, especially in a matter as delicate and dangerous as Kevin Black. There was no way she would be able to find the man on her own and she sure as hell wasn't going to crawl back to Seamus with her tail between her legs. There was only one option... one she hoped still had connections with lawless men and where to find them.

"Eddie? It's Veronica. I need your help."

Within the hour, Eddie was at their door. His loud knock startled Veronica. She peered through the peephole to make sure it was him. He was alone, dressed in the same workman's outfit he'd worn at the museum. She swung open the door and invited him in, quickly bolting the lock and securing the chain.

"Eddie, did you ever run into a guy named Kevin Black when you were, you know, working? He used to ride with the Devil Hogs. Long black hair, light blue eyes." Her brow furrowed at the thought of him.

Eddie rumpled Jenny's hair and tugged at her ear phones. "Hi Jenny." He waved his enormous hand in front of her face. She flashed a quick smile, revealing her broken front tooth. Moving to the edge of the bed to join the conversation, her bare feet barely reached the floor. She raked her chipped toe-nails through the patterned industrial carpet.

"Kevin Black," he laughed. "Yeah, I know him." Eddie sat down at the desk and rubbed his hands together. "I think the more important question is, how do you know him?"

"We dated briefly, very briefly, back in the late 70s." She paced the room. "And I'm the one who turned him."

"You turned Kevin Black?" Eddie bolted from his chair. "That's huge."

"Yes, I turned him. Just like I turned you. Why does that surprise you?"

He sat back down with a smile on his face. "We ran in the same circles back in the day. My connections were a bit more discreet about their business dealings. His weren't. How in the world did someone like you hook up with him?"

"Contrary to what you may think, Eddie, I'm not a saint. Far from it." She plopped down on the edge of the other bed and kicked her shoes off. "Okay. Long story short. Good looking bad boy likes old chick and old chick likes feeling young and alive again. She ignores all signs that being with him is a very bad idea."

Eddie raised his brows in disbelief. "Did he know what you were?"

"No. It only lasted a year and he was either drunk or high half the time. We weren't doing a lot of daytime activities if you catch my drift." She glanced over at Jenny. "One night after closing, we were at his bar and in walks one of his lieutenants or whatever they're called. I forget. Anyway, I think his name was Randy Rogers."

"Randy's still around." Eddie's voice deepened.

"Great. That's wonderful. He's such a charming fellow. So, Randy pulls out his gun and shoots me point blank in the head. I, of course, recovered. Scared the shit out of both of them. Randy keeps firing, a little less steady this time, and accidentally shoots Kevin. Randy takes off and leaves me with the mess."

"Sounds like something Randy would do." Eddie took a deep breath. "I've cleaned up a lot of Randy's messes."

"I turned Kevin to punish him. As crazy as it sounds, I had feelings for the man. I wanted him to suffer as much as I had."

"So where is the douchebag? Let's go get him." Jenny interrupted.

"I need to make amends to him, not kill him."

"He's here in Detroit, but you won't get near him," Eddie said. "He's still the same cocky asshole he always was, but now he's untouchable, thanks to you and your magical kissing powers."

"Is he still riding with the Devil Hogs?"

"No, not the Devil Hogs. Now they call themselves the Dark Lords. He really let that vampire shit go to his head."

"You have any way to get a hold of him?" Veronica's heart leapt in her chest as the situation became startlingly more real.

Eddie made a so-so gesture. "He used to use me for emergency cleanups, but not much lately."

"They sell drugs, these Dark Lords?" Jenny asked. "Like meth?"

"No. Don't even think about it. I promised Carl to watch over you and I'm not going to let you buy drugs from a bunch of psychos."

Eddie waved off the idea. "She wouldn't be buying from him, anyway. Unless she's got a million lying around and wants to go into business."

"All I've got is a debit card." Jenny returned to her phone.

"Well, then where do I find him? Do you know where he hangs out? Where he lives? Do you know any of that?"

"I'm sorry, but I don't. He called me when he needed my services and never with the same number. Seamus might know."

That wasn't what Veronica wanted to hear. "Seamus isn't very happy with me right now."

"Did you tell him about Mary?" Jenny asked.

Eddie got deadly serious at the mention of her name. "What about Mary?"

"He called me from Mary's phone. Says I'm on his naughty list because I wouldn't take his deal. Did you?"

"I never turned anyone, but I did a few questionable things for Seamus's spooks locally. That's how I found you. He promised that if I did exactly what I was told to do, I could become mortal again. And that's exactly what happened. I just didn't expect it to be quite that easy."

"Why did you agree to it?"

Eddie had the good grace to look slightly guilty at that. "He kept me well supplied with food. I trusted him. I had no reason not to. He seemed to know what was what and he had blood. Lots of it. I don't know about you, Veronica, but I was hungry." He coughed.

"I know." She bent forward and clasped her head between her hands. Tears welled in her eyes. "He has my daughter." Her voice cracked and she reached for her trusty towel.

"Oh, god. Listen. He needs us. I take that back. He needs you, just as much as you need him."

"Seamus seems to know Kevin. Says I won't be able to get near him without his help."

Eddie sat back with a thoughtful expression. "You won't. But maybe we can get Kevin to come to you."

48

Veronica approached the counter of Sun City Tan, while Jenny thumbed through a dog-eared magazine at the front bench. A leather-faced blonde stubbed out her cigarette and flung open the front door, sounding a buzzer throughout the tiny reception area.

"Smoke break. Sorry to keep you gals waiting. Is this your first time with us?" A plume of smoke rose from her lined lips.

"No, ma'am," Veronica said. "She won't be tanning, but I will. I prefer the sunless tanning. You do that here?"

"Yes, ma'am. Did you shave and exfoliate this morning?" The woman eyed Veronica's face skeptically as if hoping to dissuade her.

"Nope. I can't manage to do either of those things." Veronica set her purse on the counter. "Here's the deal. I want to be as unrecognizable as you can make me. I want to leave here looking like I've been dumped in the dirt."

The woman shuffled behind the counter, chuckling softly to herself. "Dirt, huh?"

"Or Cheetos dust. I really don't mind if I end up looking smeary and uneven. In fact, I prefer it if I look that way." She pulled out her wallet and laid a twenty on the counter.

"It's thirty-five." The woman rubbed her dark, freckled arm, tapping her acrylic nails on the counter. "Is this some sort of joke or something?"

"Put it on this." Jenny placed her debit card on the counter.

"No, this is absolutely not a joke. I take my spray tanning very seriously."

The woman slid Jenny's Visa through the card machine. "Sign here." She sighed and squinted up at Veronica.

Jenny leaned forward and scribbled her name on the slip. "She'll tip you with cash if you do what she wants." Jenny leaned in and whispered in Veronica's ear. "Whatever you do, don't kill her."

"Okay, let's do this." The woman ambled from behind the counter with a heavy sigh. "But don't bite my head off if you don't like how it looks."

Veronica smiled. "Wouldn't dream of it."

49

"You're not convincing anybody, dude. Your skin looks way more dirty than your clothes." Jenny squatted in a patch of dried mud masquerading as a lawn. "That's why everyone thinks we're full of shit and won't let us hang." She rubbed her jeans with handfuls of the parched earth, then rolled around in it for good measure.

"We are full of shit. Why are you doing that?" Veronica stared down at Jenny over the newly acquired contents of her shopping cart.

"This is what my theater teacher would call method acting. If we want people to believe we're homeless, we need to get dirty. We need to smell!"

"No one is ever going to believe that we're homeless. I should have never listened to Eddie's crazy idea. If Kevin likes to hunt, he'll have to hunt me in my hotel room." Veronica looked towards the overpass. A small group of people gathered in front of three makeshift tents. Near them, a man holding a cardboard sign peered passively at the drivers held captive by the red light on the service road.

"I'm ready whenever you are." Jenny rose from the dirt and stretched her arms to the sky.

"I've done some ridiculous things in my life, but pretending to be homeless to attract an ex-boyfriend is a new low for me." Veronica kneeled into the dirt, then laid on her back. She tentatively moved her arms and legs back and forth, making a dirt angel. "I will be so glad when all of this is over." Her cheap, mismatched thrift store clothing now looked as mottled as the complexion of her spray-tanned face.

"Me too, because honestly, all this wandering around without a bed or a shower kind of sucks. The only thing sustaining my interest is the fact that I don't have to go to rehab." Jenny ran her fingers through her unkempt hair. "I take that back. Watching you get your first taste of bacon is going to be totally worth it." Jenny climbed up on the cart and posed for takeoff. "Time's ticking, woman. Let's roll."

Veronica stared up into the darkening, cloudless sky. "It doesn't even seem like bacon is a possibility. And Ingrid. What have I..."

"You are one apology away from bacon and your daughter, bitch. Let's do this before I book a room at the no-tell motel down the block." Jenny pushed the cart forward and drifted slowly down the sidewalk.

Veronica maneuvered herself into a standing position and walked slowly behind the rickety cart. Even though Jenny was raised in a McMansion with a full-time soccer mom, she would have a much easier time fitting in on the street with the many addicts rooted in its cracks and crevices.

A chopper rumbled by and stopped at the light. Veronica turned to look at the leather-clad rider. His salt-and-pepper hair was tightly cropped, but his neatly trimmed goatee was pure white. There was no way it could be Kevin, but there was a strange familiarity about him. He handed something small to the man holding the sign. It was more than likely drugs, as he quickly deposited it in the front pocket of his tattered, drooping denims. As soon as the light turned green, the bike peeled out like a fire had been lit under it.

"Why do men do that? Do they think they're impressing us with their ability to make noise?" Jenny pushed the cart into the street.

Veronica checked for oncoming traffic. "They do it because they do it. The rest is just a story." She followed Jenny into the litter-strewn street. "You can't judge a person by what they look like or the dumb shit they do. Maybe he's late for his colonoscopy. We'll never know."

Jenny cleared the street and pushed forward to the tents.

Veronica allowed several feet between them, but Jenny's voice rang among the ruins. "What's up?" she said with the nonchalance of youth and inexperience. "Would it be cool if we hung here tonight?"

"Suit yourself." A young woman picked at her acne-covered chin, then pointed behind her. "The tents are off limits, unless you brought party favors."

"And when you say party favors, what do you mean by that?" Veronica sauntered behind Jenny and placed her arm protectively around her shoulder.

"Balloons and streamers. Gah, mom." Jenny rolled her eyes at the strawberry blonde. "I'm Jenny and she's just bitter."

Two men laughed. "She's funny," one said and guzzled from his sweating can of Colt 45.

The man with the sign ambled over. "If you want to stay under this pass, you have to earn your keep. It's a good spot and we don't let just anybody stay here." He held out the greasy, well-worn sign.

Veronica didn't trust Jenny alone with these strangers. "Why don't you do it for a while and I'll do it after."

Jenny grabbed the dirty sign and read the message scrawled in black marker. "Homeless and Hungry. Anything Helps. Bless you."

"Is this your first time?"

Jenny nodded.

"Just stand there and look sad. You look just homeless enough that you'll probably make bank. I'm Jess, that's Peaches, and those two clowns are BJ and PJ. They're brothers."

Jenny waved meekly at them. "Jenny."

Jess smiled with expectation as Jenny trotted across the street and stood at the end of the median. A black SUV pulled up to the light. The tinted driver's window rolled down and a white braceleted arm handed over a bottle of water and a crisp bill. As the vehicle drove off Jenny waved the twenty in the air. "Can you believe it? She gave me a twenty!"

Jess reached into his pocket and handed a tiny baggie to Peaches. She jumped to her feet and ducked into the largest tent.

Veronica watched another driver extend their arm towards Jenny.

She eyed the patch of concrete next to Jess and gingerly set herself down. The whole area stunk of urine and desperation.

"You two together?" Jess asked.

"Yes. She's my daughter." Veronica flashed him a look.

"Have you tried the shelter over on Third Avenue? It might be more up your alley." He wiped his nose on the back of his hand.

"We might go there later tonight, but..."

"Their beds fill up pretty fast. If you want to eat or shower, you gotta get there early. They've got a pretty good setup." Jess looked at the tent and licked his gums.

"Yeah, but then they want to preach at you for an hour. If I want to go to church, I'll go to a goddamn church." BJ crushed his beer can and popped open another. "You want one?" He held out a beer to Veronica. His red filmy eyes made her sick to her stomach.

"Thank you, but I'm good. So, Jess. That guy on the bike..."

"What about him? You need something?" Jess scratched at his poorly-tattooed arm. "They deliver."

"I saw that. Is he in some kind of motorcycle gang?"

"Yeah. A lot of them are. But it depends." His voice trailed off as he looked towards the tent.

"On what?" Veronica watched Jenny cupping her hands to take change from a guy in a blue pickup.

"On how you want to pay for whatever it is you want. What's your poison?" He leaned in closer. His body reeked of the unmistakable stench of meth.

Veronica lowered her voice. "Heroin, Oxy, whatever."

"Oh, I see, you like to chill." He looked her in the eye. "Heroin? That shit's expensive. You got money for that?" He eyed her up and down as if trying to figure out where it was hidden.

"Looks like my daughter's making out pretty well over there. What are my payment options?"

Peaches skipped out of the tent and handed the baggie back to Jess. "I'm going to the store. Any of you assholes want anything?"

Jess eyed the baggie. "You are such a fucking hog." He shoved the nearly empty bag in his jeans pocket.

She placed her hands defensively on her hips and flipped her greasy hair. "I earned it. That freak took two pints."

"Hey, it's better than having to touch his ancient dick. Am I right?" Jess handed Peaches a wad of crumpled ones. "Get me a Hot Pocket and a Coke."

Veronica listened in disbelief. Pints. After only two days of wandering the streets, they would have a way in.

50

P aranoid, Veronica watched Jenny as she slept, anxious to make sure she didn't disappear into one of the tents or onto the back of someone's bike. She didn't trust the night, nor did she trust the people within their camp.

As the sky darkened and the traffic slowed, Jess animatedly crept out of his tent like a mustachioed burglar in a vaudeville play. His exaggerated attempt at silence made Veronica feel even more on guard than usual. She acknowledged his odorous presence with a quiet, "hey."

"Can't sleep?" he replied.

"Nope. You?" She rubbed at her eyes.

"I don't think I've slept more than a few hours in over a year." He patted at his pockets, searching for something.

"Meth will do that to you."

"It doesn't do it to her. That woman could sleep through a tornado. I don't understand how she does it." Pulling out a crumpled pack of Winstons from his shirt pocket, he tapped out a cigarette and held out the pack towards Veronica.

"I don't smoke." She rubbed her chin, feeling suddenly emboldened. "Maybe it's the fact that she's donating her blood. That could tire a person out real fast."

"You're probably right. Hell, we can't even sell our blood as often as those assholes take it from her." He took another drag and ashed into the wind.

"Why do you think they want her blood? That seems sort of weird, don't you think?"

Jess sat down, eyeing the street. "I think it's some sort of biker initiation or something." He lit another cigarette. "Hell, I don't know. Can't say that I even care what they do. All I know is that they've got the best shit, and blood's a lot easier to come by than cash."

Jenny sat up, clutching a cheap fleece blanket around her shoulders. "I'll totally make a donation for some crystal. Tell them I have hemochromatosis. Apparently, they love that shit."

Veronica flashed Jenny a "shut it" look.

"I'd give you a bump, but Peaches is a greedy little bitch." He pulled a cell phone out of his pocket. "It's three, but they'll probably come pick you up if you're cool with that."

"She may be cool with that, but I'm not. I've got blood." Veronica stammered.

"Chill, lady." Jess squinted at his phone and dialed the number. "Just so you know, I get a cut for arranging this deal. That's how it works." He looked at Jenny, who nodded in agreement.

They both leaned in as Jess waited for someone to pick up. "It's Jess. I've got two." He lit a cigarette and inhaled deeply. "Yeah, they're chicks. One's older, not bad looking. Could use a shower. The younger one's…"

"Wait a second, what exactly are you arranging?" Veronica interrupted.

"Hold on." Jess muted the phone. "They ain't gonna fuck you or anything, they just don't want me sending any disgusting skanks. Pipe down." He returned to the phone. "Okay. Yeah, thanks man." He shoved the phone in his jeans pocket and turned to Jenny. "Dude's about three miles away. You ready?"

"What about me?" Veronica stood. "She's not going anywhere without me."

"You both can't fit on one bike. There's another dude coming for you and he'll be here in twenty. Chill. Seriously. She'll be fine. They're pretty fucking clinical about it. Way better than those stupid bitches down at the blood bank." He crushed the cigarette and threw it in the gutter.

Veronica felt powerless, as if she were rapidly ascending that first hill on a rickety wooden coaster and there was nothing she could do but clutch the lap bar and surrender to the drop.

"Will you excuse us?" Veronica grabbed Jenny by the arm and led her across the street.

"What is the matter with you? This is what you want, right? They're taking us right to Kevin Black." Jenny's eyes were wild, almost ravenous.

"These men are dangerous." Veronica lowered her voice. "Even before they were vampires, and I don't feel comfortable letting you go in there alone."

"Listen, as soon as I get there, I'll text you the location. You got a new phone, right?"

"Yeah, but..."

"Plus, I've got the gun in my backpack." Jenny whispered.

"That gun won't save you. It'll just piss them off. But it's not going to come to that."

"It will be fine. Where's your faith?"

Veronica forced a smile. Jenny was right. Steps one, two and three. *I can't, you can, and I'm going to let you.* She shivered at the loud thunder of a chopper in the distance. "You'll be fine," she decided out loud. "Just keep your mouth shut. And please, whatever you do, don't snort any of that shit." Veronica embraced Jenny in an awkward hug. Under the dirt, the girl reeked of iron rich blood and fear. Her scent would be intoxicating to Kevin and his crew.

"Yeah, yeah, yeah. I'll be fine, alright? Take it." She handed Veronica the backpack and looked towards the approaching bike. "He's here." She flashed her phone and quickly pocketed it. "I'll text you."

Veronica paced the underpass as the glowing screen of her phone faded to black. "What's taking so long?"

Jess dug into the baggie that the driver handed him. "Fuck if I know. They probably sent Randy. Dude drives like an eighty-five-year-old woman."

The skin on the back of her neck prickled at the sound of that name. "What does this Randy look like?"

"Like one of those ZZ Top dudes. Old, long hair, beard."

"Any tattoos?"

"Yeah, he's got this stupid swastika on his wrist."

Veronica gasped. "Oh, well, I'm Jewish. That won't work. There's no way. In fact..." She swung the backpack over her shoulder and crossed the street. "I've changed my mind. I'm going to the shelter to get clean. Tell Jenny where I went when she gets back." She darted across the darkened street to the Kwiki Mart.

Veronica's heart felt as if it had shot up into her throat as Randy pulled up to the pump, hopped off his bike and began to fuel his tank. The screen of her muted phone lit up.

Shameus is here!!! Where r u?

VERONICA CROUCHED BEHIND THE DUMPSTER, weighing her limited options. There was no way she could take the ride with Randy. He would never transport her to Kevin, and if they put two and two together, Jenny would be dumped in a landfill before dawn. She clutched the backpack to her chest and looked around the empty lot for a car to steal or a lone passenger to hijack. Not even the cashier drove a car to his shithole job. As Randy mounted his bike, she reached inside the backpack and withdrew the loaded gun.

"Excuse me, sir?" Her voice quivered.

Without looking in her direction, Randy reached into his leather jacket's pocket. "I don't have any fucking change. Get lost." He waved at Jess across the street. "Where the fuck is she?"

"Behind you!" Jess yelled back.

As Randy turned to look, Veronica raised the gun and emptied the chamber. Without a word, his body crumpled onto the blackened concrete. Inside the Kwiki Mart, the cashier bolted the door and scrambled behind the counter.

Veronica rushed to Randy's bloodied body. "Where's your phone?"

"It's you, you fucking bitch," he said with his final breath.

"Damn right it's me." She palpated his neck, wishing she'd killed him years ago when it would have made more sense.

Jess bolted from across the street. "What the hell, woman! Are you crazy? You killed him!" Winded, he stammered. "And now they're going to fucking kill me—right after they kill you." He ran his skinny fingers through his oily hair. "We need to get out of here. Now!" He paced around the bike.

Veronica patted down Randy's jacket and removed his phone and keys. Inside his boot, she pulled a large bowie knife from its sheath. "Do you know how to drive that thing?" Her voice remained calm as she raised the gun at Jess. "I asked you a question. Do you know how to drive this thing?"

He nodded and winced at the sight of Randy's battered body. "We are so fucking dead."

Sirens wailed in the distance. Jess straddled the bike as Veronica hopped on the back. "Go!"

Without the headlamp on, they whipped through the empty streets. With one arm clutched around Jess's slender waist, Veronica attempted to check her phone. Her arm still shook from the kickback of the gun. The screen remained black. There were no more texts. Nothing. According to Randy's phone, they were still twelve miles away from "Home"—312 Park Street—and Veronica couldn't afford to think about what would happen when they got there.

51

Veronica hopped off the bike at the end of Kevin's block. Jess's face looked even more pale and gaunt than before. Two streaks of tears tunneled through the grime on his cheeks.

"Ditch the bike and run, Jess. I can't guarantee that they won't come for you once they find out about Randy. Here." She handed him the gun. "The chamber's empty, but you're a smart fellow." She tightened the straps of Jenny's backpack. "I don't need it anymore."

"If you're going in that house, you're damn sure going to need it." He held it out to her. "They're going to kill you."

"Yeah, I imagine they will, but that gun won't stop them." She pushed his arm down. "Listen to me. You need to get as far away from this place as you possibly can. I've gotta go save my daughter."

Jess gunned the engine and peeled down the street, motion sensor lights from the ramshackle houses flaring as he passed.

As Veronica crunched across the dead grass of 312 Park's lawn, she knew that someone was going to die tonight, and it would more than likely be her. Seamus was already there. Shit was hitting the fan. Did he bring Ingrid? Betty? Before opening the screen door, she prayed that they'd have the moral courtesy to leave Jenny out of it. She was of no use to either of them, dead or alive.

Expecting to find the entryway to Fort Knox, Veronica was surprised and relieved to find the front door slightly ajar. To steady her rattled nerves, she squeezed the cold handle of the knife reassuringly in her palm with the blade resting against her forearm. From her experience with Desmond, she knew she had to remove the heart from the body and destroy it. But with Seamus and Kevin in the same room, it would be logistically impossible to take them both out. She hoped it wouldn't come to that. Silently she crept through the darkened entryway and padded towards the door haloed in light. From the depths of the basement, the two men's voices echoed above the pounding of her own heart.

"I KNOW A LOT OF PEOPLE. I've been watching you for a long time, Mr. Black. A looooooooong time. But, I wouldn't let that worry you. I'm not here to question you about the legality of your little business venture. In fact, I admire what you've been able to accomplish. But by the looks of your 1970s rec-room accommodations, it doesn't appear that things are going so well for you." Seamus's juvenile voice cracked. "Aren't you bored with bartering blood from junkies? It's rather pathetic, if you ask me."

Veronica closed her eyes and attempted a quiet prayer. A quivering "Help me," escaped her lips as she nudged the door open with her shoulder.

Kevin's voice boomed from below. "I don't know who the hell you are, but you need to get the fuck out of here! Now!"

Veronica flinched, tightened her grip on the knife and clomped onto the first wooden stair.

"Well, look who finally decided to show up." Seamus stood near the head of Jenny's gurney, ravenously eyeing the tubes running from each of her skinny arms. He grinned up at Veronica as she slowly descended the staircase.

"I think your little friend here is done," Seamus caressed Jenny's drawn face. "Are you intending to drain her dry, Mr. Black?"

Four men in black SWAT gear inched behind Veronica as she

rushed to Jenny's side. Large glistening knives hung from their utility belts.

"Remember me?" Seamus smiled down at Jenny's delirious face.

"Yeah, I remember you," she slurred. "I need something to drink before I pass out." Her eyes strained to focus as she licked her parched lips. "Hey V, you made…"

"Too late." He gently pinched the tip of her nose as her eyes closed.

"Oh, now I get it. You know her?" Kevin asked, backing into the wall.

"I think the million-dollar question, Mr. Black, is do you know *her*?" He pointed at Veronica, his expression giddy with anticipation. Kevin casually glanced in Veronica's direction as if she were nothing more than a bothersome waitress. He expertly removed one of the IVs from Jenny's arm and placed the bag of her blood in a cooler. "She's done. Yeah, I know her. She's all yours. Now where the hell are my men?"

"They've been detained." Seamus placed his hands on the gurney and sniffed Jenny's neck. "She smells divine. Would you mind if I…"? He held out his hand towards the cooler and snapped his fingers. Returning to Jenny, he rifled through her hoody pocket and snatched her phone. "Did you know that your little friend here is the daughter of the man who will more than likely be our next president?" He wiped the screen on his pant leg, then swiped at the screen. "The Secret Service is going to have their work cut out for them with this one."

"She's not my friend." Kevin's eyes narrowed. "What exactly do you and that bitch want from me?"

Veronica couldn't believe that she was nothing but an irksome bitch in his eyes.

"Well, for starters, I'd love a taste of this young lady's blood, if you wouldn't mind. It's been weeks since I've had anything fresh." Seamus loosened his tie.

"I don't think so." Kevin reached into his shirt pocket and retrieved his phone.

"Uh, uh, uh. I'll be taking that." The men moved forward, hands on their weapons. Seamus reached for the phone and swiped it out of Kevin's hands.

"I just need to call my driver."

"Patience, Mr. Black. Your driver has been permanently removed from this world by your ex." He nodded at Veronica.

"Something I probably should have done years ago after he shot me."

"Now about that drink," Seamus interjected.

AFTER COLD SILENCE and darting glances, Seamus sipped Jenny's warm blood from a red plastic cup.

"Now what?" Kevin crossed his arms, unfazed by Veronica's presence.

"You'll join forces with us. We could use someone like you." Seamus offered Kevin his business card.

"I'm not interested. I know all about you and your operation. The name Eddie ring a bell?" He removed the second IV from Jenny's arm and tossed the bag in the cooler.

"I wouldn't come to such a rash decision, Mr. Black. These men can end this, and you, right now."

The men drew their knives.

"Oh, you think you can kill me? Hundreds of men, all much tougher than these fucking pansies, have tried to end my life and they've all failed." Kevin walked out from behind the gurney. "I'm the fucking energizer bunny, you little twat. No matter what you do, I keep coming back."

"Yes, I can understand how you might feel that way, Mr. Black. But those tough men that you speak of? They weren't trained specifically to kill someone of your kind." Seamus smiled, revealing his yellowed fangs.

"And how is that? I've had my head blown off. I've been strangled. I've been tossed from a ten-story building and yet here I am." Kevin lifted his arms in a V, smiling a half-cocked grin.

"I asked you to get me something to drink." Jenny struggled to loosen herself from the straps.

"Oh, dear. You look absolutely dreadful." Seamus pushed her body back towards the gurney. "I wouldn't do that if I were you," he whispered. "Be a good host, Mr. Black, and provide this young lady with a beverage."

Kevin sprinted to the fridge behind the bar. "I've got Coors, Pabst, Bud and some Corona."

Jenny raised her groggy head, then let it drop back down. "Pabst!"

Kevin leaned over behind the bar, then rose clutching a 9mm. He pointed it at Seamus. "One move from any of you and..."

"And what? You'll shoot us?" Seamus laughed. He set the red cup down on top of a *Penthouse* magazine on top of the coffee table. "Don't be ridiculous, Mr. Black. Why don't you have a seat?" He motioned to Veronica. "You too, slowpoke."

The four armed men led Kevin to a tattered recliner. He glared as Veronica took a seat next to Seamus.

"There, there. Now isn't this better? A little civilized discourse is good for the soul. Speaking of spirits, shall we have a drink? There's plenty left." He turned to Veronica. "Your companion is quite tasty. It's no wonder you've kept her around." He pushed his glasses up the bridge of his nose to get a better look at her face. "What happened?"

"Spray tan." She wiped the skin of her face with the back of her hand, as if it were smudged. "And I don't plan on drinking her blood ever again."

"Good luck with that. If I were you, I wouldn't be going back to that tanning place anytime soon." He scooted from her as if she were contagious.

"Can you stop this stupid bullshit and tell me what it is you two want from me?" Kevin clutched the arms of the chair, his knuckles whitening. Long, white fangs pierced his bottom lip.

"I'm done talking, but I believe Ms. Bouchard, this clever and might I add extremely resourceful gal, has a few things she'd like to say to you." He rested his hand underneath his chin, flashing a devilish side eye at Veronica. "Go on, dear. He's clueless."

"Hello?" Jenny's hoarse voice cut through the quiet room. "I need something to drink. Douchey McDoucherson over there took two pints. And that's not fucking cool. Is anybody listening to me?"

"And those pints were delicious, young lady!" Seamus took

another sip and snapped his fingers at the armed men. "Get the young lady something to drink. Pronto!"

One of the men stormed over to the fridge, swung open the door and noisily rummaged through its contents. "It's all beer, Mr. Sansbury."

"That's perfect." Jenny shouted.

Veronica braced herself against the back of the couch. She wanted to divert her eyes from Kevin's indifference. His betrayal stung as if it happened yesterday. *So much for forgiveness.* In her stony silence, she surveyed his cold expression, hoping he would express just the tiniest bit of remorse for what he'd done that night, but he acted as if they'd never met. Anger was a source of fuel, but it was now imperative to let that go.

From this moment forward, she wouldn't be the one to drink the poison and expect him to die. They'd share a cup. She cleared her throat and he turned to look at her. "What I'm about to say to you, Kevin, is going to injure you and possibly others. Especially now that he decided to show up." Veronica waved a trembling arm at Seamus. "But I have no control over that. Nor do you. Here's what I do have control over. Are you ready?" Her eyes widened.

He sank back in his chair. "Nothing that ever came out of your mouth mattered more than what I stuck in it, including Randy's gun."

Veronica battled to compose herself. If she reacted to his ugly words, he would win. She had to simply respond and cut the cord of resentment that tied them together. She leaned forward and directed her gaze to Kevin's ice blue eyes. "I've realized some things about myself over the last forty-five years and I've recently come to the conclusion that I am no better than you or anyone else. In fact, I'm equally as selfish and self-centered as you are. But, I'm tired of this way of life. I'm ready to go home, whether that's Texas or the great hereafter."

"You done?" Kevin smirked. "Because…"

"Actually, I'm not done. What you did to me, or rather what you had Randy do to me, killed me. Not literally, of course, but on a deeper level. Call me stupid, naïve or whatever, but I thought you were in love with me. I was wrong. Dead wrong. And on that night when both of our lives changed, my biggest mistake was that I loved you enough to not want to see you die. I made a very bad decision to turn you, but that decision was made because I wanted to hurt you just as much as you'd hurt me. And because I forced my will on you and your life, I am truly sorry."

Veronica exhaled, and a lightness overtook her. As Kevin's soul exited her body, she felt as if she'd been given a shot of adrenaline. Relieved at the relative ease of the transition, she ran her tongue across the bottoms of her teeth. Her fangs were gone.

"This is going to be good, fellas. Wait for it. Wait... for... it." Seamus teased, raising his phone. He swiped the screen with his pointer finger. Click. "Nope." Click. "Not yet."

Kevin grimaced and tore at his flannel shirt. "Holy shit! I think I'm going to be sick." He ran a trembling hand across his stomach, then stared down at its unblemished flesh.

"There it is." Seamus admired the photo on his phone and held it out for Kevin to see. "Look. Recognize that charming man?"

Kevin flinched at his own reflection in the phone's screen. "How is that possible?" Kevin demanded.

"You got your soul back." Jenny attempted to sit up and took a sloppy swig from the can of Pabst. "Can we go now? I don't feel so good," she slurred.

"Yes," Veronica grabbed the arm of the couch to lift herself from its cushy clutches. "I take it we're free to go," she said to Seamus. "Is Ingrid here?" Her gaze darted around the cluttered room.

"No. She's right where you left her in California at the funeral home. As a mortal, I have no use for her, even as a bargaining chip." Seamus stood and extended his hand. "No hard feelings."

Kevin leapt for Jenny, burying his fangs into her neck as she struggled against him.

"Stop him!" Veronica screamed. One of the men grabbed her from behind and held her tight in his grasp. "What are you doing?"

"I'm afraid there's nothing we can do at this point, Ms. Bouchard. We like to see a little ruthlessness in our new recruits. It shows they have spirit." Seamus patted her on the cheek. "Now that you're mortal, you may want to get those little lines between your brows fixed. They make you look angry." He turned to the armored men. "Will you please show Ms. Bouchard the door? She is free to go."

Veronica kicked and punched at the man pulling her backwards up the stairs. "You can't just let him kill her!"

"I don't think that's what he intends to do."

Kevin lifted his bloodied face from Jenny's neck and smiled up at Veronica. "Wait. I want her to see the best part." He tore the flesh from his wrist and shoved it against Jenny's open mouth.

"No!" Veronica wailed. She struggled free from the man's grasp, tumbling back down the stairs. Her bones crackled and popped from the force of her landing.

Seamus stood above her as she lay frozen and helpless on the floor.

"My back," she whimpered, imploring him to help.

"Oh, dear. You've fallen and you can't get up. Poor girl. You need to stay exactly where you are as things are about to get rather messy." He waved at the men. "Take care of Mr. Black."

Veronica turned to look at Kevin, afraid that he'd turn her, too, but the four men surrounded him with their long knives raised. With the speed and precision of synchronized sushi chefs, they dissected his body before he had time to protest.

Horrified, Veronica struggled to raise herself off the floor, but the pain was too intense.

"What about the girl?" One of them asked, a helmet muffling his words. He held Kevin's heart at the tip of his knife.

Seamus removed a handkerchief from his breast pocket and gingerly placed it around the bloody organ and dropped it in a metal container. "I'm afraid we're going to need that if Jenny Ann Pearson ever wants her soul back. My dear Veronica, your friend is coming with us." Seamus grinned down at her. "It's for the best."

"But what about me?" Feelings of abandonment and self-pity settled in her pores.

"911 will be here as soon as we depart. Not a word about any of this, my dear. Do you understand?"

"But..."

"There is no but. I'll take care of Texas." He patted her on the head as if she were a dog begging for a treat.

The four men stepped over Veronica's frozen body and clomped up the rickety stairs. "Getting old is a bitch, but you got exactly what you wished for. Welcome to mediocrity!" Seamus laughed.

Veronica attempted to move her head in Jenny's direction. "Jenny? Are you in there?"

"Yeah, I'm here." Her voice sounded distant, as if she were stoned and sitting at the bottom of a well. "I feel really weird. I think they put something in that beer."

"Come here. Let me look at you."

As directed, Jenny wobbled over and dropped down next to Veronica. Jenny's neck was bloody, but the gaping wound had healed.

"I am so sorry for what he did to you. Hell, I'm sorry I dragged you into all of this. I should have let you go do your own thing at the airport. This is all my fault. Everything that's happened to you is my fault." She squeezed Jenny's arm, forcing back tears. "I swear to you, we're going to get them." Her voice became a paranoid whisper. "We're going to get them for what they let happen to you." If that was even possible now.

"Am I a vampire? Is that what just happened?" Jenny slowly ran a dirty finger along the bottom of her front teeth. "You don't need to feel bad. I think it's going to be okay. Think of it this way, it's kind of like I'm going to rehab, just different." Jenny sniffed Veronica's bloodied face. "Are you mortal? You smell really good."

"Yes, but as you can clearly see, I'm hurt." Veronica struggled to roll onto her side. "I don't know how I'm going to make it out of here."

Jenny eyed Veronica's dead weight and the enormity of the staircase. "Me neither. I'm fucking weak. Do you want me to turn you so you can have super powers?"

"No!" Veronica gasped in pain as she attempted to shield her neck from Jenny's advancing mouth. "Absolutely not. I'm not going backwards. I'll figure it out. I always do."

Jenny rose, as if sleepwalking, and trudged up the steps.

"You'll be okay, Jenny!" Veronica called out as if to convince herself of that fact.

Jenny stopped and turned to Veronica with a blank expression. "I'm sorry that you're hurt, but I'm starving, and he's got the food." And unlike Ingrid, who began this whole mess years ago, Jenny did not consider Veronica a dining option. Instead, she pushed through the heavy door and left.

Veronica steadied her breath, waiting for a crew of EMTs to come bounding down the stairs to her rescue. She attempted to call out for help, but the pain in her lungs was excruciating. As Jenny's footsteps faded, she concentrated on the sound of her own ragged breath. Above her, a door slammed shut.

A million nightmare visions raced through her mind. Kevin's men could be back any minute and there was nothing she could do to defend herself. How would she explain the dissected man on the shag carpeting once the police showed?

Mustering all the strength she had left, she rolled onto her side and slowly pushed herself up from the matted carpet. Running a trembling hand beneath her sweat-soaked shirt, she found the source of her pain —three ribs jutting forward. A muscle spasm seized her torso as she attempted to rise to her knees. Yelps of pain echoed in the empty, beer-soaked basement.

"Help me," she exhaled. Tears streamed from her eyes as she considered the enormity of the staircase.

But this was not the time nor the place to have a pity party. She wiped her face with the sleeve of her dirty shirt. Even though mortality didn't meet her expectation, she'd achieved it and was oddly calmed by an overwhelming sense of gratitude. Her life, no matter how unmanageable, was her own, and it would end—just not today.

We admitted that we were powerless.

Not today.

That our lives had become unmanageable.

Not. Today.

With stoic determination, Veronica fixed her gaze on the door at the top of the stairs and inched her broken body towards the first step.

EPILOGUE

SIX MONTHS LATER

Veronica swore up and down with her hand placed on the Bible, even going so far as to post ridiculous videos of herself stepping out into the scorching July sun, but she still couldn't convince any of the others she'd found on the dark web to meet during the day. She chalked it up to lives governed by habit, stubbornness and maybe a heaping helping of fear. She knew all too well that when you are convinced that you and maybe only a few others with a very shameful secret exist, it's not exactly easy to step out on faith and trust someone you've never met in person. It didn't help that she arranged for the newly formed Ninth Steppers to meet in the basement of a Catholic Church. Old mythologies, no matter how much photographic proof you offered, were going to be a real pain in the ass to break with this particular recovery group.

Veronica checked the time on her fitness watch—7:39. She tapped the screen like a drug-addicted rat hoping for another randomly delivered reward. Eight thousand steps. It vibrated against her wrist, flashing Paula's number. She grabbed her phone from the depths of her purse.

"Hey, I'm putting you on speaker, so don't swear or admit felonious acts."

"Long time no talk there, Ronnie. How's Pflugerville treating you?"

"We love it. Ingrid's applying to UT for the fall, which is kind of a long shot since she barely passed her GED, but God works in mysterious ways." Veronica moved several metal chairs into a circle. "I even started my own business!"

"You got out of nursing?"

"Yep. I'm doing Swedish Death Cleaning. It's a thing. My friend Julie told me about it when we were cleaning out all of her ex-husband's shit from her house."

"Sounds kind of morbid."

"It's just getting rid of a bunch of your stuff so your family doesn't have to do it when you die. I'm working my ass off. Literally. I've lost almost twenty pounds."

"Good for you! Have you found a group yet?"

Veronica placed a brand new Blue Book on each of the rickety chairs. "As a matter of fact, I have, and I started it. The first meeting is in like eight minutes, so I should probably go. I'll call you later tonight if that's okay."

"It is. Talk to you later."

To kill the remaining minutes, she brewed a cup of green tea in the microwave. For the three who swore they'd show—Darklord66, Vamp2000 and Paleface18—she set out three travel mugs, courtesy of Seamus. The annoying little twerp wanted new recruits and, since not every vampire wanted mortality, Veronica was more than willing to keep things amicable between them. After all, he was keeping Jenny safely removed from her father's presidential campaign, which was currently in full Texas swing. Until the Albanian text could be deciphered, Jenny remained undead, which was far less problematic than Jenny alive. With Kevin's heart and maybe something as simple as a sprinkle of garlic, she would be renewed to her former self. Until then, she was well supplied with blood.

Veronica eyed the clock and sipped from her tea as she paced the room. In the hall, she could hear two distinct footsteps. Smiling didn't come naturally to her, but she was determined to change that.

A young man, no older than eighteen, with a blonde buzz cut and tanned skin entered the room. "Veronica?"

"Darklord66?" She giggled.

He extended his arm to shake her hand. "How'd you know?"

"I had a feeling. Was there someone with you?"

Frank appeared in the door frame with a sheepish grin.

"Sorry. I only saw your car in the lot and I thought you might like some company. Plus Ingrid's attempting to cook some vegan nonsense and that's never a good thing."

"Dark..."

"It's Bryan." The man interrupted.

"Bryan, this is my husband Frank. Thanks for looking out for me, honey." She quickly kissed him on the cheek. "He has some control issues."

"Don't we all?" Bryan lifted the virgin text from the chair and took a seat.

"The first step is acknowledging you have a problem, Bryan. And it appears that you're already there." Veronica took a seat and opened her notebook. "And with that, let's start with a moment of silence, followed by the Serenity Prayer."

God...

ACKNOWLEDGMENTS

Writing is a lonely endeavor, so when you are lucky enough to have people enter the picture who want to read, encourage, comment or represent you in a professional capacity, it is rather humbling/exciting.

Big thanks go out to the following people. (If you are reading this and your name is not on this page, blame it on my menopausal mental fog and don't take it personally. Despite all outward appearances, I am a hot mess.) Bob Mecoy, Ora McCully, Paula Rose, TwylaBeth Lambert, Jodi Thompson, Tex Thompson, Carra Henry, Michelle O'Neal, Trayce Primm and all the folks at the DFW Writer's Workshop for listening, offering feedback, and laughing through my weird-ass reads. I think I was just as surprised as everyone else to be writing a book about a menopausal vampire, and here we are.

To Erik, Lola and Nik, thanks for being my biggest supporters. Nik, if you'd never brought up the vampire at the tanning salon, Veronica wouldn't exist, so my biggest thanks go out to you and your teenage imagination.

Last, but certainly not least, I would like to thank you. If you're reading this, you've reached "The End."

If you enjoyed this book and would like to support the creation of further literary adventures, please do one or more of the following:

- Leave a review on your favorite book review site
- Tell a friend about the book and author
- Ask your local library to put Pamela Skjolsvik's work on the shelf
- Recommend Fawkes Press books to your local bookstore

VISIT US ONLINE

www.PamelaSkjolsvik.com

www.FawkesPress.com

FAWKES PRESS

CPSIA information can be obtained
at www.ICGtesting.com
Printed in the USA
LVHW051104291020
670168LV00002B/378